SELLOUT

OTHER BOOKS BY JEFF PUTNAM

By the Wayside
Good Men
Bottoms Up

SELLOUT

A NOVEL BY

Jeff Putnam

BASKERVILLE
PUBLISHERS, INC.

This book is a work of fiction.
Names, characters, places and incidents are either the product of the author's imagination or are used fictitiously. Any resemblance to actual events or locales or persons, living or dead, is entirely coincidental.

Baskerville Publishers, Inc.
7616 LBJ Freeway, Suite 220
Dallas, TX 75251-1008

Library of Congress Cataloging-in-Publication Data

Putnam, Jeff.
Sellout / Jeff Putnam.
p. cm.
ISBN 1-880909-35-9
I. Title
PR6066.U8S44 1995
813'.54--dc20 95-10933
CIP

Manufactured in the United States of America
First Printing, 1995

IN MEMORIAM

Alan Miller

BEFORE

When tears came my mother held the letters away. She passed each one to my brother and me unsmudged.

Here were all the names I remembered from the Christmas card lists. Names of people I knew, and some I had only met, and some I had only heard about. There were people I'd never heard of. These were the friends my father had made over the dozen years of our estrangement, the neighbors my parents had known at other California addresses as well as their present neighbors, friends from church or the beach club, even a tradesman or two.

Never had I felt such a gulf between my father and me. Seeing him in his last sleep I'd felt one with his flesh, I'd felt the trembling flame of his life leap to join the dancing flames of mine. Yet I didn't know the man who was being remembered in these letters. He had been loved for qualities that had never mattered in his relations with me. No one remembered him as I did.

"He once told me how long the Bancrofts lived," wrote one old friend. "I remember feeling pleased that I'd be able to share my old age with him. What a loss to us all! What a crushing loss for you, dear one..."

Here with my mother in a living room flooded with light I

was moved by the loyalty and kindness of my father's friends, and I couldn't help thinking how different it would have been if I or one of my friends had died. Not a single letter of condolence would have been sent. None of the people I knew gave death more than a passing thought. People who died were spoken of as if they had done something foolhardy.

Thoughts of death gave pause and people my age had to keep moving: recklessness was our beauty. Life was only precious when we were taking a curve on two wheels. I admired the people a few decades ahead who appreciated life more than I did. Knowing that they were ready to say goodbye to so much that they loved, their steady warmth was inspiring.

As for the goodness of my parents' friends—I didn't need to see all these letters. I'd known them as a child. Their views about man and the world had been sentimental, but comforting. In contrast, the radicalism which had been ever more exciting to me and my friends had become increasingly uncomfortable.

The sentimentality of my parents' friends was peculiarly American. It survived from an age when there was optimism in the land, when an entire nation had gone to war and an entire nation had danced in the streets when there was peace. In spite of the hardships of the Great Depression, which had profoundly affected my parents' lives, I couldn't help feeling that they remembered the period fondly. There had been a wistful look in my father's eye when he told my brother and me, "People helped each other then."

I hadn't known my parents very well. I hadn't been able to understand the old sayings that they applied to my behavior, I couldn't see the importance of the dreams they had for me. I had scoffed at their sentiments and the trust they had in the goodness of other people. I had repudiated their faith in God and their country, and refused their love. With the passing of my father I no longer felt oppressed by his ideas. On the contrary, though I would never share them, they'd become precious to me. I was sad that he would no longer be able to uphold the things he believed, and afraid that his friends would soon be gone, and with them a feeling for my country—for an America I'd never known.

I felt prematurely adrift back in my San Francisco apartment with a few days to go on the rent, notice given by Teresa, the manager anxious to have us out so there would be no more singing to disturb the working people who had been on time with their rent for decades.

She'd gone back to Wolfgang, who had just returned from a voyage to the Orient, the one he'd taken after she went back to me and we took this apartment. We both loved her, she loved us both. I'd been her singing partner and we'd done each other some good, but we were "at different places in our careers." That was the euphemism which covered relationships between singers whose prospects were different because of age, talent, ambition, luck, money, contacts, education, looks or experience.

Teresa had more experience than I but, because coloraturas had to be very young to qualify for important national auditions, some people might have thought she was going nowhere. The only paying work I'd had besides church solos and funerals had been in roles for small companies. I'd had good notices but not enough to inspire confidence at the big houses.

Making it as singers was an even tougher fight because things were whispered about us that tended to reinforce doubts that had been raised by our résumés. A lot of important ears had had the word "Wolfgang" whispered into them after they'd been impressed by one of Teresa's audition arias. The word whispered about me was "drinker."

Wolfgang didn't meddle in Teresa's career but she worked full time to help pay for the one-man revolution he was waging. She'd canceled an engagement when there was TV news coverage of one his unjust arrests. Last year, the bicentennial, hadn't gone well for him. He had failed completely to show the world that the America celebrating and the America celebrated had little in common. He hadn't been to jail yet this year but he was brimming with backtalk.

My advice to Teresa had always been: don't list all the straight jobs you were doing from forty to ninety hours a week—just put the singing work and education. Then it would appear that she spent the rest of her time rehearsing or taking classes. But no, she was proud of all she could handle. Teresa always got her way in arguments with me. I think I was smarter, but she was more passionate, and passion carried us along.

My résumé was full of lies to cover the fact that I had been, for quite a few years, a bad drinker. Much worse than anyone would have guessed to look at me. I'd taken all the help there was for people with "my problem," but it took a miracle to save me. I didn't believe in miracles, but for some reason I had begun to dislike nights before almost as much as mornings after. If it was a mojo it must have been Teresa's. A spell of some kind she'd arranged Faust-like. I looked so much younger I was again getting career advice.

My problem now was to keep separate the people who still thought I had a problem from the ones who were looking at my résumé. My résumé looked good to people who hired artists to do something besides art. In the opera world, however, the name Gordon Bancroft had been tied to a number of anecdotes involving falls or unconsciousness onstage, and some might have been true.

The smart thing to do with the money my mother gave me when dad died was head for Europe. During a three-month trip to France last summer with my pal Alex Hilliard I'd already made inquiries, calling myself Jeremy Locke, and there were people ready to hear me... People so impressed to have met an American who spoke good French that they had pointedly disregarded my résumé. This squared with what I had heard from other singers: the French system was very easy to penetrate. If you had the voice and the roles, you were in. There, if someone had said something about my drinking, especially now that I didn't drink to excess, they'd have been thought insane.

I'd have bought my ticket to France in L.A. and not even gone back to San Francisco for my clothes if the apple pie-baking executrix had shared my enthusiasm. Dad hadn't left me any money, but both my mother and my brother Tom wanted an even split with me. I agreed it made sense for her to withhold most of the money she'd earmarked for me for one year. She wanted to see how I would handle the sum she was giving me right away. If there was any left a year from now, or if, by another miracle, I'd made money on some sort of investment, she'd give me as much as Tom was getting. Then I found out the money would be tied up in probate for a year anyway and all my mother's incentives were hot air.

"Bank the money," Tom advised. "If you've got any left when the rest clears probate, you'll get your share. Mom wants to give you a break..."

On Interstate 5 in my father's old Mercedes I got the idea for a restaurant. I'd look for a place that had possibilities for musical performance. Not opera all the time, I'd lead up to it with chamber music. Some way to make use of all the talent available to perform for the money a restaurant could afford to pay... That took in nearly everyone in the Bay Area who didn't have advance bookings.

I needed to get in touch with Hilliard for help with restaurant chores. He was supposed to be in love with a nurse called Sarah who took care of quadriplegics. An odd match, unless Sarah liked to take her work home with her. Hilliard was deliberate in action and what was on his mind made him stare a lot. I hadn't met Sarah yet but it was bound to happen. To help him as a painter I always gave myself carte blanche. With Sarah on my side I could convince Hilliard that my restaurant represented an outlet for his art, a place to show—the end of an impasse that was annoying everyone, but particularly those who believed in him as I did—and Sarah, presumably.

I had worked as a waiter a lot, even when I was on the bottle, and knew a lot about restaurants. I realized that no one would show up to hear music, no matter how good, unless the food were a draw, too.

No doubt the problems I faced were staggering—even Teresa would have thought so—but I'd had good luck ignoring problems that everyone but me thought were insurmountable. A kind of cussedness had come over me when dad gave up on me years ago. I'd been stubborn about everything I tried to do, sure that someday I would be able to show how far I had come on my own. When there was nothing to show for so long I'd been secretly glad that my father was out of touch. Oddly, I felt him right beside me now and was glad to have him. I had the money to try to build something I cared about, and the cussedness to see it through, and the daring that comes from having nothing to prove.

Yes, nothing to prove, because it was a different father I had with me now. He was the presence I remembered at a time when I'd been excited about what I could accomplish, and he had, too. I felt nothing like the child I had been, however, needing to be told if what I had done was any good. A shell of the child was more like it. Empty of so much, but determined. And the father who was with me was the man who had always loved me, though cursed by ideas of the right thing to do, so that the darkness I brought upon myself he had brought upon himself, too.

After the bank I reached Carrie. She was happy with her job and her Italian boyfriend, Vito (she said right away). Advice was what I wanted, I told her. It was flattering that she agreed to meet without hearing about my money.

Carrie had been born of English parents in Shanghai. Her father had done puppet shows all over the eastern world, I guess for British soldiers, but Carrie didn't like to talk about her parents, who had divorced and perhaps disappointed her in other ways. She had a trained voice but she'd never wanted a singing career—too unsteady. She'd married into the bar business, divorced and stayed behind the bar. She drank too much, was unfazed by the vilest behavior from customers she didn't know well, wouldn't tolerate gentle kidding from her friends, loved to give advice to people in trouble and anything else she had to give. In short, a barmaid. We must have had fun singing duets here and there along the way because Carrie had always been glad to partner me.

Her fresh English beauty was still there. No, she was paler. More desirable to me, perhaps, now that she showed signs of having been attained.

It was four in the afternoon. She had arrived first and killed a pint waiting. I got her another pint straight off and she went deep into it while I told her my restaurant idea. I didn't have enough money to build a restaurant or buy licenses, but I could go in with a bar owner who had done food service once and still had some equipment in...

"I don't know. This might be just what you're looking for, or you could be blaming me for the rest of your life."

"Let's hear it."

"The Fife and Drum. He needs someone to get his restaurant going. There used to be a good one there years ago, upstairs."

"Brian, wasn't it? Didn't he put us out?"

"He couldn't take our singing, but that won't be a problem now."

"I could have opera?"

"Maybe so, if you're cagey. His mind is gone. All he cares about is wrestling on television and his India stories. He'd give you the premises for nothing."

"Would he know what he was doing?"

"Probably not, but his wife would. She keeps an eye on things. Days his daughter is behind the bar—Fiona. Too young for you to remember. Eight years ago, was it? Fiona is as hard as nails. There's another daughter, older, but you won't see her."

"A young daughter who is hard as nails might not be the right one to approach. What would the wife be like?"

"Emma—whew! Some call her a nympho, but I don't believe there is such a thing..."

This might have been Carrie's way of teasing me. I smiled back.

"She's out to have some fun, though, to make up for the way she's been shut out by Brian."

"So who has the power?"

"Between his binges Brian has a lot of power and he'll find fault with everything you're doing."

"You worked for him, Carrie?"

"Twice, and that's not all. I could tell stories, but that would just scare you off. The point is he'll never remember what he's promised you when he's drunk, so as long as what you're asking won't cost him, he'll take you for a friend. He's learned to be suspicious of people who try to hold him to his word. My advice is, do everything you can to make Brian your friend while the ladies are waiting for him to die, but be sure to give them everything they want while Brian's drying out or passed out."

I consulted my warm pint. I had no doubt now that Carrie was telling the truth, but it made me queasy that the Fife and Drum was the best she thought I could do. I couldn't shake the impression that a huge joke was being played on me, even if Carrie wasn't in on it. Yet the Fife and Drum had an interior no amount of scuffling could have changed. A fireplace upstairs and down—I remembered it as if I'd been there yesterday. Redolent firewood to help the smell. Best of all, the big dining room upstairs was rectangular and theater-sized.

Getting her another pint I started feeling ashamed of my timidity. So what if Brian and his dotty family were at each other's throats? I'd have employees; no one would tell me how to run my end if I hammered out the right agreement going in. Hilliard could be motivated; buying some paintings would give him a push. Sid Peckham had come to mind because he'd flunked his bar exam just before my trip to L.A. Yet he was much too bright to have flunked for not knowing enough law. He needed to be stoned to do his best work and must have been afraid his examiners would catch on. On the few occasions I'd seen him when he wasn't stoned he had been oblique. Anything you said to him caused a faint look of pain, probably because everything that had happened in the last few years was just a blur to him when his head was on right.

Sid had dealt dope off and on for a long time, but he was also completely at ease with people who still thought brandy and cigars were the *sine qua non* of the good life. He could have been called a politician or a prince, a salesman or a con artist, but no one could deny he liked people.

Anyway, now that I'd thought of Sid for my number two man I didn't want to look further for some reason.

"Carrie?" I put down her Guinness with its pillowy, persistent head. "Would three bearded guys be all right? I've just had this one going a month but I'd like to keep it. The others have had their beards forever, long hair, the whole bit..."

"Sure. Facial hair is still in. Anyway, I don't know when I've seen Brian Steele lately without a growth of beard."

Of course there would be plenty to laugh about. Of course everything was a joke about what I wanted to do and everyone who heard about it from me would be smiling to themselves the way Carrie was doing.

"Tell me honestly, Carrie... Did you think of the Fife because of my reputation? It's the best I can do?"

"Not at all. I know this business. Brian's no sweetie, but he's fairly honest, even generous at times. If they're an eccentric lot, well, what about you bearded guys? What about that program of yours? There's no way you can make them get rid of the pool table. Let's see—dart tournaments, flower boxes, a kettle on the hob... and you want to add opera. That's quite a mix. I forgot! What kind of food is it you're doing?"

"Well, it's a pub, isn't it? If that's where I go into business, we'll do pub food."

She considered me a moment, then started laughing so hard she got some of her old color back.

Facing Hilliard was going to be harder than I had thought. I never broke the ice when he was avoiding me. Yet the windfall from my father was a perfect reason to come by. If I didn't owe him money at the moment I could always make him think I did.

Sarah was the reason he was staying out of sight. She had to be perfect for me, he always pulled this when he became interested in a woman with views and interests like mine. Sarah and I were practically colleagues: I'd worked in an emergency room, cared for the dying. Been an attendant in a charnel house. Once spelled a male nurse who needed a vacation, spent a week caring for a quad, but I'd have to save that story for a time when Sarah and I had trampled out a place for intimacy.

I vowed to spend as much on Hilliard's art as it would take to buy his loyalty to my restaurant venture. In the process I'd acquire some beautiful art to decorate with. No doubt, thematically, Hilliard's stuff was grim, but the colors were bright. The colors would be the main thing at the Fife and Drum, I felt. If I didn't get the Fife I'd find a restaurant to suit the paintings. Grim themes wouldn't bother people who went out at night to eat—the sorts who could be turned back by something like a theme were home eating TV dinners and lording it over the universe with their channel-changers.

SARAH. So much to tell you now I've met you at last. What can I? Recall times we were alone, or together, the three of us. This notebook paying homage to your presence in my life, recording feelings you couldn't have expected me to have; enlarging contexts you remember, telling you things that were said or thought before you arrived, after you had gone. That part of your past with me in it gaining in significance...

What I've been doing for years: writing a poem each day no matter how uproarious my circumstances. Something with the best of me in it.

Must I always share disgrace with vermin?
While empty bottles gather, and boisterous neighbors
Assail the walls with oaths, and make me sermons
On the undiscovered worth of their useless labors?
While their incidental food assaults the nose
In onslaughts, and the loud resort of doors
Continues whether misery comes or goes,
And despair is ever drumming on the floors?
I see that the drink which brought me to this pass
Cannot be done without if I'm to endure
The clamor of life among this troubled class
Of madmen, brutes and simpletons: the poor.

I'll take my place beside them, scared to death,
But first I must have something on my breath.

Making me squirm you have entered the small room I shared with a man called Sheridan, who must have a few years left, and will therefore be sitting in my restaurant often enough to meet you betimes.

Hard work to stay in the restaurant business will smother my poetry. But weren't all the ABABs to convince women I was more than a black zero for alcoholic drinks to go down and operatic sounds to come out? No need to convince you with what I do here. Unread, unopened, this notebook will speak for me, dark with entries, bulky with insertions.

Still, this isn't for you to see until you reciprocate my interest. If your interest is still Alex or someone else or someones you will never learn of these pages devoted to you. Your exalted place in my thoughts will be proved by what I have written here, and our being together, finally, will seem less incidental. All the time with me here you will not have been a star, an icon frozen ideally or pornographically, but a person ever more knowable, ever poised to surprise me.

Late at night I will write, numbness filling each gap in thought like sand. Or when I wake early, fighting my stomach to think of you—a stomach that stalks my attention like a cat who thinks that everything the day holds in store, and everything I have to do, has something to do with food. Soon this will be all too true. Then I'll have a day off when my restaurant is established—a time to put food—times, temperatures, tastes—completely out of mind. By then a habitual glutton, my attention will feast on you.

The kidding before you came that Tuesday: Hilliard—"Alex"—hadn't shown so much interest in the same woman for so long since—college? I started knowing him right after college.

He said how tall you were, how you "towered" over him in heels. I told him to carry you a lot. Not the fireman's carry. "Cradle her. Make her think of a threshold. With that upper body strength of yours you're the best thing that ever happened to her." Try doing it in a chair, I told him, hiking you into the air and bouncing you like a rubber doll. After a week of that treatment you'd be taking things down from top shelves as if it were *your* fault that they were out of sight for him.

He divined my interest in you and reminded me that you were down to earth, didn't like opera, didn't like the phony waiters in expensive restaurants, suggesting these dislikes of yours didn't leave me much room to operate.

I told him not to be too sure. Those were places where women wore high heels.

He told me you and he had plans to go out, you were expected from work. He stood, meaning I should go.

After you arrived I saw the quick questioning look you gave him when he mentioned your plans for the evening. A shock to realize he could lie to me.

I'd held on till you arrived by discussing my plans for his work in the restaurant I was opening. Wall space where food would be served, room in the bar after I softened the owner.

H. was disappointed the Fife and Drum was where I hoped to have my restaurant, may have felt deceived. "The low-class Brits in that toilet will throw darts at my stuff," he said. "They trash what they don't like."

My music would drive them out, I said. Not opera... (I couldn't tell him everything yet. He claimed to like opera in the distance but it wasn't true. After having been his roommate I could hum something and make his hair stand on end.) He should forget the music and think how his paintings would look in a place with fireplaces and flower pots, copper and pewter utensils right out of an old still life. How like "a bloody pheasant on a hook."

You came and were lovelier than I had imagined. I was pleased not to have mentioned yet that I was willing to buy the art I was putting up, or some of it. Originally, my fallback position if his "no" to my restaurant was unconditional.

Thanks to having you on my side he was able to see himself serving people. (Caring what they thought? Cleaning up after them? Seeing his value in a pile of coins?) He may have cooled since, but you had him excited about trying something new—I wouldn't have been able to do that. Great kidders, we are also great at keeping each other from kidding ourselves.

The celebration was worth it, unexpected. In retrospect, why was I paying to celebrate *his* receipt of *my* big check? No, I'm glad I did something in a big way while I still had all this money to spend. The sad truth is: the generosity I've always liked in myself has been drying up. Unless the money is earmarked for Xanadu.

You were unguarded, said so much about your patients. My first opening, whether or not you knew Hilliard couldn't stand the sight of blood... Thought people with health problems should be a separate horizontal society... Would react as to a zombie if one turned up in his headlights raising a braceleted hand, gown billowing behind...

Herewith in full the experience I began to relate before Hilliard, man of the hour, shouted me down. Setting: a charnel house or "old folks home." The hero: Mr. Roberts, the railroad man.

It was easier to imagine him driving spikes than working as a Pullman porter. His stroke (everyone said "CVA") had turned him into a block of wood. Not in a fetal position from neglect like some others. Straight as a mummy. Immobilized by bands of muscle that stood out under his black skin. Nothing he could *do,* little to be done. He lay like a section of rusty track when I came in. Alive in there, though. Energy poured from him.

I squeezed his hands first, then the muscles of his arms and shoulders, gazing into his eyes. Rubbed his legs and feet, trying to warm his sluggish blood. Told him what I was trying to do. Before I left spent long minutes looking into his eyes, my hands braced lightly against his mighty, stricken arms.

The love in his eyes was a shining, not an invitation, but I went ahead. The pupils were tunnels deep into his past, made a hole in his life, seemed to reach so deep and far the man Roberts was lost in them. There were seas in his eyes, but the surface was dry.

My eyes were closed to him, though he could see the start of tears. I forced emptiness into my eyes and throat, thrust aside the projects of my mind. It wasn't good enough. He never connected with something I might have had inside. I was content there was nothing, it made it easier to leave.

I bowed slightly before I left and was acknowledged as by someone sleeping when an insect comes and leaves. Ten or fifteen minutes a day was all I had to spare the man whose mind moved like an ocean under ice. Still, I may have been the only nurse who just came to see him, and he had no visitors from outside.

He slept on, the workers worked, fellow patients who had never suspected his existence died. Awaiting transportation the dead patients were wheeled into the break room, a wonderful expression of consideration for those of us who'd cared for Mr. or Mrs. Once Somebody. Sometimes for hours a corpse, covered by a sheet, would share the small room with steel and plastic chairs, now inaccessible, and a glossy red machine that said—"Have a Coke!"

I knew it had happened to you, too. Continuing about your tasks feeling a shell of yourself, everything inside scooped out. The fear, achy and acid, that kept making you aware of your own body as if you were all joints. Nothing working right within, everything accurate without. Or else the wonderful, well-oiled ease of health, gloating limbs, grinning loins. In spite of all the confused messages, a quiet mind. The will to take it as if you had no choice.

I started wanting to be lost with you sometime that night.

Then there was Hilliard, with beer in his beard, drumming his fingers—your "Alex," who probably as I write has at least once carried you cradled in his arms from the easy chair up front to the hard one in the hall, and bounced you like a rubber doll. Good old Alex waiting for us to get tired of our "sentimental humanitarianism," as he put it, and tell him which of his paintings he ought to hang first. Would his winos be too grim for English taste? Were his wrecking yards too dark? His meat lockers too grisly? Shouldn't he try for a thread of consistency to characterize his *oeuvre*?

The Fife and Drum had been the glory of the neighborhood ten years ago. The neighborhood had become more fashionable. Going to the Fife had not.

It was a tavern in the Tudor style with some purple dust lying around. Vestiges of someone's dream. Mullioned windows. A fireplace just inside, varnished furniture taking the glow around. Flowers in the windows that had survived the smoke and the slop thrown into the pots every evening by merrymakers. Streetside were the flowerboxes Carrie had mentioned, but where Brian's missus saw flowers, passersby saw a box.

Beyond the raised area of the fireplace and the easy chairs there was a gloomy section with brown picnic tables. Drawings too dark to make out, maps and spurious heraldry adorned the walls lit by creamy Christmas tree lights put up at intervals behind a greasy shade.

The maps had been legible back when food had been served

here. Now when there was a thud on one of these tables that wasn't another drink being put down it was likely the boiled head of an imbiber.

Going to the back there was a pool table under a blinding light and seating appropriate to a hamburger stand. Another choice was a grand staircase to the upstairs dining room, lounge bar and snug where there was another fireplace, but no amount of fireside cheer could affect the entrenched mustiness up there. On your way down and out of the place (forever, unless down and out was a heading you liked) you'd find the kitchen on your right all the way aft, then an area devoted to clanging electronic games, and finally the main bar, long and straight and heavily scarred.

My first trips were disturbing. Nursing a pint I had strolled about the place making mental notes, but I was never asked what I thought I was doing. Also, people who knew perfectly well who I was saw nothing amiss in my reemergence after eight years and had conveniently forgotten my name. I played along, of course. Asked for my drinks, drank them in silence, pissed and left like the very best sort of customer.

Hilliard was pulling his beard a lot.

"I knew my life was in for a detour of some kind as soon as you pulled up in that car. Look, I'll do the artwork. You can have all the paintings you need to hang with the ones you bought—I'll hang them. I'll make slides and create designs for your menu cover, postcards, sandwich boards, anything you want. I'll lay out your flyers. But waiting tables isn't my bag. Sure, I'm broke, could use the job..." Frantic beardpulling. "What do I know about restaurant work? I don't even know which side of the plate the fork goes on."

"I'll teach you everything you don't know. Just think, when I'm finished with you you'll have a skill, Hilliard. When your work isn't selling you can wait tables to pay for your art supplies. This could be something to fall back on in your old age."

"There won't be some kind of uniform, will there?"

"Of course not."

"Jeans and sweatshirt?"

His uniform. I nodded.

"You said I wouldn't have to shave my beard. I'll have to trim it, I suppose."

"Leave it alone. I'm hiring *you*, beard, blue jeans and all. You're going to wait tables for me."

"I guess so."

"But first we have got to get this place in shape. I told you about the kitchen. And we've got certain problems with water supply so I'll need you to solder copper pipe, that sort of thing."

"Piece of cake." Suspicion sloughed off his forehead.

"I need you to help me figure out the grease trap."

"I don't know. How do you know so much about this place if you haven't even got the guy to go in with you yet?"

"I went over it with a restaurant man I used to work for, a chef in his own place. All I had to do was ask Brian's daughter if I could take a look at the kitchen. 'Sure, go ahead.' And no one came to see why I didn't come out sooner. I'd call that a good sign."

"The English women might be OK. And the men don't fight as much as the Irish." Suddenly his eyes went wide. "You'd better find out how many Scots are coming in!"

"Don't try to talk yourself out of this, Alex." I was calling him Alex now, too. I thought he should have a first name when he met the owner. "Customers come and go. Pretty soon a lot of them will be ours."

I had grave reservations about the other guy I wanted to hire—Peckham. For one thing he thought he was smarter than I was, an irritating quality in an employee. For another I was sure he'd pass himself off as owner of the place while he was out taking care of his tables, sure that no one would have the temerity to meet the chef or reason to thank him. If only I didn't have to do all the cooking... When I could afford a chef, Peckham would have to go. His entire restaurant career had passed before my eyes before I hired him.

There were compelling reasons to hire him. He may have flunked his bar exam, but surely he knew enough to keep me from getting into a bad agreement with Brian in the first place, and knew what to do if Brian didn't honor his obligations. The latter was knowledge I was pretty sure I'd need to judge from what Carrie had said about him.

Peckham was a goodlooking man my height with a flowing red beard, curly red hair and native wit and charm that had made him a success with the ladies and even some men his age. His friends weren't the sort to hang out where pool was played but I was hoping he'd attract enough of them to start a clique at the other end of the place, a small group with their backs turned that would get so big, pool would be smothered by "excuse me"s.

The women who went for Peckham were a common California type I've heard referred to as "the New Woman." These ladies kept abreast of cool things to think and say and do, and cool ways to be. A lot of them were already attorneys themselves. There were college profs, designers, middle management people, a lady mechanic who had her own shop and a golfer who had been on the tour. Not one of them knew how to cook.

How could I be so sure? Because Peckham thought he was a great cook and no woman who cared about him would take away his apron. In retrospect his legendary ability as a cook was probably another reason I should have considered him a poor risk to fairly represent what was on the plates he was carrying.

I never gave a moment's thought to letting Sid Peckham take over the kitchen. He admitted that he would have been a tyrant there.

"Being cooped up in a small commercial kitchen would probably alter my personality. Where would I be if no one wanted to come back to see me? No, I belong out in front where I can make friends for the place. And as for the food, if you'll listen to my advice all of your offerings will be winners. You'll only be changing the menu to challenge yourself, like a real chef."

Since Peckham was a few years my junior, being patronized

by him always bothered me. Still, I liked him, I'd always counted him a friend. It was hard to resist his charm even though he thought he'd cornered the market.

I knew I didn't have to let Peckham dictate the terms of his employment. His dope-dealing business was falling off and he was hard up. He'd put himself through law school dealing dope. He'd smoked a good bit of it himself, which may explain why it took him five years to make it through. Now that he didn't have a new crop of classmates to sell to he was trying not to see himself as another shifty-eyed dope dealer hanging around the campus having to act friendly to people he didn't want to know. Meanwhile his former clients were becoming hotshot lawyers somewhere else and could order their dope from prominent citizens.

"Peckham, this is your chance to try the old charm on some new faces. You can tell them you're a lawyer, you can tell them you're a part-owner. Hustle the women if you want. If all our customers have the highest regard for you and commiserate with you for having to work as a waiter, nothing would make me happier. But the job is putting plates down, not giving legal advice. Try not to forget that."

"What about *your* legal problems?"

"I was too hasty. On that score you can expect me to pick your brains down to the last axon."

"Rather frightening. The other guys are converting their legal knowledge into imported cars and I'm road meat."

"Another thing. All the people who buy weed from you? Not while you're on duty, OK? Not here."

"You forbid me to prospect for new business?"

"I know how you get your business. I can't keep you from making friends."

"It's a deal then. I put down plates, make friends for the place and act as your lawyer for nothing. You pay me minimum wage, feed me once per shift and give me zero benefits."

I gave him my forty-page prospectus.

"Study this. Give me your ideas by eight tonight. If it's all OK we move on Brian tomorrow morning right after wrestling and before the churches let out."

"He's receptive then?" Sid had heard about Brian's excesses.

"That's the word. Don't try to make me think you had your hopes up. I'm going to try to get through to him before he's completely sodden, that's all."

Brian went to sit in the window when the wrestling stopped. We left him alone for a while because he seemed to be waiting for someone and we were hoping it was his wife.

He was short and scrawnier than I remembered. Eight years ago he'd affected long scarves, driven a sports car fast, and I'd been reminded of RAF pilots, which may have been what he intended.

Small darting eyes, small hands, a short moustache that looked sumptuous on his narrow face. Moustache and head hair were black. Since he was in his fifties I promised myself a closer look the next time his head was on the bar.

It was decided that I should make the first approach alone. "He might remember you," said Hilliard.

"You won't have to tell him you want something right away," said Peckham. "You'll have other things to talk about."

"That's just what I'm afraid of. It's not enough to hope his memory is playing tricks. The tricks have to be in my favor."

"Sit down," said Brian, without looking at me. "What are you coming around again for, Bancroft? My girl tells me you've been snooping in my kitchen. Came back with someone who looked like a building inspector. Shouldn't go around scaring people like that."

"Brian, I've got a proposition..."

"Forget it. I've never had anything but trouble from partners."

"A partnership isn't what I had in mind."

He shot me a look. The morning light couldn't have been so unkind. He hadn't been waiting for his wife, he'd been waiting to die.

"You wouldn't want to buy me out?" I couldn't decide whether it was hope or terror on his face. They might have looked the same. "Are you having an affair with my wife?"

"I haven't laid eyes on her."

"So much the better. She's at the age where she thinks she hasn't got much time left to enjoy sex so she's careless when it comes to names and backgrounds. She can't even keep the faces straight. She used to be so good with names..."

"Sounds like you're coming off a family quarrel."

"Not at all. We've become close friends in our old age. I'm coming off a twenty-day drinking spree. Pretty soon I'll have to take more than three days off to rest up for the next one."

"I must say you're in excellent shape for a nonstop drinker in his fifties."

"Who told you I was fifty? One of those bitches behind the bar? This is more than I can take. It's bad enough that my wife picks up her one-night stands in here. Now I've got a daughter that tells my age to perfect strangers."

"Maybe we can talk business another time."

"Now is fine. What's on your mind?"

I told him everything in a rush, emphasizing the improvements I wanted to make.

"I like all of it but the music."

"You'd be surprised how many people like chamber music these days."

"Could be, but you're the only one who ever set foot in here. Don't worry, I could never forget you. Coming in here with Carrie, singing your heads off. No singing at all, I want that in writing! All right, I'll have a look at your proposal. Not today... But I'll have it read before next time. Those two boys going to work for you? Bring them along, too, we'll go over the whole thing for Emma. She's a German-Swiss, you know, and on that account alone she's a bit thicker than most, but since she really doesn't want ideas to mean much to her she's a master at finding fault. Suspicion with her is an art. So be ready to fight for the things you want, and prepare yourselves to start liking some things you don't even know you want yet..."

Brian had Emma all wrong. At our first meeting only her deep breaths harassed us. It was hard putting anything on the table without having to deal with her bosom. Being unable to refer to it openly made everything else we had to say sound insincere.

Perhaps Brian had been setting me up for some laughs, wanting to see how far I would go getting Emma to approve of my ideas before I realized she was an imbecile. Right off he told us, "Emma's got a good head for business," but then he started to giggle.

Hilliard and Brian seemed to be getting along. Hilliard never had a problem with anybody. At the hint of one he clammed up. When you thought something was eating him it was time to take a hard look at yourself.

"Oh, I'm just gonna keep on doing my art," he told Brian when asked about his special contribution. "Little touches here and there might help. All he wants me to do is dump the food down in front of people, and I can handle that."

Emma beamed and rested her left one on his forearm.

"What about you? You actually graduated from law school? I should tell you straight off, I hate lawyers."

"Everyone does, but most people could use some free legal advice."

Now it was Brian's turn to brighten.

I went through my pitch all over again while Brian studied my proposal with trembling hands, glasses down at the end of his nose. I doubted it was the first time he'd looked at it.

There was a hush when I was done and Emma was the cause of it with her ruminant eyes and her cud of celery. Something was brewing, but it wasn't suspicion.

"Vot jew tink, Brine? Dieser vunnerful boys?"

Brian didn't, obviously, but he did think some of our ideas had merit. "Now live music... We tried that once before." He closed his eyes and shuddered. "This wouldn't be the place. There's no way to buck the union. I'd never go through that again. Anyway, I should have told you sooner, the upstairs is out of the question unless the dumbwaiter can be repaired. The lowest estimate I've been given to get everything to code is over eight thousand dollars..."

We were in disarray. Sid couldn't even clear his throat, a lawyer's stock in trade. Without the dumbwaiter there was no hope of carrying food upstairs, not in the evening with all the people standing around. I'd taken the dumbwaiter for granted...

"Why didn't you tell me before now?"

"How was I to know that a sum like that would be too much for you to spend?"

He had me there. Until today I'd been going by what my friend the chef had told me I'd need to get the kitchen to code. Small as the kitchen was, he'd been impressed by all the equipment that was in.

I looked at my prospectus on the table and thought of all the drafts the language had gone through to give it selling power. I wanted to tear it up then and there, but there was Sid's legal work to consider. He might want to go in with me somewhere else.

"I'll tell you what, though," Brian was still at it, "if you boys want to start a restaurant here, I'm not against the idea."

He waited for his words to sink in, then he must have thought that would take too long.

"I can see you've got a lot of time invested in your idea, but let's be realistic. We've a younger crowd these days. They like the noisy machines. Loud music. I can't see where chamber music fits in with a pool-playing crowd."

"I can't either," I growled. "That's the point. In time our crowd would have pushed your crowd right out the door. This place would have been respectable again."

"Dot vould be nice."

I loved his Emma.

"Come out of the clouds," said Brian. "Since when is Gordon Bancroft an expert on the bar business?"

"I don't have to be to know we're doomed with this place as it is. What kind of restaurant are we going to have without the upstairs? You want people to eat our food on picnic tables where all this drinking is going on?"

"No reason people shouldn't want something to eat when they pop in for a drink." There was a shy grin on his face that reminded me that Brian had once been a child. "Why should I lose them to another place when they get hungry? And they could hold more of my booze with something in their stomachs."

"You're talking about feeding pool-players. A hamburger joint..."

"Not exactly..."

But his wife cut him off. "A pub lunch vould be nice. Bongers und mosh."

Brian was looking daggers at her. I realized that they'd already made up their minds how they planned to use us. The proposal would have been a waste of time even if the dumbwaiter had been functional.

Peckham had on a big, sarcastic smile. "Bangers and mash? Sausages and mashed potatoes, right?" He was more offended than I. He'd once chewed me out in my own home for eating cheese and fruit cold instead of at room temperature.

"Try different things. See what goes over. If you can come up with a successful menu, that would be the time to fix the dumbwaiter and start operating upstairs..."

Hilliard and Peckham and I were looking at each other trying to think how to respond when a high voice at tremendous volume stopped everything.

"There you are!"

She was headed straight for our table. Some early drinkers had made way, their pint glasses clutched against their chests.

"At least you're not drinking..."

Brian was already responding to her beauty.

"Teresa, this is a business meeting..."

"Let her sit down," said Brian cheerily. "Have a drink! Your ears aren't too tender for anything we'll say here!"

With a sinking heart I saw Wolfgang looking after her from the bar, wearing his liberty cap emblazoned "Death to Tyrants," while beside him the Weasel, red-capped as well, was ordering a pint.

With the barest nod to acknowledge the small man who was

making her welcome Teresa sat at the picnic table adjoining us. Her eyes were now fixed on me and she was beginning to look hurt.

"If this is an example of the sort of people you'll be bringing with you, I should reconsider what I said about the music and let you have a tape at teatime..." Something was already starting to bother him, though. "She drinks, doesn't she?"

Teresa turned to him slowly and sucked in her eyelids. Mechanically subtle, her affronted look was bosom-piercing in the balcony.

"Perhaps it's a bit early," said Brian, "but we'd like to offer you something."

Now Teresa was baffled. She'd finally noticed that our own table was barren of alcoholic drinks. Water glasses of water, a plate of celery... rabbit food... In this case bar fruit for Bloody Marys. Brian never spent for anything that was good for you. He left his pretzels out until the salt rubbed off.

"I'm fine, thank you." Teresa muttered. "Thank you!"

"Sister ist dis?"

"It's his ex-old lady," said Hilliard.

"They sing together," said Peckham, who had seen Teresa onstage with me but scarcely knew her.

"We don't allow the kind of thing that Bancroft does in here, you understand." The furrows on Brian's head deepened. Then to me, "Did you invite her here to change my mind?"

"I didn't... I don't know how she found me!"

"You should be ashamed!" She was back on top volume. "Sneaking out of our apartment without telling me! No forwarding address! We had to ask your little friend in the corner store. We knew you'd be afraid to skip right in front of your creditors."

"Teresa..."

She was looking to the rest for confirmation of my infamy. They were looking to the tall redcap approaching us fast, waving a specimen of American currency.

"Who is this now?" said Brian.

"That's her husband," said Hilliard, ever helpful. "He's a kraut too."

"Vot a hensome men," said Emma while Brian looked from her to Wolfgang to see if one and one made two.

"A German!" said Teresa, genuinely delighted. "Oh, please speak German to him! In German he's the politest man you ever met! He's never said a cross word!"

"Can the crap, *Maus*," said Wolfgang to his wife while holding the bill—it was a five spot—in Brian's face. "Ever see one of these? You're the pop, right?"

Brian was at a loss for words. The blood that had come to his face revealed a rash, or skin that was angry from a recent shave.

Wolfgang frequently had this effect on people, especially when he came too close and there was garlic on his breath. For over two years now there had been garlic on his breath every day because I'd told him of its healthful properties. He adopted the health practices of people who led charmed lives and then carried them to extremes. This brandishing of what he wanted you to see and then thrusting it so close to your face you couldn't see it was also characteristic.

Wolfgang was well over six feet and had his grey hair in a braid exactly like George Washington's on the 25-cent piece. He wore homemade square-toed shoes with square silver buckles, sported a liberty cap, often inscribed, and a white shirt, sometimes with an early American flag sewn over the pocket. His most recent arrest had been last year when, as the bicentennial dawned, he had retired all the flags on Civic Center Plaza and run up a dozen of his own—large replicas of the *Don't Tread On Me* flag, the Liberty Tree flag and others of interest to the handful of people who still cared about the America that was when there was an America to care about. Before the "banksters and gangsters," as Wolfgang would have it, had "swindled us out of our patrimony." For Wolfgang the Founding Fathers were the only fathers America would ever have and anyone acting in their spirit was a rightful heir.

Brian glanced at the five-dollar bill and pushed away the huge hand it was in. Then he looked more and more carefully at Wolfgang. Is there any reason I shouldn't be laughing? he seemed to be asking himself as he polled us with his eyes. Peckham, too, seemed to be straining to control himself. Emma was still staring up in admiration. Hilliard was looking at his hands frowning, I was a complete blank and Teresa appeared about to cry.

"I know what that is, I've seen bags of those. More to the point, what are you? Are they having a parade outside?"

Laughter was a common response to Wolfgang when he was outnumbered, but it never fazed him.

"Take a closer look, pal."

I don't know why Wolfgang's gangsterese wasn't more menacing. Maybe it was the German accent. I remember explaining to women who found it charming that he'd learned English from watching gangster films. In truth Wolfgang was capable of English that would make teabiscuits look fresher, doilies whiter. However, in a nation where all the top dogs were gangsters, as he explained to me once, "one speaks gangster." A classic infiltration strategy.

"Back off, you!" Brian stormed, sitting up straighter and trying to escape the huge hand with its "cabbage." "Your money is no better than anyone else's!"

"Yes it *is!*"

Since Teresa had a thing for big voices it was easy to see how Wolfgang had won her heart.

"Brine, gib der men a chonce!"

"Humor him, why don't you, Brian." Peckham's first words of advice.

Brian sagged wonderfully with feigned boredom but his face was all wrong.

Hilliard was grinning and jerking his head up and down, quite a distraction with all the hair on it. I think he was trying to let us know he was in on the joke, whatever it was.

"I don't think this is the time, Wolfgang," Teresa said primly, looking up at him with pride, grateful his fly wasn't open and his shirt was tucked in. "They were having a business meeting."

"So much the better. That dame behind the bar is this geezer's daughter. Been here five years, never seen one of these. When I wised her up she said she ain't never heard of a U.S. Note, much less seen one!"

"Brine" had been watching his daughter for hand signals to

indicate that Wolfgang was crazy, throw him out, but she was listening to the Weasel and looking over at us wearing a beatific expression.

"What is a U.S. Note, then?" said Brian tiredly. "We were having a delightful discussion with your friends, who are planning to open a restaurant here."

"You're going to have your own restaurant, Gordon? How wonderful! Unless it's a disaster..." Thoughts of the time and place quieted her, but curiosity won out. "Is it going to be yours or will you just be working for one of these two?"

"THE REASON A U.S. NOTE IS DIFFERENT FROM A FEDERAL RESERVE NOTE IS BECAUSE IT IS LAWFUL CURRENCY!"

Teresa clapped both hands over her mouth and Brian stopped paying attention to her.

"Lawful currency, you say? Well, I'm glad to hear that if you plan to spend it in here."

Peckham laughed. Emma was so smitten she hadn't heard a word her husband said.

"You might wanna think of it as a check from the U.S. Government," said Wolfgang, patiently. "The government stands behind this money. It's worth something."

"Well, I'm glad to hear that, too."

Wolfgang withdrew the note, then flashed it again.

"Watch for the red seal! Right here where you usually see a green one. Blue, that's a silver certificate. Hang on to the red ones and the blue ones. Don't spend 'em, they're rare."

"Thank you very much. This has been frightfully interesting..."

Wolfgang had removed his U.S. Note to an inside pocket of his leather jerkin, whence he now produced a waterproof plastic pouch which he began to open on the table right where Brian had been resting his hands.

"You ain't seen nothin' yet."

"But I've seen all I want to, haven't I?" roared Brian.

Peckham was the only one who sighed. I'd been holding my breath longer than anyone, but I kept right on, hoping for a massive derailment. We'd be heading into a blind turn out of the forest when suddenly I was rolling a bloodsoaked Brian out of the weeds, his wife was tearing up clothes for a bandage, Peckham was devising a way to boil water.

"Read that!"

Wolfgang was holding a plastic-encased note in front of Brian as before, pointing without looking to a place in its upper left quadrant. The note was a "green seal."

Brian might have sensed that class would let out quicker if he tried to learn something. He recovered his halved glasses, perched them on the end of his nose and read: "'This note is legal tender for all debts, public and private, and is redeemable in lawful money at the United States Treasury, or at any Federal Reserve Bank.' That sounds perfectly reasonable." Brian placed his glasses on the table.

"To me, too," said Wolfgang with satisfaction. "But you won't see any notes like that in here. They're as rare as the red seals. What you will see is this!"

He pulled a wadded note out of his pants pocket and flung it down in front of Brian, where it unwadded slightly.

"What am I supposed to do now?"

"Read what's on there."

Brian subdued the note with one hand and skated on it with the other.

"Here!" Wolfgang stabbed the note three times, creating a noise that turned the Weasel, who grinned and pointed, evidently summarizing for Fiona what her father had learned so far.

"The print is larger. I can read it without my glasses." Brian looked up to see if he were on the right track. "'This note is legal tender for all debts public and private.' I get it. They've made it shorter to give it bounce."

Brian looked to Peckham for approval; Peckham's cackle was already looking for Brian.

"He thinks it's a joke." Wolfgang's disbelief was no joke, however. "Maybe you think it isn't your problem, pal, because you're not a citizen. But the reason they changed the wording on the note is because people actually went down to treasury offices to redeem these notes for lawful money. I went down a lotta times. And what did I find out? It's all a shuck job. The swindlers will laugh right in your face. They ain't about to give you what they say they will right on the face of that bill. They didn't even have any lawful money in stock. Hadn't for quite a while. 'We don't keep it on hand,' they told me."

"Vy din't du go zu Vashington?"

"Speak German to him," said Teresa. "It calms him down."

Emma restated her question in rapid German, and said much more besides that hadn't come up in any of my German conversation courses.

Teresa's prescription was working, as always. Wolfgang was storing his materials in his jerkin, and there was a soft melancholy in his voice I loved as much as Teresa.

"By the way, she's a Swiss," said Brian, braying. "But here, sit down with her, you have a lot to talk about. She hasn't had any German sausage in quite some time."

Instead Wolfgang sat down opposite his own wife wearing a look of stupefaction, resolutely mute.

"Go on." Brian was elbowing Emma. "Take him off in a corner, somewhere. Get him to spend some of that worthless money. I'm trying to run a bar, here," he looked disgustedly down both tables, "in case you forgot to notice. But how could you know a thing like that, when you come upon a crowd this size at table and nobody's drinking?" He was asking Teresa this question. There was more fury in his voice when he turned to Wolfgang. "How about the Chancellor of the Exchequer, here. You a drinking man, *pal*? Care for a pint to drown your sorrows?"

"No!" Teresa shouted. "Don't get him started, he'll never shut up!"

"Thanks for the warning. I withdraw the offer."

"That's not so," I told Teresa, irritated that the scenario with Wolfgang and Emma off in the corner together might not have a chance. "When he drinks with Germans he's a bartender's dream! He drinks the place dry without raising his voice. Then at closing time he bundles his papers and leaves like a finance minister."

"Emma? I don't mind," said Brian, "as long as you're where I can see four hands on the table."

"Shot op! Vot jew tink?" She backhanded Brian and he'd have been on the deck if he hadn't caught the lip of the table with his legs. When he'd righted himself I felt the sheepishness of his look was calculating. In truth he was pleased with himself for getting through to her with this jibe.

"I don't mind if you want to sit in on our meeting..." Brian told Teresa confidently while measuring the extent of the lump on his forehead with the fingers of both hands. From its small circumference and well-defined depression I related the wound to a ring on Emma's right hand. Garnet? Ruby? Whatever, it was bulging out of a bronze mountain upon which much history had been written. All but Wolfgang were tittery with appreciation.

"We don't want to tie up your meeting one more second than necessary," Teresa began hurriedly, Bo-Peep to Brian over clasped hands. "But I haven't seen Gordon, here, in weeks and I've been combing the city for him. The Weasel spotted him headed for your place... Forgive me for bursting in the way I did... I was so glad to see him! And I'm even happier to see that he didn't come to drink, but to talk business."

She looked at me with no change of expression, but I played along, used to her histrionics. She meant what she had to say to me when we were alone; in front of a crowd this size it was all bullshit.

"It is your restaurant, isn't it?" Black eyes opaque, still too much white.

"Yes."

"I knew it. You were the best behaved. How could you think of something like a restaurant without asking me? After all I've done for you!"

"I didn't think you'd approve."

"You were right. It's a crazy idea. If you're going into something with these two they'll skin you alive."

"Now wait a minute!" said Peckham.

"That's right, you and the little Englishman. I didn't mean you, Hilliard."

Brian's eyes had narrowed and seemed to be saying *I respect you. You've got a head for business.* Then when he looked sideways at Wolfgang, *How'd you end up with this fruitcake?*

"That's right, Gordon. Say what you will, a restaurant isn't your thing. It's for greaseballs like my cousins..."

"Vot skin? Vot greaseballs?"

"Shh!" said Brian. "You've been fed! What restaurant do your cousins have, dear?"

"Never mind. Up in North Beach. Two. They wouldn't want to know you."

"Teresa, you're insulting the man I want for a partner. Believe it or not I was trying to make a good impression on him today."

"If he doesn't know about your drinking, you're misrepresenting yourself. I shouldn't let this happen."

"Where do you get off telling Bancroft what's in his best interest?" said Peckham.

"Bancroft doesn't have a drinking problem any more," said Hilliard. "I can vouch for him even if she won't."

"You can all relax on that score," said Brian, weighing in with his boyish grin. "Problem drinkers are welcome in my place. I'm one myself!... It's just good business." He was suddenly serious and appealing to Wolfgang of all people. "What's a problem for some people is money in the bank for me. So if you ever feel like doing some German drinking, as your friend puts it, come on in and get yourself properly pissed."

"You can't talk to my husband like that! You think because you've enticed Gordon you can get him too... I warn you! If you ever do anything to compromise his dignity..."

"Teresa, this is really off the subject..." I began.

"I have friends who look out for me, you know," she went on. "And if I want them to, they'll look out for *him!*"

"I have a few friends in that line myself," said Brian, "also in North Beach. They don't make pizzas, either..."

"Enough!" I said, rather loudly for me, winning a look of sudden hope from the bewildered Emma. "If Wolfgang wants to make a fool of himself, it's his business, not Brian's. And if I want to make a fool of myself in the restaurant business, I have the right."

"Like hell," she said, hammering the table with one exquisite fist. "Do you know how many times I've helped him out when he was in jail or about to be thrown out of some cheap hotel?" Looking at everyone in turn she was clearly referring to me now, not Wolfgang. "Where did you get the money to open a restaurant, anyway?"

"My father died."

The sound was so sudden and high-pitched that all of us started back as one. From where Fiona and the Weasel were looking on we were a burst pod.

"I know how you take this kind of news, Teresa. He loved you."

"So sorry," said Brian, one grey spotted hand darting to the red and blue backs of mine.

Suddenly Teresa had squeezed between me and the table and thrown her arms around my neck.

"Hold me, Gordon. I can't take it."

She rubbed her tears on my cheek and kissed them off again. She pulled away and made room for her emotions.

"My God! The poor one. How old was he? Sixty-one? What a mockery. Did he still eat bacon? Did he go back to smoking? Did your mother drive him to it in some way? What am I saying? Your poor mother! Why aren't you with your mother in her time of grief? What are you doing in this evil place?"

"There you go again," said Brian. "We're people, you know, whatever you might think of our habits. I had a father once."

"I lost my father when I was nine," said Hilliard. "It completely fucked up my life. Bancroft fucked up his life before he lost his father, so it might be easier for him to adjust."

"Why aren't you with your mother?" Teresa repeated.

"She sent me on my way. My brother's with her. You know I make her nervous."

"But your brother is no one to rely on in a crisis. A businessman? She needs somebody with feelings..."

"She needs the benefit of a good night's sleep in her own bed."

"What has she got against businessmen?" Brian asked Wolfgang.

Wolfgang shrugged. "Sorry to hear about your old man," he

told me in the same tone of voice he spoke German.

"I knew something like this would happen if I abandoned you!"

"A congenital aneurysm would rupture?"

"When?"

"The day after you left."

"That long ago and you never told me? What did I do to make you despise me so?"

"I didn't tell you because I didn't want Wolfgang to think I was maneuvering to get you back in my corner."

"That's your name? Wolfgang? Pleasure to have met you. Would you consider a reply this time? What has your wife got against businessmen?"

"Did he forgive you on his deathbed, at least?" Teresa went on, oblivious to the niceties of melancholy.

There was a chance Teresa was so innocent because, from an early age, she had been thought too sweet to be given a straight answer. Or perhaps types who needed illusions wanted her to share theirs because her expressive gift made them so nearly real. Everyone who'd ever said "I love you" to her fell in the latter category—so many people that Teresa felt universally loved and had lapsed into unwariness. Still, she was capable of towering rages sometimes if it was driven home to her that someone didn't like her very much. Wolfgang's strategy was simple: he was using the illusion of universal complicity in doom to raise his capital as a comfort-provider. As for me, I lied to her regularly just to see what would happen, varying her diet of the ecstatic and miraculous.

"A few hours before he went he came out of his coma to tell me I was forgiven everything. He even decided I should inherit. I've got too much money all of a sudden not to offer you something. Take it all if you want."

"How can you talk of money at a time like this? Do you think I want your stinking money?" She looked down the table, shaking her head. Didn't that beat all?

"If you've got some money, though, you ought to let me invest it for you. I could get you a parcel in Oregon up by ours. Lakefront! And they send you money when they log it."

"Beware of real estate deals like that, Bancroft!" said Brian, coming over the table so that I could smell his sour breath. For my part I was breathing easy for the first time since Teresa et al came in—sure that Brian wanted me, "needed someone to get his restaurant going," just as Carrie had said. And if he was nonplussed by friends like Teresa and Wolfgang, I might have a lot more say in the kind of place I was going to run than he wanted me to think I had...

"Brian's right," said Peckham. "I wouldn't let her get her hands on your loot for a shaky investment like that."

"Why not a shop?" Why did she keep looking for support from the others? She didn't realize she was trying to take the bread out of their mouths? "What do you know a lot about? Books! You're a poet, Gordon! What better place than a bookstore to pursue your interest?"

"I love to read poetry and write it but I'd never get the chance in a bookstore. The people who hang out there only like to talk about it."

"You're right, that was hasty. An art gallery? A print shop? No one knows more about cheese."

"This is it, Teresa. I've got my heart set on this place."

"You poor boy!"

"Boy" was a bit much, but I was beyond being embarrassed. While she was kneeling beside me, crushing my arm into her bosom and clutching a handful of my hair, I told the rest that this strangely erotic behavior was perfectly natural for an Italian such as Teresa when there was a death in the family—anyone's family. And my father had been particularly fond of her...

"All right, then." She jumped to her feet. "I can't stop you, and it wouldn't be right for me to. But I can help you... If things go wrong, you'll need investors."

"That's the spirit!" said Brian.

"I feel a responsibility to see that you don't throw money away on crackpot ideas. Are you planning to have entertainment, for instance?"

"That was the whole idea to begin with," I said, sad at the thought of what was coming. "To open a place where you and I could sing. Sonja. Stanley. Jørgen. All the good singers who are being shut out because they're short or one leg is longer than the other."

"Never! Are you an idiot?"

"Bravo!" shouted Brian, clapping his hands.

"People don't like loud music in small spaces. They don't like people holding their mouths open like that while they're eating, either. The inside of a mouth is disgusting up close in bright light. I have a brother who's a dentist. Does he think about eating while he's working on a patient? Do you think he's working up an appetite?"

"To judge by his waistline..."

"Nonsense! If you want people to come here for the food, keep the music out of it. Something on a tape is fine, so faint you can't really tell what it is."

"I knew this girl had a head on her!" exclaimed Brian. "If you want to invest some money that will really make a difference in this place..."

"I'm investing with Bancroft. I would never put money in a bar." She faced me one last time, summoning courage for all to see. "I know you can be successful. Even here. Your poor father!"

When she started for the door Wolfgang scrambled to his feet to follow, and the Weasel left a glass on the bar with beer in it to follow Wolfgang.

"Who's the little one with the cap? Does he make the bombs?" Brian wasn't laughing now.

"He tags along and looks out for Wolfgang. Nobody knows what he really does. That's why they call him 'The Weasel.'"

"Are they dangerous? Tell me the truth."

"Not... No. I mean, they could be. If you were abusing the public trust..."

"Nothing to worry about there," said Brian, much relieved. "I might cut a few corners running a public house..."

"Wolfgang is sincere, you know. He's got the goods on the power elite. Two trailers and two garages crammed with papers." The papers had taken over his house again—that was what Teresa has gone back to. He'd brought so many paper trails together that America for him was a huge parking lot of wrongdoing. No place for the fat cats to hide. Nothing to do but take the heat.

Brian whistled low. "He is dangerous. I'd better bar him just to keep out the people who want him dead."

"Oh, it's not like that. Way back when I first met him he was a quiet guy with natural dignity. He plays the buffoon so people will ignore him and let him get on with his work."

He'd been a garbageman for more than a year—to look at the mail certain people were throwing away. The FBI kept tabs on his movements and I once had to testify to Postal Inspectors that he was incapable of sending, much less making, a letter-bomb.

"He's just a crank, then, not a bomber...?"

"So far as I know he's never harmed another soul. I don't think he's capable of it. Teresa used to punch him out before she understood what he was trying to do. He's been a longhaired pacifist ever since his India days, right after the Korean War, when he lived with the Sikhs..."

"Why didn't you say so? He's all right, then. We've a lot in common. I think he's misunderstood is what. His wife has damaged his pride. She's the one with the money, eh? I'm sure he's not lazy. I know the Jerries... It must have been time-consuming amassing all that paper. So when his wife comes up with all the green stuff to keep them going he has to find a way to make it worthless. Karl Marx would have done the same. What a man won't do for the love of a beautiful woman!"

Brian parked an arm on his wife's upper back and brought her blonde head closer tugging an earlobe. While the three of us gaped, a smile glided across her face. She closed her eyes when he blew gently into her ear.

"Du bist ein guter Mensch..." she cooed.

"Parcheesi," he whispered back, doing something to her thigh. "Parcheesi." Aside, with a gleam in his eye: "It's a board game. We have our nights at home, too, once in a while."

Emma, purring, bent down to play-bite and Brian presented his ear, tilting his head slightly.

A huge rush of sound was making our teeth knock together: the Rolling Stones singing *Jumping Jack Flash*.

"Fiona, turn off that rubbish!" Brian bellowed. "We're having a meeting!"

She took her time about it, but she obeyed.

And we did have a short, uneventful meeting after Brian and Emma were disentangled.

Brian wanted reassurance about the music. He sympathized with the dream of being an opera impresario that had led me to think I wanted to open a restaurant. Would "restaurant man" be a comedown for me? If not he'd donate his premises upstairs and down for food service, the use of his kitchen, and the use of the name The Fife and Drum for our restaurant. Our only start-up costs would involve getting past the health inspector; it would take a few thousand to get his kitchen to code. "You know what needs doing. According to my daughter you've spent hours in there."

I told him my partners didn't have any stake in doing music. I couldn't shut them out of an opportunity because it wasn't everything that I wanted. I had his word, then, that the big dining room would be ours someday?

He insisted we could begin service upstairs whenever we were ready. We wouldn't have to fix the dumbwaiter if we didn't mind running the orders up the stairs...

"Boys, let's be honest." My stomach began to churn. "We haven't had food in this place for years. It might be a while before the twits coming in these days see fit to give your food a try. Bring your friends! The more eccentric, the better. British people have a special fondness for eccentrics, as you know. Promote the place any way you want! Remember one thing, though. It's drinkers we want in here, people looking for the bottom of a glass. The women working for me forget that sometimes... even my *liebchen*, here. We don't want a bunch of aesthetes hanging around, soaking up the atmosphere and merely moistening their lips..."

We left promising to think over Brian's offer, but I knew then that we were going to accept it. He'd been in business for twenty years; his advice rang true. Novices in any business always had big ideas about what they could accomplish and we knew ourselves well enough to admit we were no different.

Even without the dumbwaiter to give us headaches, getting our kitchen ready was a lot more work than I had bargained for. After lengthy visits from a health inspector who refused my offers of a drink I learned that my sink wasn't to code because it didn't have three tubs, my grease filters had to be replaced, I needed more flashing over the stoves and new ventilation ducts, I needed to run hot water to the restrooms...

So many helpful suggestions to help me get started. Then after I had taken them there were new ones the inspector had forgotten the last time. He was no toper and Brian scorned a meeting with him.

I soon saw that Brian rarely met anyone who came to his place for something besides a drink. Deliverymen didn't exist for him. He had the most highly-developed ability to vanish of any small, unkempt person I'd ever known.

The restrooms were over by the pool area. The toilet in the men's was maddeningly slow. You had to wait five minutes to make sure you weren't leaving something for the next guy. Every time I watched one of its long-drawn-out curtsies I thought of my twelve-pound sledge. But this was something that worked, I should have been grateful.

At first I was worried that my friends wouldn't hang on until our opening since I was only paying them subsistence wages. All they got to eat were the sometimes less-than-appetizing results of cooking tests.

Keeping Sid Peckham out of my hair turned out to be costly, but worth it. I let him do the buying. Of course he had to get in on the cooking tests and the tastings, but that was all I let him do on the premises. When I was talking to Sid I referred to the labors of Hilliard, my friend Sheridan and me as "shitwork."

"What really counts is to get this place equipped right, and Sid—you know how little I've got to spend. Don't keep coming back with things I've left off the list. You've got the menu plan and you know I don't need *crêpe* pans, for instance."

"I couldn't resist when I saw the price. I know we'll be serving *crêpes* here when the opera crowd arrives. They'll go over great when we've made, say, a terrace out of the pool area and broken through to the outside."

"Sure, serving the ladies off that alley. Great idea, Sid. That alley might be short of atmosphere, but it's got history. It's still got stuff in it your grandfather puked up."

"Just a thought. It takes vision to see what could happen to that alley."

"It sure does. Looking up at that pile of junk it takes a hell of an imagination to think of that back alley and food at the same time. You know how to cure a sick imagination like yours, Peckham? Spend your own money to fix up a dump like this and see how much thought you give to back alleys!"

Sheridan got along well with Hilliard and did a lot of work—more than I did myself, in fact, since I was less than helpful in matters of plumbing and electricity.

Sheridan expected to be on board now that I had a place of my own. We'd been through a lot together, we'd even been through a car wreck that was my fault, but damn it all, Sheridan was clumsy when he drank and he was only sober one day in twenty.

It's hard to tell someone he's clumsy—almost as bad as talking about baldness to someone who wears a hairpiece.

"You know how you are when you drink, Sheridan."

"How? How am I? What do you mean by that, Bancroft? Christ, if you don't drink the way you used to it's because you've been thrown out of every bar in town. I'm only unwelcome in seven bars, and I've been here twelve years. Who's the bad drinker?"

"It's true, man. You haven't got a bad mouth when you drink. You slobber, but you're polite when you can get the words out."

"Lay off him, Bancroft," said Hilliard, putting his torch out with a pop and sitting up to hear to the rest of this.

"Slobber? You son of a bitch, I don't slobber! When did I slobber? I want witnesses! Hilliard?"

"Well... I don't know, Bancroft, maybe he doesn't always."

"Why do you two have it in for me all of a sudden?"

"Because you were hinting around that you're closer to me than Sid Peckham and should have been my choice to run this restaurant with Hilliard and me. At least I could have asked you... Isn't that what you said?"

"It was pretty shabby treatment, Bancroft, but I've come to expect that from you. Let's face it, Sid's got a law degree and I never finished grad school in English. I know that's all you need him for—to keep you from screwing up with the law."

I'd been an idiot not to take this line and stick with it. "You're right, Sheridan. Sid's a little slicker than you are, that's all. He's a lawyer, a gladhander. He's light on his feet."

"What have feet got to do with it?"

"You've seen how trial lawyers move. Don't they have a lot in common with waiters the way they buzz around to get in your face?"

"You don't think I would move fast enough?"

"Sheridan, aren't you working for Bubba in the roofing trade?"

"Sure, but how do you think I like risking my life every day?"

"...Making five times more money than you ever would working for me?"

"What would I need money for if I could get free drinks?"

This kind of wrangling went on whenever Sheridan came to help. To make matters worse he wouldn't accept any money for his work. I gave him plenty to drink, but I had stolen most of it from the walk-in freezer since I was already at war with the bar over the cost of drinks for my employees.

Sheridan stuck around and was our best customer for three months or so after we opened, then he went back to New York. It was a lie about him being in San Francisco for twelve years. Ever since I could remember he'd been going to New York and staying long enough to consider himself a New Yorker again by the time he came back. I got the feeling that he might stay in New York for good this time, and that I might have something to do with his decision, and this was a feeling I didn't like no matter how much it pained me to see Sheridan drinking too much when he came around, knocking things over on the bar and crashing into empty tables on his way to the john.

Brian had been zero help while we were fixing up the kitchen. He came in once to show us something about how the big reefers were wired, took 440 volts and staggered out telling us which electricians not to use and wishing us luck. We were treated with exaggerated respect by his daughter and the night barmaids even though they wouldn't lower the cost of our drinks.

Hilliard, Peckham and I spent a lot of time discussing Brian's motives in giving us a free hand.

"He told me he never gave the kitchen a thought, it was his partner's concern," Sid related. "I believe him. I don't think there's anything suspicious about him staying away."

"Maybe not," said Hilliard, "but it's sure suspicious the way that daughter of his is acting. I get the feeling we're being set up. But it's Bancroft's money, so how do they think they're going to screw me?"

"Tell you what I think, guys. He's amazed to see someone putting money into his place and he doesn't want his surprise to show. He's crossing his fingers until we're a going concern..."

But Brian didn't even come to our grand opening.

GRAND OPENING proclaimed our banner—wide as the building. Huge red vinyl letters on a white background, distracting to Polish people as far away as Milwaukee. Hilliard had made the banner, of course, but Sheridan claimed to have helped. I helped Hilliard hang it to show Sheridan I wasn't afraid of heights; really, to preempt the usefulness he was so eager to demonstrate whenever anything dangerous or difficult needed doing.

I hated our sign by six o'clock. By then even the potvaliant-seeming Sheridan didn't want to risk taking it down.

Until today we'd given away a good bit of food at odd times

and there had always been takers. Now we had our hours of service on a sandwich board outside (carpentry by Sheridan, lettering by Hilliard)—11:30 AM to 2:30 PM, 5 PM to Midnight.

Here it was 6 PM and we'd only been able to give away a bowl of mulligatawny soup to a wino named Frank who spit his first mouthful onto the adjoining barstool and said it tasted like shit. Peckham, who had served him, asked if he knew what mulligatawny soup was supposed to taste like.

"Hey, I didn't mean nuthin'. Don't take it personal. Maybe it goes over great wherever it came from, but you'd better get the rest of it outta here, the smell is making me sick. I spent a nice piece of change getting a heat on today and I don't want to have to start over on an empty stomach."

So the first food to go out of our kitchen now that we were officially open came right back again. It was borne to one of our stainless steel counters and gone in one swallow down a huge, perfectly circular mouth which communicated with a garbage can.

"Some of these people must know enough to eat before they load up on drinks," I grumbled. "Everybody knew that when I was a wino."

"It's a lower class of wino we're seeing these days," offered Peckham.

"Look, I cooked this shit—it won't do for me to buttonhole everyone I can find out there and beg them to try it. Peckham, go out there and tell them what a chance they're taking with their health. Tell them they've got to take in protein when they drink or the liver starts using it's own to process what they're drinking. Some doctor told me that, once. It may not be true but she made me buy it."

Peckham demurred. "It's Saturday night. They're just waiting to blow the roof off this place. Then they'll get numb. Then they'll get irrational. I just don't see an opening for us. For damn sure it's not the time to discuss their health."

"All right, why don't we do a giant cheeseboard with Appenzeller, Stilton, and Vermont White Cheddar. Chop up an apple for color, take it around with nothing but napkins and toothpicks. Could you handle that? If enough of them were eating something of ours they'd get used to the idea of food coming out of this kitchen. How can they turn down cheese, where the only sign of us is where we cut it? Come on, Peckham. Try Russian service, from the left. Invite them to take a napkin first, then hold up the little quiver of toothpicks and tell them to spear as many hunks as they would like... Make a game of it!"

Peckham wasn't enthusiastic, but the food was free, after all—this wouldn't be anything like selling. I duly created three heaps of bite-sized cheese chunks, sectioned an apple and he was on his way.

He was back before I'd cleaned up.

"No sale. A hunk here, a hunk there. They waved away the napkin and grabbed with their fingers."

"Isn't this the same crowd we see around here during the day?"

"I got it," said Hilliard. "We didn't give a shit about them before today and they didn't look that hopeless. Now that we expect something of them we're taking a harder look. I bet if we were giving away hot dogs they'd all be gone by now..."

"You may have a point, Hilliard, but don't let these heresies be heard outside this kitchen. Didn't you tell me Sarah was coming? And she might bring some friends..."

"She said she'd try to make it. What she does for a living, they don't schedule things around bars..."

After fifteen minutes making our clean kitchen cleaner I'd had enough.

"Hilliard, Peckham, we've got to go all out to give something away. Put those paper lunch menus around like placemats and tell them, tonight, tonight only, they can have anything they want for free. Cracked crab, cherrystones... Or if it's one of those little broken-down Brits, talk up the meat pies... Tell the Germans about our wursts... The Italians about our *cioppino*."

"You see any Italians out there, Peckham?" asked Hilliard.

"I didn't and I doubt I will, unless they're friends of Brian's. Italians aren't big drinkers."

"Tell the Scandinavians about our open-faced sandwiches then."

"How do you tell a Scandinavian?" asked Hilliard.

"If it makes you uncomfortable to approach someone on a hunch, ask. Ask! Are you Scandinavian by chance? If he says he is or is by extraction, if he says anything positive, you say, 'How about an open-faced sandwich, then?' But even if he says, 'No, get lost,' you can say, 'Too bad. I was going to offer you one of our open-faced sandwiches.' Does that make any sense?"

No reply, but they left with a stack of our lunch menus. I decided to follow and see how they were doing. As I feared they were putting them out without saying a word.

"Free food, folks! Anything on the menu for free! You'll never get another chance!" I strolled about in my spotless apron shouting at the top of my lungs. Some of the customers were putting their heads together as if to consider what I'd had to say, but backs were all I was getting, not a single face.

Right after I returned to my kitchen I heard Hilliard hollering after me. "Chef! Chef! Someone wants to speak to the chef!"

I followed Hilliard back into the smoke-filled bedlam. It was Gerhard Woerner, a guy I'd known when I was waiting tables years ago at a French place up near Broadway. I'd heard that he'd left to work in Monte Carlo.

He jumped up to hug me and brought another world of good smells with him.

"What brought you to this place?" I was asking, involuntarily. "I don't know why I said that, I'm trying to get a restaurant going here."

"So I see!"

I remembered the years I'd been kidded with that grin and longed to be the person I had been, and for the world to be as I saw it then. If the intervening years had been less a miasma and more like an arcade I would have punched out all the supporting columns.

"Tell me to fix you the best thing on the menu! Jesus, I can't even give the food away..."

"Not to people like this. But I see what you're after. If you can run them off, this is a nice property, *ja*."

"Then eat something! Give them a preview of what this place is going to look like after the invasion."

"I can't, my good friend. I'm stuffed to here. I couldn't even look at more food."

"Why'd you come in, then? This isn't someplace you go..."

"Old comrade, I'm sorry—I was slumming!"

"You've been here before, though, surely..."

"In its days of glory. I didn't expect it to be so clean, I tell you honestly. This is very good what you are doing!"

"Well, it was good to see you. Maybe when the people who come here are as clean as the floor you'll have a cup of soup with me."

"I will! But where are you going? Don't pretend you have work to do. Your kitchen is spotless. *Alles in Ordnung, sicherlich.* I asked Blackbeard to get you because... I wonder if you would give me a game of chess. I remember those games we used to have in the afternoon trying to stay sober for the evening rushwork..."

Chess had been but one of many ways we young, single waiters had passed the afternoons between split shifts. Of course Gerhard and I had gotten dead drunk then, too, often enough; it was probably one such afternoon that had cost me my job and ended our chess games.

A surprisingly clean chess set was kept behind the bar, no pieces missing.

"How'd you know about the chess set if you were just slumming?"

I was setting up the pieces.

"All bars have chess..."

"Not when they cater to a crowd like this. You were ashamed to be seen here, weren't you?"

"Gordon! Really, not... All right, I live nearby, the gay places don't amuse me any more, the drinks are demn cheap here, the atmosphere is what I like, these others leave me alone—especially these low-class British people who don't even look around the room when they are alone and start making an exclusive group when they are two. You notice this?"

I nodded. "I live in the neighborhood, too, now, so I'll expect to see a lot of you. When you've been having a bad day you can always drop by and beat Bancroft at a game of chess!"

"Ha ha. *Ja, sicher...*"

Gerhard always beat me at chess. He may well have been a rated player, but he wasn't the big ego my remark implied. He didn't identify his openings by name and talk about his moves the way players did who imagined themselves reinventing the game. He liked to talk about things in general while he played, draw people out and hear their real views. In the southern U.S. he'd have been killed—one less troublemaker. The real reason he came to places like the Fife was because booze was king here, the customers came to drink and everything else was beside the point. These people never came to blows because they didn't see eye to eye on some issue of political, historic, aesthetic or athletic significance. Nearly always, when there was a fight, it was because somebody had got the math wrong pertaining to whose turn it was to buy a drink.

Gerhard had a lot to tell me about his wanderings over the last six, seven years. Indeed, he had gone to Monte Carlo to work as a waiter, thence to Switzerland to run a ski lodge, back home for a while to reassure himself that he'd been right to leave. Then he'd been Chief Steward on a cruise ship. He'd worked as a waiter all over the planet doing more or less the same things while his customers asked more of him in a host of different languages. Only the food was different. What people ate, how they prepared it—these were the crucial factors identifying the races of man...

How could a history of China be written without an understanding of the conflicts between the noodle-loving North and the rice-loving South? Or of Italy with its noodle-loving South and rice-loving North? It was easy to explain the preferences of different cultures for different cooking oils in terms of the food sources available, but how to explain the deadly choices of certain branches of the family of man and the healthful choices of others, when healthful or deadly alternatives existed for both groups? Had it ever occurred to me that human beings were nothing but pawns in a battle between the redemptive and demonic forces of nature?

No, I told him, but I was sure that Gurdjieff was right in describing the race of man as food for the moon. Actually, this prescription didn't make much sense to me but it stopped Gerhard in his tracks, and he hadn't been the first one.

"Can you imagine that dairy products... Dairy products!... This is exotic food in the Far East? Milk? Cheese?"

"You don't see any problem in it, do you?"

"Of course! This is the whole problem, don't you see?"

"You want to be able to order bratwurst on the street in Mangalore?"

This would have seemed quite a leap to a kibitzer, but we'd had this discussion in a less refined form seven years ago.

"I should be able to order anything at any time! I don't want to need the same people every day when I get hungry. Thank them for more of the same. 'Very good, very good, mama-san. Taste is the same as yesterday. Long life to you!' Why should I have to get on a demn airplane just because I'm in the mood for bratwurst? In this day and age? What is this global willage, all bullshits? Sometime I feel like a *confit de canard*, sometime a *paëlla*, sometimes a *rijstaffel*, sometimes a *bockwurst* or even one of your focking hotdogs."

"If you're in the mood for *bockwurst* you came to the right place."

"This is no joke, you know. Guard your queen. Who makes this *bockwurst* of yours?"

"Heinrich Hupfnagel, a craftsman."

"Don't tell me this nonsense, he is a friend of mine. He used to make violins in Germany. Here he lost everything because of a bad marriage and two worthless sons. He couldn't get backing for a violinmaker's shop so he started making sausages. We Germans say there are tears in his sausage. Before cooking you must punch little holes to let them cry..."

"But they're perfectly good to eat!"

"Magnificent, but not now. I'm still full. I predict mate in six."

"Please, Gerhard. One beautiful succulent white sausage with red cabbage and a boiled potato flecked with parsley."

"This traditional garnishment is very good for passing Germans. However, what is a great, great pity: Americans with no knowledge of our cuisine will reject a white sausage. They will think you have taken a red sausage and frightened it somehow."

A fellow with a tweed Norfolk jacket and an absurd hat with matching oatmeal had just come in and was looking the place up and down. He wanted to give the impression that he was looking for someone but I spotted him for a tourist who had seen our GRAND OPENING sign and wanted to avail himself of a food giveaway. I too now saw certain checkmate and was in no mood to feed someone I was certain never to see again. He'd be lucky to get the right directions.

"All the more reason you've got to try one of Heinrich's lachrymose *bockwürste*. Someone is sure to see you and figure they're OK. You're the best-dressed man in the whole place."

The tourist left and Gerhard announced mate.

"Another game next time," said Gerhard, grinning again. "If I stay you are trying so hard to ram a white sausage down my throat you are not giving me a good game. No white sausage, Bancroft, I give you for nothing this wery waluable adwice..."

Gerhard had been in the states for years and could speak the King's English as vell as Volfgang vhenever he vanted. The son of a bitch. He lived on *Schadenfreude* and tonight he'd had his fill. But he gave me a goodbye hug, the only sincere thing he'd done besides crush me at chess—because of his germ phobia, hugs were hard for him. My "spotless" apron—I still would have called it that—was to Gerhard a record of all the filthy places I'd been and the unhygienic uses to which I'd put my hands.

Suddenly it occurred to me that I'd made him hungry with all the talk of sausage and he'd left to visit a place he knew in the neighborhood to have some. I wanted to send someone after him to make sure he vanished in a residential doorway.

Such whims were bombarding me constantly. I knew I could never give in to them, I had to keep fighting off the feeling that people were trying to hurt me by ignoring my food. When someone wanted some I had to be careful not to act as if they were doing me a favor, disguise my gratitude. Whether they ate or not, it was all the same to me. It was their loss if they didn't—lucky for them if they got the chance. But what was the big deal after all? A little food went down a human gob tonight instead of the hole on the steel counter next to my drainboard. A little money had changed hands.

All the livelong day I tried to talk myself into a blasé attitude but my dreams at night were another matter, or call them nightmares: rounding up a hundred people at random out on the street, herding them to The Fife and Drum at gunpoint, posting guards at all the exits so no one escaped without trying every item on the menu... That's right, even if it took days. The waiters would shoot anyone caught trying to go to the can. My maître d', Werner Erhard, would be patrolling the floor at all times to make sure the plates were clean. Was everything all right? Did you enjoy your dinner? Strange how my maître d' resembled my old friend Gerhard Woerner, the man who ended culinary discrimination by urging the nations of the world into a food fight, wurst versus hotdog, mussel versus clam, rice versus noodle—to hasten the day when earthlings could get whatever they wanted to eat wherever they happened to be on the globe—one man, one menu...

Before Sarah stumbled in a bit past ten with three exhausted coworkers we'd had two orders for mulligatawny soup an hour apart, two bowls per order, so that a total of four Englishmen had consented to eat with us, all quite sodden but comparatively well-dressed. All claimed to know what mulligatawny soup was and pronounced our version of it delicious. We were present to hear all the compliments, needless to say, and to watch each spoonful of soup tipped into their faces.

At the sight of Sarah I forgot all my petty schemes to cook for people I didn't know. Let them all drink themselves to death. But I'd lock myself in the walk-in reefer and freeze to death before I let her talk me out of cooking something and serving it to her and her friends, preferably something different for each.

I took bread to their table to hear what Peckham was telling them. He'd thoughtfully put them in the middle of the room, near the railing that separated the raised area near the fire. People came to nurse a drink in this area, where thirst wasn't causing such a commotion. Among the poor sods at the Fife, as in life, quiet, more temperate sorts appeared slightly more prosperous and a great deal more miserable.

Sarah and company were just plain miserable, and Sid knew it, but instead of calling attention to his excellent reasons for being more miserable than they (as he did with me when I was miserable) he had removed contiguous chairs at nearby tables, told them "the service rush is over" to cover the fact that there were no signs that food had ever been consumed in this room, glossed over the fact that he was giving them a lunch menu ("Everything is free!") and given his set speech about the political enlightenment of our pubkeeper in having an Irish standby like Guinness in an English place. Peckham believed it when he was telling people why we were the future; amazing considering the writing on the wall which was staring him in the face.

These ladies were Guinness drinkers. Bravo, Sarah.

"Take their food order right after you set their drinks down," I whispered to Peckham while he was picking up at the bar. "They're about to pass out from overwork. One pint of this shit and they'll forget they were ever hungry in the first place."

Peckham agreed and I loved him so much for agreeing that I went back to the kitchen and let him take care of the nurses all by himself. I told Hilliard to help him out and get rid of any drunks who tried to hustle them. Hilliard was dying for a reason not to be Peckham's busboy. Best if he sat down with the women, but that wasn't his style either. Lounging nearby, keeping an eye on things, able to respond to Sarah without raising his voice: without fail, when he had nothing to do, Hilliard always looked as if he knew exactly what he was doing.

When the orders came I was jumping out of my skin. These nurses may have been exhausted when they came in but our menu had revived them. They knew the cost of the things I was giving away! Probably none of them had ever eaten this well when she went out alone. And Sarah hadn't been eating this well on dates with Hilliard. Hilliard couldn't put down a plate of clams without looking away—couldn't touch them unless they were completely closed. He'd never even seen some of the food

I was serving until I brought out the ingredients for our first cooking tests.

Soon my stewpot was bubbling, the rich aroma of my crab casserole was filling my workplace, two baker's dozens of cherrystone clams had been slaughtered, a double order of calves' sweetbreads with mushrooms, splashed with sherry, was sauteing. I was putting the finishing touches on a crab Louie that deserved to be called Louis and brought with fanfare out of one of the town's best kitchens.

When I had the orders ready a look around made me even prouder of my plates. To hear the doom and gloom crowd, customers like ours—working people, poor people, drunks, degenerates, weirdos—couldn't appreciate good food, didn't even know what it was when they could afford it. When one of them had a windfall he went out for a burger and maybe paid for a new tattoo on his leg or a new accessory for his car. He wouldn't dream of spending on something that would turn to shit in a matter of hours.

One knocker (a lawyer friend of Peckham's who hadn't yet moved on) said: "Are you trying to change their eating habits? What do you care about their health? Why get rid of a beer gut when someone's just going to stick a shiv in it anyway? Why try to foster a taste in the finer things when they'll pauperize their families to indulge it?" And he told Peckham: "Bancroft just wants all the fancy shit on the menu because it's what *he* wants to eat."

I knew he was mostly right, but I wondered what he would have thought to have seen me swing into action to give Sarah and her friends a taste treat. Maybe my egotism was no different than Gerhard's, but our conditions of life were reversed: he got to see the world but kvetched because he couldn't at all times have exactly what he wanted to eat; I always had what I wanted to eat, but I complained (not very loudly yet, but I would) that I was stuck in my galley nineteen hours a day and the world was passing me by.

Let people make of my motives what they would, when Sarah came in I had no thought but to please her, even if she took the appearance and quality of her food as a given, no different than it would have been for any other customer. Even if Hilliard took all the credit for the pleasant time she had, or Peckham. Even if she forgot me back in the kitchen, even if she forgot to have one of "my men" tell me goodnight... knowing she was there made all the difference in how willingly and well I did my job. Sometimes I would watch from afar while she devoured the food I'd fancied up in special ways. All of my special touches found their way into the notebook where they were joined with things that were different about her dress that day, or if she were wearing her uniform, with stories from work or front-page news.

When Sarah was around I was a chef, this was my restaurant and there was nothing funny about any of it.

"I'm kind of disappointed," I told Fiona when Brian still hadn't turned up the morning after our grand opening. "He seemed so enthusiastic while things were in the planning stage."

"He's off on a tear. You should be grateful he's not here to fuck up everything. If you only knew how grateful you should be."

Tardily I canvassed the neighborhood merchants to know their opinion of the Fife and what they might like to see me serve. And did they know the owner? Brian was known in all two hundred bars within a half-mile radius, no need to produce a picture.

"The English runt with the mustache? Sure I know him. We used to let him in here until he started spending all his time with his head in the toilet..."

"Oh, Brian, sure. He put his head through our plate glass window, right there. Can't remember why, might have been an old football move. He came right on back when they let him out of emergency, no apology or nothin'. I'm glad to let him owe me if that's what's keepin' him away."

"Do I know him? Let me tell you, fella, he was the only drunk I ever known who was comfortable with the DTs. I mean it, all the creepy-crawly things he would see were like pets to him."

It was the same everywhere. No one had anything good to say. The ones who hadn't seen him in a while were surprised that he was alive. The ones who knew he was alive were insulted that I was looking for him in their place.

Perhaps I'd been unable to write Brian off at first glance because I could remember looking in a mirror during my drinking days and saying to myself, "I know what people will think, but it's just not true." In addition, my memories of Brian went back to a time when he was a flamboyant drunk in a sports car, as well as someone who could show me the door or have me barred whenever he was tired of my company—whether or not I was guilty of a slip of the tongue or, shall we say, a slip of the stomach. The fact that he had only put me out for singing had meant to me that he was deeper than most bar owners. It was a time when I was inclined to worship anybody who thought I had it in me to rise above my appearance.

I now realized that Brian had put up with me because drink had made him blind to my attire, perhaps even to my addiction. I'd mirrored his excesses and contributed to his delusions about ordinary society.

"Nothing has to be on paper," Sid had told us over and over, but with less conviction now that our doors were open. Perhaps laziness was the main reason we had to live with a bunch of vague oral agreements.

Take the "linked percentages" Sid and Brian had "hammered out." To me it had sounded a lot as if Peckham had intended for Brian's bar business and our restaurant to go down together. In any case the first I heard of the scheme was when I found out we were committed to it. Sid gave me a superior smile and interrupted me before I'd worked up a head of steam.

"We're just giving him a small percentage of our take. The same percentage of his will be a lot more money. It's a handout to help us get going. And it's insurance that each side has an interest in seeing the other prosper."

Brian's daughter had heard nothing about linkage.

"You're out of your mind," said Fiona. "I don't care what my father told you, no way you're getting a percentage."

"Peckham says that your father's promises are legally—"

"Take us to court if you want to make yourself a laughing-stock. My father can't remember what he says from one day to the next, but drunk or sober he knows what he ought to have said, and he'll insist he said it."

Fiona softened when she saw my expression of defeat.

"Relax. Now that you've spent a good sum of money on our place we'd have a hard time chucking you out."

All along Brian's family and its hangers-on had been nibbling at my Stilton cheese and pocketing cherrystone clams to make up for the wine I was stealing from the walk-in reefer. I had thought this was a pleasant way to live with each other, but Peckham was sore about linkage in any form at this point and wanted the last word.

"We'll chain our reefers shut when we leave. They won't lock up the walk-in, that would be too inconvenient for them. We'll never drink enough of their booze to offset the advantage of having us here."

The day chains went around our boxes all the wine disappeared from the walk-in. Amazingly, space had been found for it in the reach-in lockers behind the bar. And Fiona informed me that I would no longer be served at the bar.

"I had a long talk with my father on the phone last night...."

"Where is he?"

"At his apartment, resting. He never answers the phone, that's why you haven't been able to reach him. He called me."

"And told you not to serve me?"

"Not exactly. He said that by oral agreement he only let you start a restaurant here if you promised to stay on the wagon. You've got quite a reputation. Maybe he's been hearing things about you in the bars."

"I've no doubt that he's been hearing things in bars since that's where he's been spending all his time, but everything concerning me is pure fantasy."

"Well, we have to respect his wishes. It's his place. No more drinks for you over the bar."

"Has it occurred to you that not once since we started serving have I sat at your bar for drinks?"

"I assumed you had an agreement with my dad and last night I found out what it was."

"Hilliard and Peckham are still free to enjoy your hospitality?"

"Of course. They're never a problem. Everyone seems to like them. In fact, they might even be good for business."

"How do you feel, Bancroft?" Sid wanted to know later. "Obviously they're trying to humiliate you. Any chance we could continue as we are, as if this edict has no importance? You never wanted to be a regular at the bar."

"But what about when his friends come by?" Hilliard objected, "or somebody he wants to hire? When he wants to impress somebody, you know, it might look bad for him not to get served in his own place."

I'd made up my mind listening to Sid. "We'll go on just the way we are. I don't mind bringing my own. It'll be a step up in quality. Stealing from each other is childish. It's been an embarrassment to us from the start. All right, but even though this war has been kid stuff, I want you guys to remember we're playing for keeps."

"We are?" said Hilliard. "Not me. I don't take any of this seriously. I go out there with my tray and people actually want the stuff on it, but I can't get over the idea that the whole thing is some kind of joke."

"That's because of those trays you use," Peckham said acidly.

"Which you should never have bought in the first place," I told him.

"Ever see salts and peppers stored any other way? Your sugars and creamers? How was I to know that Hilliard would refuse to carry a waiter's tray?"

"I feel more comfortable with these little brown ones," Hilliard said then, and not for the first time. "I'm used to carrying 'em. High school, in the army. I always thought it looked ridiculous—some guy flying around with a great big tray up over his head. The carts are more dignified."

This wasn't a dig at Sid, however, who loved to fly around with a loaded tray. Hilliard had wondered from the start why we couldn't serve from a gueridon the way it was done in French places.

In answer Peckham had roared with laughter and I'd waved my hand to take in a roomful of people playing pool, Fussball or tripping on first generation visual heroin; people standing around in groups laughing at what they thought they were hearing over the loud music, spilling on themselves, in all probability pissing themselves without knowing or caring: our clientele. Younger since we came, less British, but brutish as ever—in studied contrast to the genteel customers in the gay bars down the street.

I rigged up my own bar in the kitchen, a marble counter near the stove. Fiona couldn't complain about all the people sitting on cans of industrial cleaner and drinking with me since they had come to the kitchen of their own accord carrying bar drinks. In effect I'd extended the Fife's capacity.

In my cozy den the profane shouts of the barroom muted the puling on the jukebox. People came and left with stories. Most of them were true, I thought, since that was the point of letting your hair down in the kitchen. A small haven of veracity.

But there were further hostilities. From the time I put my pots on in the morning until the first customers arrived I felt like singing in Italian, but the moment I made a sound one of the girls behind the bar would turn up the jukebox full blast, a reprise of last night's onslaught, sharp-edged for lack of a hubbub, more excruciating than the worst hangover.

Feeney the swamper was right in the middle of these musical contests grinding away with his mop. He was out of time with the music. "I can't tell you not to sing," he said glumly. "And I'm not going to tell them to turn it down. Now that each of you is paying half my salary I guess I have to put up with the sound till this floor shines. You won't catch me wasting any time."

The bread man came and left giving me strange looks, the cheese man. Even when our morning drinkers arrived it wasn't a sure thing that the pandemonium would stop. None of our chronic alcoholics seemed to mind what was going on as long as they could get a glass to their lips.

When Hilliard and Peckham showed up Fiona and I were less overwhelming. It was a tacit agreement which produced an uneasy truce. I hummed at my work, she kept the volume down—down to nothing if something listenable had come up and the quarter was our customer's.

Sid's lawyer's instincts and Hilliard's artist's instincts told them the same thing.

"There are bad vibes out there you could cut with a knife." Hilliard.

"Exactly," said Sid. "We've got to do something. Some guy at the bar asked Fiona about our food and she just shrugged and walked away."

"Yeah, walking away. They all do it. That's why we're late picking up or getting the orders working."

"What can we do about it?" I wanted to know.

Silence.

"What I thought. We're up against it. The best we can do is call in our friends. When the numbers go against them they might back down. I don't think we can force them to be nice, but we can make it easier."

I kept telling myself, "Our doors are open," "This is a restaurant," but in spite of myself I couldn't help wondering if Fiona wasn't right about us. Peckham was a dud lawyer, Hilliard was some kind of artist, I was a crazy opera singer and the restaurant we were trying to run was an incipient fiasco.

I saw precious little of Sarah after our Grand Opening. Hilliard was much too cagey to have Sarah meet him at the restaurant when they were going out of an evening. All too often I was hearing from him, "Sarah says hello," after one of his wild nights with her.

I lived through him. While I had my eye on little pieces of food in pots Hilliard did art all morning, did a little work for me, did art all afternoon, did a little work for me, went home and drank beer and played with Sarah till the middle of the night. I say "a little work for me" because Hilliard always moved at the same unhurried pace no matter how busy we were. Quick movements would have interfered with his digestion. All he did was eat all the time, sometimes right off the customers' plates, if something caught his eye. Not just leavings. He left the kitchen eating.

Once before our grand opening Hilliard and Sarah had wanted me to go to the Palace of the Legion of Honor with them and since it was a Sunday we caught Ludwig Altman's weekly recital, a real treat. Around all the great art we belonged to each other. She gave us each a hand to hold while we were strolling. When I took her hand during the recital, however, she gave me a squeeze... and let go.

Hilliard had a life and a woman and all I did was work, work, work. But I didn't hate him at all. I looked forward to seeing the art he'd been doing when he brought his slides and in the rare times we were alone I enjoyed hearing him tell me about Sarah.

Hacking away at a lamb's carcass, cleaning crabs every day, Sarah was nothing but a dream of beauty, already hazy. I was thirsty for any detail that Hilliard could provide, anything I could cling to. A lock of hair would have been enough to satisfy me, or as Jacques Brel would have it, the shadow of her shadow, the shadow of her dog...

Work, work, work. Fight, fight, fight. Not just with Fiona

and the other bitches behind the bar. I had my hands full with Peckham, too. I had known from the first he was going to make trouble so I had to make sure he knew I was boss. I guess I'm saying the fights were my fault. I could have let him go his way until it was time to fire him, but I got my kicks winning arguments with him. Getting Peckham to admit he was wrong was practically a crusade with me. Or getting him so worked up when he was right about something that he lost control of himself... A crusade or a vice.

Predictably, tension gripped us when our first restaurant critic showed up. A big name, almost as important as Herb Caen.

I waited on him since I was the only experienced waiter and Peckham didn't even get the chance to hear what I had to say.

When he found his first bone in my lamb stew you'd have thought he'd struck gold.

He summoned me by waving the little bone. "Look at this! This is a rib!"

"Only one? There's half a breast in there."

"You don't leave bones floating around in a stew, my good man. Somebody could break his teeth on them unsuspecting."

"I usually warn my customers the first time they try a bowl. I thought you'd recognize the recipe."

"Don't tell me where you got it."

"I'm surprised you don't already know. It's traditional! Irish lamb stew, but you can understand why I don't call it Irish in this place."

"No, I can't. The British adore things Irish. It's the Irish who have the chips on their shoulders."

"Some might say, 'crosses to bear.'"

"Some might."

He got down to business.

"Do you know what I can do to you for this?"

He held the relic of lamb between us as though I'd been trying to vampirize him.

"Yes, you can refuse to pay. You can sue me for damage to your teeth."

"In my column, you fool!"

"You could write nasty things about the place, but seeing

what an asshole you are I'd probably get some customers on the strength of your disdain. You don't believe me? You're somebody people love to hate. Half your readers are probably that way, and if I get just one of them I'd be doing better than I am now since types who read your column don't come to this place."

He left a decent tip on the supposition that Sid belonged to the brotherhood of waiters and a bad word about a figure as important as he was in food circles would go around as fast as clap in a commune.

I thought I'd handled him well. In retrospect I probably shouldn't have told Peckham who he was. It had been distracting, while I had to deal with the critic, to know that Peckham was running around in circles back in the kitchen, clasping his hands in prayer and looking heavenward. He'd have trembled too much to serve the man, but he had watched every move I made for the slightest mistake. When the critic had started waving that bone around I knew the effect on Peckham had been like pointing a gun.

I couldn't help torturing him, though. Even though I knew exactly what Peckham would do, how he would feel and what he would say about me afterward I needed to put him through his paces. Frequently he cleaned while he was spouting off or sharpened one of my knives. The more horrified he became by the ridiculous way things were done at our place, the more he brightened our days.

The day we were visited by Mr. San Francisco's understudy he had his apron off when I got back to the kitchen.

"You've really done it this time. That man has so much power. Why did I let you fix that bowl of stew for him with bones in it? The bottom of the pot, no less. There's a fresh pot in the walk-in. In the time it would have taken to warm it up I could have told him the history of this place."

"You mean how it was a machine shop before Brian bought it?"

"Didn't you know that this was one of the buildings that survived the Great San Francisco Fire? I don't think either of you knows how to sell what we've got here. Stained glass. Tiffany shades. Two fireplaces. That journalist might have made this place his hangout if the food lived up to the decor."

"And if he was an eight-ball aficionado," I put in, "or hooked on Pong."

"You don't have the guts to admit your mistake, Bancroft. You just ran off the most powerful man in hospitality journalism... in all of Northern California! You've consigned us to the garbage heap. Which is where this place belongs, the way you're running it. But I don't have to be there with you."

"Quitting again?" Hilliard.

"You bet I am. I have too much respect for myself to fail along with this enterprise. I had a contribution to make, but as long as Bancroft thinks he knows what's best for us, we're doomed. I'll never get the chance to turn this place around."

"What you'd better turn around now is that dainty ass of yours," said I, punching another dent in one of the reach-in reefers. "You can finish those tables before you go."

All the little reefers were full of dents, though I doubt more than two of them were in earnest—the ones that didn't have anything to do with Peckham. I was never angry at Peckham, I wasn't even irritated.

Close friends were the nucleus of a clientele in all the small restaurants I knew. Going in I'd been sure of Teresa, Wolfgang and The Weasel, Sheridan and a few others. Then Sheridan went his way and other friends from the past never found their way to us because digging them up would have taken too much of my time. Wolfgang was barred by Brian because, while I was shopping, he'd tried to distribute *Infamy*, his recently updated catalogue delving into the activities of international banksters during certain military campaigns that were never called wars—most recently, the one in Vietnam. Teresa was too indignant about Wolfgang's ejection ever to set foot in our place again unless I found the time to learn new repertoire with her. As Teresa saw it, Brian was monopolizing my time now, and she deserved at least half of it—if I cared half as much for her as I did for Brian.

Teresa's friends, even though they knew me well, would never set foot in my parlor without Teresa any more than The Weasel would without Wolfgang.

Hilliard had a lot of friends, people he'd worked with when he'd sold art supplies, people he'd gone to school with, fellow artists. If we ever saw one I think it was by accident. I don't know why he was so worthless promoting the place. I know he told people straight out what he was doing—I'd heard him telling them. Maybe his friends felt embarrassed for him.

As for Peckham and his New Women—he wouldn't have dreamed letting them near our place. Serving our customers only deepened the shame he felt to be in the same room with them.

It was left to me to pack the place with friends who weren't close yet. In theory, I was the one to do it. I probably knew five thousand San Franciscans by this time, a matter of having worked so many jobs, sung so many places, patronized so many bars—particularly the Irish dens.

I'd had my ups and downs with Hennessey over the years but I had been a pet of the salt-of-the-earth types in his bar, the tradesmen and artisans, the roaring boys, the culchies from the west and the Dublin jackeens. A ready explanation for this seemingly strange marriage of ould sods and an American like me was quite simply my love of Irish literature—I could quote pages of Joyce—and my singing voice.

Were I to put my head in the door today one of the regulars was sure to ask me to sing while my first Guinness was high in the glass. "Give us a blast, Gardon." Sometimes I did go on at great length, the times Feeney was on—no relation to our swamper—who winked a lot.

An Irish crowd was my first choice to pack the place, and McLanolin was my first choice among Irishmen. He sang himself.

McLanolin was excited by the idea that his protégé had his own place and planned to have opera someday. When I reached him at the Abbey he promised to come by, raise a few pints, have a bowl of stew with us. A few days later he made good.

"Give us a blast, Gardon!"

He'd waited to surprise me, there was nothing but foam in

his raised glass.

"You've had enough," Fiona called out.

"He wasn't asking for another drink," said I. "That's the way he asks me to give him a song. He's an old friend of mine."

"Then so much the better if he doesn't get served in here. We can't stop you from singing but we can stop people from encouraging you."

"You'll want to watch what you say to my friend, missy. I'm a singer meself. You could be askin' for a duet."

"Sing a note and I'm calling the police."

"Sure and it's a cold day in hell the police will arrest a man for singing with the little voice God gave him, and his friends askin' him to."

She went to the phone.

"Sorry, Gardon, I've got to be gettin' on. I don't know if the peelers'll have me, but they might run me record, and I owe a few hundred in parking tickets I can't affard to pay."

We never saw another Irishman who was a friend of mine. And we knew where we stood with Fiona and company at this point.

We involved our patrons. They were to ignore bad treatment by the bar staff... Consult with us... Remember that they were valued customers... Yes, we knew exactly what Fiona was up to, but where was Brian to set her straight? Where did we stand with him? Was he alive?

We needed customers. Irishmen were too obstreperous? What was the other end of the spectrum, little old ladies?

I called up little old ladies I'd worked with and they duly toddled in and insisted I serve them and tied me up with impossibly complicated stories about what had happened at the office since I'd left. Because they made me uncomfortable Fiona never had a problem with my little old ladies and I was stuck with them.

Peckham and Hilliard wouldn't go near one of their tables. The moment one of them came in my friends poked their heads into the kitchen and sang out, "Agnes is here," "Gladys is here," or whatever, and I had to adjust my cooking fires, degrease my hands, run my fingers through my hair and become that nice young man who used to work with these old birds, never forgotten, sorely missed.

Brian came back on a Tuesday afternoon when I was alone in the kitchen and Hilliard and Peckham were taking their afternoon break. I didn't emerge to find him at the bar until I'd heard the broken glass. It wasn't the sound of glassware breaking, which had become routine.

The first thing wrong was an artificial arm projecting out of the television. So much for the endless game shows and sports. The next thing wrong was a burly fellow with one arm trying to strangle Brian and seeming to succeed to judge by Brian's dark color and the fact that he was supine on the bar with both legs in the air. The third thing wrong was Fiona watching all this from behind the bar with her arms folded.

"Go ahead and kill the bastard, Tony," I heard her saying as I came up. "Stay out of this, Bancroft. This is an argument between friends."

"The hell it is, he's killing him."

I got Tony in a hammerlock and he turned dark red, too, but now Fiona was holding a full bottle over my head.

"Let him go or you're the one who's going to get it."

I pulled out of range and gave Tony a left to the midsection, wide open on his armless side. The blow doubled him up and he was in position for Brian to claw at his eyes.

For a moment Fiona seemed to be looking for a clear shot at her father's head with the whiskey bottle, but it was all happening too fast. I was raining blows all over Tony and he had to let go of Brian to swing at me. The moment he did, with more energy than I thought he had left, Brian was off the bar and clinging to Tony's back. Tony could have shrugged him off if his legs hadn't been entangled in the barstool. With Brian helping the momentum of his blow it was inevitable that he go down, and he did, with Brian still on top of him.

I'd sidestepped the two of them and was in a good position

to kick one of them in the head and end the fight, but the question was—which one? Allowing for her considerable hatred of Brian, he must have done something uncommonly vile for Fiona to shout encouragement to his murderer.

Before I could make up my mind which assailant to stun, Brian had bitten off a piece of Tony's ear, there was blood all over the floor, and Fiona was phoning for a cab to take Tony to the hospital. In great pain and with a couple of damp bar towels wrapped around his head, the fight was out of Tony. Brian had drunk a tumbler of whiskey when he realized his life was out of danger and lay passed out in his favorite window-seat with Tony's blood on his mouth.

The cab driver had had a look at Brian through the window when he came for his fare. "I can't take him," was the first thing he said. "I'm not an ambulance." Then he saw Tony coming toward him. "At least you can walk."

"Something Brian did cost him that arm?" I wondered aloud when Tony had left.

"None of your business, Bancroft. I told you, they're old friends. Tony's one of the family."

When Hilliard and Peckham returned to set up for dinner Fiona directed their attention to the "action art" above the bar.

"Whose arm?" Sid wanted to know.

"I missed the fight," one of the drunks told him, "but Brian took it off some big guy and your boss here pitched it through the TV screen. No more game shows. Now we got art."

I took my friends in back to set them straight. I couldn't believe what Peckham concluded.

"You think they've got Mafia connections through Brian?"

"Didn't she say 'family?' Family quarrels that end in murder, murder between friends, that's how the mob behaves."

"This place is the California connection for the English Mafia?" Hilliard's face showed satisfaction that Peckham's unreasonable fears were out of the closet.

"Tony was English, too?" Sid wanted to know.

"He didn't say anything. But his groans were 'oh' not 'ow.'"

"Well," said Peckham, relaxing a little, "if he's a wanted man he's sure going to be easy to find missing an arm, an ear and his powers of speech."

"A Mafia miss man!" Hilliard.

Peckham acknowledged him with a brief smile. "Tony is short for Anthony and ninety-nine percent of those mob guys are Anthony something. If Brian's related to him there's a good chance he's mob, too."

"They wouldn't let a guy into the mob who's drunk alla time," said Hilliard, serious now.

"I'm with you, Hilliard," I said. "But you've got to admit drunkenness would be a great cover for someone in the drug trade, for example. And think how much time he used to spend in that upstairs office. Do we really know what was going on up there?"

"Sure we do," said Sid. "He was pouring drugstore whiskey into empty bottles of the good stuff."

We'd all caught him doing it. That was the extent of Brian's working contribution to his establishment: increasing the value of his inventory.

At one in the morning Hilliard, Peckham and I took Brian his breakfast-lunch-dinner. We found him upstairs in the lounge bar on a sofa he'd pulled up to the fireplace, trembling under a stack of tablecloths.

"Sorry we haven't had a chance to talk before this," he quavered. The fire was generating so much heat that the building was creaking, though the night wasn't particularly cold.

Brian didn't know anybody named Tony. So far as he knew he only served two-fisted drinkers in the bar, no one-armed people at all.

"We have other things to discuss, but first have a little soup. Mulligatawny. You once told us it was your favorite."

"My wife's?" He brightened, or something in him brightened. One ember in a dying fire.

"She gave us the recipe, along with the one for cock-a-leekie."

"You boys know how to repay a favor, I'll say that for you. I've forgotten what I did to deserve this, but thanks all the same." He put up a small grey hand. "I couldn't, I try never to eat before the sun comes up. Put it aside for me, will you?"

"Brian, we need to talk to you about your wife and Fiona."

"What a curse for a man my age. If you've got one of them pregnant be sure to tell her she can expect no help from me."

"We're concerned about our agreement with you," Peckham put in. "Fiona doesn't even know about it."

"I'm sorry... What's your name again?"

"I'm Sid Peckham, the lawyer."

"Well, Mr. Peckham, if you're a lawyer, I'm sure you'll understand why any agreement I mean to keep has to be in writing."

Sid's eyes flashed. "I think we can all understand that well enough. Do you recall your obligations under our joint venture agreement? You were to contribute the premises, your liquor license, and seven percent of your receipts."

"None of that belongs to you. What is this?"

"Do we or do we not have the right to run a restaurant here?"

"You boys are running a restaurant? I think that's a fine idea. Just what this place needs, I've been saying so for years. We used to have Indian food here, by the way. Are you boys fond of curries? I know where you can find an Indian boy who does beautiful curries and he'll work for half what you'd have to pay a fry cook anywhere else."

"How did you figure we came up here with soup if we weren't running a restaurant?" Hilliard asked evenly.

"I thought my wife sent you. You know my wife? This wouldn't be the first time she's thrown me to the dogs and sent someone over with soup when she wants to be friends again. No, this is the first I've heard of your restaurant, but I think it's a fine idea. I've been saying so for years. What you'll want to do is ask my wife for her recipes. She's got one for mulligatawny soup that is the glory of the British Empire."

I shot Hilliard a look to countermand what he was planning to do with the soup.

"We'll talk again when you're feeling better," I told him, signalling for an exit. "Maybe we'll try you at dawn with the mulligatawny."

"She sent you!" he screamed, sitting bolt upright. His back was to the fire as we departed and since we had been considerate enough not to turn on any lights when we came, he was in silhouette. His mustache and the caked blood still around his lips made his mouth seem a large hole.

On the way downstairs Peckham was telling us all was not lost. "In the state he's in he'll agree to anything. We'll get him to sign something this time."

"Nothing he signs will hold up in court," I insisted. "Anyone in his right mind can see that Brian is out of his. It's time to get Fiona on our side. At least she knows who we are. Brian will have to do something drastic, though—something to convince her all enmity is forgotten, we're serious about taking her side. We might have to start cooking something she likes."

"There's no shame in a good burger," said Peckham, reviving.

"Anything but that..."

"It's all in the grade of meat and the seasoning."

"I don't care how good it is. I can't serve burgers and attract an opera crowd, don't you get it yet? Do you think I'm killing myself back there so more shitheads will come swarming in and I can make a few more bucks off their sodden asses?"

"If you brought in opera, they'd go elsewhere."

"All right, Peckham, if all else fails, you'll get your chance, but show a little patience first, a little loyalty. Your desperation threshold is higher than mine."

Brian's behavior did become drastic, though he wouldn't have thought so. He began living upstairs at The Fife and Drum.

He was at home. There were two sofas in front of the fire to give him a choice of warm, soft places to pass out. His office was up there to remind him of his possible importance to the world. He had dragged up enough hard stuff to last him a lifetime (if he didn't stop drinking). The upstairs toilet worked if he could find it.

We'd have carried him a meal three times a day and a newspaper if that would have been enough to keep him off the stairs. But Brian liked company in his misery and the bar downstairs was full from noon on. When his pangs of loneliness came while he could walk he'd come creaking down to us, order a bowl of mulligatawny and cozy up to the bar.

I never inquired into Brian's personal life—there was no need, it was right on top of us—but apparently he and his wife hadn't lived together for a long time. She was tired of mopping up after him. She would let him languish for two weeks at a stretch before she'd heed anyone's complaints. At the end of two weeks even Fiona was complaining... As was Deirdre, her older sister.

Ominously Deirdre was helping out behind the bar in the evening, ending a family quarrel that had been going on for years. I thought it obvious by the way Deirdre behaved when her father came stinking into the bar that she would be as glad as Fiona when Brian's drinking finished him off. When Deirdre got him his drink the glass was always extra full, and of course Brian loved her for that and got tears in his eyes.

When Brian was so ripe he'd have put a vulture off its feed, Emma arrived—the only woman alive who had the stomach to wash two week's shit off his pathetic little ass. The rest of us were too squeamish to get within ten feet of him.

The woeful sounds which issued from the stairwell were amusing to customers who knew what was going on. Brian wailed that he was in pain, insulted, ashamed, but he was giving in. When the scrubbing was finished he followed her out like a little boy without saying goodbye.

What went on at his apartment was anyone's guess, but I couldn't imagine him doing calisthenics and eating health foods. In a day or two he'd be back with a good heat on and the entire process would repeat itself.

Hilliard wasn't speaking to Brian by this time, but Sid and I kept trying to reason with him.

"How about it, Brian, don't you think you'd be more comfortable at home tonight?"

"I'm doing fine, boys. Don't worry about me."

"We could give you a lift if you'd rather not drive."

"No need to go to the trouble. I've got everything I want right here."

"Brian, the customers are starting to complain..."

"Let 'em go elsewhere to drink. They're a no-good lot."

"We mean our customers, the people who are trying to eat."

"I've never said a word to them, boys. They're not my type. They come in here and eat your food at a low price, but they don't give my bar any business. Let 'em spend some money before they start finding fault with my place."

In spite of Brian's daughters we were developing a clientele. Brian himself would have noticed if he weren't blind drunk all the time. Brave souls who'd never darkened his door before were coming to stay a while and bringing their friends. Even Brian's daughters must have realized that we were in business to stay, and that it would profit them to get along with us and be a little less unfriendly to the friends we'd made for the place.

However, Deirdre was so obnoxious that we had to put off making common cause with her and her sister. She considered us opportunists trying to wrest control of the place from Brian—failures, fly-by-nights.

Fiona was a dark, bosomy beauty. Deirdre was a bony nag with a turned-down mouth who had the annoying habit of making everything she said a question.

"That's your customer at the corner table by the bar, innit?"

(She'd been ignoring someone waving his arms for five minutes.)

"It's a cheeseboard for that twit in the green sweater, innit?"

(Green sweater had had the audacity to order it from her.)

"Took you by surprise, that empty plate, now, dinnit?"

(The rest of the party had left a lot of food.)

I even caught her recommending other restaurants to indecisive bar customers. "Want to try the new fish-and-chips place down the street, then?"

Deirdre and Fiona knew exactly what to do in any circumstance. When either was on duty it was like having God guard his own temple. Yet our offerings and our customers were almost always found wanting, even when they were just what the place needed. Oh, Sheridan could do no wrong. He ate a little soup, a bite of this or that, and managed to spend a tidy sum over the long hours of inexorable consumption that he called his life. When he decided to go back to New York we gave him a big sendoff and Deirdre bought him a drink.

Instead of a big loss of revenue when Sheridan was gone we were surprised to notice that a crowd of slightly less committed drinkers had sprung up to take his place. I actually overheard Peckham telling someone that "business was good." Hilliard and I were starting to hate our customers and all the money we were raking in just seemed to be marrying us to them.

Some of our biggest problems came as friends. Such a problem was Burl, someone I'd met in the drunk tank years ago who was now working at a famous place down the street as a bouncer.

I'd never figured him out—it was often the case with legends. Once in a cheap hotel, the first time I went to his room, he had bid me enter while he was in bed with some young guy. My first inkling he liked boys! He must have got started that way in prison. He'd spent a good part of his adult life in prison prior to going over to the good guys, at least marginally, by becoming a bouncer. Prison was where he had learned to bend steel. He never told me what he'd done to land him there, but I doubt it was serious. With Burl something as innocent as shopping could end in mayhem before he'd bought anything. Aisles, shelves, crowds, the difficulty of picking something out... Getting in and out of a public conveyance... Going through a turnstile or a revolving door... Everyday life was fraught with danger when he was around. There wasn't any danger to him unless he stepped in front of a locomotive.

It's not often you run into someone 400 lbs. and well-muscled.

The fellows much over 300 are usually soft, glandular cases. Burly Boy was hard as a rock. His thighs were as big around as a man's waist, his biceps as big around as most thighs. He could eject troublemakers with one hand, picking them up by the collar, arm out straight before him, and marching them to the street dangling in front of him.

I'd never seen him encounter resistance. The Forty-Niners probably had sense enough to steer clear of him when they went out on the town. He was a gentle soul in spite of the rough stuff he had to do for a living. He didn't give people the heave-ho when he got them outside, he just dropped them.

It was hard to think of him as a lover unless sex for him was a matter of what the boys did to him while he was running one finger through their hair. I'd observed that whatever Burl did with them hadn't changed their way of walking. In his room there had been piles of poetry dedicated to him or written about him by a prison lover, which must have meant that he was gentle in bed, if there was a bed.

Burly Boy thought he'd found a place to hang out. Fine if he came alone. The daughters wouldn't have guessed he was queer by the way he and I got on. But no, he wanted to while away his free time in the Fife with the young men he was seeing and he had no qualms about letting them sit on his lap. He had no qualms about fondling their genitals or French-kissing them. This could get tedious... He had no qualms about doing whatever he wanted to do whenever he wanted to do it because who was fool enough to try to stop him? For all I know no one had ever had the guts even to hint to him that some of the things he liked to do were objectionable to watch. Burl may have had a warped view of how he was perceived by the rest of the world—may have thought the type of the nellie Goliath was the crowning achievement of Evolution.

Brian Steele was not a brave man. Brian Steele had never done an honorable thing in his life, except by way of foolhardiness, as he was doing now. Brian Steele was telling the mighty Burl that he was unwelcome in his bar, that he and his "catamites" could take their custom elsewhere.

"Hey, there. You. The big one. What do you think you're

doing with that boy? Get the hell out of here. I don't want any poufters in my place. I won't allow that sort of thing. Hear me? Out."

At first Burl just ignored Brian, and why not? So did everyone else. But Brian had a nightstick behind the bar and it was hard to ignore Brian's attempts to use the nightstick.

Burl took it away from him.

Brian approached with a loaded forty-five which was also kept behind the bar.

Burl took that away too. This was all in a day's work for Burl.

"I could have shot you just now."

"Thanks for not doing that. I don't have much use for people who shoot at me."

"With a bullet between your eyes you'd think twice about coming in here and molesting young boys."

"We came here together. David, do you object to any of the things I've been doing since we came?"

"How could I? I'm so in love with you I'm just all syrupy inside."

"There. Could you leave us alone now? I'll return the gun when we're ready to leave."

The Steele girls were in a strange position. They didn't like Burl hanging around playing with his boyfriend, but they didn't want to protect their father from a fatal beating by complicating the issue. Love, respect, material support—the girls had been deprived of nearly everything they might have expected of a father. It wasn't all their fault that they were monsters. Seeing them stuck between Burl and their father I came close to feeling sorry for them once or twice.

"You don't seem to want my business," Burl told me after one of his run-ins with Brian.

"You've got it all wrong. We love having you come. Shame to lose you because of Brian's sensibilities. You'd think someone who drinks like that would be more tolerant."

"You would, wouldn't you?"

"He's unreasonable, no question. Something went wrong in his childhood, maybe. We'll never know for sure what's eating him because his memory is shot."

"Do you think you could talk to him for me? Ask him to be more polite to the boys I bring in. I can't get through to him. This is San Francisco, a gay neighborhood. He's the weirdo in this part of town. I'm not gonna have him discriminate against me because of my sexual preference."

"Of course not. Tell you what, if you'd stay away from this window area... Hang on, hear me out! It's not that I'm afraid to put you and your boyfriend on display. That's Brian's favorite place to sit and watch the world go by. Anyone but you would be asked to move..."

"Is that all it is? Why didn't somebody say so?"

"You tend to come here in the afternoon and stay till it's time for you to go to work in the evening, right? The time you like to come is when Brian is fully awake and feeling strong enough to face the day. When he comes down and finds his window seat empty the way he's used to doing, and starts reading the day's paper and drinking his vodka and orange juice the way he has for the last twenty years he won't even know you're in the room. I don't care if you're sucking off two of your boyfriends through a straw...."

"OK. You won't hide me in the back, though? I'm not looking for privacy."

My problem, exactly. "No, Burl, we'll put you any place you'd like..."

We did, and Brian objected as vehemently as ever, and his daughters were just as confused, and even my little old ladies had something to say about it, but had to agree with me that we didn't want the police mixed up in anything that happened in our place. Dope deals were going down all the time out in the alley, while Brian's barmaids looked the other way. To be sure, they'd have called the police right away if Peckham ever tried to make a sale. The dealers they were protecting were boyfriends, evidently, or friends of boyfriends... People who rooted for the same teams... I didn't bother trying to figure out the exact nature of arrangements the girls had made...

When Burl stopped coming in we didn't want to know the reason, either. He was alive, still throwing people out of the place down the street, a huge natural foods cafeteria that was open all night and catered to people from all walks of life, from hookers and pimps and drag queens to spoiled rich kids and trendy types dressed to a cutting edge. What all of them had in common was not needing to work for a living. Burl had apparently worked hard all his life (pumping iron in a prison-yard was work), hated the types he had to control and did his best to hold them to standards of behavior that could be said to apply to hardworking, solid-citizen types. He only fondled young men when he came to us.

We had our share of obnoxious customers. All right, maybe we had more than our share, since we were a haven for anyone who wasn't homosexual, and people who came with "not homosexual" to recommend them were often the dregs of humanity.

What really rankled during the time we were trying to establish ourselves was having Brian upstairs. Fair weather or foul his fireplace was always going, and so what if his nest was flooded, as it was once because of clogged roof drains (and the downstairs in its turn), and so what if the sofa he was on was a kind of island for a while? He had his whiskey and his fire to keep him warm and he never got up to pee any more. The tides came and went, life went on. Mulligatawny for lunch washed down with vodka and orange... Liqueurs of many different colors in little glasses while he whiled away the festive evening hours... Whiskey all night till he passed out again.

After a few months of the above regimen and in spite of Emma's bimonthly cleanups, Brian lost all sense of time and his appearances downstairs were embarrassing. Before I could head him off I would see him teetering through my lunch crowd in front of the hearth to take one of the window seats he favored and read his paper. Heads turned; noses wrinkled; mastication stopped; lips were sealed; nausea reached a rolling boil.

We were advised that a derelict had wandered in and the best that I could do was to explain that the "derelict" was well-known to us.

"He becomes violent if you try to run him off. To tell you the truth, he's the father of that poor girl behind the bar. A millionaire with a drinking problem. He'll be all right in a few days. Would you like me to change your seat?"

I was likely to lose these customers anyway, especially when the poor girl in question would volunteer, "He owns the place!"

The low point came one Wednesday when I had a good crowd in the middle of their lunch and Brian came storming down the stairs yelling, "Get them off me!"

It's incredible to me now that we could have lived with Brian's behavior for any amount of time. I suppose what made it possible was the stubbornness of my illusions about what the future might bring, which were in turn due to months of dreaming and the accurate plans I had drawn of the restaurant with music that I wanted to have someday, plans that could be realized as soon as I had the money to fix the dumbwaiter and refurbish the big room upstairs—and Brian was keen that I should do so. All I could do was wait for a change in his disposition, however, because regardless of the shape I found him in, he always promised to be more cooperative than his daughters.

After four months in business we decided to take Sunday off. Hilliard and Peckham weren't hurting for a day off as bad as I was. They'd had plenty of time to themselves everyday. The day off was their suggestion, however.

"You're a classic case of burnout, Bancroft," Peckham told me.

"He's right." Hilliard.

When these two agreed on anything there was no taking a different side.

"Taking off Sunday wouldn't hurt our lunch business..."

During my first day off I tried a program of sensory deprivation that lasted till noon.

Feeling resentful of all the Californians who were skipping through the woods together or lounging naked in their hot tubs I emerged from my miasma onto the blinding streets. Currents of self-gratification were so strong as I set off I felt as if I were swimming against a school of herring. When I reached the Fife I intended to cook myself a princely crab omelet, and garnish it with a refusal to cook anything for anyone else, even someone starving who was willing to double my price.

It was too beautiful for any but the hard-core murderers of their own souls to be sitting in a pisspot watching sports on television so I was scarcely noticed on my way in.

What was this? Someone had come to see me moments ago, she was using the restroom. She? Me? The barmaid (Mary Ann) went on to say "she" was looking for a job. More humiliation.

"Did you tell her I couldn't afford her?"

"I don't get mixed up in your business."

Then lightning struck and I wanted to kiss Mary Ann.

Her name was Nina and she had to be a refugee—no one but a refugee would fail to see that the kitchen at the Fife gave the lie to all the talk about a land of opportunity. It wasn't a place to stop five minutes unless you were on the lam.

Nina was French-Vietnamese. She'd cooked in a Vietnamese restaurant back in Paris where she'd lived with her French husband. Separated, she was in America with her two children. The husband hadn't adapted to American life and had gone back to France. She, too, thought she would like to return if she could save the money. She could have her job back. Her family ran the restaurant.

"Your husband wouldn't help with your fare?"

We were already conversing in French, and though she didn't know it yet, she was hired.

"He's not doing well. He used to work in the fashion business and got in trouble with drugs. He doesn't want to go back to that milieu, but that might be his only opportunity unless I return with enough money to help him get ahead in his métier."

"I'd like you to work here. Trouble is, I can't afford you. Things aren't going that well for me, either."

She smiled at me like someone who understood my troubles. Perhaps she already knew that I was going to reverse myself. Pinocchio was a better liar. "Look, I'd give anything to have you here to help me out. I'm not paying myself much right now, but

I could stand a pay cut. I live in this place and haven't got time to spend money."

"I don't want to cause you a hardship..." Still smiling.

"Are you kidding? This place would take off with you back here. People are afraid to eat things I cook because I don't wear white clothes... Not even a hat. Oh, I don't know what it is... People can't imagine me cooking anything."

"If I can feed my children here perhaps I could accept a small salary."

"Of course! The whole family! But I won't pay you anything less than you would have been willing to accept when you came in. Could I ask you to dinner tonight? Is there anyone to watch the kids?"

"What about your restaurant? It seems you're alone."

"We're taking Sunday off. I've got two guys working for me. I was on the verge of firing one of them to make room for you, but it's hard to imagine firing anybody. I don't think I could. It might be easier to turn someone over to the police."

Her approving look changed to one of real fear.

"Police gave you and your husband trouble?"

"No. I'm afraid of them, yes. I don't have the permission to work in your country."

"Maybe they'd pay your way back to France if you got caught."

"I've heard this. Surely they wouldn't arrest a woman with children?"

"I would think not. How old are your kids, by the way?"

"Mai is eleven, Nguyen seven. Mai is a great help to me caring for Nguyen. My little boy is spoiled."

"Perhaps you'll let me meet them after dinner. Will you accept my offer of employment? You'll be the cook and I'll help you. I'll do anything you say, but I'm afraid I'll have to stick with my menu for a while. You might not like this kind of cooking."

"I saw your menu before I asked for work. I've been here over a year and such food is no longer strange to me. We're quite French, actually. You'll find us different from the refugees."

"Well, that's good to hear, because I don't want to hate myself for watching you work hard. But you haven't really said yes to my proposals. Don't worry about the job yet. Have dinner with me and I'll talk you into it."

"But I do say yes to the job and I accept your invitation to dinner. We can talk of other things."

It wasn't just her beauty... Her gentle manner, her sincerity... I was charmed. I couldn't think of anything else the rest of the day. And I was having wonderful, selfish thoughts about changes in the place. No longer would I be walking around with clenched teeth, dreading my doom and supervising it at the same time. Nina represented a chance to care for someone without destroying myself.

In the short time we'd been in business I'd already been propositioned by five or six women who said they could cook and had their burners on high. Some of them had been serious, I suppose, but I distrusted American women—especially those who told me they made wonderful brownies or bragged about their meat loaf. Nina could cook in a French, Vietnamese or Chinese style as she chose. She didn't have to boast. All she had to tell me was that she'd worked as a cook in France.

After she had the hours straight and I'd shown her the kitchen Nina gave me her address and left. Mercifully, because I was starving and had been ashamed to start cooking in front of her.

My omelet was too full of crab to close but I was tired of being down on myself. Nina was intelligent, beautiful, even chic—a smart cookie all the way. She must have liked *something* about me.

To hell with her husband, I was telling myself as I called at the address she'd daintily written on a scrap of paper. To hell with what the kids will think...

The kids weren't even home. A neighbor was caring for them.

I'd trimmed my beard and put on a tweed coat that didn't have food on it, a clean shirt and slacks with a crease. Made a reservation at a classy seafood place. Wisely. If her clothes reflected Jean-Pierre's fashion sense, he knew what he was doing. Or perhaps it was Nina's knowledge of *couture* that had been guiding Jean-Pierre.

Before we'd finished our meal the French words were really coming. Hers were intoxicating now that she was speaking softly, sure of my interest.

She thought the meal was fine, felt that she was starting to know me. She asked if I'd like to come up for a while before she picked up the kids.

I went along, wondering if I should. It was the usual thing in France to find out about feelings by putting them to the test right away, like trying on a gift of clothes. I was worried that my feelings for her weren't the right sort to round out the evening.

What I was dealing with in spite of her beauty and the French we enjoyed speaking was Vietnam guilt. Stupid? Maybe so, but it wouldn't go away.

I hadn't gone to Vietnam, I'd just agonized for too long. What's more, I wouldn't have gone, I was a traitor. Vietnam had ruined the American dream for me, or say it had brought me out of it. I despised the advantages of being an American because I was aware that I only had them because I was a WASP. I despised American bullying abroad so much that I might seriously have considered helping the Viet Cong to kill *me*.

Courtesy of Wolfgang I'd been infected with idealism, the ideas of Jefferson and other heroes of the early days. The bald truth of American skullduggery had bowled me over; Wolfgang's evidence concerning the Southeast Asia Redevelopment Bank, for example, had been conclusive. Since I had often been drunk in those days, issuing my opinions in a loud voice, I fully expected to have been shot out of hand by one of the patriotic organizations, torn limb from limb by the legions of the American Legion, the Veterans of Foreign Wars, the Daughters of the American Revolution, or their running dogs, especially the ones who took the American flag with them wherever they went as a tattoo or a decal. I knew I was a danger to society and I fully expected society to be a danger to me.

Did I want Nina? Yes. Sex and politics went hand in hand. I

could have got it on with a Nazi torturer. The woman wasn't made who couldn't arouse me under the right circumstances.

Then I'd be able to get it up if I slept with Nina? There was a good chance. Since I'd given up the heavy drinking I was having the biggest erections of my life.

Was her frailness a problem? A desire not to hurt that would insult a woman who wanted the shit fucked out of her? (So many women wanted it that way these days.) No problem. She only looked frail. Small courtesies had disclosed a firm back, a solid left arm.

Did I feel my attention to her would antagonize her children? Children had never stopped me in the past, even when they were pounding on the bedroom door.

Were there qualms about taking advantage of someone who needed a job so bad? Making her feel like a whore for sleeping with me? I was untested in this area, but I was quite sure I wasn't the sort of employer who would take advantage of insecure employees this way. Even so it was comforting to recall how many of my former bosses had become involved with their employees. Let's face it, I hadn't had a woman in what for me was an eternity. A terminal disease wouldn't have deterred me. I'd have been in a hurry to get in her while her body was still warm.

But there was more. The stiff way she was sitting with her tits out like that. What was I thinking of? A movie scene? She was like a girl turning her first trick in a whorehouse, waiting for the appraising gaze to pass.

I took a chance and pulled her onto my lap. Lose the employee, lose the friend, but I still thought my chances of getting laid were good since she was French.

I caught a look of surprise and delight. We kissed deep right away, more aggressively with each passing second.

"It's been so long... It's so good to hold a man again..."

She stayed in my lap to have sex. She was agile as a cat, and in spite of her greedy lips, very in time with me, fully in charge of the rhythms that came and went. She sounded like the whores in France last summer. It was a set speech with all of them, I was beginning to think. Something they learned from their mothers.

Our time together was brief and I fully expected never to see her again. In the first flush of love a Frenchwoman expected to be sexually occupied all night. But Nina came to work the next morning with shining eyes. She put her kids before her sex needs, then, and she put work ahead of ease. These were the ways she remained an Oriental in spite of all her years in France.

On my next Sunday off I moved out of my studio apartment, forfeiting my deposit. That same day Hilliard's paintings, which had been piled at my apartment, went onto the walls at Nina's place. For the first time in what seemed like ages I had a genuine reason to celebrate and the time.

I had my own room, my own bed—for Mai's sake, who was curious about the exact arrangement her mother and I had made. A perfect arrangement, was what. *Pratique.* I could help as much as I wanted, have as much family life as I wanted, withdraw whenever the kids wanted to talk about their real dad or their former or future lives in France. School would be out soon and they wouldn't have to be hidden at their Vietnamese "grandmother's" during the day.

When the children were in bed Nina was there in the big bed for me, not as someone burning with desire for illicit pleasure, but as someone grateful, whose greatest delight was in her ability to please me. I knew that role; I'd played it many times, grateful to some woman for the roof, the bottle, the bed. I'd hated myself then; I'd been brought up to despise dependency in any form.

Nina was a proud person, fiercely protective of her children, resourceful in supporting them. And she appeared not to give a thought to taking help from me. The way she gave herself sexually went beyond something practical. Were all insinuation stripped from the word, *professional* would have described her. And her abundant health and energy came through. I was blessed in having her and forced myself not to think why, for how long and what I should do or how I should feel when she was gone.

Since Brian's very existence was preventing me from having a place of my own upstairs, forcing me to continue dealing with the living dead downstairs, it would have been logical to stay depressed and bitter. My long workdays were still full of headaches.

Nina completely changed how I felt about my work, and had a big effect on Peckham and Hilliard, as well—more gradual, to begin with, of course, because they couldn't play around with her when they were supposed to be working.

Peckham thought we were "creating a private world by speaking French." He was jealous and told me frankly that he had always been looking for an Oriental woman who could speak German, his only foreign language.

Hilliard had known right away that I was serious about Nina, and was hopeful, for him. "She must be a lousy mother to let you stay at her place, but I've got to admit she can cook."

"Thanks, Hilliard, I'll pass that along."

"I don't care."

"Which one of her new dishes do you like the most?"

"I don't know."

"Well, for once I don't mind you cleaning the customers' plates. I don't want her to see her food coming back."

"No problem."

"Don't let anyone see you, though. That's got all the class of picking your nose out there. Maybe it's only one of our drunks who sees you, or one of the idiots who comes to play video games, but if we act like slobs, walk around scratching our asses, we're going to make them feel at home. I want to see the kind of behavior that will shame them into staying away."

"Come off it. The drunks were out there soaking it up long before we came and they'll be here when we're gone, just the same. Dream about opera all you want. Some things don't change."

Crab had been featured on our menu from the time we opened. For one thing, I was nuts about it and had to have some every day to make life worthwhile.

"If we featured anything but crab we'd be sure to have spoilage," I'd told Peckham, who favored more variety in the menu. "We can't sell leftovers, but I'll eat anything with crab in it, even if it's been left out all night."

"Yes, but you're the only person in the world who would, and that's what has me worried. Our particular public happens to be turned off by crab and we've got to stop trying to force it on them."

"Sure you couldn't eat more yourself?"

"I couldn't eat five pounds a day the way you do. I get sick thinking about it."

"I get hungry. In five pounds there's a lot of untorn claw meat."

"Another thing. If you'd buy it frozen we could keep it. Not only the crab but all of our seafood. I don't care how sophisticated the dining public is in this town, they don't expect fresh seafood any more, not at our prices."

"Screw your dining public, then. Screw anyone who doesn't know the difference between fresh and frozen..."

"I'll have to quit if you won't reconsider. I think that's a shame in view of all I've given to this enterprise—and all you've given."

"What would really be a shame is to compromise on quality until we're on the same level as our clientele. What about that redfaced German guy who came in last night? Now there was a real diner. Maybe he'll tell his friends in Swabia."

"He came in by mistake. He was so drunk he couldn't see straight, that's why his face was red. True, he liked your crab, but I'm certain he'll never remember eating it or stopping here. Sober, he'd know enough to stay away."

Of course my *tête-à-têtes* with Peckham did nothing to deter the pro-crab tendencies of my menu. The Louie was now a regular feature and deviled crab or a crab casserole of some kind turned up as a special at least five days out of six. Cracked crab with mayonnaise was what I was eating seven days out of seven, but I was willing to share. In spite of Peckham's clucking I was beginning to move my crabs to a small band of addicts who were almost as fanatical as I was.

Cleaning crab had been hard work. Their little pink buildings were well-constructed, the marble counter had been cold on my arms. The juice made my fingers sting, aggravating the wounds I'd received from previous demolitions.

Hard work, but the high point of my day before Nina started. Oh, the cleaning continued, there were even more crab dishes on my menu when Nina realized that I was as crabhappy as her countrymen. We bought more crab and cleaned more, but the ritual was gone and the work no longer took me an afternoon.

The first time Nina saw me at work in my own way she burst out laughing. I understood why when she set to work. She could clean a crab twice as fast as I, and alas, she showed me some of the tricks. Suddenly my afternoons were full of disagreeable chores that Nina had assigned me.

It was no secret to our customers that I was taking orders now—Sid Peckham made sure of that. The knowledge that Nina was doing all the cooking reassured them. Our kitchen was all the rage and anything from it was touted as the best of its kind around the neighborhood.

Nina took all the credit, quietly center stage. Off in the dark, smiles peeped like little mushrooms on Peckham's face from time to time, on Hilliard's, even on mine.

I was getting a taste of fatherhood these days and Nguyen made it sweet. His affection was obvious. Mai seemed to be watching from a distance. She wanted to be very sure of me if I was going to be replacing her father, even for the time it took for her mother to make a stake for France. She told me that she was mad at her father for deserting them and hurting her mother, but she still loved him. "He needs to be a success before he can enjoy us. That's what Mama says."

"Do you believe it? Wouldn't it be enough to have a good job, a little time off?"

"No one gave him a job over here. He won't work in a restaurant."

"San Francisco's not the town," I said. Nina came in to listen. "Jobs are so scarce in San Francisco you have to be a criminal or work at McDonald's."

"I'd work at McDonald's," said Mai.

"Be a criminal," said Nguyen.

"Europeans get work in the best restaurants," said Nina. "Do you suppose all of them have *cartes de séjour?*"

"I don't know. Anyway, it's too bad Jean-Pierre got discouraged. I think he could have been a designer for one of the big stores. With one good contact..."

Nina's apartment was full of heavy old furniture that a succession of tenants had left behind. There was a landing behind the kitchen where Nina and the children tended flowering plants. The place felt as if it had been lived in for a long time—by me!

I'd lived with families before, I knew the routines. Husband and wife fight. Kids cry, run out to play. Adults make up by making love. Kids run in to tell mommy what made them cry. Adults resent kids for bringing discord, kids resent adults for taking their injuries in stride. Everyone takes sides, everyone resents what he has to give up to achieve equilibrium, everyone needs to fight to feel alive. More pain and breakage. Peace and darkness descend, new scabs are formed. Again for the millionth time the sun makes a huge rubbery splat on the stone steps outside and all the birds start at once, right where they left off yesterday. The morning paper is full of meaningless murder, meaningless diplomacy. The children sleep on, their faces godlike, and the adults wish they could follow them through life with a gun, on point or close behind. The coffee wouldn't be quite so bitter if you had time to really clean the pot. Family life. The old routines.

There were flareups, but we felt good sitting around together.

I was aware that Nina's family was on loan to me from Jean-Pierre, that I was a visitor to family life—on vacation, and having a lot more fun than the real fathers pulling on their pants in the cold morning.

I no longer shouted at Hilliard for carrying his cafeteria tray too high or putting plates down with his thumb in the sauce. Rather, I thought he was amusing even if he were costing us a star for service in some restaurant guide.

Peckham and I no longer quarreled over niceties of cuisine. I still felt a frenzy coming on when he wasted time over his orders to harmonize the colors of the garnishes, but when he started doing his little dance around a plate to look at it from different angles I no longer threw a towel at him.

My labors in the kitchen were no longer Sisyphean. Small talk with my partners was no longer being made between clenched teeth, nor were my occasional supplications when Brian was running off our customers. The way his health was going I'd soon be able to carry him upstairs when there was shit in his pants, box him and make a present of him to himself.

When the children were asleep late Saturday evening Nina and I came undone. We felt no need to explain the way we tore at each other. It was an understanding between animals.

Now that Nina was in the picture Hilliard wasn't keeping Sarah on such a tight lead. When I'd find myself keeping her company while she was waiting for him to show up she made a point of getting me to talk about Nina and applauded anything good I had to say about her. It goes without saying that where underdogs were concerned Sarah was something like the world-champion champion.

Sarah wanted to believe good things about me as a match for Nina, and it was downright annoying at times.

"I want to hear you admit how much you love that lady. She's in a bad situation. No papers, two kids, forced to work for low wages. Don't you think you have more to offer than the husband who walked out?"

"You think she should get a divorce to have me on her hands and keep working at our place? Anyway, I'm paying her more than twice what I ever made."

"She's more than doubled your business, hasn't she?"

"I'm giving her a huge raise when we go upstairs. Big if. Brian is still up there trying to drink himself to death and hassling the poets who come to read there once a week."

"Hilliard never told me there were poetry readings. I write poetry."

"That's why he never told you. You probably really do write it. The people at those readings... Come to one. I can't describe what it is they write. I recognize some of the words."

"So Nina's just a plaything."

"Enough! Stop trying to make me feel sorry for her. Whatever she is to me I am to her. If we've got to give ourselves titles call it Masturbation Assistant. Our sex isn't taking us anywhere new. It's pleasant and harmless and it makes our work easier."

"I don't see how you can have a relationship and withhold love."

"Of course I love her. But that's the impossible part. We don't want our love to grow, and it's not just the kids. She really loves her husband, just as I really love you, if truth be told. She's even worried about what her parents would think."

Sarah looked worried herself to hear this from me, but she brightened when Hilliard came. Hilliard never mentioned any of her concerns to me so I was quite sure that she wasn't telling him what we discussed. He'd have been on me in a minute if he thought I were upsetting her.

SARAH— It's been two weeks since I wrote anything in this notebook. I haven't needed to. Then today you nagged me about Nina and I revealed myself to you. I told you I loved you and the moment I did I realized I'd been lying about my feelings for Nina, about our importance to each other, about all of it.

You were hinting I should marry Nina. Perhaps I'm a worm not to. The longer we're together the more obvious it is to me that her husband is a worse man even than I am, so selfish in pursuing his career that he's willing to put his wife through this ordeal indefinitely. In France the *salaud* eats for nothing with Nina's parents, at their restaurant.

Nina wants to go back, then she doesn't. For the kids she believes she must. She insists Jean-Pierre is a great father to them. Mai wants to be reunited with him and I overheard her telling her mother she would go back alone to be with Jean-Pierre. So this is a pretty mess we're in.

If I made a life with Nina she and I would live like contented animals. I would grow fat and think a lot about new ways to season my food or my sex life. I would hoist my sluggish self into various seats, pulling the kids into my lap to watch what they are watching. I'd hoist myself into various conveyances and pull the kids after me, to go where there is something they want me to see with them, or something I've got to see them do. After years of being appreciated as a soft, accessible creature with a favorite chair I would be respected. Letters would arrive. Invitations. The phone would ring frequently and my tired announcement of myself would be reassuring to callers who want nothing from me, nothing but what they have come to expect. Like Johnny Carson behind his desk or Richard Nixon with his arms upraised in a V, an image of me wearing an apron would persist in a small number of minds after I retire from society, then from life...

No, Sarah, I don't see anything like this in store for me. Not with Nina, you or anyone. I am a better father to Nguyen because I am filling in for someone. My generosity is more genuine because no one expects it of me. Nina's body is nothing like a property to be held and occupied, answering all my needs for pleasure, security, identity, belonging. She is a door, a drug. With her I don't want to find, I want to forget.

Someday the door won't be there. There will be another door for her, for me. She never wanted to own me either, she just wanted to use me. Yet we have the highest respect for each other as artists... cooks, if you like, making the best use of the material at hand, creating memorable moments and appearances, adding spice, playing tricks on the appetite, never getting our fill of each other.

I'm sure of what I have with Nina as I could never be of anything that could happen between us. Every wild thing would be possible with you, too. That's been true for me too often. It didn't make a difference with all those women and I doubt it would with you. When I think of what I have with Nina what I want with you seems childish: to dwell in you, to protect you and be responsible for you, to be a resource and make survival easier for you. All very childish from the Oriental point of view. And yes, there are probably deep disturbances in my life which cause me to ask so much of another, to ask so much chaos and cause so much confusion.

Still, there might be something too exquisite about passing into bliss through each other's portals, eye to eye, as Nina and I do. There's nothing jolly between the seigneur and the serving girl. I see the rictus of a Sade, a life devoured by dreams. And where Nina and I are concerned the practical and useful could easily encompass the forbidden practices of the world's great sensuous gluttons. I can be led anywhere for the sake of knowing, but I already know full well that death is what lends excitement to all these games. Death is the payoff, and degradation wins no reprieve.

The trouble with practical arrangements with a sensual payoff has to do with the wish you see in her eye. With the omnipresent mind planning everything, changing things on the spot, never satisfied. I realize that I am creating a romantic construct with this endless devotional writing. Of course you are not what I make of you. You are not what *you* think you are, either. Do I need you to be something you're not? Am I changing you to suit some romantic illusion? No doubt. I need to worship somebody, somebody good. Your goodness was apparent from the day I met you. I'm still blinded by it. Were I not I'd have made my move and risked my friendship with Hilliard to win you.

I can't get over the feeling I'm taking part in a practical joke under someone else's direction. I have no sense that the joke is on you or on me, however. Nor am I anxious to see the final moves played and find out exactly what's going on. The little voice that tells me what to write would never have permitted any of this romantic folderol up to the moment I met you.

So far, my grand notions of you have all been accommodated. You continue to make me admire you, and when you come right up to me full of trust and the outdoors you take my breath away. My goal is the same as when I started to write about you, or to you: to make the waiting worthwhile. To hold out the hope that passion will help me to lose my mind. To remind myself of the possibility of life so lost that there aren't any doors because there aren't any sides. I think what I have in mind is a stroll, hand in hand. A sunny place with some trees.

The weekly poetry readings at The Fife and Drum were being produced by Alf Greenway, a much-published poet with a ponytail whose silences attracted mobs. Young things of both sexes just out of college kept him busy reading their poetry. When he wasn't curled around a tree's worth of poetry he organized poetry readings. He looked for new talent and old talent, went on his belly to plead for publication, wrote grant applications for poets and lobbied legislatures, raised their political consciousness, armed them.

He got me to spring for a sound system in exchange for letting Sarah read a poem. In addition he was to back me when I approached Brian about letting Hilliard, "the Pickwickian antirealist," put more of his art around.

"I'll take your word that both your friends are top notch. But one poem only, please, we don't want to corrupt the selection process. There's a long waiting list to read. Pleasure doing business with you." He'd said it to thousands by now. Why did I feel so good to be one of them?

He walked away with my self-esteem. Once I'd been an idealist pushing too hard, never the type to ask for special treatment—a hardhearted egalitarian, sure that the walls would fall as long as I was right. Teresa had been the same. If only she could have found a way to get by with slightly less integrity she could have screwed her way to the top by now, started over and done it again under another name.

The sight of the poets was exciting. Greenway had been right in his pitch—types like this could change our image.

All of them were poets, of course. Only poets listened to poetry in these latter days. The men were ultra handsome, the women must have figured that all males drooled after puberty. Except for being a foot taller Sarah didn't stand out in this company. I think she was glad of that.

She was only going to read one. The opus was folded where she sat with Hilliard and me. I didn't want a preview, but Hilliard was jumpy for some reason. A poem about him...?

This was the third weekly reading—and the first one fully attended, but there was already a highly evolved order of bullshit.There was a lectern with its Gordon Bancroft Memorial Microphone attached. Greenway sat behind it in an easy chair with his legs crossed, a sandal dangling from his big toe. He only glanced at the women who were shifting their weight before the lectern. Mostly he lolled in his chair with his eyes closed or his pupils rolled all the way back. In some mysterious way he seemed to be in rapture or agony, but not asleep.

Brian's tables and chairs had been gathered at one end of the room, closer than I would have put them when I began service up here. These were fine spindle-backed chairs and the tables were as hefty as our picnic tables, but straight-legged and lacquered. Some of the poets were ragged but all were intent, Greenway's was the only lolling body.

Into the middle of a poem by the fourth reader (no one seemed to know the order on Greenway's list, but all were ready to go) Brian wandered in.

Since he'd been missing all afternoon I was glad to see him. The others who knew who he was were not, and those who'd never seen him before were most worried of all.

"For the love of Jesus." He'd stopped well inside the room. Weaving. He looked around. "Caw... Can you tell me what the hell is going on?"

"We're having another poetry reading, Mr. Steele," said the hale and hearty Greenway, bouncing up from his chair. He was on Brian in two strides, trying to escort him to a table.

Brian knocked his hand away. "...The hell you think you're doing? We're the same sex. Are you an imbecile?"

Someone laughed at this. Brian spun away, nearly fell, caught sight of the table that Greenway had been pointing him toward. Holding himself straight, with his shirttail out and puke on his shoes, buffeted by a tempest of silent attention, he wobbled to the table and leaned against a chairback, looking queasy. What must he have seen? Beards being pulled, pipes being pointed, lapels being fingered—conferences, all eyes on him. "What do they expect of me?" he must have wondered. Suddenly he jumped back and wheeled, pointing a finger.

"...The hell are *you*?"

He was pointing at Greenway.

"Alfred Greenway."

"...You think you're doing uninvited in my house?"

"Having one of the poetry readings we spoke about."

"Poetry?"

I stood to explain.

"Are you...?"

"Bancroft," I roared. "Your only friend."

"What are you doing here? You're not a poet, are you?"

"No, I came to hear the others. In particular, Sarah, here."

"That's more like it. I recognize her. Well, let her read then. I won't stop you. But when she's done I insist that you patrons of the arts buy a drink from me."

"Laurie, why don't we let you finish after the featured

reader?" said Greenway through his grinning mechanism. "I don't think he'll last that long."

Clever as he was at making people like him I thought Alf had made a big mistake.

"What do you mean 'last,'" said Brian, spitting out the last word as if it were something green he'd just found in his lung. "I'll outlast you, you longhaired little git."

"Sarah? Sarah Schwartzman will read," said Greenway, as calm as someone trying to keep order among children. Bored-seeming, in fact, as if he'd been through all this a thousand times.

Hilliard, whose cheeks had blazed when Brian wandered in, was now white with fear. He couldn't bear to look at Sarah. Probably he'd never heard one of her poems before and was terrified that he was about to be ashamed of her.

The mumbling while Sarah went to the lectern meant that even the poets who thought Brian had been raving were now aware that he was pushing drinks because he owned the bar. Sarah must have noticed that all the faces turned to her were too resolute. She was in a contest with Brian for their attention and they were treating her like the underdog!

"My poem is untitled," she said into the microphone, perfectly modulating her voice so that she seemed to be whispering into our ears. "But it's dedicated to Alex Hilliard, the artist whose paintings are collected here and will remain on display."

She looked from the wrecking yard to the shipping yard to the flophouses *après le déluge*, with winos sprawled out in front or wadded into recesses. Her throat seized at the sight of so much familiar and unfamiliar absurdity. She looked at her large feet. She looked at Hilliard, who was bright red again. She managed not to change expression when she noticed Brian where he lay on his table, head on his right arm, eyes unblinking.

The setting sun has gilded all the leaves and boughs above.
Below the golden ocean moans, and glitters red, and heaves.
A breeze has just begun to stir and the straggling clouds to glide.
A chill is in the air that has begun to reach our bones.
We cannot long remain here, such a wild place in the dark.

Our unacknowledged thought the same we gather things we brought
And dedicate our last look round to the brightest, farthest sight
Where the sun still lurks at the edge of the earth and melts into the tide.
The darkness now encloses us and no one passing by
Could see us softly making love with our eyes upon the sky.

"Bravo!" shouted Hilliard. Out of embarrassment for him a few others applauded with a semblance of spontaneity—I was one. Then the polite applause started, a demonstration that was exactly the same for every poet, produced by people whose real feelings were and always would be a secret, though they would let you screw them if you wanted.

"I don't buy it," Brian said as soon as Greenway had raised his hand for quiet and Sarah had nearly reached our table.

Brian was leaving his seat, taking the floor. The general intake of breath which greeted his first step was a lot stronger than "Oh, no!"

"You Yanks could learn a thing or two about poetry," he was saying.

Amid the hostile buzzing the words "throw him out" could be heard.

"Criticism is hard to take, but take it in the spirit it's given."

Looking directly at Sarah, who was standing in front of her place at table, wringing her hands, he said, "The sincerity is unmistakable in your little piece. There's even some metrical control and a heightening of imagistic power. The long, even lines invoke remoteness and aloneness and so forth. One can almost hear the seawater gurgling in a little place between the rocks..."

"Mr. Steele," said Greenway into the microphone, "this isn't a workshop, this is a reading. No one expects to be criticized."

"How can they be helped, then? How can any of you expect to get the hang of something like poetry if you can't take criticism? Anyway, I own this place, and it's time I introduced myself to you nice young people. Brian Steele. Glad to have you. Drink more, please! I was young once myself..."

"Mr. Steele..."

"Let me finish, I haven't even come to the main fault in that last poem. How hateful for logic to intrude this way, my dear, but how do you and this lucky fellow of yours both keep your eyes on the sky while you shag each other?"

Hilliard was in a good mood, fortunately. Perhaps pleased to see Greenway with his hands full and amazed by Brian's sudden rebound into near sobriety. Some would object that a very drunk person is incapable of sincere interest in anything. In this case I was convinced that Brian was sincerely trying to help Sarah with her poetry and that his chief criticism was right on target.

When she'd said that last line I had been wondering the same thing. And I had a lot more to go on than Brian. It was preposterous to think of Hilliard rolling on the ground the way Sarah had described—"on the edge of the earth," indeed! Maybe if there were a massive sea wall, streetlights nearby, he was parked on blacktop. But "such a wild place in the dark"—not on your life. Hilliard was afraid of the dark in his backyard.

The next big howler was the publicity for Hilliard's sexual imagination which would make him look good to one of these poetesses when Sarah dumped him. I was all for Sarah's romantic outlook, it was what I expected of her. The homage I was writing, the mawkish hopes that kept me going... If Sarah didn't possess a stalwart romantic side I would have been wasting a hell of a lot of time... I might as well have joined our drunks at the bar every night.

It was the only explanation I could accept: she was romanticizing a time she'd had with Hilliard. Actually, there had been plenty of light... A full moon... He probably had that lantern along that he kept in his truck. I could even accept the thought of Hilliard copulating on dry ground in his usual dogged, journeyman style, but the thought of the sky being there for both of them... If he'd been with Nina he might have managed it... Having her in his lap facing away... Both of them watching the stars come out over the horizon. But anyone with a grain of experience, even Brian!, knew that the shapes were all wrong... Unless he were in her asshole... That would have explained his red face right enough! But even though Sarah was Jewish and probably could manage a little chutzpa in the right circumstances I balked at believing her capable of writing a romantic poem about being cornholed and then reading it to a room full of people who might have been indifferent poets but were much too sexually attractive not to be sophisticated.

"I'm with Brian," I interjected, stentorian enough to be heard in the hubbub. "I think the end needs work."

Sarah bridled next to me, but I didn't want to face her till I'd had my say.

"The poem makes it clear the *author* is looking at the sky, which puts her lover in the missionary position... That's where the poetry goes out of it."

I got a slap on the back from Hilliard to thank me for the laughs he was still having. Something flipped out of my periphery where Sarah was still sitting. The poem being put in that big purse that served her as briefcase and overnight bag. I grabbed her arm and turned her.

"You can't leave till you've heard the others," I said under my breath. "Sorry I said it. I was just trying to humor him. Can't you see the spot I'm in?"

She tore her arm free while the author of my supposed predicament was lurching toward us.

"I meant every word, dear," Brian gurgled. "It was the most beautiful poem I'd ever heard until the last line. Gordon has a point."

"Mr. Steele? Mr. Bancroft? Ms. Schwartzman? Could we please go on? We have a full roster of poets we haven't heard from. Our featured poet has come all the way from Austin, Texas..."

Brian had turned to deal with this interruption but began to sag when it didn't make sense.

"Then he'll want something to drink. Look, we're having so much fun hearing your poetry tonight, why don't I sell you bar drinks at a special price..."

"I can well understand why someone might want to leave at

this point and have a few at your bar," said Greenway, "but those of us who came for a poetry reading want to hear poetry read. Does that make sense? What they do later is up to them..."

"I'll tell you what they'll do," said Brian. "They'll go someplace else to talk about all the fun they had... You've been making it sound as if all this poetry was my idea. Bunch of American swots garbling the words in *my* language... Hah! This is the kind of thing they do down at the Main Library on Sunday afternoon, are you aware of that?"

Brian spat on floor—something I'd never seen him do voluntarily.

"Look, we've done publicity for this event," said Greenway, "we've gone to great expense..."

"Fiddlesticks!" Brian shouted. "The only person who's gone to any expense is Bancroft, here..."

I was glad of the plug, and amazed that Brian had remembered what I told him about the sound system.

"We created a flyer with the name of *your* restaurant on it," said Greenway patiently, but cracks were beginning to show in his self-control. Though the room behind him was empty he was looking over his shoulder at regular intervals.

"Now you've really got things turned around," said Brian, raging now. With all the reasons I had to hate the guy, I felt proud of him. "Is there anything you know how to do besides poetry? Apparently Bancroft is running a small sandwich shop downstairs, and I recommend it highly, but try not to forget that this is a public house, a bar to you, a place where alcoholic beverages are consumed. Look, the size of the crowd doesn't usually warrant it on a Wednesday night, but I'll open the upstairs lounge and give you kids a special price for all your drinks. A drythroated poetry reading? Never heard of such a thing!"

Wisely, Greenway let Brian have his way. He must have realized that Brian would have to negotiate the stairs down to beg the keys to open the upstairs register. It was never a sure thing that he'd arrive at the bottom of the stairs in one piece when he was this far gone. And anyone who knew the place at all had heard Brian wangling the keys, his daughters stoutly refusing. Perhaps Greenway knew Brian well enough to realize that no matter where Brian went or for what reason he had to have a drink before he got what he came for, and after a mere one drink what he came for frequently lost its significance. The key would be sitting in front of him all night but Brian would never once remember why.

No more than a minute after Brian had pulled the huge oak doors closed behind him, while reader six was still clearing her throat, Nina came in carrying a big tray of canapés: salmon caviar on egg, crab rangoon, watercress sandwiches, stuffed deviled crab, crab dip and chips...

I sensed Greenway's gorge rising and with it the mounting curiosity of his audience as to whether or not what had just arrived was the free lunch of legend. (I doubted that any of our poets had missed lunch, but I was equally sure that no one present would turn down a second lunch, just because it was supper time, or for that matter, their third breakfast of the day, as long as it was free.)

Before Greenway could say anything to stop her she'd set her tray down on the very table Brian had just abandoned and slid it in front of the low platform which separated Greenway and his readers from the rest of us.

"*Bon appetit!*" she said with a little salute, backing prettily from the room, the snap of the door just missing her swirling skirt.

As in *The Night of the Living Dead*, a film that had had special meaning for me since I'd gone into business, a good dozen poets, all men, were on their feet responding magnetically to the attractive food laid out before them. Greenway himself rose tiredly and inspected the offerings. When he swept up a small cracker adorned with bright yellow egg and bright orange caviar it was as if a signal had been given. All the rest of the assemblage, mostly women, followed after to get their share before it was all gone.

When the doors were next flung open all the poets were standing in the center of the room eating. Behind Brian there was loud march music in the lounge.

"Bring the food along! Bancroft? Help them! They'll need something to wash that down with, hey?"

"I'll buy the first round," I called out, motioning for Sarah and Hilliard to join me. "Drinks are on me."

Everyone on our side of the room was decamping, even the hippie from Austin who was the featured reader.

When the poets had adjourned to the lounge bar Brian's march music was changed for a tape of reels and modal Scottish sounds, which might have been martial, too, but were easier on the ears. Brian was holding forth behind the bar, so overwhelmed with gratitude over the size of the house having their first round that he was letting Hilliard and me carry their drinks. I doubted that there was anyone in these ranks brave enough to buy the house their second round but surely a few of the big drinkers would be getting started.

My food was quickly forgotten along with my generosity when Alf Greenway had herded all the poets back into the reading room after one drink. The readings were back on track and no one felt shy about shushing Brian.

Brian had consoled himself for the sudden exit of all his customers by locking up my money and fixing himself a killer drink. He wandered in while the featured poet was finishing his reading (he was applauded politely but something was very wrong with a trip from Texas to read such stuff) and began a disturbance when Laurie tried to get through the same poem he had interrupted earlier that evening. *Déjà vu* was nothing new to Brian—it was happening all the time. He may have felt uncomfortable when it wasn't happening, as if he'd finally been cast adrift in some uncharted realm.

This time a well-dressed young poet stood to call Brian off even before Greenway had thought of how to handle him. "We're here to hear what Laurie has to say," said the young man. "We're not here to hear what you have to say."

"You need help," exulted Brian. "Try something like, 'Here gathered are we/ To hear poetry/ If the poet's not Laurie/ You're going to be sorry.' Get the idea? Put the rhyming words at the *end* of the line. Pity you weren't brought up as I was."

Brian was so merry by now he was wandering about the room with his huge highball, leaving his scent at every table. He routed all the poets at the round table by sitting on the edge to keep his feet.

The poets he ran off sat somewhere else. Not one person tried to leave. The loyalty of Greenway's crowd amazed me: if he'd made an offer I'd have given him my restaurant for a song. Having the right crowd was just as important as having the right thing to eat. What did it matter if their poetry was any good? It was sure to get better. These young people had patience; it was the outstanding trait they had demonstrated tonight. What about Greenway inspired such loyalty, though? The poets didn't all dress the same way. In fact there were very few dressed like him, in the style I'd heard described as "Santa Fe" (nothing to do with the railroad).

The poets were waiting Brian out, God bless them. He seemed a good bet to wander out shortly.

Instead, in a voice that needed no microphone, he intoned:

God of our fathers, known of old—
Lord of our far-flung battle-line
Beneath whose awful Hand we hold
(raised glass)
Dominion over palm and pine—
(lowered glass to drink)
Lord God of Hosts, be with us yet,
Lest we forget, lest we forget!

Brian had drifted toward the door. Greenway and a number of his poets squirmed in their seats.

The tumult and the shouting dies—
The captains and the kings depart—
(drank again)
Still stands Thine ancient sacrifice,
(toasted the man last addressed)
An humble and a contrite heart.

Lord God of Hosts, be with us yet,
Lest we forget, lest we forget!

His quiet delivery, choked by emotion, made me think of the child he must have been when he learned these verses and uncertainty was keeping back the words.

He left, head high and shoulders back. The heavy door drifted shut behind him, stopping the troops in the distance.

No amount of applause would have brought Brian back. Whenever he'd had enough of a situation he began to brace himself for something better to do, and left as if he were well rid of you. Minutes later you came across him in some dark corner, writhing. You never found him on his knees in one of our restrooms. The disgrace!

Uneasiness of all kinds was rampant when Brian hired Carrie back. We weren't consulted but by now we were used to having Brian and his daughters do as they pleased, and having it cost us.

We needed another barmaid when Carrie came. Fiona was "bummed out from bartending" and wanted to continue her education "at least as far as Deirdre." Rumor had it that Brian too was "bummed out" because he was paying for Fiona's projected Poli Sci spree.

If we hadn't been watching Brian go down the tubes for so long Carrie would have been a good example of the perils of too much drink. While she was pottering behind the bar her voice could be heard now and then in a snatch of song. No more self-conscious than a parrot she would deliver a catchy but irrelevant message and run out of words.

Nina thought Carrie had suffered in some way she couldn't tell us about. Nina's maternal side was irrepressible around our sadsacks. Take her soup! she'd say whenever she got word of Carrie's distress, promptly reheating a bowl and stirring in a monologue.

Sid's reaction to Carrie was what made everyone so uneasy.

"She was brought up in China by British parents," he raved, sounding like a book jacket. "She lived in Hong Kong. She spent time in Burma, India, Siam. Her mother danced, played the piano, sang. Her father was head of a troupe of Shakespearians. When he ran out of funds to produce his plays he founded a puppet theater and took all the parts himself. That's a background."

I'd never underestimated the past behind Carrie's wide, moist eyes. It accounted for her distracted air, her fragile hold on reality—in this case, glassware.

Sid had it in his head that Brian was responsible for Carrie's mental condition. When he found out that Carrie had worked for him in the past he was sure that Brian had only hired her back to witness her complete ruin. It was one thing for Brian to destroy himself and the good name of everyone close to him—shit by association—but to preside over the ruin of someone as beautiful and gifted as Carrie...

Brian was spending his days in the bar now that Carrie was back, haranguing her. Sid was speaking for Carrie, as good at retorts as he was at torts. Encouraged, Carrie's bartender boyfriend Vito began to denounce Brian for letting his place go to hell and paying such low wages to someone of Carrie's caliber, whose drawing power was the only thing keeping him in business.

The wrangling was interminable. Brian told Carrie that she was through at least once a day, but it was easy for her to pretend she didn't know what he was saying, because *he* didn't. None of us paid attention to Brian's opinions any more, but that treatment encouraged the number and loudness of them until there was nothing to do but argue. The customers argued with him, Carrie shouted him down, Deirdre threw things at him. He began to realize he didn't have a friend in the world, an unfortunate realization for someone who had strong paranoid tendencies to begin with.

When Brian was in his office he put his army band music on such high volume that he had everyone in step within a radius of five blocks. No doubt he needed the music that loud to cope with all the threats that were piling up on his desk.

It was afternoon when Peckham and I paid him a visit.

"Office" wasn't the right word. Dumpsters were as well organized. I'd had glimpses of the place when Brian had first come to stay with us and had noted a messy desk and a wing chair. Now only the top of the chair was visible, one corner of the desk. When he half-propped himself up to greet us Brian appeared to be treading water in a sea of newsprint and correspondence.

Peckham and I kept losing our footing on the empty bottles that had sunk to the bottom.

Brian's red eyes were all that were alive. His shirt and sweater had the appearance of papier-mâché. His hair and his half-inch beard were clogged with the same colored syrups that had immobilized his clothing. The smell of vomit never clung to Brian, perhaps because he threw up his drinks before they had a chance to sour. Then again, the primary smell of urine might have monopolized any nose but Emma's.

"Have a seat, boys. Good of you to come up. Have a drink!"

The army stopped marching. Brian was fishing for a bottle.

"Never mind," I told him. "Too early for us. We've got to serve dinner." I caught Peckham's eye. "God knows we're trying hard not to think of it."

"Puts you off your feed," said Brian with a yellow grin, looking around. "That's why I take my rations with you down there. It's what you Americans say about business and pleasure. Drinking is a serious business with me, eating is nothing but... Heh, heh, I guess it's moderately serious, too, hard as it is to get anything down. Wait!"

"What?"

"You're Gordon Bancroft! Carrie's been serving you at my bar!"

"Yes." It was true. If anything she would have welcomed me more effusively if she had been aware of Brian's edict.

"But that's in violation of our agreement. I agreed to let you cook for me as long as you never drank at the bar."

"We never agreed to any such thing. True, Fiona has always acted as if we had."

"Your lawyer friend must have known. He worked on the details of the joint venture with me. Wait... Aren't you the man himself? Peckham, isn't it?"

Peckham was far away. Coming to your senses in a place like this was quite an awakening.

"Yes, I'm Peckham. Maybe you did say something about not serving him. Sorry, Gordon, I may have thought he was kidding."

Satisfied he was right Brian sat back and the sea of paper heaved and enclosed him. Hamster-like he reappeared.

"Go ahead, Bancroft. Never mind the provisions. You're handling yourself better now. I'm glad you boys came to see me. We've got business to discuss. The opportunity of a lifetime has come our way."

Dread mounted in Peckham and me while Brian foraged in his desk drawers for something to drink.

"An avant-garde theater wants to rent the upstairs. What they're willing to pay in rent will cover my costs for the whole building! Hey?"

The point of the drink was a toast.

"What about our restaurant?" Sid blurted, cheeks ablaze.

"You mean your sandwich trade? That's what I wanted to talk to you about. My new tenants are willing to let you sell sandwiches to the theater crowd. I'll be selling 'em drinks. Before, after the show we'll be mobbed. You could put your sandwiches in a basket on the bar... Don't worry, they'll pop out during intermission and you could charge whatever you like for a snack of some kind. Isn't this thrilling?"

"A lot of avant-garde shows don't have an intermission," I said gloomily.

"That room was ours! You knew we were going to expand upstairs!" More unlawyerlike all the time.

"Piffle. I waited some months for you boys to make your move, now, didn't I? Seemed like you were doing well downstairs. Your business has picked up. But there's still plenty of room to serve all your customers. I had no idea you were still dreaming of a restaurant up here. If you'd been doing something about the dumbwaiter..."

"How soon before the avant-garde takes over?" I asked, feeling numb.

"Any day now. They're waiting for me to move. How would you boys like to help me move a bed in here?"

We left before Peckham had aired any more of his grievances. I was sure he had dreamed that he and Carrie would take over the restaurant someday. Now he was irrevocably a waiter and would-be lawyer and our clientele would remain the same as Brian's. But a theater would be going in, and if Brian caused the thespians as much trouble as he had caused me, they'd depart soon enough and leave their improvements. I still *felt* as if I'd just weathered a big setback, but with the future so murky there was no reason to give up hope.

Business fell off while we were waiting for the avant-garde to arrive.

Alf Greenway got wind of the change and took his poetry readings elsewhere. A note turned up on my butcher block thanking me for the sound system and promising to pay me something as soon as he came into some money with my name on it.

Alert to the slightest change in us as they would have been to a hair in their casseroles, our customers began to lose their appetites.

Sid was the most demoralized. "Up to now we didn't need the punks and zombies. We were cooking for the ten percent with tastebuds, hoping to take them upstairs with us. Now there's no getting around it—if we can't keep the zombies happy, we're finished. Being polite to them now that we need them is killing me."

Nina took him to task. "Customers are all the same. I don't like this word 'zombie.' And what is 'punk' for you?"

"Punk is what Hilliard calls the young zeros and party animals," I told her. "It's not the right word, but you can't blame him. It would be a shame if American English lost a word like punk because of the punkers. He doesn't mean those gentle people with the green hair who are shouting 'no future' and mutilating themselves."

"Yes, in France these are the punks."

"And he doesn't mean the lost souls who are taking it in the ass in prison."

The more I told Nina about our customers, the more confused she became. Heretofore she'd thought that the young people eating her food were students, starving artists, thrifty hippies and the like. She'd been imbued with the notion that a restaurant was meant to offer people a good time and profit from it. But the way she saw it now Peckham, Hilliard and I resembled pushers handing out our product and taking money for it with cynicism and distaste.

"I could go for that analogy if we were serving them hamburgers—anything bad for them, more and more of it, getting richer while they got sicker. Actually, maybe we're helping them," I said grimly. "Maybe there's some satisfaction in giving them an antidote to that stuff of Brian's." She nodded, eager for more. "Maybe some of them will develop a taste for good food and start going to restaurants where they can't put their cigarettes out on the floor."

"No! They will stay with us here, but to taste our food better, stop smoking!"

I loved her innocence. It made me feel good to think she needed my protection. But she was still a danger to herself.

"Wake up, Nina. We're talking about zombies. Zombies don't stop smoking. Try as hard as you like, you'll never convince one that anything he likes to do is bad for him. Some of them are so far gone that they think they can cross the street whenever they like. True, most of them make it, but leading a charmed life is the essence of being a zombie. Let's take their money, but for God's sake, let's not try to reform them!"

With great pride in his accomplishment Peckham told me that he had persuaded Carrie to relay anything she heard regarding the upstairs premises. She was on our side, then—fully aware of how we were being screwed.

When he told me this I had shrugged it off. I didn't doubt that Carrie was an excellent fly on the wall, but I did rather expect that when she got down off the wall she'd tell us about flies.

I couldn't have been more mistaken.

"Emma and Deirdre have been against the avant-garde group from the start." Peckham was agog with the news he had for me. "The deal is with Brian and wouldn't mean a cent more for the bar downstairs."

"How do they plan to scotch it?"

"Fiona and Deirdre have sent Emma to Switzerland. This isn't the first time. Every couple of years Emma revisits her alpine pastures. She calls it a pilgrimage. The point is, Brian would never have been able to relocate without her help. Now the girls are intent on fixing up his office and the theater's already looking elsewhere. They've got nothing on paper with Brian. The big room is ours again!"

I thanked Peckham for the good news, if that's what it was.

As for Hilliard, when the avant-garde veered away from us at the last minute, far from feeling relief, he was sorry we wouldn't get to sell a few more sandwiches.

II

I knew by the way Brian lurched into the kitchen that he had another big plan.

"Why the long faces, can't you see this is good news? Remember when I was trying to get that avant-garde theater in here a few months back? Did I ever tell you—seems they would only have been able to put in a 99-seat theater to keep from paying top union wage. Not enough seats to pay for anything but one-man shows. As soon as they started telling me about the union rules I knew they were through. Next thing you know they'd be trying to unionize me!"

He scouted for a smile but all four of us were waiting to hear his good news.

"Boys—and you too, dear—I'm taking the Fife and Drum in a new direction, one dear to my heart. My daughters are going to fight me. I'm counting on your loyalty. For years I've admired the dinner theatres you find in America far out on your farm roads, overlooking waterfalls. Places the unions have forgotten. Places where young American voices are raised in song and banjos are strumming..."

Hilliard and Peckham groaned. I laughed.

"I feel I have an obligation to let you boys serve your dinners upstairs. I know how much it would mean to you to have a room of your own..."

"What sort of theater is it going to be?" Peckham.

"As far as I know, the first event of its kind in a dinnerhouse. Ladies wrestling!"

I laughed louder than before.

"Think of it, boys. Something you can't even see on Cable TV. I picture women as big as my wife, jolly big boobies, all of it, but the muscle would have to be there, too—and a flair for wrestling. I know the chap who promotes some of the big boys on Sunday morning and he said he'd have me a show within a week. All we've got to do now is fix up a small ring. Small because these girls aren't going anyplace. You see, in our dinnerhouse matches no one will be thrown from the ring. Your diners have nothing to worry about on that score."

"I don't suppose there's a chance that a little sweat might go flying." Peckham muttered. "Anyway, why aren't they wrestling in mud? That would certainly keep us on our toes."

"You miss the point, lad! We'll have trained athletes, not some sex show for people who don't care about wrestling. Girls who are properly trained won't even come out of their clothes. A spectacle of this kind can be completely self-contained as long as the girls know what they're doing. Just in case, though, we can put the tables on tiers above the arena, three sides..."

"That sounds expensive," said Peckham. "Gordon, wouldn't you like to speak to this? We couldn't set up a restaurant at a moment's notice..."

"Is there any chance we could go into this together?" I asked Brian.

"I was hoping we would, because I wouldn't like to bring in restaurant people I've never worked with. I've got more tables and chairs in storage, and I've got risers from the time we were doing fashion shows. The way I see it the big expense will be warming ovens and the dumbwaiter, of course... a few hundred dollars."

I'd been carrying my eight-thousand-dollar dumbwaiter load for so long that a sinking feeling followed Brian's words. Then the blood rushed to my head and flooded my arms and Brian was in more danger than he knew.

"And what's wrong with the dumbwaiter that would cost us

hundreds of dollars?" I asked, heading off Peckham.

"Oh, the motor needs an overhaul is all. The alternator? I don't understand the thing, but I know just who to call."

Peckham was shaking his fist at himself. Hilliard, trusting soul, was still flabbergasted. Nina had been smilingly out of place but Peckham's antics were making her curious. Scenes of the restaurant that could have been upstairs were flashing before my eyes.

"Great, let's get going, then," I babbled. "We'll have to clean before anything else. It's a shithouse up there."

Brian beamed at me quasi-paternally. "That's what I like about you Yanks. You spot an opportunity and you act. Bring on the Amazons! Stock the bar! We've got our work cut out for us. Remember this moment a few years from now when we have imitators. Get ready for all the naysayers who will wish they'd thought of it first... Thought of what, though? We need a catchy name."

"How about the Open Pit Burleycue," said Hilliard, astonishing us.

"The Pit is just right." Brian placed a grey hand on Hilliard's shoulder. "I like this boy."

By the time Brian had gone back upstairs Nina was making a run to the Chinese grocer and Peckham was giving me the benefit of the doubt.

"Brilliant, Bancroft! We get the upstairs fixed up and then all we've got to do is run off Brian and his warrior women. Knowing his daughters we should have lots of help. Food service continues. The place is ours. They'd be hard put legally to get us out."

"Exactly. He said tiers but I heard balcony. This goose has just laid a Golden Horseshoe. He has risers, too, and more tables and chairs in storage. Still, we'd better plan to serve around his wrestlers for a while."

"You're not serious."

"No, curious. Let's take a look at the demography here. We're one of two straight bars in a gay neighborhood—but you could say that of almost any straight place in San Francisco. From everything I've read, the lesbian population is expanding at double or triple the rate of the rest of us, and not because of people coming out of the closet. Girls are no longer stigmatized for wanting to suck a pussy, even by their friends in junior high school. They're as relaxed about it as they would be about frenching one of their pimply boyfriends, or if they're not, they will be soon, and it might be a good time to get on the bandwagon, or up in the bleachers."

"Maybe there's something wrong with me," said Hilliard, "but it already turns me on a little to think of women trying to hurt each other while I'm having my dinner."

"Sorry to burst your bubble..." Peckham, sharpeyed. "Responsible women aren't interested in wrestling. Women in general aren't interested, lesbian or what have you. The only people in the world who are interested in exploitative shit like women's wrestling are degenerate idiots like Brian, chauvinists from colonial outposts who say 'boy.'"

"I don't say 'boy,'" said Hilliard, "but I think it might be interesting to see really huge women go at it. From my own experience I'd say your average woman could really give you your money's worth in a fight."

"Moot point. You could never have food service and wrestling at the same time in a so-called dinnerhouse. The Health Department would close you."

"Hold on. Isn't the usual thing at a dinnerhouse, you feed the folks, then give them a show? What's wrong with doing the same thing here? If it's a package the wrestling fans will have to eat what we put before them, and I have enough faith in Nina's cooking to think that they'll be coming back for more no matter who's on the card."

Peckham had turned the bright pink color which meant that words were failing him. "That's the last time I ever respect you as a musician. All those years of classical training!"

"Yeah, well, I've had a few years' experience trying to get my way, too, and I don't expect an opera theater to get handed to me by someone like Brian." I let this sink in. Then I went on more quietly. "Look, I've had lesbian friends who are big on sports. Taking sides, egging each other on—go to their bars if you don't think they're ripe for something like this."

"Let's see what kind of people they are," said Hilliard. "I say they're a step up even if they're a bunch of vicious bitches."

I was only half-dreaming when I imagined franchises in all the major cities with Nina's food and my kind of music and even servers with long beards. Brian's wrestlers at the grand opening to attract the sort of customer we'd been after all along, operalovers with a sense of humor. They were out there. In spite of appearances and the ample olfactory evidence most operalovers weren't half-pickled snobs who were much too serious about things like stage business, and thought an opera could be spoiled because of a horse pissing on stage or a balcony coming down on a diva's head.

You'd have expected someone who couldn't get around to wiping his ass to have problems with procrastination; I didn't expect to see any wrestling for some time. But Brian moved faster than I would have thought. He took up residence in his office, put on some march music and peered out again and again to watch the illegal immigrants he'd hired scour the upstairs dining room, lounge and snug.

With Nina doing most of the cooking I could keep one eye on the dining room. Shortly after Brian had approached us about the wrestling I caught Peckham letting a customer flamboyantly unwrap a fish and chips order and start eating it at one of our tables. The customer must have felt glad to escape with his life by the time I had him outside with his fish stuffed into his jacket pocket. Peckham was the reason I was so angry, but I let the incident pass without giving it to him. If I publicized my feeling that treason was afoot I wouldn't get to know who was planning what.

When Peckham asked if we could talk somewhere quiet I was on my guard. I took him down the street.

"It's Carrie again," he said. "Or Vito to be exact. I've found out Brian wants to use him to run the bar in his new place. So far he hasn't said no. I'm not sure Carrie wants him to."

"How could that be bad for you? If Vito throws in with Brian, Carrie will get tired of him fast."

"You don't know Carrie. She's deeply involved with this guy and he's not doing her a bit of good. With him upstairs..."

"With him upstairs you're afraid you might have to get behind the new place to stay in with Carrie, instead of going over to Deirdre and Emma and waiting till Brian and I lose our ass to step in and run the whole show the way you've always wanted."

"I'm sorry you feel that way."

"What way? Like I'm about to lose my ass?"

"I'm sorry you feel that I'm not behind you."

"Oh, I feel you behind me all right. That's why I'm always watching my back."

"I wish you every success and I'd never think of stepping in unless you wanted to get out of the business. I just don't think I could be much help to you in the kind of place you've got in mind."

"No, you wouldn't be able to step outside and do your dope deals."

"I promised you I'd never do any personal business here and I've kept my word."

"Yeah, well, I've been keeping an eye on you. You've been buttering up clowns like that Harry character and those three guys from Jersey that latched onto us. You've been gladhanding all over the place, and there's no reason to. They're already our customers. All they need to hear from you is the sound of their plates being put down, and that's all they were hearing until a couple of days ago."

"It was Deirdre's idea. I should try to get to know the customers better, especially the ones they don't know too well themselves. That's why I wanted to talk to you today, the real reason. I thought I'd only be able to sound you out, but you seem to know what's going on so I'll tell you everything. I think Nina should cook for the restaurant upstairs and you should manage it. I want to take over food service for the bar and go with a new menu that's heavy on hamburgers."

"Peckham, you poor chump. I knew all along they'd throw their support to us if we served hamburgers. That's all they eat. To think of the lectures I sat through about palates and cuisines."

"There's no disgrace in serving a first-rate hamburger. We've only got a third of the people who come here eating our food. If I can put out the right hamburger I'll have them all. It's just good business."

"You want to scrap the old menu and all of the things Nina's been cooking?"

"No, all I really need is room on the griddle. I can cook the orders and run them out. It'll mean more work for me and I'd want my salary to reflect that. I don't care what happens to my tips. I expect them to stay the same in spite of increased volume. People sometimes forget they're being served by a waiter when you hand them a hamburger. Look, I'm not for any change in the way we handle our revenue. I'll still keep the daily journal for you and do your books—and I won't charge more for the heavier transaction load. The people who patronize this place will be getting the food they've always wanted. You'll have a dinnerhouse upstairs, which was what *you* always wanted. If Brian hadn't fooled us about the dumbwaiter we'd have been serving up there all along and wrestling would never have been an issue."

"Brian snookered us and someday I'll get even. Still, who can blame him for wanting to hang onto a space like that? He's had offers ever since his old partner left. He was just waiting for the right one."

"Too bad he didn't take on the avant-garde."

"We'll see. As for your offer, sure, I'll go along, but you'll have to think of yourself as a paid operator, not a lessee—you'd know the right word. You're just running part of an operation that belongs to me—at least for now."

"That's the way I want it."

"What about this business with Vito, then—was that just a way of getting to talk to me?"

"No. He's got me worried. I don't want him working here

the same hours as Carrie. That means they'll have time off together and it'll be next to impossible for me to make my move."

"For all your scheming you're not very shrewd. If they've got time on their hands they'll fight. As it is, with one being the best customer of the other all day and half the night, there's no way to go for the jugular. I don't give 'em a week if they've got to worry about each other while they're at work. Some woman will be perched in front of Vito up there..."

"Some lesbian, though. That won't do any good."

"Carrie knows better. The minute you go to work behind a bar you have to start fighting off people who want to get in your pants."

Sid thought for a moment. "One more thing. Who gets Hilliard?"

"You know him better than that. He won't jump ship."

"What if the lesbians want waitresses?"

"We'll let Hilliard make up his own mind. I'll be able to work him in somehow no matter what happens, but if he wants to stay with the hamburger crowd, well, fine."

Sid started perfecting his hamburgers the next day, making a hell of a fuss to get them right.

I'd known all along that Sid wasn't the man to run something as stubbornly imperfectible as a restaurant.

Perfectionism was what inspired him, but all it inspired him to do was dabble. Sid had a good critical mind and knew enough history to realize that he would never do anything heroic. However, dabbling made the comparison to great men possible. No matter how cockeyed, when he laid out one of his schemes you couldn't help thinking how long it must have taken him to acquire so much knowledge.

I doubt if he was as miserable about imperfection as he let on. All perfectionists wanted to be encouraged to keep trying. They alone knew that their efforts were doomed to failure.

Deirdre and the other barmaids thought Sid's hamburgers

tasted great, but they were always able to find some tiny flaw. Nina tasted Sid's hamburgers but had no basis for comparison. Hilliard tried one and said, "Tastes like a hamburger," but he and Peckham were cooler to each other now that they were no longer workmates.

Nina didn't begrudge Peckham the griddle since all we were frying these days were our German wursts, and wurst fell from favor the minute word went out that we had hamburgers.

Sales of all our menu items plummeted as one after the other our quasi-customers ordered hamburgers, or whathaveyouburgers. There was no menu to curb their fancies and Peckham was always up to a challenge. He ran around like a madman serving his hamburgers and bestowing superior looks upon Hilliard and me whenever he caught us watching.

Fortunately work was proceeding apace upstairs. Now that signs of Brian had been expunged and he was keeping to his office, the bar up there contained the best seats in the house. Vito was indeed tending it, and by thc time our ring was built and the tiered seating was in, he had a following.

The elevator man told us there was nothing wrong with the dumbwaiter but a bad switch, though it had been out of service for so long it did need an overhaul. Since Peckham had no plans to serve anything but soup-salad-sandwiches we were able to relocate equipment and material that eased our construction costs in the upstairs serving area. In short, my expenses to get things going at the Pit were piddling.

My other worries came to nothing as well. So many women wanted to wrestle that we had to hold auditions. The lesbian community responded warmly to the concept of women wrestling. I'd gone to the top with my ideas, to the executive offices of the same Lesbian Political Action Committee that had all the politicians smiling. There a panel of prominent lesbians assured me that as long as straight men stayed away there couldn't possibly be anything degrading about women wrestling. "Goodnatured combat between women has long been considered impossible by the sexist press," said the letter of endorsement I was given. "We believe that the promotion of activities such as Mr. Bancroft's is in the interest of good, clean fun and should offend no right-thinking restaurant patron."

I was flying high. The only legitimacy I'd ever craved was within the lesbian movement itself. Then if an influential lesbian turned against us—because of a liaison with one of our wrestlers, for example—I'd be able to call upon her sisters to defend my contribution to the lesbian lifestyle. But what if our wrestlers discovered a yen for each other while wrestling?

"The way I see it," said Hilliard, "well, all of them are big, right? How often do you see a couple of big ones go for each other? The big ones are supposed to go for the ones that look like normal women. It's the normal-looking dykes who are crazy in my book."

"You're going to blow it for us if you don't watch your mouth, Hilliard."

"I'm talking to you. I'd never call one a dyke to her face."

"But you've got to remember there's nothing abnormal about what they like or what they do. They're not crazy. They like the same things in a woman that we do, is that so hard to understand? Think of them as pals."

"You're right. Hey, I like all the ones we've met so far. Especially the wrestlers. You're wrong if you think they're all gay. It just doesn't bother them to have women in love with them. They're no different than any other performer in wanting people to admire them. No one stops to sex the applause."

"I just hope that kind of admiration is all we've got to worry about."

"You're afraid they'll go too far and bring the cops?"

"I'm not worried about the police. I'm not even worried about guilt and hypocrisy. I'm worried about jealousy. We most certainly will have at least one woman out in the audience who is in love with one of our wrestlers and one who is in love with the other. But it's not only the big backers I'm worried about, it's their friends."

"You're afraid everyone will get into it."

"You bet I am."

"A brawl. They'll smash up all that expensive shit we bought for them to eat with. They'll jump into the ring, or the wrestlers will jump out. Give their fans a hand."

"That's why it'll never do to let Brian be the referee. He's been looking forward to it. You see how excited he got at the last audition. But he could never throw a spectator out of the ring and he could never break up a match when they start killing each other."

"I knew it was the wrong move to let him in on it."

"It's his idea, for chrissakes. He's waited all his life for something like this."

"Make him the emcee. 'In this corner at two hundred and fifty pounds, Tiffany...'"

"You've got it. The only way these dames would ever accept a man in control is if he's a tired little joke like Brian. I'll sell him on it. Sure, he'll make the announcements and hang around to declare the winner. One thing you've got to give him, he knows wrestling."

Nina, Hilliard and I worked like crazy to get the place ready. Pleasant work, really, since Brian had a warehouse full of things to donate and work was mostly taking what we needed, transporting it, trying it, making it permanent. Happily, we had our tiered seating without spending a penny of my money. Such was the unreality of what we were doing or planning that the preparatory work was rather like staging a complicated practical joke.

Decor was never a problem thanks to Hilliard's *Gutter*, probably as long as Monet's *Waterlilies*, which followed the upper tier of seats and covered three walls. The subject matter was soggy leaves clinging to a wet street. Recently fallen, bright with color, there was nothing depressing about their rainy journey to catchbasin and storm drain. The familiar values of landscape painting were present. The foreground was full of intricate natural shapes, while the curb, vast but vaguely tactile, filled the distance like a cloudy sky.

The sound system went in, the lighting went up: soft for dining, harsh spots for the action. Our ideas for ring design came from the manager of a boxing gym, except that we instinctively opted for a three-foot height.

I was going to try out an innovation that had originally appeared on my forty-page prospectus, when, hard as it was to acknowledge now, I'd been wooing Brian: to avoid conversation (shouting) which would detract from musical performance we would use a menu written large on a chalkboard, each item numbered. Paper placemats would be order forms so that appetizers, salads, entrees and desserts would arrive at each numbered place as things asked for in writing. Nina and I were going to serve a full house banquet-style without wasting anything, and we couldn't go wrong no matter how loud the music was.

"I don't care how you put the food down," I told Hilliard. "I'm tired of hassling with you over the size tray you're willing to carry. I'll find you a dessert cart, something on that order. Better yet, a warming oven like the ones used for room service."

"Now you're talking. That'll look good."

"It's slow, Hilliard. And they'll get heavy, too, when you have to keep pushing them up those ramps. Try a tray once and you'll forget about your cumbersome cart."

"I don't know. I better stick with the cart."

In the back of my mind I knew he was right. Whenever I heard a crash out in the bar it was always Hilliard. He'd have been holding his little tray out in front of him with both hands, but he was a magnet for staggering drunks.

Peckham came up to tell me none of my ideas was any good.

"Paper placemats! What kind of class is that?"

"What kind did you expect in a place like ours?"

"You've missed the point entirely, Bancroft. Now I realize you're just blindly following Brian. I thought there was hope for you when I heard about the tablecloths and tuxedos. I know what camp is. But you can't have tablecloths with paper napkins. Tacky tacky."

I just smiled. All of Peckham's pronouncements were much easier to take now that he was a hamburger man.

The first day of wrestling season Nina and I both felt the tension start to build from the moment we came awake. The kids felt it and acted afraid for us when we dropped them off. Ms. Truong opened the door wider then came half outside to look long at us over their heads as if she never expected to see us again.

It was a rare sunny morning, the streets bright as steel. The car was warmer than usual inside without the heat on and not even damp. The engine seemed to have called up reserves of power, sensing our need to escape.

Having everything nailed down can be a mistake. It's helpful to have huge insoluble problems to wrestle with on performance days so that last minute details don't have time to mount a concerted attack. Oh, this was going to be a performance to rival the best of them, never knowing till the last moment whether I'd be winging it or flat on my face. How well I remembered the brazen waiting for the curtain or the lights to go up, unsure of my lines or bereft of a single word of dialogue, waiting for the terrified look of a colleague to wring the words from me, the gestures. Unable to look the conductor or the prompter in the eye, but aware of the batons or fingers replicated on the teleprompter... A puppet being jerked around.

It was a mistake to make comparisons. As much as I was pulling for things to go well, an appalling fiasco might have been just what our first-night audience was looking for. I couldn't be the judge of any of it, merely a kind of bailiff. All I had to do was take myself seriously and stay out of fights.

Nina would perform well, I knew. She'd be ahead of the orders no matter how busy we got. We were having two seatings to start, so for Nina there'd be a brief period of calculation at the beginning of each comparable to moments in the western movies she loved when the attacking Indians made their numbers known at the tops of surrounding hills. But with our new set menu she could precook and plate the entrees herself. There wasn't room in the kitchen for anyone to help since Peckham was still operating on the "every customer is king" system, darting in and out with productive sideswipes and finishing swoops.

All I had to worry about at the moment were red lights, green lights and no left turns. Nina's food would arrive on time gushing promises, entrees so mouthwatering that no one would think of mass murder, even with all the little carcasses the same size, their scorched wings or amputated legs all pointing the same way...

The show was my own once the food arrived from Nina. If I'd been too idealistic in entrusting an old wino with the job of dishing up vegetables there in the staging area beside the dumbwaiter, I'd find out tonight. Perhaps my trust had been misplaced but I remembered how grateful I had been to encounter people who thought I could add and subtract when I was being offered work as a "recovering alcoholic." As long as employers thought I was the best worker they'd ever had I was never less than that. Of course none of my new hires had experience doing what I was asking of them, and I'd never asked anyone else. We were all flying by the seat of our pants, and the desiccated string bean I had working as a bouncer, an inspired choice at the time, might have been just as gloomy as I was at the moment thinking what was in store for him tonight.

If worst came to worst Hilliard would take care of the final plate preparation and I could run all the orders myself. If worst came to worst... What an innocent recipe. It made the worst sound like one unfortunate surprise, one thing gone wrong. I could cook up dozens of worst-case scenarios between this block and the next, but that's why Nina was the chef. She only cooked food and left scenarios in their natural state.

My off-street parking place was blocked again, but this happened too often to be an omen. All over town it was all the rage to be the opposite of civic-minded. The not-civic-minded rang doorbells to make sure nobody was home before they blocked your driveway. The cops couldn't be everywhere at once, especially at this early hour when they were all in the same place having coffee.

Count your blessings, O Bancroft, I told myself again today.

No menu to run off any more, no last minute purchases down at the Wharf or around the corner at the Chinese grocer's, no long hours cutting up food and stirring it in pots, no worries about the daily journal that never seemed to reflect all the money I was actually spending (Peckham was keeping the journal and I was providing him receipts), no worries about whether Hilliard and Peckham would report for work, leaving me to run lunch orders to the nice ladies from the Red Cross with blood on my apron.

For the first time since we'd been in business there was a crowd of morning drinkers upstairs, and Brian hadn't come down to read his morning paper, but was entertaining our new customers in his boudoir.

Vito was behind the bar, nonchalant as ever, and there was no reason for him to be at work this early. And Carrie? Here?

Vito was ebullient when he saw me. "Word's out. We're going to be mobbed. Tonight it's going to be unbelievable."

This was the first time Carrie had thrown us overt support.

"You gonna stay? We sure need you."

"Didn't think I'd have to ask. Pay me the same as Vito if you want."

"You're ready to stay past tonight, though? You want to work up here?"

She nodded. "I didn't have my heart in it downstairs, Bancroft—Christ! I just got tired of Sid Peckham making his moves. And I can only take Deirdre in small doses."

I hauled her halfway over the bar to plant one on her cheek.

When the track lighting perfectly illuminated the ring at the flip of a switch, and softly illuminated the upper tier of tables, relief came upon me in a kind of swoon. Why had I been worked up all morning? All opening nights were a disaster to those doing the opening. How much would customers really know about what was going wrong? Weren't the best tippers at the Fife genteel lunch customers rewarding Hilliard's hard-hat serving style?

I climbed into the ring, threw myself on my back and pretended to take a nap. Since it was impossible not to worry about something, and anything could go wrong, I focused on Brian. Directly or indirectly he was sure to be behind most of the things that were about to go wrong. I knew this from experience, from common sense, from intuition. From little birdies.

To be forewarned about Brian, however, was to be disarmed. Like British people everywhere he was at his best in an emergency.

But was there really nothing to worry about in the fact that Brian imagined a very different crowd for our event than the one in attendance?

There was the occasional male face to deceive him. "Ladies only" would have embarrassed the large number of lesbians who were politically active against all kinds of discrimination. "Don't worry," my chief advisor had told me, "when we turn out in force the males will stay away."

"What about the beer-drinking, dirty-undershirt type who gets off on seeing women degraded?"

"If he gets out of line, throw him out. You shouldn't have any problem keeping order from what you've told me."

She had been pleased to learn that our wrestlers were in charge of security.

Anyway, as I pictured the men in our opening night crowd it was impossible to imagine something as coarse as a shout emerging from between their thin, malicious lips.

Right on schedule—all my worries these days were briefly embryonic self-fulfilling prophecies—I heard Brian's whiny tenor over the belly laughs of the lesbians at the bar, complaining to Vito about the lack of cigar smoke.

"These buggers look like poufs, like types I've always been trying to keep out of this place. And who are these short-haired women?"

Here I was in the next room, separated from him by a crowd of the short-hairs in question, and he was coming through as loud and clear as a referee counting me out.

"Wrestling fans, for godssakes," Vito growled. "Don't tell me you didn't know it's the ladies who get off on women wrestling?"

"Chaps down at the bar were trying to tell me our club was going to be for ladies only and I laughed in their faces. Who'd have believed such a turnout? And still seven hours to go before the action. Should anyone need me I'll be at the downstairs bar. If you see Bancroft tell him the redbeard should send up four dozen hamburgers, chop-chop. If they don't get something in their stomachs none of these ladies will be left standing by the time the fun starts. Damn it, hasn't Bancroft any common sense?"

I raised my head to watch him flash past the open arena doors and start for the stairs, broad-shouldered short-hairs making way.

"As the owner of the Fife and Drum...bleu bleu bleu bleu..."

Brian teetered in the center of the spot, bent over his microphone, coughing and drooling. Our co-host, a near-bimbo named Tricia, snatched the microphone away and said nice things about Brian, how grateful everyone was, how the classy show we were about to see wouldn't be out of place *here* (gesturing to take in our faux-medieval surroundings)...

Brian wasn't having any, he was trying to get the microphone back. He wanted to tell everyone how grateful he was, too, perhaps, but his urgency to have the mike betrayed sentiments more deeply felt than those of the emcee and presenter. One of the wrestler-bouncers (Candy) slid through the ropes on all fours and erected six feet of herself right behind Brian. A titter passed through the crowd at the sight of Brian, rumpled and disgruntled, in front of the giantess, whose hands were slowly advancing to the scruff of the neck. Green bile hurtled forth as she lifted him kicking over the ropes. Loud applause, led by our grateful wrestlers, got louder when Candy dropped him next to the ring.

Candy watched Brian for movement. Content that he'd be

quiet a while, she smiled and nodded to the understudy emcee (Tricia), who would never wait in the wings again.

"How unfortunate. Mr. Steele was trying to welcome you to his pub and dinner theater for a unique wrestling event. He's sure you're gonna enjoy tonight's program. Let's meet our first wrestlers..."

Here they were in different-colored one-piece bathing suits with matching rubber caps completely concealing their hair. Tricia made the introductions kowtowing, and introduced the managers, too, who rubbed their wrestlers' backs and patted their fannies as they followed them to the center of the ring.

"Thank you for your applause. You will notice I'm not saying how much these women weigh. The steering committee feels it would be demeaning for these young athletes to reveal their weight or their age. We do have an informal weigh-in before each match, however, to make sure these women are within fifty pounds of each other..."

Hilliard and I were looking on from behind. Now we were looking at each other.

"She's gonna go through that song and dance every night?"

"Hilliard, she's as green as we are. Give the poor girl a break."

The crowd roared. Brian must have been up to something. I joined the gawkers who had crowded up from the Fife and watched the managers and the emcee leave the ring, the referee enter (Carla, a grey-haired ex-marine) and instruct the Norns. Thus I was able to see our fan's faces when the music began.

Since I had been inveighing against loud music for the past year I'm sure there were onlookers who were shocked to realize that I had organized this onslaught. Melchior as big as all outdoors! Melchior god-size! These folks might have thought they knew something about opera, but they'd never heard the like of this.

There were shouts of "What the fuck!" "What the fuck is that?" and "Who the fuck is that?" These voices were a crow-like squawking since Melchior covered everything musical in other voices. The fans were dumbstruck. Our new cocktail waitress (Lulu, British, vouched for by Carrie) stood transfixed as well. Business as usual was at a standstill.

It was the moment for our Brobdingnagian Brunnhildes to square off and try to kill each other, and they did, their war whoops barely audible as Siegfried was forging his mighty sword. (First up at the start of every match was the *Schwertlied,* with Melchior pounding his magic sword, Nothung, into shape, the ring in his voice proclaiming his hammer to heaven.) The wrestlers thundered on the hollow, built-up ring-stage, their body-slams audible in spite of my bone-jarring quadraphonic system.

When I opened my eyes I was flipped into a time I'd only imagined. The pink-fleshed contestants, the whooping and clapping, the Hogarthian swilling, the music of Wagner, Melchior with his voice of a jolly god...

Wagner had been an anti-Semite. His music had sickened my old Jewish friends at the Community Center, some of whom would leave the room when it was being played or practiced. Yes, it showed in the music at times, the signature of megalomania: fear of inadequacy. An unbalanced mind was striving to create a new balance; heroism was being institutionalized out of an excessive need to control. Wagner's noblest battles were with himself, it seemed. His need to wrest beauty from himself was so great that it lent gravity to the artistic record of his struggle and enabled his hearers to overlook the silliness that plagued his poetry.

Wagner the megalomaniac and small-minded racist was deified by the Nazi louts—closet vulgarians false to all notions of excellence in people or music. (One phrase of Schmidt or Kipnis outshone anything Speer was able to manage.) Yet hearing Furtwängler's slow tempi, the incredible musical discipline of the German orchestras... Add the voices of a Melchior, a Flagstad... Could such a *row of pearls* (one early description of *bel canto*) have been cast before swine? Yes, a thousand times. And the barbarian hordes, rebaptized the *majority*, were shouting *aves* again. The swine leading the swine.

Away, gloom. This wasn't the time. It was the hour of Melchior, the hero with a heart of gold and a belly full of beer. Allegiances didn't matter with singers—Gigli stood shoulder to shoulder with the blackshirts, Ruffo refused to sing for them, but both were a perfect embodiment of the human spirit, if they were human at all. I thought them gods, but if not, they were still too exalted to be claimed by the society of the privileged, and certainly not by politicians.

Away gloom. The show had to go on or the curtain would ring down on my dreams. This crowd had come to see female flesh, lots of it, shuddering in torment, twisted, torn. From this tangle of suet and muscle was it possible that the hand raised in victory would belong to the strongest combatant, the most persevering, the most heroic? Would the spirit of the music prevail and bring our women up to the level of the Wagnerian hero who was overcoming the fearsome challenges of the music with his inexhaustible freshness of tone?

Fool! A voice I recognized from the local Public Broadcasting System was giving a companion the lowdown on Melchior during what ought to have been the blissful aftermath.

"Jolly Danish giant...swilling beer offstage...walked off during Parsifal to play a hand of cards..."

I was in the aisle shouting down at him.

"Swilling beer? A game of cards?" With a broad gesture I indicated the somewhat abashed gladiatrices still standing ringside. My own voice seemed to be singing out over the hubbub. Surprised faces were turning to me and starting to lose their afterglow.

"Is that how the giants of the century are to be remembered? To hear you tell it, and I've heard you much too often, the greats never let art stand in the way of their vices." I was fast reaching Wolfgang's decibel level. "Types like you don't stop at opera, either. No respected biographer can deal with Thomas Jefferson any more without mentioning the slave he might have slept with. Even if he did, was he less of a musician because of that, less of a scholar, less of a lawyer, less of a statesman, less of a paleontologist, less of a botanist, less of an architect, less of an inventor, less of a man? No, you fix on a failing that would make the pipsqueaks of our day feel better about themselves. It's the same thing with Melchior. The stories of Wagner are piffle. Let his heroes and gods run around all they want in their animal skins, with horns on their heads and iron brassieres. It was all just as silly to Melchior as it is to us now, but there's nothing silly about what he made of this material. Nothing nobler is possible for our kind."

With the broadest possible gesture I indicated the ring again. Faces there but I took my eyes away before I could read them.

"The *story* is that these girls..." Let it stand! "...hate each other, want vengeance, are old rivals. Do you believe any of this shit? Did you see them moments ago, hugging each other? Regardless of what you think is going on, something else is going on, something spiritual!"

Applause from the sisterhood, but I didn't pause to take credit for it.

"Sure he had card games going while he enacted Wagner's tales of mischief among the gods! Sure he stepped offstage for a beer when one of his co-stars had ten minutes of music ahead of her! But this behavior should never be used to introduce him to strangers. Eccentricities, no more important to his listeners than his gigantic stature or the ridiculous costumes he wore. Let him be known be the sublime music that was pouring forth!"

Giggles. Laughs. Hearty applause. Raised glances. Removed dinner jackets revealing undershirts. The emcee tapping the microphone to restore order. Brian lurching to his feet and raising a hand to mark the beginning of a new speech. Brian taken down by an ankle sweep.

Not even one of our wrestlers, merely a concerned citizen with feet. Applause. Delirium.

Then the applause began to die down and the emcee was telling me "the show must go on" by the way she held the microphone to one side in the flat of her hand. Yet the faces beginning to turn to me wanted more of something.

I gestured to the grapplesses lurking by the pantry door, waiting to spring into action as soon as they were announced.

"Can my meaning be lost on a crowd like this, full of so-called lesbians? As a species nearly all of us have sex of some kind, and all of us have to eat. Should we have to answer to 'cheese-nibbler' or 'bacon-eater?' Why is the particular way we might like to have sex so important—so important that we have to be identified with it, and have to go before the world with a placard around our necks?... So that the wildest notions might be formed about us, by children for example, by people who don't know us at all, but have a host of implanted ideas about the kind of people we are. By handing over intimate details about our sex lives to the hoi polloi certain journalists..." (a glance at the critic beneath) "...are feeding the dishonorable need of the dullard to feel superior to his more talented brothers and sisters by virtue of his innate normality... which is nothing but lack of imagination. In fact our little kinks and peccadilloes should never be used to identify us... they don't belong in a dossier any more than they do on the front page..."

I had them now.

"But enough, enough! Carla grows impatient. The show must go on. More wrestling awaits you, more dedicated athletes are preparing to honor a tradition that began in Ancient Greece. And please remember that the drunken, card-playing Melchior," I looked daggers at the bemused critic tapping the table beneath, "the hero you will hear singing along, is not only personifying the struggle of mere man against the immortal gods, but blazing the way for all of us here to find spiritual glory in all-out combat!"

A standing ovation? For me? I came around to the front of the ring where Brian stirred and fixed me with a demented expression I'd noticed before when beggars on their last legs, or leg, were both asking and refusing succor. I blew a few kisses and bustled behind the ring again where Hilliard was waiting beside the double doors. Melchior was singing and the next wrestlers hadn't even been introduced—couldn't be without stopping the music and starting over!

The wino handling lights and music had fooled me. I'd seen the face of someone intelligent once, a pillar of the community or at least a trusted right-hand man. I hadn't asked him what he did before the bottle cut the legs out from under him: a fatal mistake.

Brian was up to something. The emcee was tapping the microphone to restore order, saying 'please' into it. Brian was in the ring, raising his hand, about to speak! This time Carla took him down herself... More applause, irrespective of her amplified exhortations. So much hot air in the room at the moment that the roof bulged, we could somehow feel it threatening at any moment to become unsealed and rattle like a kettle lid. What was that? Ah, in the silence between Melchiors, the din of the jukebox downstairs at maximum volume. But no amount of tired chaos from below could cover our bubbles and squeaks.

The wino made a fast-forwarding mistake so that the next match began with the dreamy sweetness of Lohengrin. As with college wrestling there were long clinches, long pregnancies during which the combatants might have forgotten what they were planning, even what they were doing. Their immobilizing holds may have begun to seem like an intense embrace between waves of pain, an apologetic and comforting countersignal to their aggressive impulses.

At just the wrong moment, *kommt er dann heim*, when goose bumps were arising, hair standing on end, Brian stirred again, made his knees and walked on them, raising himself at intervals just enough to peer over the mat. Twitching convulsively, he feasted his eyes on the taut fabric clutching buttocks and cleaving labial hillocks.

Where Brian was kneeling the rest of us didn't exist. His entire world was sprawled on the mat before his eyes, in need of his advice. Over the soft passages he could be heard shouting: "Leglock... Nelson... Flying mare..."

Rhythmic pulsations were the only sign of life. The tangled bodies appeared to be one creature trying to get its breath. Since the match was going nowhere the crowd was calling for some action regarding Brian, and the same woman who had swept his ankles away raised him to his feet, or would have, had he been able to stand, then went aloft with him for a modified airplane spin. After she had bounced him off the side of the ring (cloth on plywood) he was quite unconscious. She acknowledged the cheers of the crowd with raised, clasped hands, but quickly took her seat again. An impromptu audition from an underweight, aspiring wrestler?

The rhythmic pulsations continued. The crowd noise subsided before one of the rubber-clad heads had budged an inch. The rest of us didn't exist for the wrestlers, either. They were in their own little world of hair follicles, wheals and papules.

Melchior was wasting his breath. But then my new hire (I'd already forgotten his name... Jimmy?) advanced the tape again. Incredible! Perhaps he thought he needed to inject some life into the proceedings. I went behind the curtain in the vestibule of the wrestlers' dressing room where Wizard-of-Oz-like he was manipulating the controls. After explaining his mistake I fired him and warned him off the premises, jug and all, wondering the while if the bitches downstairs had supplied him. It was hard for me to believe that even such a specimen as "Jimmy," who'd fallen so far and landed so hard, would have had the chutzpa to show up for his first day on a new job with a gallon jug of wine under his arm.

Brian stayed passed out until the first series of matches was over and it was time to serve. I put on the hour-long tape of Debussy and Fauré which would provide background music—scarcely audible to eardrums that had been pounded so hard and long by the heroic Dane.

When I emerged the faces of our fans told me all I wanted to know—and just what I had hoped! We'd surpassed their expectations! And they were hungry. Drinks were going back half-full on the little serving trays. Fans were straightening their chairs, squaring their place settings, writing on their placemats, buzzing so loudly that Debussy was nothing but a faint crackle overhead, a picnic sound of birds.

The wino who was readying salads and appetizers was someone trying to get ahead in the food service business. He'd told me as much the day I hired him and now he'd made me a believer. For anything to go wrong from this point until the entrees arrived Hilliard would have to give crab cocktails to people asking for limestone lettuce, or duck *pâté au poivre* to people who wanted *crabe argenteuil*.

Hilliard put all his food around without a hitch. What he lacked in carrying power he made up in geniality and in his unerring eye for plate placement. I hadn't worked a full shift as a waiter in quite some time, so it was all I could do to match Hilliard's warmth and fuzzy unobtrusiveness. Down in my kitchen I was accustomed to getting things right with brutal speed and having people stay out of my way. Now I had to wait for people to get out of the way, I couldn't singe their arms with hot serving dishes, I couldn't even knee them.

Nina sent the entrees right on time: plump and blistered brown. With the possibility of a mistaken order eliminated, I could approach the tables with plates all over my arms, and discharge them in rapid order with no more than a glance beneath. Hilliard was perfect, too— stately, even. Lulu was working out fine. Nina had done the impossible and told me afterward that she'd never had a problem, even with Peckham cooking hamburgers ten at a time. The sound system had functioned perfectly once I'd eliminated human error in the person of Jimmy. The emcee had stopped the speeches. None of the wrestlers had been hurt, and all had turned out to be gracious winners and losers as well as a valuable security resource. Brian had stayed passed out during the show, and hadn't bothered to come to when we moved him to the lounge bar and left him where the floor was warm in front of the fire.

My own reception was just as amazingly onesided. Stiff I may have been, and insufficiently ingratiating, yet at some tables I was welcomed as a conquering hero for the speech I had given. The marriage of wrestling and Wagner which was mostly my idea was "brilliant," as was the inspired use of Brian as a kind of clownish lightning rod to draw off the charge of sexism which lay heavy in the air. Yes, that's what our good patrons had decided about Brian. As owner of the place he'd been uncontainable, so we'd turned him loose for the general amusement and let him improvise. We were still running the show and under our management women's wrestling would be taken seriously as a sport, would sweep the country in company with our serious music and serious cuisine. Why not? All of it made perfect sense to me at the moment, flush with a victory I didn't deserve and hadn't foreseen.

Much later we had help from our new clientele in cleaning up the colossal mess. One of the V.I.P.s was excited about the newsletter.

Ah, well, I thought. They're all the rage, these newsletters. Couldn't take a step without being handed one, and the steps themselves, no matter where you were going with them, were certain to have been commemorated in someone's newsletter.

"Great," I told her. It wasn't the first time.

"It would be cool if we could have your help."

"So I've heard, but what kind of help?"

"I was told you were some kinda poet. Had poetry on your menus once..."

"When I xeroxed the lunch menu every day, just to keep my hand in. Haven't done that in a while. I don't think of myself as a poet these days. Anyway, you don't want poems to celebrate the kind of thing we've got now. Melchior's the man. I'll be on the lookout for less well-known passages so you regulars don't get bored. What about Flagstad, though? Talk about a meaty tone. For dessert I could score you some Wunderlich. Being the person responsible for bringing those voices back before the public—that's enough for me. That means more than anything I could possibly write."

She flung her wadded tablecloths upon the pile. "We were thinking of the kind of thing you said in that speech during the first match. It might be cool to have someone explain what the sisters are really doing up there. It would mean a lot to all of us to see wrestling the way we do it get the respect it deserves."

"Something like a pamphlet, then, to advertise?"

"I guess. We could have interviews with the wrestlers, though. Some people might be surprised to find out what good minds they got."

"A fan magazine?"

"Like, hey? Why not? Anyway, if you won't do it, as long as you don't mind if one of us does, that's cool."

I told her I didn't mind. I didn't mind anything at this point.

Nina was long gone by the time I finished cleaning up, but my new-found lesbian friends weren't, including two of the wrestlers. I knew the feeling. There was nothing better than hanging around in the dressing room after an opera, taking plenty of time getting your makeup off, slowing the transition back to street-noise, puddles and "Spare change?"

The wrestler named Paula wanted to go to the place around the corner for coffee. Not the natural foods cafeteria where Burl kept the peace, but the little doughnut shop where pedophiles went for "chicken." No one who knew what was going on could enjoy a cup of coffee there, much less one of their greasy doughnuts. Never mind, I told myself. I was a danger to choke on highmindedness every time I recalled the speech that had gone over so well.

Two large people on little stools, having to sit sideways, no room for our knees under the small counters facing the wall—not a cause for attention, even when she began to eat jelly doughnuts to draw me out. Instead I watched a "chicken hawk" outside signal to one of the boys. Six of them were waiting together, now five: severe chopped hair, earrings, pimples and pallor; assertive, nervous voices, laughter too prolonged. Only a mother could love them, and some poor mother somewhere probably still did. But they weren't as necessary to their mothers as they were to the man in the raincoat who had just stopped to dangle his car keys. "You know what's going on..."

She nodded, still chewing, the sort of acknowledgment I'd have expected from one of these teenaged boys if I'd told him his life expectancy according to the latest study.

"Can we get out of here?" I asked. "I guess I'm too tired to hang around in a place like this. You're a day sleeper, I'll bet."

She shook her head, still chewing.

"What do you do as a regular thing?"

"Oh, you know. Bartend. I used to be a pet groomer, mostly dogs. Good money in it but I had a difference of opinion with the woman who owned the shop. How about you?"

"What do I do besides wait tables in a wrestling club?" She nodded. "Let's see. Well, I used to cook there. I wish I could say, 'sing opera.' I've made some money at it but not enough to go around saying that's what I do for a living."

"That explains a lot, though. Your partner into that, too?

Besides paintin'?"

"No. Painting is it."

"At least I knew you guys weren't restaurant material." She started on doughnut number two, looking at me flirtatiously. Right after swallowing, with a kind of sigh, she leaned forward and flipped her elbows to straighten out her warmup jacket. Staring fixedly at my right knee she began to test it with little squeezes.

"You don't know how much this turns me on." Both hands now, both knees.

"Me, too, but four a.m. is a lot different than two to the woman I live with."

"I never saw you with anyone tonight..."

"She was down in the kitchen. The chef."

"How come she didn't come up to see the show when she was done cookin' for everyone? That seems a little weird to me. You had someone all along, and she never saw us during rehearsal or opening night. No one ever told me about her. I met the other one's ol' lady. Hillyer's. Wow. Your lady pretty as that?"

"Very pretty, but not at all like Sarah. Probably not your type. But she's got nothing against wrestling, and I'll make sure she comes up to see you wrestle next time. I'll tell her you're a special friend."

On that note I got her a refill, paid, and left her with her remaining doughnuts. She might have been vaguely grateful. As for me, seldom had I been so glad of a cold and drizzly San Francisco night, a bone-tired body, a chance to go home and sleep a few hours before morning's grisly mess was good enough again.

My feet were quick under me, my chest less complicated. All the wrestling had surely had an effect... So many striving, near-naked bodies... And Paula had affected me with the need in her eyes. But for once I hadn't been hostage to my body's perverse caprices. For once I'd seen disaster ahead and taken a logical step back instead of a huge leap forward with my eyes closed.

My first tip of the hat to the middle-aged man I might become—to the possibility of old age? What I had to live for, suddenly, was more sweet air.

The morning after our season opener was delicious with the smell of bacon frying. Nina had let a couple of Sundays go by without bacon as a way of punishing my tendency to expect miracles from her. She'd waited patiently for the Sunday when I was least deserving of special treatment.

Barefoot to investigate. Bacon. Waffles. Maple syrup. Sectioned grapefruit halves. When someone who cooked for a living cooked at home... This was tantamount to receiving a long personal letter from T.S. Eliot.

She wanted to goof off *(flâner)* all day. We were going to take the kids to the zoo.

The kids already knew or they would have been cheering the news. Well, if they expected it, I had no choice, but my energy level was quickly subnormal again.

But why? Why resist? It was the thought that I wasn't doing everything possible to stave off disaster at the restaurant, the workaholic's waking nightmare. "If I'm not busy every second, there will be hell to pay. However, if I'm busy every second, anything bad that happens can't be helped." I'd been listening to this maniac all year.

If Jean-Pierre fell off the earth I'd marry Nina in a minute and let the Fife make us all millionaires. The money I hadn't earned and didn't deserve would straighten out all the messes in my life. With a mere two or three years of hard work and clean living, momentum would take me the rest of the way. Or I could turn my back on moneygrubbing and be the famous singer or lowly shopkeeper that Teresa saw in me, selling songs or cheese or books all day... Then I'd dash home, slip into my apron and be a smiling cook, masseur, raconteur, and of course lover, when Sarah came home whipped from one of her depressing shifts at the hospital. Why limit myself?

The kids had poked at their celebration breakfast. Nguyen was such a conservative eater that he turned up his nose at most American fast food in spite of all the drugs in it that kept American kids coming back for more until they were stringy-haired, pimply-faced adolescents. Both of them were big-eyed watching me eat, though. Jumping up and down and, coached by Nina, telling me to take my time.

Soon it was off to the crumpled edge of the continent in my dad's old car. Sun in the morning again. The fog would roll in before I had to think of work. The wrestlers skin to skin. Brian stumbling in and out of the action, women shouting for his head... Sunday night, and there'd be another sellout crowd, I knew it.

The kids had been before with their mother. The moment we were inside they were pulling in different directions. We had to do it all in one day... or until we were hungry again, probably early afternoon... No problem, this wasn't the one in the Bronx or San Diego. Not such a bad deal for some of these animals, though. I'd been here years ago tripping on mescaline and sung to the animals. All the mommies and daddies with kids along holding blue ice cream had avoided me and some of them might have alerted the keepers that there was a man serenading their rhinos... I'm sure the reason no one tried to put me out was because the rhinos were responding...

Why hadn't I thought of this before? In a flash I saw myself as a hero to the kids—someone of substance, finally. I got each one by the arm and dragged them off to the rhinos' mock heroic world. On the way I tried to remember the other animals who had liked my style. The llamas, alpacas, guanacos, whichever. Fans from the word go, flirting with me. But the female rhino flirting was something the kids would never forget. The behavior of lovesick rhinos would be known to a large circle of friends by the time I arrived to take French operahouses by storm and charm the Parisians with their thick hides...

There they were, munching, head down, not a care in the world. The bird who liked to peck the lice off them had been imported too, a package deal. What ungainly contraptions they were as they stood there between the grass and their huge turds, snuffling and grinding.

I would have bet anything the female would remember me from last time. She'd trot over and make big eyes at me as of old. How many millions of two-legged voiceless Pinkertons had come and gone! Probably she never looked at the brightly-colored species that was craning its neck at her over and over, not any more. I was pretty sure I'd given her *Intorno all' idol mio* of Cesti, a standby practice aria of those days with which I tried to imitate the legato singing of Gigli.

When my voice rifled through the enclosure both kids leapt away and took refuge in a mob composed mostly of other mommies and daddies, and those soon to enjoy that status, or thinking about it. Contemporary versions of the romantics I'd seen in the fifties at Playland in Rye, New York. Italian girls named Cele with two much makeup accepting bluehaired trophies won for them by guys named Vinny.

I'd aimed for the big one, who erected her ears right away. Could I be sure she was female? All kinds of sloppy tissue was hanging out of her ass. But so what if it was a swain as long as it would lower its prehistoric head and bat its eyes.

I turned up the volume and the onlookers edged away from me another step or two.

"Look, dad! He likes it!" No word from Nguyen yet, but it was the little boy next to him and they were jumping up and down together.

No question. Flogged by its tail, the rhino's loins were starting to register on the Richter scale. Weak-kneed, head wobbling side to side, she trotted up—better I thought of it as a she, it fit the song. She was tilting her lowered head coquettishly, but the rhino I had aroused years ago had rolled her eyes. I was finishing the song, hadn't sung the second verse in ages. *"Al mio ben che riposa..."* Launched. Good enough. The words came of their own accord when I was inspired, and I *was* inspired, I had a crowd now. Even Mai would have to admit I was the reason so many people were staying in front of the rhinos' pen. A happening song here, folks, a happening rhino.

Bertha's boxcar head was down, lolling to the side. She was batting her left eye. Swung her head the other way, let it loll back slowly, batted her eyes again. The kids were going wild. Flashbulbs were going off, but nothing broke the spell—a bomb going off wouldn't have frightened away my conquest. There was some question in my mind about how long I should keep this up. Would she register disappointment in some way if I stopped? What had happened the last time?

I'd had a good warmup. Staying in the same key I launched Iago's creed, *Credo in un dio crudel che m'ha creato simile a se!* I pointed at the poor creature as if she were my god and I were triumphant about the horrible discovery that I was just like her. Aha, she was no different than the little brown darling at my side. Love songs had to be soft. There had to be a little cool silk in the tone.

Bertha was backing off now. The crowd sensed a problem in our relationship, a potentially embarrassing squabble. No doubt I'd disappointed some high hopes. After all, I hadn't merely found my way to Bertha's heart with my ditty—I'd hooked up with her after wandering back through many millions of years of evolution. Before I'd opened my throat to her we'd had nothing in common, even the most ardent sentimentalists in the crowd, sniffly little girls among them, would have been quick to say so. Could there have been any clearer demonstration of the fact that evolved creatures quite different in their physical aspect still had a soul in common—and that music was a form of communication between souls?

After the rhino had backed off about halfway to the little patch of grass and dung where she'd first perked up her ears, the crowd scattered and I had only to contend with a couple of fans—middle-aged men from Des Moines or someplace, with cameras around their necks, full of questions about opera.

"No, it's a special love song I sing to her... The attraction was amazing some years ago, but we're only friends now and I sing to her for old times' sake. You can imagine how hard it has been, with everyone against us from the beginning."

Nina laughed with me at the sight of the men bustling away.

I had two affectionate kids beside me as we moved on, their beautiful French tinkling, interrupted by a periodic, somewhat guttural "too much" from Nguyen, who had developed a special fondness for the phrase. It didn't take them long to ask if there were other species that might be susceptible to my charms...

After the rhino the llamas were like a bunch of whores trying to hurry you into a decision, preening, stretching, watching for signs of interest in the most subtle, sidewise way. With the llamas music held them in sway a priori, there was no attraction process. They were interested in the singer who could make such music, it was he they had dreamt of while rotating their teeth inside their little camel mouths and looking dewy-eyed into the distance for the mountains that were never there anymore.

Where the kids had been awed by the rhino's raptus, they cawed with delighted recognition now. The streets of Paris were full of such creatures. Flirtation in the cafes obeyed the same rules. In spite of resolute frontality, maintained by the waiters between seatings, as if all that could possibly be important to their customers would be *en face*, via the corners of customers' eyes gentle ripples of flirtatious interest were launched which reeled sideways and sometimes, ever so minutely, touched upon tables behind to the left or the right. Whereas the rhino had been responding with sincere affection the kids might have wondered about these dodos. *Hein?* Or think of emus with their long straight necks and small, flat heads (though any head would have seemed small after Bertha's).

"A bunch of turkeys," I told the kids in French.

"Exactement," said Nguyen, giving me another brief preview of the man he would be someday, hollowing his cheeks, sticking out his lips. The expression I'd seen when Frenchmen were calling to their animals in mock outrage, utterly delighted with their misbehavior.

We had a late lunch at a little Vietnamese restaurant on the Sunset side of the park just up from the ocean. I riffled through the day's stored moments even as I smiled at the kids tasting food they'd almost forgotten, creating an orgy of attention in our little corner. Their food had transported them so far. I was reminded of times I watched late at night on tiptoe as they stirred in their sleep—so completely mine, so completely lost.

Mai tried to spoil everything later by perversely talking about how soon they would have to go home... "Home" in her mouth was always France, our apartment was "that dump." She saw the look of hurt on her mother's face, and on mine too, I think, and was reassured to know she belonged where she thought she belonged. More than once I'd watched her burn with shame—momentarily much more of a woman than she was—at the thought of her mother having to confess our relationship to her father... Yet she would never have allowed her mother to conceal such a thing from Jean-Pierre. She agreed that daddy would understand their situation. It wouldn't have been normal for mommy to live without a man, with just part of a family—not feeling whole, no matter how important the kids were to her. And she loved Mr. Bancroft nearly as much as her daddy... Ah, but no hotfaced tears would be shed for the soon-to-be-bereft Mr. Bancroft. Childhood was fast coming to an end for Mai and she was quite capable of articulating the irrefutable opinion that Mr. Bancroft was using her mother to make his restaurant a success, and taking advantage of her loneliness and helplessness as someone stranded in an alien culture to offer her physical comfort. (Unlike much older adolescent Americans Mai already knew everything that was possible between men and women in bed, but rather like most girls of eleven she was a prude and put a ridiculously high price on her mother's favors.)

I bumped around the city for a while, extending the trip home, savoring our truce, remembering all the moments and flavors—refusing to consider how right or wrong Mai might have been about her mother and me. The time for hidden motives was past. If Brian couldn't figure out a way to screw me, so much money would be pouring in from the Open Pit that I'd be able to say goodbye to all of my dear ones very soon... True, the kitchen would go to hell again without Nina... But maybe not. We had a good routine, surely it could be taught. There was no reason to fiddle with the menu any more. Great if we could find someone with enough talent to vary it, not just a routine, by-the-numbers sort of cook. But what did it matter? Did I care so much about my "product" any more?

Not so much, I feared. About Melchior, yes. My joy in hearing his Pentagruelian voice... and in forcing so many people into his way. It was a different goal than I had set out with, but so what? A direction was more important than a goal. I'd only wanted to do live opera performance (eventually) because I thought it would create excitement, wake the odd person here and there to the possibilities of the human voice. Surely Melchior had done just that, creating opera fans out of wrestling fans. What would be the next step? Concert readings of an opera with unabated wrestling to replace the action? Ballroom dancing to operatic backgrounds? Striptease? Anything was possible, but somehow nothing I could cook up seemed as plausible when I pictured its implementation after Nina had left for good. Anyway, morale started to sag in my campaign to create a taste for life's finer things after the way the rabble in the Fife had hurled themselves upon Peckham's burger bandwagon...

For the thousandth time I tried to wiggle into a scenario wherein Nina would remain in the restaurant...The obvious arrangement would be to invite Jean-Pierre back to the States. Pay Nina enough to support them both and let Jean-Pierre bide his time as a designer. Until now we had invoked immigration problems to explain to ourselves how such a scenario would be unlikely, but I'd never believed such problems would be insurmountable. I knew that she didn't want Jean-Pierre to know me, to know just how she'd earned all the money she'd be taking back to France with her. And she didn't want her kids raised so far from all the loved ones in her family and the friends they missed and schools they knew.

The sooner they left, the better, that's what it always came to. A quick and clean departure, and the hell with what happened in the restaurant. I could start cooking again... God help me... Maybe if I stayed in touch with her long distance she could talk me through the hard parts. But there wouldn't be any Melchior down there in the kitchen, and I was spoiled, let's face it. I knew I could never face that jukebox again.

Two more days of windfall receipts emboldened Nina to tell me she'd booked the kids on a flight to Paris some weeks ago to take advantage of a discount. She didn't have to explain that she'd have been on the flight as well if we hadn't been serving a full house. She'd been on the phone to her family. All of them would be there to welcome the kids back. They'd miss her terribly, she couldn't stand to be estranged from them for too long either... But if I were willing to give her a percentage of the receipts for one more month... We'd talked about such an arrangement before...

Sure we had, when I was desperate to keep her. But I agreed to a healthy percentage as a farewell present. She'd be glad to break in her replacement. Better if I found someone right away. Gratitude was bubbling in her again, more than I'd seen since her first days on the job when she had told me how wonderful it was to be earning money again, how safe she felt in the passenger seat of my car, what a good father I would be for her kids. Her way of showing gratitude was the same now as it had been then: extra-long sessions of lovemaking with her insisting that I remain immobile on my back and leave everything to her... Tit for tat again. So what? It was the confidence she had that her body would always be a precious gift that caused it to be such a precious gift... It was her feeling that she knew exactly how to please me that made my flesh so quick to respond. Even though I probably wasn't exactly who she thought I was I'd never caught her at guesswork. Perhaps the complicated rigamarole she practiced in the name of "taking care of a man" was the cumulative result of years of experiment, and her artistry wasn't so much a factor as the fact that all her men had responded to the same things.

Yes, in spite of the maelstrom that lay behind her expertise, Nina's secret was simple, I thought. She had learned to give without obligating. She never seemed indecisive, gave an impression of craving. There was a restlessness about her, a sudden ferocity, that set her apart from any so-called "pro."

All her obvious experience excited me, let it be said. If ever a woman were the least bit clumsy about an act that might be labeled "degrading"—after the merest whiff of the possibility that she was a virgin, that is—nothing more would be possible with her.

However, passion changed everything. Someone passionate was never degraded.

Perhaps I was better prepared than most to understand this simple truth about life thanks to years of carelessness. Never look back! You will never again be the person you were the night before! You become, therefore, passionate to be someone else, to escape the identifying labels like "degrading"... Hence all the experimentation, which led to trying on the same old caps with different people.

On the way to the airport she got so carried away explaining to the children how hard it was for me that I had self-pitying tears in my eyes... "Poor Gordon won't be able to follow you to France as I will be doing in a mere month!" "Poor Gordon will have to stay here and make sure his gambling casino keeps making money..." Yes, they were faithfully to report to all relatives that I was running a gambling casino. We'd been successful in keeping them away from the Open Pit at night and they hadn't been forced to understand exactly what was going on there. Apparently her relatives had a soft spot for gambling, but wouldn't have been any more able than the kids to understand what passed for entertainment in my "club." Her folks thought all Americans were gangsters. (God knows what she'd already told them about me.) "Poor Gordon... But he'll visit us in France, little ones. We can count on him... Someday..." I was still feeling sorry for myself. Busses were notoriously quick when running over our loved ones. No time for a yelp, the deed was done.

The giant winged busses approached the airport again and again to regurgitate and feed. In spite of the deafening noise and magisterial movements out on the tarmac they were unreal to me as I huddled with my little adopted family for the last time. As we waited to see which of the monsters came to us everything that was happening had been planned long in advance, had been tried a million times before and gone off without a hitch.

Nguyen let me molest the soft skin of his neck for five seconds instead of two. Mai merely shook hands at first, but then she gave me her cheek as she had done when we first knew each other. Nina had given up trying to control herself. I was used to outbursts that washed makeup onto her blouse, stuck the fabric to her skin, made you wonder how many children she'd lost before these two became all she had left. Even the hardhearted veterans of departure and farewell who were crowding up behind us (the kids were to be put on first, with their ID badges dangling) were starting to look unsure of what exactly it was they were about to do with themselves. Fortunately the flight crew in charge of boarding children got them the hell out of there before everyone was completely miserable, actually tearing Nguyen's hands from his mother's wrap.

My heart was aching for Nina, but oddly I felt nothing but relief as I watched the kids disappear, already showing delight with their new French-speaking escorts (or trying to get their escorts to say something in French). I knew they'd love flying over the ocean this time because they loved their destination. The neighborhood would begin to disgorge faces made glad by their return. Their friends would seek them out and old mischief would be remembered, new mischief embarked upon. Whenever they missed their mother the reassuring word would be soon, soon... or rather *bientôt, mes petits...*

The next few days would be an eternity of suffering for Nina, I thought; then she would begin to number them and numb herself, tiring her body to the point that even dreams of the kids wouldn't have a chance in the time she had away from the place.

I was right about the next few days, but Nina was more resilient than I had thought. She might have learned something from Jean-Pierre about ducking in and out of responsibilities. I would have said, from me, but I'd had my shoulder to the wheel the whole time she'd known me.

How would Nina have responded, had she known? She knew of the words I wrote in the notebook from time to time, and thought I was keeping a diary, since the entries were under no particular head and my handwriting was too crabbed for her, or the most sleuthlike native speaker of English, to read. Had she found it wasn't a diary, what would she have made of a homage? Some harmless literary exercise, then, not so different than the sewing that busied her in moments alone.

For a long time her French nature had been uppermost in her dealings with me— her almost pathological need to be cheerful, even flirtatious, while bustling about in the gassy kitchen of the Fife like a maggot in the chamber of a carcass. Utterly French was the way she delivered the goods when we pulled the covers over us at night or went at it with the door closed, in streetlight. No matter what she was doing, unwrapping herself, offering herself, taking me inside herself, she always paused many times to look me in the eye, and kept the eye contact while she slowly resumed what she was doing... till everything was in flames again and there were screams in the night. The children had slept like stones. Only the neighbors knew, presumably, but we'd never met face to face and they had their own screams to worry about. Hilliard and I had heard the same sounds next door to us in French hotels, which might have explained Nina's nonchalance after.

Now her Vietnamese side was uppermost. In spite of her nimbleness and her undeniable competence to get the orders right and get them up to us on time, I thought of a water buffalo in a furrow whenever I came upon her working. Her downward-tilted forehead poured so much patience it swept the legs out from under me. The authority I had derived from having her "help" me, do what I required of her, made my flesh crawl.

There was nothing I could do to help. There was only room for one person to work here unless all the workers were bent over a counter or a range, that is, working—something Peckham, with his swipes and pirouettes, had yet to learn. Her prep work was everywhere. To touch anything on the counters only made more work for her.

Instead, sometimes several times a night, I went below and stopped her from working. Put my arms around her and went still. With the near sounds of cooking, the howls of the wrestling fans overhead, and the familiar jukebox madness blasting through the swinging doors, I pressed her to me and immobilized her. The sobs in her small body were like hiccups. Her hands dug into my back so that she hung from me by her trembling arms. Her rather wide, wet face was indescribably tender where it was bone to bone with my lower jaw. What were we doing here? Who were these crazy people? What was she doing so far from her children, her culture, the streets and the smells she knew, the sounds of morning and evening, the sounds of others that were her sounds, too?

There was a time to cling and a time to stop clinging. And each time life went on she was a bit closer to the edge of the earth, to the end of life as she had known it with me. Reborn as the wife and young mother who'd suffered Jean-Pierre's folly, reborn as the charming girl she still was, among people who could appreciate her charm, she would sink back into ordinary life with a great sigh. *Pas possible*, her tales of two-hundred-pound women wrestlers in a restaurant. And the food was good? *Pas possible.* She'd have had more luck with her tale of The Baritone and The Rhinoceros.

Brian loved the lavish falsity of the commercial wrestling he saw on television and was able to make a fairly accurate comparison of it to the kind of thing going on at the Pit. True, we lacked the colorful costumes the men had, the hairdos, the swagger, the chutzpa to snatch microphones away from the emcee and broadcast threats to each other, the ultra flexible rules, the retinues, above all the improbable holds and aerial moves. In fact, there was very little action in our matches after the initial takedown. Nearly everyone in the audience and on the staff, with the possible exception of some of the winos I'd hired, had been to college and had a passing acquaintance with the look and spirit of college wrestling. Our wrestling was strictly according to college rules, therefore it was in earnest. Deadly serious. And sometimes, if it hadn't been for the waves of inspiration emanating from Melchior's Wagnerian crises, and from other supreme operatic moments via other great interpreters, our program would have been quite dull to certain people, I'm sure.

To Brian? Well, he was quick to point out the lack of bravado at our matches. "I'm afraid these girls of ours don't know anything about show biz," he said to me sadly once. "Here I thought you Yanks had invented it." So smashed that it was a miracle he was alive at all he was still able to appreciate the fact that our wrestlers were competing: no one ever stepped into the ring without wanting to win, whatever the odds. As a longtime aficionado of the kind of thing on television perhaps he respected the determination our women displayed, staying with each other move by move, lightning quick to readjust to the slightest change in parity (as opposed to his old favorites who stood in the center of the ring trying to look dazed while their opponents leapt upon them from a corner turnbuckle twelve feet away).

With all that might have been said in his favor as a fan, though, if one could discount the smell of him and the way he dogged the women, Brian still wasn't able to persuade himself that our wrestlers were doing all they could to win. Why did they *never* disentangle and take to the air, where gravity would be in their favor? Why all the tedious grappling, eh? He didn't think it would be seemly for them to throw illegal chops and punches the way the bad boys did in the Big Show, or pull each other's hair (the shower caps were "sensible"), but he did think our "girls" lacked a killer instinct and could have been much more dangerous to each other with the right instruction.

While Brian was giving instruction as part of his clown routine or as an outspoken little heap Hilliard and I would shout for his head from time to time, almost goodnaturedly. When the wrestlers gave me interviews for the newsletter, however, I was surprised to find their feelings strongly roused against him. I was Brian's only serious backer. Here I'd thought he was the last word in camp! There was no such thing as camp for one.

I'd tried to wiggle out of doing a newsletter at all, but it wasn't possible while we were turning so many people away. As a plus the interviews were held in the gladitorial sanctum, the former pantry, a steamy place where it was pleasant to chat with the Amazons between bouts.

Some of the women might have had a shred of modesty—but it was literally a shred, a *cache-sexe* of one sort or another to keep the little white tails of their Tampaxes from showing. Most were completely at ease in the nude, strolling about that way after matches. While they were having their rubdowns, capping off and pulling on their one-piece suits I listened to their desultory opinions, reactions to opinion, dreams, desires, and bits and pieces of their life histories, feeling as if I were being read to from a candy wrapper.

OPEN PIT NEWSLETTER
by Gordon Bancroft

In this first number we'd like to introduce some of the star wrestlers from the Open Pit (right on top of the world-famous Fife and Drum Pub, in San Francisco). With me at the moment are four of today's six winners—Jennifer, Tinka, Paula and Cass.

GB: Let's start things off by asking what wrestling really means to you. Paula? How does it feel out there?

P: I been wrestling all my life, ever since I was a tomboy, and I still don't understand why I get off on it so much.

T: Body odor is a problem for me in long matches and my opponents can sense when I'm getting desperate. Mr. Steele shouldn't be allowed to stand right next to the ring, shouting with that breath of his. He's all that stands between me and job satisfaction, if stand is the right word.

Paula and Tinka are statuesque blondes and close friends off the mat. The green-eyed Tinka, who has just uncapped her shoulder-length blonde hair, met Paula at a strength contest when they were just out of their teens. Now Jennifer is speaking, a broadshouldered brunette.

J: I was a swimmer, All-American High School, freestyle, butterfly. It's like you hear and you don't hear the crowd noise. During the turns? That's what it's like to have someone's ass in your face out there. It's OK, I guess. Actually, there are things about my job I really like.

Cass wants to get into this, a tall woman with straight dark hair who is on the wiry side compared to the other wrestlers here tonight. She's known for tremendous speed and endurance. She was a hippie ten years ago and says she still is, proud that she has never worn makeup or carried a purse.

C: I dunno, man, I might get into something else. I must be sick to like this so much. OK, the money's good, no complaint there, but let's face it, what the bitches are really getting off on is seeing us get hurt—

GB: By bitches you mean all the fans, the fans—

C: All of them. They get off on seeing us get hurt, and that's degrading, man. Trouble is, it makes me fight like hell to realize I've got a roomful of people against me. I must be some kind of fucking exhibitionist at heart. I don't know.

Since there is a demand for it from those who have joined the Pit Club, I ask the four stars how they would feel about wrestling nude.

C: I've done it before. It's cool. It would be really good for me, 'cause I'd know there were women out there getting turned on. I'd be able to pick and choose my lovers, and that sure beats meeting them in bars or at the nude beach.

T: I might have a problem. I used to be bothered by the way my ass looks from behind. But I've been getting really good feedback from the women who come up to me after my matches.

Even when it's someone as well-educated as I, I can tell when it's my body that has them interested, and that's very liberating for me.

J: I swam nude with my brothers when I was a kid. I was a tomboy. I don't think I really care what people think about my body. I still believe in God and that's what He gave me—

T: He? He? Where've you been, Jen'—

J: That's right, He. Tinka's into goddess worship. Her privilege. I believe in religious freedom, but I'm a Catholic. Anyway, my build is a turn-on to some women, but I've never tried to look sexy in my life, so help me God.

P: I never gave bein' nekkid much thought since my first job was dancin' in a titty bar. Men, women been after my body ever since I can remember and I got molested a lot even before I had boobs. As far as I can see my body's always been the way I've made my livin', and I've had a lot of good times with it and so have a lot of other people, so I think of it as a kind of a friend that's never let me down and it wouldn't say very much for my character if I was to be ashamed of it, now would it?

I ask if the women are happy with working conditions here at the Open Pit.

C: I don't call this work, man. It's just a little gig for me and there's other shit I do. This is a nice place, but that Brian—wow. At first I thought he was funny wandering around with a drink in one hand and his prick in the other sayin', "Ever try the airplane spin?" But he's starting to get on my nerves.

J: It means a lot to me to stay in shape and it's a double plus that my job is such a good workout. If the sport continues to catch on and I can keep my popularity I'd like to go to school during the day and learn physical therapy.

T: The working conditions are fine but I'd like to make several recommendations. One, you need a real doctor in the house because none of us knows her own strength. Two, the room is too drafty. Be nice if we could wear a robe before and after, but I can understand why not, we've got our meat to parade. Three, the so-called owner, but I might get in trouble saying what needs to be done.

P: Best job I ever had. I know everyone's down on Mr. Steele, but imagine someone who drinks that much still havin' a twinkle in his eye and tryin' to be nice. It's like a miracle. Just think how bad he must feel!

Casual conversation with the stars reveals that Jennifer's hobby is skydiving while Tinka's is rock gardens and bonsai. Jennifer sleeps alone with her teddy. Cass once worked on a suicide prevention hotline. Paula was a great bass fisherwoman in East Texas, and goes for stripers here in San Francisco Bay. (She says, "It ain't the same.")

Stay tuned for more information on your favorite ring stars in the next issue of THE OPEN PIT NEWSLETTER.

Success was mine for the time being, but I knew perfectly well I didn't deserve it, and I knew it could be snatched from me at any moment. I'd already exceeded my expectations going in, and was nonchalant about anything that might befall me by staying on.

I thought I could keep things going when Nina left. She was training a replacement, and the replacement had been a customer of Peckham's once (getting her dope from him, not our food). Her name was Melanie, and I didn't trust her. Though Nina assured me she didn't dislike or distrust me I got the feeling she'd quit on the spot if I ever gave her an order. Still, I had a history of being wrong about chefs. When I'd worked as a waiter it often happened that the ones I was sure hated me turned out to be my best friends in the place.

Brian was the reason I couldn't take my success seriously—the same old reason. Because of him I could never sell the business. I had the food and the entertainment charge, he had the drinks. But he still had the building and was donating the premises.

Now he needed me, though. As long as we had our food and wrestling programs his bar would be busy, and as long as his bar was busy his daughters couldn't have him declared incompetent. And if he dropped dead? We were out of business the moment he hit the floor.

All during Nina's last month we never saw the last of him at night without wondering if we'd see more of him tomorrow. Then there he was, reading his newspaper at the Pit Stop before the first seating, turning the pages with a trembling hand, surrounded by his potions.

We were rooting for him to stay alive, but we never let him know. Brian's will to survive derived from his ability to disappoint people's expectations and desires. A kindness without ulterior motive might have killed him! Quietly, then, we were all rather proud of him for being such a tough old bird, proud as we watched him wobble on like the sole survivor of an oilspill.

Our first month's profit was more money than I'd seen in my life. My success was so real to me at that point that I was a little down on myself not to have seen what was coming.

Fiona was back working downstairs, and not on a break from school. She meant business. Carrie was still working upstairs beside Vito, and there hadn't been anything more serious than a tiff since the grand opening. Vito had always known how Peckham felt about Carrie, and Carrie knew only too well, but she was still shocked and annoyed when Peckham started coming up to "visit." Sure, he said he wanted to see how we were doing, but the real reason he was hanging around was to make small talk with Carrie. To bask in her atmosphere.

"What's the matter with your friend, coming on to me when the man I live with is working right beside me?"

"You did the right thing to tell him to fuck off, but are you sure you never felt anything for him at all?"

"I know he's a nice guy underneath, but he's always trying to prove how smart he is. He's condescending."

"That's an occupational hazard down there."

"Look, I don't mind telling him to go away, but maybe you could talk to him."

"Oh, I'll talk to him. But Brian is the one who has me worried, especially now that Emma has turned out to be a wrestling fan.

(All too true. A fixture in the front row, oblivious to her husband and the women in the audience. She laughed inappropriately, drank beer and acted as if she didn't understand the question when attendees found out who she was and wanted to hear about life with Brian—"before.")

"Why do you put up with so much shit from him?" I asked Carrie point blank.

"He helped my family when we came to America. Gave me my first job. Sure, he took advantage, but he's not the worst guy I ever met."

"That must have been a long time ago."

"Brian was in a lot better shape. Still a son of a bitch."

"He wanted to make you feel obligated."

"He was never that subtle. I couldn't be alone with him for two seconds. He'd try to force me."

"So your father beat hell out of him."

"No, he was after me, too."

"Jesus Christ!"

"It wasn't as bad as it sounds. He didn't want Brian to have me. He hated Brian for putting him in his debt."

"That's what happens, all right. Oh, I don't know, Carrie. Nothing could cause me to lose respect for you, but it's hard to imagine you with Brian."

"Oh, it's hard for me, too. Lucky for us both we were drinking so much that if anything ever happened between us, I don't remember it."

I knew enough about Carrie and Brian to have headed off what happened. Sure I did, but I'd never thought of them as people whose behavior could be changed. I must have thought of their behavior, if I thought about it at all, as secondary to a mania that had to run its course.

Brian's hostility to Carrie was just what Carrie had hinted once: a sign that he still had a hankering, still "loved" her in some primitive, possessive way. Brian probably belonged to that sizable class of men obsessed with some practice like peeping or dressing up in their wives' clothing—or some game like golf or collectible like baseball cards or toy like model trains—who were no less proprietary about their wives because they were "busy" out on the golf course or in their playrooms. Such men were harmless as long as their wives were home a lot.

From a greater distance, thinking more clearly, it became clear to me that Brian was randy from thinking about that night's wrestling program and Carrie, more beautiful by far than any of our wrestlers and so touchable to most, had whetted his appetite for something risqué, something besides the visual banquet that had been laid out for him night after night, then just as quickly put away before a single morsel had been next to his lips. No doubt his wretchedness had been exacerbated by the memory of better days, when his fingertips had prowled Carrie's dermis at will, even when she was conscious.

Whatever. What happened: As soon as Carrie started upstairs there had been more of the abuse Brian had been dishing out all along, and let it be said, more of Carrie's counter-torment—letting men besides Vito squeeze her buttocks or pat them in a seigneurial manner, and lately by letting the lesbians kiss her, squeeze her and tell her what they'd like to do to her if only she would reciprocate their feelings. The lust for her was palpable, breathable. Everything said and done by the bar customers was strategic, and so was the way Carrie teased them. She couldn't have been any more strategic clad in a gauzy fabric with winking sequins and pasties.

Vito was one reason the matter got out of hand. Vito had worked all over. He'd probably dealt with drunks as bad as Brian before, hard as that is to believe about someone so clothes-conscious. Rarely did he say anything but "Hey!" when Brian was out of line, but that was enough. A quiet, hangdog type like Vito could make people jump when he cleared his throat... So why didn't Vito see it coming?

It took one of our regular beered-up lesbians to put an end to Brian's abuse. All of our regulars were plenty fed up by the time Bobbie crowned him with a full bottle of Bombay gin and fractured his skull.

According to Vito, Bobbie may have actually seen his cock when he pulled it out. Still smiling about the incident, he told me the thing had been half-erect.

Vito's views made sense. "No one woulda hurt him for what he was sayin' about Carrie. They all know his brain's gone. But they're sensitive about seein' a pecker, some of these dames. Makes you wonder what was done to 'em."

"Carrie laughed when he showed it to her?"

"Sure she did. So did I! Wouldn't you? I mean, you could feel sorry for him if it was someone besides Brian. Probably the first time in twenty years he was offering to make somebody happy."

"I don't know..."

"Sure. Brian's never been off the tit. You got something, he wants it. That's the first time I ever saw him come across like, 'Here's somethin' for you.'"

Brian left us by ambulance. We believed his attacker, who swore she hadn't tried to kill him. There were heavier bottles close at hand. Some probably wouldn't have shattered at all, but quickly broken through his calcium-depleted cranium.

The police came with the rescue workers and were told by fourteen female witnesses and one male that the victim, in a state of obvious sexual arousal, had attacked a customer and was struck down in self-defense. "In Carrie's defense" would have been too hard to explain. And there hadn't been any attack, of course, but Brian was well-known to these officers.

"Attacked this lady with his cock out? We hadn't seen him in a while. Thought he was doing better. Anyway, even if he dies, we'll believe anything you say."

"We've had a problem with him for years," one of the patrolmen told me over a beer. "He gets so drunk he can't stand up and we run him home or drop him off here."

"Bad drinker, but he never hurt a soul. Well-behaved, I'd say." This from the junior officer. "Now a sex thing. He must be in the last stages."

"He smelled like hell. Let's face it, if you didn't know him you'd take him for a derelict. A hard-on, though. Who'd have believed it? Someone in his shape, you can't really blame him for wanting to show it off. Sure nobody wants to bring charges?"

"Positive," I told them. "We all know him. Know enough to expect anything. If they can sober him up while they're saving his life we'd like to find out what kind of guy he is."

"Don't be so sure," said the junior man.

"He's not gonna turn himself around after a few weeks in the hospital. It might be a good time to talk to him, though. See if he'll check into one of the dry-out houses."

"You don't need him for anything here, do you?"

"He does a little buying, payroll. We can keep things going without power of attorney. His daughters are running the place downstairs in his name."

"Don't visit right away. If he lives through the head injury he'll still have to be detoxified. Tell your bar people it's gonna be a crime to serve him."

Brian was able to talk when I first saw him five days later, but I wasn't. I was hurting to keep from laughing. His tape turban was one thing—it made his face look smaller than ever. Ferret-sized. The other was the first thing he said to me.

"She wanted it! I could see it in her eyes before she started laughing! She had to laugh it off in front of all those people, but just for a second I saw her eyes the way they used to be when I'd grab her juicy little blackhaired cunt!"

A nearby nurse was legging it away. Now that I felt my visit might be curtailed I was able to get a grip on myself.

"How are you, Brian?"

"I had DTs my third and fourth days, or so my doctors told me. I don't remember much. My skull is cracked and it would hurt like hell if I weren't so full of medicine. I don't feel a thing, that's the truth. Not fuck-all. Physick has come a long way in this country. Bancroft, I'm counting on you to get some spirit to me when they take me off this medication. By the way, how's the fight game? Any new talent? Same old crowds?"

"We've been having a full house right along. Things couldn't be rosier. I'm going to pay Carrie and Vito for you and deduct the same as I do on my own payroll. Your daughters haven't stuck their noses in yet, so I've started a separate account for your bar receipts. I expect them to move in and try to mingle your receipts with theirs, but Vito's running the tape and keeping a copy. This time we'll make it hard for the little bitches to cheat you..."

"Good lad! I knew I could count on you! Bancroft, you have what it takes to be a partner. Keep on, keep on. My other partners were the scum of the earth, they affected my judgment. If only I had known there was someone like you out there!"

The whitecoats were coming. "Next time don't forget my medicine," he whispered. "Just a half-pint or so to start. It will take time to build up my tolerance again."

"The man is terminally ill," his doctor told me out in the hall. "All the most terrifying manifestations of advanced alcoholism are present and on top of that he's cracked his skull. If he has any other family you ought to make sure they come today, while he's comparatively appropriate."

"Could you tell me who's been? I'm not family."

"The Swiss woman. Edna?"

"That would be Emma, his wife. No Italians with roses?"

"Only his wife. Frankly, she wasn't much good with him. She must realize that Mr. Steele is not likely to improve in any case, but has no chance at all if she keeps shouting at him. She seems to want to reform his character, but I really can't see what good that will do if it costs him his life."

"You're evidently not a religious man, nor am I, but she may be under the impression that if her husband repents of his sins,

God will see his case in a better light."

"There are people who still believe that?"

I nodded and shrugged.

"We sure don't see many of 'em here at County Hospital!"

It was the day on Nina's ticket. If we left now there would be ample time for check-in. Melanie was ready to take over. There had been less and less wrong with her work as the days passed. This would be her first day on her own and I'd rested well the night before.

I gave Nina a ton of severance pay and she put it in her shoes. (I was paranoid about my country's currency restrictions.) Nina cried from the time we began the drive. As soon as she became composed enough to speak she swore that she loved me and began crying all over again. "We'll see each other in France again," she said between monsoons. "Someday we'll be together."

It was an elaborate production. I knew it hurt her to be leaving me this way; it hurt me, too. But I could tell she was also relieved to be going home. She'd blubber her way on board and start smiling again as soon as her plane was in the air. Her resilience cheered me, even though circumstances required that I take it for granted. I loved the way she refused to acknowledge the daily obstacles she had been forced to overcome. Let's face it, I loved *her.*

I had tears in my eyes when I last saw her, and again when I thought of the day we met. That was how I saw her when she came into my thoughts, brazening out her request for a job, though she was an undocumented worker.

In the fourteen months since my father died I'd had little to be grateful for—or that was my warped view. By herself, however, Nina had balanced everything that had gone wrong. It made me tired to look ahead and imagine what it might take to keep things running right.

"Are you family?" asked the burly nurse in a whisper, barring the way into Brian's room.

"No. His business partner."

She screwed up her eyes as she considered this, wondering where she had seen me before.

"Oh. Doesn't he have any?"

"I'm surprised his wife hasn't called. Emma?"

"Not while I've been on duty. I hope to God I've got more support than that if I have to fight to stay alive. That's right," she folded her hands over her imposing bosom. "He might make it. I bet you didn't think he would when you were trying to decide whether or not to visit."

"Maybe she comes when you're off shift."

"No, he hasn't been able to see anyone till today."

"You mean, my last trip here, yesterday, was unauthorized?"

"As far as I'm concerned. Who let you in? He wouldn't have been able to see anyone till today. He didn't make sense! You know all about his drinking, I take it."

I nodded. "But the blow on his head?"

"Oh, it's not as bad as he thinks. There's a tendency to blame his mental condition on that fracture, but pretty soon his head will stop hurting and he'll have to deal with the biggest reason he's not a healthy man. Go on in. Take it slow, is all. He's under heavy sedation."

I'd never known him when he wasn't heavily sedated, but he was even more chipper than the last time. I was reminded of our first meetings between binges.

The bandage might have been smaller but it still made his head twice as big, and with his emaciated body gave him a faintly spermatozoid appearance. I had the impression that with a little push he'd have followed his head anywhere.

"Bancroft? Good you came. Could have come sooner. How long has it been? I've lost all track of time."

"Six days. I was here yesterday."

"You were? Sorry about that. Did I recognize you?"

"Right away, don't worry about your *compos mentis*. You'd had a touch of the DTs."

"So I'm told. Well, I can welcome you properly today at least. How are things in the fight game. Any new meat? Still pulling in the fans?"

"Same old 'meat,' but the crowds are marginally bigger, if anything. Hanging off the ceiling. We're a big hit."

"Bravo! Splendid! If you can keep my daughters away from my bar receipts, I'll... I'll... I'll be in your debt. You can have... three wishes, let's say, as long as they're within reason."

"I'm just acting in my own best interests," I hastened to tell him. "I wouldn't have done anything differently if you were on vacation at the moment, or dead."

"Don't count on me buying it any time soon. Amazing what they can do to put a man right these days. One wonders how they were able to save so much of my mind..."

He waited for me to demur, then went on cheerfully: "In my father's day you didn't go in and out of DTs the way you pop off to an amusement park. Anyway, damned inconvenient of me, this DT business. And I'm sorry the wrestling will have to go..."

Could it be...? I felt the burden of all I thought I would have to say being lifted. I felt myself floating after it.

Brian was shaking his white helmet. "I've been such a fool." Bright as a little boy looking up from water that he has just learned not to fear: unmistakably the awe of the old man fallen in love.

"Such a fool."

Ah, my cue. "How, do you suppose?"

"All the years I thought I couldn't function with a woman again."

"And now you've fallen for one of your nurses."

He looked up hurt. "She fell for me, in fact." A shy smile. "She told me it wasn't love," he went on, all misty under his white helmet, "which was all right with me. You see, she's half my age. She just likes to play with it. Can you imagine, the first time John Thomas has stood up straight in years!"

"Is it really? Word has it you were ready for action when

Bobbie crowned you."

"Was I really?" Pain crossed his face. "Ah, well. Better I give all the credit to Angela here. Who was Bobbie, though? Someone jealous of Carrie? Wasn't it Carrie who charged me?"

"Nobody did."

"What am I doing here then?"

"Recovering from a near-fatal blow."

"Nonsense. I've got my own apartment! What bloody difference does it make where I lie around with a bloody bandage on my head?"

"What about Angela, though?"

"You might have a point there. You don't suppose she's grown so attached to it she'd follow me? You're a poet as I recall. You might know about this kind of thing..."

During my next visit, finding Brian more lucid still, I tried to clear up the mystery surrounding certain past associations.

"One-armed Tony?" A bitter smile. "He's a Mafia hit-man. My wife and daughters hired him to take care of me."

"With one bare hand and that little stump?"

"That's how he can operate openly. No one suspects him. If I had been stupid enough to really take care of him, what kind of sympathy would I get in court? Thrashing a cripple? When you think of it, biting his ear off was brilliant strategy for someone who had no choice."

"I was never told the whole story, but Fiona once suggested that you were old friends."

"They all say that when you're winning. He was my bookie. He paid for the fireplace upstairs and our first family automobile, a Healy 3000 MK II. Wonderful machine."

"So you never had a falling out before he tried to kill you?"

"We could have remained the best of friends, but he was delusional. Claimed I owed him money. Thought he was a loan shark, I guess, but couldn't inspire enough fear to make a go of it."

"But he was a murderer for hire?"

"If they only knew! His victims, I mean. I don't think the coppers were even on to him. I'm sure he paid them off as a cost of doing business. That's the way it is—you ever notice? When someone is paying you more than you're worth—and isn't hush money or blackmail the easiest money there is?—you want to think the best of them! When you want someone to be your victim, it's harder for you to see yourself as theirs. That's how a lot of people fell afoul of Tony, though I don't think he took down many coppers... He was putting their children through school, after all. That's what went wrong with Carrie and me when it comes right down to it. If Tony had been putting her through school with my winnings she'd never have said a word about the way he made a living. But nothing was ever good enough for that cavilling slut. With Tony and Carrie sucking my blood simultaneously it was a miracle I had enough left to buy my wife a potted plant once in a while."

"Perhaps I've been given wrong information. Surely it was just a fling between you and Carrie. How much damage could she do in that short time?"

"Ask her where she got her front teeth!" His color was in bright contrast to his bandage now. Sallow as he was when I'd come in, the bandage had looked positively dirty. Now it was unmistakably recent.

"Surely..."

"Without me she'd have been afraid to sing a note! She'd have cleared the front row with those stubby brown pegs of hers."

I was a naif about things like false teeth. It was disappointing to realize that Carrie's beautiful set of incisors, which I had always presumed to have been her own, had obligated her to Brian.

"You look surprised. She's still sucking my blood!"

"Hardly. She's a big hit with our new customers. Why do you make her life miserable?"

"Because she's an ungrateful little bitch, that's why! When she first presented herself to me she was nothing but a bit of crumpet. I should have had her put it in writing... She didn't have the cheek to ask for cash! I'd have paid her double the going rate, and I don't care how beautiful she is, her fanny couldn't sing opera... Couldn't even hold a tune, much less massive equipment like mine. But no, cash was too much like a tip, even if she was holding out her hand for it."

"She likes the tips well enough at the bar!"

"Quite right! I've noticed! But then, she always did. Even when she was innocent..." He was about to shed tears of bitterness while wearing a smile, something I'd never seen before. "She couldn't work behind a bar, nobody could have stood her... The arrogance! No, first it was her father. Nothing in it for her, mind you! She wouldn't think of selling you her fanny for personal gain! No, it was all for her father. He didn't have money to repair his puppets. There were bookings if only he could pay for a paint job and some hip replacements... I think he was trying to replace his own hip, the greedy, lying bastard! It's no secret she was supporting him. Can you imagine? Trying to make me think my money was going for puppets when I was putting food on the table for the lot of 'em. Then having to put up with her father's surly manner with me because I was defiling his daughter. Fouling the nest! We had been friends in India, you see. I should have known better. What sort of man would try to earn a living with puppet shows in a place like Calcutta? I'm surprised she came to me with both her legs. No, he was too devious to put her on the street that way. All the diseases she got from the rabble getting between her legs wouldn't reflect badly on him. Everybody was dying of something in India, that's why everyone was pissed all the time. That's where she contracted syphilis..."

"No!"

"I hope you don't think her memory was devoured by mere drink! An old wives' tale. She's a syphilitic if I ever saw one. Her father's child. Look, Bancroft, this is all very interesting, but I have a special visitor coming..."

I was half-convinced on the way out of the hospital, then dismissed everything by the time I was behind the wheel. Brian had always made a lot of sense when he was delusional. He could be eloquent then. Much of what I'd heard could have been disinformation to stir up trouble. If he was as shrewd as I thought, he realized he was in a bad position to run things from his hospital bed with no one but me to carry out his orders. If he kept us on edge with each other there was less chance we'd get together and realize that all of us, including his daughters, had common interests antithetical to his.

What were his interests, then? To live long enough to see all of us, or some of us, or merely one of us, if that were the best he could do, reduced to wretchedness comparable to the sort Carrie or her father had known, so that he could simultaneously enslave and redeem us as he had the important people in his past. His wife and daughters, Carrie and her father, had managed to nibble away at his substance and carve out little niches for themselves. Brian wanted his prestige back, his lordliness restored. He wanted so much success for himself that his children would be more childlike, his employees more dependent. He needed to die a martyr to make up for all the petty martyrs he had made with his own outrageous needs. And I would be his righthand man, his eyes, his legs, his brain, his mouth... I was to be the one who restored his patriarchy. He would live again through me, running everything from the soiled swivel chair in his cluttered office, while the bands played on.

Brian may only have been a lord in his twisted dreams, and I a prince in mine, but my promotion was flattering. If Brian knew who I was and thought he needed me I could use my influence to manipulate him and create a meaningful future for myself, and Hilliard and Carrie, too, if I was careful. There was only one catch. If Brian recovered enough to reenter our lives as a medical problem inhabiting the upstairs premises of his bar, his days were indeed numbered and so were ours. However, if I could keep him alive, reasonably fit, and convinced that a bedridden state would be ideal for him—a real bed, this time, far from the Fife and the Pit—there was hope for all of us, and even a sliver for Brian, which was all he deserved.

It would be a struggle to convince Brian I knew what was best for him if one of the quacks at county pronounced him fit. To make matters worse, he was rumored to have constructed a pleasure dome in the attic above the downstairs bar. While he was passed out I'd observed some of what was in there with a flashlight, but the catwalks were flung boards, and so irregular as to convince me that he'd filled the attic and crawlspace with obvious booby-traps to warn off building inspectors and insurance people. Romex wires were running all over the place like pale nerve tissue, and it was demoralizing to realize that so much illegal wiring could be spotted with a flashlight. Anyway, if there were a pleasure dome of some kind, or even a small hideout in there, Brian had secret access to it, I had been wasting my time. Then as now I put off knowing everything I had to know about the premises for the time when Brian disappeared completely and left us holding the bag and fighting for our lives. When it happened, as it was sure to (my dealings with Brian had taught me to take worst-case scenarios for granted), we'd have help from the police in making sense of his half-life, and his building's.

To put Nina out of mind—to put women in general out of mind and avoid finding Miss Right in the bookstores, coffeehouses and parks where she was lurking with a dozen others just like her—I started coming to work before lunch and helping Peckham serve hamburgers upstairs. He was swamped down in the Fife and Vito and Carrie had a full house up in my place from noon on. These days I always had a dozen ulterior motives going at the same time. One of the main ones at the moment had to do with keeping an eye on the melancholy, cow-like Melanie in order to learn how she was getting all the orders out so effortlessly. If she could do it, I could, and who knows, I might have to. If she was able to feed so many people fast and well, she could be lured to greener pastures at any moment. I was paying her as much as I paid Nina—but there was always someone bigger who could pay more.

Sarah had called while I was closing the kitchen on a Friday night to tell me that Hilliard had disappeared again. I didn't give the call much thought. Hilliard was disappearing a lot lately during the day, and I never knew what he was up to at night, because he never stayed to close the place with me unless he had a lot on his mind and wanted me to drink with him. But he was always on time to help me set up for the first show, start moving drinks, and prepare for the dinner onslaught. So when he burst into the kitchen the next day, looking as wild as I'd ever seen him, I wasn't alarmed.

"I did it, Bancroft! I've got a studio at Artaud! Enormous, and I'm only sharing with one guy—Scanlon!"

Project Artaud was an enormous warehouse or factory that had become a kind of artists' cooperative full of huge well-lit studios for which there was a long waiting list.

"Sarah's been in a sweat, man. You weren't in her bed last night, or she wasn't in yours, or something. You'd better call her."

"I know. I blew it. We had a party there. Sarah wouldn't have hacked it, tired from work. Bunch of artists. Can we talk?"

Out into the alley. Street noise and filth. Now for what he was ashamed of.

"Yeah, I was with someone. It didn't start that way, but after she latched onto me I couldn't stop it, ya know? I didn't know what to tell Sarah."

"Call her now. She's worried sick. Tell her about the studio. You got drunk at the party and passed out there. There isn't a phone in yet."

"Right! She's got to buy that."

But he was still worried.

"She was from Virginia." The girl with the latch. "I cast her in plaster. Scanlon helped me. That was before the party. Trouble is, she's got a studio there, or lives in someone's. Sarah's sure to find out. You know how she is. She'll say I've betrayed her."

Secretly I was exulting, so sure of victory that I could afford a little *noblesse*.

"Couldn't Sarah move in with you? Isn't there room?"

"There's room, but I don't know. You've been to Artaud, you know how many people are there, what kind they are. And Scanlon's there. Sarah would never be able to live with someone like that." I'd run into Scanlon a dozen times, I guess, and he always went to pick up a guitar when I came around, or was already holding one.

"But Miss Virginia isn't scared of him, I take it."

"I've got a problem..."

That night we left the mess from the last service, picked up Sarah in Hilliard's truck and went to see the new studio. Sarah fumed for a while when she got in beside him. Hilliard had spoken to her three times that day, but there was nothing he wanted me to know about his explanations. He must have been sticking by the story I gave him. It was my duty to shut up, as he was doing. It was an awful silence, and I was glad when Sarah broke it... at first...

"If I'd known you were going to be gone all night I would have asked Gordon to come over," she said while I contemplated Hilliard's always-open glove compartment.

Now the silence was unbearable.

"I'm surprised it hasn't happened before this," said Hilliard.

"Given my history of throwing myself at every man I meet..."

"No, Bancroft's not just anybody." Hear, hear. "You guys have a lot in common."

"The kind of work we do?" She was puzzled.

"I was going to stay out of this, but I can't let that stand. The obvious thing Sarah and I have in common is our liking for you, Hilliard."

"Glad I heard that!" Sarah. "Good thing nothing ever happened if that's all that's between us!"

"Couldn't we just forget the whole thing?" Hilliard wanted

to know. "I fucked up, Sarah, OK? Maybe you could think of some way for me to make it up to you. Or if it'll make you feel better to get it on with Bancroft or somebody, go ahead, but let's just not talk about it any more..."

We smouldered the rest of the way with nothing but sudden useless movements or too-loud interjections to show how we felt.

Hilliard took us around the building first to disorient us. In a place like this you could film *The Castle* and *The Trial* simultaneously and there was room for two of Orson Welles.

Hilliard let us in. Scanlon was there with a woman, playing his guitar in the dark. Sarah must have known who he was, because she was as oblivious of him as he was of her. Meeting her for the first time nobody could have been oblivious of Sarah, not even somebody deep into drugs.

We were in Hilliard Heaven. His face lit up the moment we were inside. Half a studio was still heaven to him because of the sunlight that would stream in on two sides. Here in the dark now, the mournful streetlight of this deserted industrial district was more romantic than weird.

Hilliard should have given Scanlon credit for the casting, but no. With the overhead lights on he let Sarah walk right up to the impression of a woman with an amazing figure and oafishly took credit for the fine job he'd done. The evidence was still fresh... Firm, full breasts pressed into the soft plaster. A dense record of her pubic hair, fringed with scribbles. It didn't take much of an imagination to think of Hilliard helping her clean up.

Sarah kept staring, her face a death mask. Hilliard kept grinning like an idiot, since pride of accomplishment with him was about as discreet and fleeting as a case of eczema. I walked around them in circles, swooping in, trying to get a little magnetism going. Scanlon picked at his guitar with the kind of wary precision I associated with the removal of bras.

Back in the car Hilliard knew something was wrong, bless his sensitive soul. But he still wanted us to admit we were awed.

"I'm very happy for you," Sarah told him quietly. "It's just what you've always wanted."

"I hope it will be." Off and running again. "I tried to get in the first year and it was too much dough. Then when I had it there was a waiting list a mile long. Scanlon does his art every day. He's a selfish prick and I know he'll steal from me, but he'll be on time with the rent. He knows what he's got."

We seemed to be headed to my place. I wanted Sarah to ask to be dropped off alone at hers so I could call her. She ought to have been ready to confide in me if she really saw what she was getting into. From now on when Hilliard wanted a fling all he'd have to do was walk next door or leave his own door open and wait for someone to wander in. Art-hungry females moved through the huge building all day and night, a succession of languid ricochets. One could come spinning through Hilliard's door and out of her clothes in a brushstroke.

Too soon. They were just waiting to get rid of me so they could lacerate each other in earnest. I could hear them over the engine noise as they pulled away.

It was three days before I visited Brian again, and he'd signed himself into a month-long dry-out program. His head bandage was smaller but he looked a lot worse now that he was no longer flying high on medication. I had expected to be asked where the bottle was as soon as the nurse left us alone.

I wasn't.

"You don't know what I've been through. Fighting for my life! My suffering should be a lesson to you, Bancroft. When I think of all the crap I've had to take from people because I was too drunk to command their respect. Do you have any idea how much the drinking man is despised?"

"Here?"

"No. Back out there in everyday life. Except at lunchtime, nine out of ten people would rather do business with a man who's sober than a man who's been drinking. I never knew that before."

"I'm sure those nine would be less squeamish if they were

dealing with someone in the bar business."

"That's right. You'd think so, wouldn't you? But listen to this: a majority of the general public thinks booze smells bad, especially on someone's breath."

"Yeah, but after they've had a few they don't know the difference. It's the same with garlic and goat cheese."

"Good point. I'll bring it up at the next meeting. If everyone has a little drink in him, nobody smells bad. I like the way you see things, Bancroft. I'm tired of people who are always negative."

"Me, too, but I'm used to it in hospitals. The only way to command respect in a hospital if you're only a patient is to sign out against medical advice."

"They're still running tests. I don't want to die before they find out everything that's wrong with me. Can you imagine thinking, 'What's wrong with me' right up to the end?"

"I can't imagine you thinking it. Booze will be the cause of anything bad that has happened to you, Brian."

"Do you think so? I'd been meaning to ask you, do you really think I was drinking too much?"

"That's a tough one. Some people might have thought so when you wet your pants without knowing it or went around with shit in them for days at a time. But if you're a person who enjoys that kind of life, who's to say you've had too much?"

"What if you're so busy enjoying life that you forget to change clothes? That was always my excuse. Clothes don't make the man, you know."

"Now there's a lucky break. Think what might have become of you!"

"Are you sure you didn't mind the way I was behaving just a little bit? I wasn't too domineering, selfish, messianic, quarrelsome, nasty?"

"No. As far as I was concerned you were just a drunk little bugger with shit in his pants."

"Watch what you say, Bancroft. I'm still your employer."

"I think you're confusing me with Vito. That's one of the reasons I came, by the way..."

"I may not be your employer, but I can see to it that every

penny you've spent on my building is wasted."

"That's why I'm glad you're going to be on ice for a month."

"Wasn't I easier to get along with when I was drinking?"

"No. Much easier now that you're locked up. Feel free to say anything you want."

He thought for a moment. "Do you care whether I live or die?"

"Of course I do."

He drummed his fingers. "Why?"

"I guess you don't want to hear the practical reasons. You've got the building, and you're the only one who can hold off your daughters. But I've enjoyed you on a personal level."

"How could you? I remember clearly that your customers would get up and leave when I came by. It didn't mean anything to me at the time, but things like that are coming back to haunt me now. How was I enjoyable?"

"Why do people still like the Marx brothers? I don't know, the people you ran off were the ones who look better in retreat."

"At least I never tried to sit with them and bore them with my stories."

"This is true." The nurse was back. Female, thirties, attractive, but no sweetcakes. "Nurse, Mr. Steele has important business with me and I'm sure it's good for his peace of mind that he doesn't feel too cut off from his affairs. A few minutes more?"

She left smiling. There was nothing nurses in a place like this liked better than proof that the drunks in their keeping were important men, upper-echelon types with one tiny flaw.

"What's wrong with our business?"

"Vito's had it. He's leaving his job. Carrie. Maybe the town."

"This really is my lucky day. What did you do to him?"

"It's all Carrie's doing. I've seen it coming. Vito never said anything while the customers were fondling her, but he was hurting inside. I like Vito..."

"I don't."

"I like Vito because he's good at what he does and ever since I've known the guy I don't think I've heard him pass judgment on another... Well, he didn't always have nice things to say about you, but that was when you were abusing Carrie..."

"Stop! I won't have it! I may have done awful things I don't know about when I was drinking too much, but I stand by anything I said to her. She ruined my life."

"Have it your way. But losing Vito is going to hurt, whatever you say. Of course Peckham is dying to come upstairs and work the bar beside her. He'd give up his hamburgers for a chance like that. It's a touchy situation."

"Peckham? Hamburgers?"

"You'll remember him when you come back. Everything is under control for the moment. The account I've opened is swollen. Your bar receipts are upwards of two grand a day..."

"In that little bar?"

"Don't forget all the wrestling fans up there. You've got quite a capacity now, thanks to us."

"Don't talk about my capacity," he said, looking glumly at his belly. "I realize you're talking about seats, but use another word..."

"The Pit is a sellout in so many ways I couldn't begin to tell you."

"That's wonderful," he said, congratulating me on my good fortune and looking in my eyes long enough to realize that it was his good fortune, too. "I have complete confidence in you." He put his small, still tremulous hand on top of mine. It was cold and covered with spots and sparse black hair. The fingers were pink and clean and the nails had a nice shape. It was a hand that might have comforted someone, and it made me sad to think how little it had in fifty-some-odd years, and how little chance there was of it doing so again.

"Bancroft? You never did say why you cared about me except that I was amusing to you. Was there nothing more?"

"Isn't that enough? I feel an obligation to anyone that can make me laugh. Without the laughs even the women and the children and the work don't mean anything."

He chewed on this for a while, wishing it were sweeter.

"I don't know. Would I be a successful businessman if I'd spent my life yukking it up with people like you?"

I didn't visit Brian again while he was detoxifying. The visiting hours were stringent and miserly, it was too much of a hardship, even though I wasn't busy all the time any more and was on the verge of advising old golf partners that I was ready to start playing again. Anyway, it was business as usual around the Pit, even though Peckham may have been howling his head off downstairs. Carrie had told him to "keep the fuck away" while she was on shift. Her pal Lulu had taken Vito's place, a leggy East Anglian who gave new spice to the increasingly brazen games our regulars were playing. The new cocktail waitress, Hilary, was another friend—Carrie could contact hundreds of women she'd worked with and usually find you a replacement in minutes.

Brian came back in the middle of another sellout evening wearing a cycling helmet and taking small, careful steps. Hilliard's first words to me were: "He looks like someone pretending to be sober. But he's not. It's the real Brian."

"What's he like, then?" News of Brian's arrival had reached Hilliard first and he'd helped the old man up the stairs.

"Too early to say. Hasn't said anything about the job we're doing. Just small talk. Very polite."

Brian hadn't wanted to see the show and was cleaning up his office—work for three German maids in their prime. He was all business when he came to me.

"I want to see some more clothes on those girls."

"You're not serious." But he was. "I don't have to tell you how boring this style of wrestling is to most people." Because he'd told me as much a million times! But now there was nothing like that on his mind. "Chance exposure of one of those little pink places might be the main thing that's keeping us in business, Brian."

"Do you take me for an idiot? It's not much more than a month I've been away and the redblooded wrestling fans, the sort I used to be, are all gone."

"Let's hear your tune when you see the balance in the account I opened for you."

"I don't care about the money. I may have wasted my youth and middle age but today is the first day of the rest of my life. It's not too late for me to be a morally decent human being. There are plenty of ways to make a living without degrading young women, or encouraging people to poison themselves."

"Give me a lease and you can live the rest of your life any way you want. God knows it would be brave for you to stay... committed to this business... sober. God knows my thoughts often turn to jumping one of those healthy young warriors... Jumping right in there with them and putting it into every crack I can find..."

"See a therapist. Work it out. I had such impure thoughts once myself."

"You're no longer interested in healthy young women?"

"I'm no longer interested in taking advantage of them. I have a position to maintain. I want to keep people's respect. I want to be able to respect myself again the way I did before all the big crowds started arriving."

We had a new seating to take care of. Brian promised not to pull any plugs until the end of the second show, at which time we'd get comfortable in his new office, put on a pot of Ovaltine and discuss the meaning of life.

In the intervening two hours I alerted Hilliard and even Peckham. They should expect the worst. I almost went so far as to ask Fiona's help and Deirdre's. Surely they'd seen him this way right after the straitjacket...

Carrie was my only hope. "Has he gone through anything like this before?"

"He was awful to us when he went on the wagon. Somebody has him on drugs. He was as polite to me just now as he would have been to a perfect stranger. If this isn't a miracle, it's at least a mixed blessing."

"It might be too early to count blessings."

"You sound like Alex. Let's give Brian a chance. Just because I need a drink to get through the day, I don't wish that kind of life on anyone else."

"Carrie, give me a triple Black Jack neat. I'm the one who needs a drink tonight."

"I can smell it on you from here!" Brian told me as soon as we were comfortable. "Open the door a crack. Are you sure you'll be able to talk business?"

"Not if you doubt my mind is clear. I've got important things to talk to you about, but they can keep. All I want from you is an assurance that until we talk you won't do anything to dismantle the business."

"You're forgetting what I told you earlier. I'm for mantling, not dismantling."

"The wrestling is my baby, Brian. I've had a lot of success with it. It's making money for everyone involved and it isn't morally repugnant to me in any way."

"I shouldn't wonder. I wouldn't expect a whiskey-swilling, skirt-chasing type like you to see it for what it is." His eyes glittered. "You're no better than a ponce. You're talking to a man who has raised two daughters!" There was a conviction in his voice I'd only heard before when he was delusional from too much drink. "How do you suppose they feel having a father who's running a sex show for perverts right above their heads?"

"I know exactly how they feel because you've already told me. They want a cut from you, or they want you to croak so they can have it all."

"How dare you talk about my daughters that way?"

"How dare you change your tune about those sleazy bitches after all they've put me through?"

"You're shouting! Are you aware that you've lost control of your voice with all that you've had to drink?"

"Are you aware that you're about to go through that window?"

"I'll call the police!"

"On your way down?"

He came off the ground like someone half his size. Then I

forced him down on his knees beside an office chair, sat next to him and with one hand around his throat and the other under his cycling helmet, pulled his head back.

"Now you listen to me, you son of a bitch, and do as I say or I'll break you in two. All your life you've been getting your way and making people miserable with the way you want to run things. Well, I took care of this place for you while you were incapacitated... FOR YOU, goddammit. I never had any interest in watching these pituitary cases wrestle each other. YOU WERE THE ONE who sold us on having wrestling here. I AM THE ONE who made a success of your idea. Now you want to destroy my work. All right, fine. I'm ready to move on. I'm sick to death with all the headaches this place has given me from day one, primarily because I had to go along with you on everything to keep from being screwed out of my investment by those daughters of yours. You want me out? I'm ready to go. But you're going to make me a settlement. You're not going to fuck me out of everything I've done, all the equipment, the remodeling, the work..."

"Bncrft! Ffffft!"

I took my hand from his throat and made a fist right by his nose.

"Hear me out," he said, sounding quite sane. "I've had a chance to think. I grant you, a lot of it was confabulation. There are gaps. But I know I shafted you on the dumbwaiter, if you'll pardon the pun." He gave me one of his boyish smiles then. I took my fist away and got tears in my eyes. After the scare I'd just given this poor, sick man it was my turn to be dragged away screaming.

He looked puzzled by the change in me, but went on. "I got to thinking about that thick business plan you showed us when you first became interested in this place. You wanted a coffeehouse up here as I recall. Chamber music..."

"Not a coffeehouse. A restaurant with chamber music."

"A restaurant, then. And I'm sure you wanted to sell liquor, too. It's not lost on me that my liquor license was one of the reasons you wanted to venture with me. This may not have been exactly what you intended, and I may have some of my facts wrong, but hear me out. What about a nondrinking atmosphere...Wait!"

I'd merely changed my expression, but had been making a powerful statement all the same.

"The money might not be so bad as you think. You wanted to do music, isn't that so? Chamber music? Why not music and food the way you once wanted. Hot spiced cider. I've got an old espresso machine at home. All sorts of restaurant equipment to add to what you've got. I could be a real partner and help you make a go of it in the sort of place I describe. Forget the Fife and Drum. We'd wall it off. Let my daughters go to hell. I know perfectly well they'll do everything to block me if I turn my back on the moneymaker we've got here..."

"A moment ago you were standing up for them."

"I was pulling your leg, for godssakes! Weren't you the one who told me that the only reason you weren't angry with me after all the times I embarrassed you or ran off your customers was because I was so entertaining?"

"True. I did say something like that. Congratulations."

"Don't worry, I understand why it's so easy to fly off the handle. Who wants to close down an operation as successful as this? I just think it would be the best thing for both of us. You've got the ideas, the talent, the enthusiasm. You've done well with the food, too, and that's something I would never want to get into. I've got the experience, the premises and licenses, and if you'll help me to stay on the wagon... I know it's a lot to ask, but I wonder if you'd consider doing your drinking somewhere else from now on..."

"Eighty-sixed again."

"I couldn't go that far after all you've done. As a favor to me, perhaps? It may not be easy for me to stay on the straight and narrow. Bugger, I know it won't be. I've never been there before."

I helped him to his feet, walked him around the desk, helped him sit.

"I don't know," I began when I'd returned to my chair. "I've gone more than halfway ever since I got involved in this place. I'm not sure I'm overjoyed that halfway seems far enough for you... But sure, it's an improvement. How about I ask a favor, too, though? Do you think you have it in you to try to do something my way for a change? Just this once?"

He nodded slowly, unblinking. His manner would have had real authority without the brightly colored helmet (red, white and blue).

"I've been involved in a lot of community opera productions. Most of them were so-so, but not for the lack of local singing talent. Maybe you've heard of the Old Spaghetti Factory, Donald Pippin, et al. He's probably done more for opera than anyone in this town. He does concert readings, though, and we're set up to do a bit more here. In fact, we're perfectly set up for a real dinner theater. We'd need to fill the room eventually, but we've got enough seats to start. There's room for props where the wrestlers dress. We've got all the lighting we'll ever need. We could do grand opera in full costume. A small orchestra or two pianos. No chorus, but some important operas don't have them. I'll be honest with you: it was what I always wanted. Success of any other kind was just another step closer to the goal."

"Which you didn't expect to reach until I died..."

"Not that simple. You'd have had to take the rest of your family with you."

"Quite right. But you wouldn't have to worry about them if I'd give you my support."

"Of course not. I wouldn't have to worry about anything but producing an opera in this place on short notice. To someone in another field that might seem like a piece of cake. Pippin has been doing it so long he's made it look easy. Anyway, there you have it. What do you think?"

"So it wasn't chamber music you wanted?"

"I didn't think I could slip opera past you after all the times you'd put me out for singing it..."

"I'm not a fan, but I won't stand in your way."

We shook on it.

Sugar plums were trying to dance in my head but first I had to tell Carrie and make sure she didn't expect me to give her leads.

"We're going to do opera," I told her, oblivious to the wrestling fans all over the place. "I just cleared it with Brian."

"Which one?"

"*Lucia* to start." Seconds after the go-ahead I'd known I'd have to revive the *Lucia* I'd done with Teresa and Jørgen at the Community Opera Center.

"I knew that part," said Carrie, looking into the distance. "Were you going to ask me?"

"Of course!"

"Sweet of you, Gordon, but I could never take a chance on my memory. Doubt I could even get through the mad scene. It's great news, though. I'll help any way I can. If there's a small part for me in one of the next ones, it would be something to work for..."

Now I was really flying.

There were still plates on the tables when I started making phone calls. Bubbling over, knew I was, hoped my enthusiasm was contagious.

It wasn't. I couldn't believe the apathy I encountered with my first call.

"Bancroft, it's midnight..."

Right, a time when people might be expected to be dreaming of better days—musicians more than most. Ballet dancers, painters, sculptors—artists of every sort who subsisted on possibilities, promises, glimpses, tastes... foreshadowings that almost never led to anything concrete.

My first call had been to a guy named Chandler who played a lot of flute. Some time back, when I'd spoken to him about the chamber music I intended to produce at the Fife someday, he'd been interested. A woodwind quintet had been my first choice to provide the right background for my exotic crab dishes and festering cheeses—clear as a mountain stream, perhaps the same thing Brian had momentarily had in mind when he imagined his dinner theatre perched near a waterfall with the single difference that I heard the old-world music of Schubert and he heard banjos.

"I dunno Bancroft. It's so late. I teach tomorrow." I was about to cross his name out of my address book. I'd given him my spiel. Christ, I was going to pay, and not just the twenty bucks we'd discussed for chamber music.

"A little orchestra... You could lead them... I'd feed you... Drinks after... No, I can't pay scale—are you crazy? But you were interested in doing chamber music for twenty bucks. Why do you sound bored now? Are you stoned?"

"No, just sleepy. Can't we talk in the morning?"

"No. I've got to put this thing together while the owner of the premises is still receptive. What's wrong with fifty bucks each for a three-hour, four-hour gig? To pay it I'll have to have my singers go unpaid or pass the hat. Why are you instrumentalists all so greedy?"

"We're not greedy. I promised you a woodwind quintet. The Chandler Quintet. We could build a name for ourselves. Playing backup for an opera of yours we'd be faceless. It wouldn't matter who played as long as they knew where *one* was and played in tune. That's why all of us charge more for accompaniment. It doesn't do shit for our careers. Lots of practice to get our name in tiny print in a part of the program nobody reads. Sure, you singers take less money, but you're mentioned in the papers, you've got a role to put on your résumé, and who knows, someone might hear you and offer you a booking somewhere for decent dough."

"But not somewhere around here because we'll be paying better than anybody. I can't believe what a moneygrubbing, self-promoting asshole you are, Chandler. Here I'm offering you a chance to give this town something it sorely needs..."

"You're just trying to give a break to your singer friends and give yourself a crack at leading roles when no one else will have you because they never know when you're going to show up drunk on your ass."

"That's in the past. I've got my act together now. So read about me in the papers. Besides, I won't cast myself if I can find someone better. I've got enough to do running the whole show. And running orders. Or cooking them."

"You're doing the cooking, too?"

"You're right if you think I've been in a lot of places you'd be afraid to put those lilywhite fingers of yours. All right, Chandler, I won't bother you again..."

After hanging up it occurred to me that Chandler was highly respected by local instrumentalists and could hurt me a lot worse than I could hurt him. Diplomacy had never been my strong point. How could anyone refuse a chance to give the people of this town more of something like opera? San Francisco was the nation's premier gay wildlife preserve, and gays were the country's most important resource of knowledgeable support for opera. An audience for my productions was assured, even if our early crowds were full of disappointed wrestling fans. Too optimistically, perhaps, I was counting on a few wrestling fans who'd learned to love opera from listening to Melchior and the other heroes I'd had on top volume for the last two months.

I called Anneliese last, because I could leave a message anytime without disturbing her. She'd been a coach for Lotte Lehmann down at the Music Academy of the West. I'd worked with a her a few times in local productions. I could get her if she hadn't been twisted by her recent marriage.

Unpaid I'd done three operas with Anneliese at the COC, and twice received favorable reviews in the *Chronicle*. Our *Lucia* had drawn two hundred people, all of whom would have been unlikely customers at the Fife or the Pit. Yet the production was recent enough to dust off in a week or so as long as I could get the singers together to repeat their roles.

I would take the part of Enrico, since no one else wanted it, here or anywhere. I specialized in ungrateful roles, for obvious reasons. (Enrico is one of opera's standard hothead brothers who disapproves of his sister's love interest. All his big singing is in the first half of the show; by the end he's just one more guy in a kilt.)

Teresa had been our Lucia, of course, and though she was slow learning a big part, once she'd performed it, she knew it cold forever.

I had worries about the Raimundo, but just before dad died I'd run into a Russian guy with one of those legendary bass voices so deep you'd swear he was bringing up bowel sounds. I'd detected a generous soul. Even if he turned out to be less generous than he had seemed, Teresa could help me recruit him just by coming along and letting him know she was going to be in the show.

If the Russian had left town I was in trouble. There was another Russian import I'd actually sung with a couple of times. He'd been around forever, too, and could speak English without an accent. He was a lousy musician, but Raymond was a comparatively small part. The reason I dreaded using him was because he loved the sound of his voice so much that he was a distraction, and I'd always had trouble keeping a straight face while watching his public masturbations. It was fine to laugh in the audience with the sleeve of your coat jammed in your mouth, but on stage with him it was fatal, especially when (as Rigoletto) I'd just hired him to murder my employer, or when he'd just murdered my daughter by mistake. His name was Vladimir and I'd known the first-mentioned Russian basso as Volodya. I had the phone number for neither and Information was no help so I was being torn limb from limb all night by the two Vladimirs.

If it weren't for sweet dreams about the tenor who would be my Edgardo I probably wouldn't have slept at all. His name was Jørgen (pronounced *urine*), an Americanized Norwegian who washed windows all day on the downtown skyscrapers, singing to seagulls and frightening office girls. He had a fierce Viking face and seemed to chew his words, though not because they were hard for him to say. He had a big, horsy mouth with hair all around it and his expression while singing and weird pose of body might have been tolerated in the way certain baseball pitchers were permitted to keep a garish windup. All a matter of comfort, important to both singers and pitchers since both were asked to remember and create at the same time; neither was given sufficient time to search his mind or plan anything.

Jørgen was tall, unlike most tenors, but he was true to type in being quite mad. "Crazy like a tenor" is idiomatic in some countries, as are speculations about the damage done to their brains by piercing high notes. Savants had held forth in long treatises about imbalances in the sensorium arising from the fact that emotions of female intensity were being reinforced by a heavily-muscled masculine torso and transmuted by a small, muscular larynx into sounds that produced an identity crisis. Thanks to such theorists, and maybe some wives, a good many people thought tenors were freaks. Tenors, on the other hand, regarded themselves as supermen who were exposed in a way that let lesser beings take the air out of them. Like all martyrs, however, they never tired of worship, and worshippers were usually rewarded in some way: knick-knacks from faraway places, get-well cards—some would eventually turn up in the will.

Jørgen was that rare bird, a natural voice. He never bothered with voice teachers' exhortations to "cover" his sound, "support it," etc.—his tool kit was empty. He never bothered with voice teachers, *period.* He resembled the idiot savant in being able to accomplish miracles of correct singing without being able to articulate a single rule to explain what he was doing. In his own mind he was probably obeying God, or if he didn't believe, giving rein to a force he felt being channeled through him. Like the great singers of the past, he knew how to get out of his own way. His genius was not in adding to his kit bag of qualities, but in taking away, since great singing depended on deriving a maximum of sound from a minimum of effort. As I understood it, with less pressure of breath the muscles involved in singing were not tight in reaction, but strong and quick to function on their own, dancing away with the singer's soul.

Alas, with huge effort today's singers could scarcely fill even a small hall. And all because of the pseudoscience, what I called cantobabble, which could be heard even in the lower grades of public schools: about "the column of air," "the dome of the soft palate," etc. In the manner of the infamous Academy of Lagado, when precepts making use of these terms didn't work, the student was meant to practice with them until they did. When the promising student hadn't sung passably after a lifetime of such practice, he or she was adjudged to have been deficient in the first place—not to have had the right vocal cords, the right suspensory mechanism, the right resonances... Structural anomalies had *prevented their voices from coming out...*

Poor human beings, especially women, always so quick to believe bad news about their bodies. Autodidacts like Jørgen and me thought the truth quite another matter: most people who could carry a tune and loved to sing could become singers, even great singers, if they could stop hampering their voices with useless muscular devotions which, though they were undertaken in the hope of "freedom," only served to capture tones which belonged to their listeners.

The great singer knew that he or she was a vessel to be emptied, whereas the Academicians paraded their excellence as if it were an animal on a lead, holding tight while they put the little creature through its paces. Instead of simply pouring sound, their internal structures, greedy for a taste of self-generated excellence, were digging in everywhere to funnel the sound more quickly to their own ears. Thus the sound the rest of us heard was altered, deformed, however delightful it might have been to the singer, perched near the source.

Now great singing, once the glory of the human race, was disappearing from the earth—in spite of the lamebrained "bravos" resounding everywhere. The critics knew that the standards of the Golden Age were no longer being attained, and the best were saying as much. The best singers knew it, too, and some, such as Alfredo Kraus, were brave enough to say so. No doubt there were many reasons for humanity's terrible loss, but the principal one was so simple as to be chilling: people had become enamored of mechanistic thinking, which could be taught, and afraid to follow feelings, which could not be. It was hard to find out what great singing felt like without being a great singer, and it was perhaps no accident that the very greatest singers of the century were self-taught, or nearly so. (Not sorts to do what they were told, but willing to search endlessly, and to endlessly refine by practice what they had mastered along the way.) I was by no means alone in my feeling that the decline in vocal art could be blamed, for the most part, on mediocre singers who had been anointed great teachers. These days, of course, universities and conservatories were anointing all over the place and voice teachers who could sing were almost as rare as medical doctors who radiated health.

Jørgen and I were considered mad because we understood instinctively that singing was something different from what all the well-intentioned, beautifully attired, royally behaved teachers were telling us it was. That it was *not* something that should happen in a small room that gave the sound back too quickly, creating and perpetuating the illusion that the voice was "out" or "free." (Until it came time to sing for a large assembly.) I sang in parks and zoos, in the countryside when I could get away, or I just pointed my nozzle over the city and stirred up the undershirt-clad Chicanos having roof parties with their radios. Jørgen sang to the skyline and heard himself back from skyscrapers blocks away. I'd have been up there with him singing duets if it hadn't been for my fear of heights.

I couldn't believe my ears.

"Teresa, this is your big chance..."

"How long have you known about this? How do I know I'm the first person you called?"

"I could have called you late last night but we'd have kept each other awake. That's what I thought then. Look, you know the part. I'd never have thought of anyone else."

"I'd consider it if they hadn't thrown Wolfgang out..."

"That was then, dammit! Brian, the little guy who did it—he's on my side now!"

"Then you're betraying Wolfgang. He'll never forgive you. Anyway, you were content for me to stay away. You never called."

"Teresa, I've been working every minute. Killing myself. Now I'm finally making money."

"You won't if you start small-time opera! Haven't you learned anything from all our shows? If you've got something that's making money... What is it you've got?"

"Wrestling."

"That's right. I heard about it. Women, though. A sex show."

"Not at all. Dead serious. Chairman Mao bathing suits."

"People are going for it?"

"With Melchior and Flagstad in the background."

"Wow. You could have invited me. There's no getting around it. You turned your back on me. After all I've done for you. I can't ever forgive you for that, Gordon."

"Don't bother. Just don't screw yourself by not taking the lead in this opera."

"Do you really think it will do my career any good to sing in a place where you've got women wrestling in bathing suits?"

"You'll have a costume. I'm getting Anneliese to play. There'll be two pianos. Jørgen as Edgardo again. You know it'll be a hit. We've got good food, you know. A full house these days. If the show got hot we'd run it for months. Years. Another *Fantasticks.*"

"I don't know... Anneliese is committed to you?"

"Not yet, but you know she will be. She's not worried about the company she keeps. She's an artist."

"And I'm not? I'm worried about what people think because I sing with you?"

"I'm sure you have been, some. But look, I'll take myself out of the production. Find someone else to do Enrico... If that would look better for you..."

"No, no, no. Are you crazy? Anyway, everyone is going to know it's your production, your restaurant. They'll think you hired me out of obligation."

"Because they figure there's money I owe you?"

"Keep your voice down! All right, I'll tell Wolfgang to meet with the little Englishman. Wolfgang will do whatever I say, so make sure your guy does the same. He called Wolfgang names the last time. And he was laughing at him during the so-called meeting. Don't think I didn't know what was going on..."

"Just making jokes to hide his bewilderment."

We set the time. I ran upstairs and woke Brian, who'd dozed

off in his office, in his swivel chair. A first! He'd never have passed out and remained on such a treacherous perch for more than a second when he was drinking.

Brian remembered Wolfgang, another feat—I almost clapped him on the back. Brian would be glad to meet with Wolfgang and tell him that, no matter what his daughters had to say about the matter, he was welcome on the premises whenever he felt like dropping in, even in the downstairs pub. He would have the run of the place, and whatever he wanted to drink or eat for nothing as long as *Lucia di Lammermoor* was playing at the Pit with his wife in the title role.

Wolfgang answered the phone when I called Teresa back; I could hear her in the background practicing the mad scene. Wolfgang yelled my message; Teresa yelled, "Get down to the Fife and Drum right away. You're meeting with Brian, that little Englishman who has the bar in Gordon's restaurant. Braid your hair, but don't wear your buckled shoes... Hurry!"

The phone was dropped. There were more instructions I couldn't make out, she was shouting the other way. Wolfgang was already legging it out the door, he could drive and braid his hair at the same time. I loved that about Teresa: she might have taken longer than some of us to make up her mind about one of my schemes, but once made up there was never a moment's hesitation about getting in deeper.

Wolfgang and Brian were closeted for so long I forgot about them and helped Hilliard with his opening duties (we took turns).

I never saw Wolfgang leave, which was just as well. Wolfgang was immutably Wolfgang and I'd already heard everything he had to say. However, the change in Brian concerned me.

Gone was the bicycle helmet when he came up. He was wearing a liberty cap.

"Sure that'll give you enough protection?" I nodded at the new headgear.

"This isn't a question of how much I can withstand, Bancroft.

It's a question of what I stand for." He took off the cap and read the inscription aloud: "REBELLION TO TYRANTS!"

The rest of the line was: "is obedience to God!" It appeared on Jefferson's great Shekinah seal and he had proposed it as America's motto. I told Brian as much.

"Oh, I know all about it. We talked of nothing else. He's completely convincing. Consider me a disciple."

"Me, too, but did you find time to discuss his wife's participation in the opera I'm producing? *Lucia?*"

"Oh, that. No problem. His wife can do whatever she wants. He's completely a modern man in that respect. There will have to be some changes, though, before our little opera house will be acceptable."

Joining forces with Brian hadn't rid me of a sinking feeling when I was about to hear his plans.

"Ah... Of course we'll need another tier of seats... The boys at AGMA never make any trouble the way the Equity people do about how many seats—"

"No worries there! Calm yourself, Bancroft. I was thinking of that frightful painting. Surely we wouldn't want to be surrounded by the closeup view of a gutter—heh, heh—while attending something as classy as bel canto opera..."

"That's not your word! I'm sorry, but how could it be? Did Wolfgang..."

"Of course he did, and that's a very small part of everything I learned."

I had a hunch... "And what would you like to see on the walls of our 'little opera house' as you call it, once Hilliard's *Gutter* is taken down?"

"It's not what I would like, it's what we're going to see. Back me on this and I'll give you everything else you want: the original American flags! The ones that *weren't* adopted! Great slogans! A reminder of what this country could have been if it hadn't been betrayed by its banking system! I don't think it would be at all out of place to have a fife and drum corps march about while the seats are filling up. The Scots are always doing that kind of thing with their pipers."

"And I suppose there'll be a souvenir stand where Wolfgang

can sell his Revolutionary War paraphernalia, his specially-designed shoes, and so forth, and hand out his pamphlets."

"We discussed that, yes. Bancroft, you don't know the kind of man I am. I don't blame you. I was so pissed the last few years I didn't know myself, either. I'd clean forgotten what brought me to this country in the first place. It was the practical, inventive side of Americans that struck a chord in me. The British way of life had always been oppressive. I needed the freedom to 'do my own thing,' as the firebrands used to say. Instead I let Emma browbeat me into flowerboxes and easy chairs and all the rest of it. Before long I'd recreated the very atmosphere I'd been trying so hard to escape—so unbearably stuffy and complacent! That woman has been the death of me, I see it now. Because of her I betrayed the principles that caused me to seek a new life here. I may not have long to live, but I've heard the call, and still have a chance to *join* before I *die! Join or die, Join or die,* Bancroft! It's your choice, too!"

"Look, I'm not going to fight you. I've always accommodated Wolfgang in everything—I'm surprised he hasn't already told you so. He can hand out his material on the Revolution, on flying saucers, he can name names and pin down all the gangsters where they sit in each other's boardrooms. All I ask is: no speeches during the intermissions, no hawking of revolutionary material in the aisles. Decorate the place any way you like as long as you leave the stage design to me. Change the name to the Raleigh Tavern..." (Long Wolfgang's dream haunt.)

"How did you guess? Exactly what it needs to be! 'The Open Pit' gives too much away, even if we were to stay with this silly wrestling business. As you may be aware, the Raleigh Tavern was the single most important place of assembly in your country's history. What was discussed there is still more important than anything decided in those huge, draughty halls of congress. And there's more, Gordon, I'm not finished. I want *this* Raleigh Tavern to be as important as the last, the beginning of the end for those who have subverted this country to their own ends by buying its leaders! Decor may not make much difference to your opera buffs. They may ignore our attempts to educate them. But they'll know that something of great importance was going on here—something far more important than entertainment. Right here in The Raleigh Tavern, a new world was being born! If only I could join you in a toast!"

"Join *and* die, eh? I'd think twice about it..."

"Please! Please! The moment's past. I may not be as weak as you think! After all, it was only a figure of speech. But firecrackers are much too dainty to express my feelings. Can you imagine how it must feel for someone like me, after so many false starts and dead ends, finally to find something to believe in?"

Tears were leaning out of his red-rimmed eyes like windows about to leap out of their casements. In spite of the conviction that shone from them, the eyes themselves were inky and would have been chilling had I not known the nature of the malady.

When Wolfgang had made a believer out of me I had been unguarded out of love for his wife. I knew I'd never be good enough for Teresa if I weren't one hundred percent behind her husband's work. If my first loyalty were to Wolfgang, however, Teresa would do everything in her power to make my devotion worthwhile. She'd reached a point where it was meaningless to be loyal to Wolfgang in the usual way of married folk, with consecration of the body. Her body meant less than nothing to Wolfgang as long as it was healthy. It was a practical matter, strictly: eat the best food, exercise, go to your spas and all your classes to stay in shape so that you can continue to support my work. For her part, Teresa, too, was dead serious about reclaiming the country for the Founding Fathers. Other than the occasional crumpled box of cookies under the front seat of her car, she was everything Wolfgang could have hoped for (and he kept quiet about the cookie boxes, as I did, if he noticed them at all). If there was to be an American Revolution in the future based on Wolfgang's ideas—or as Wolfgang saw it, a continuation of the one great and glorious American Revolution, which had been abandoned in the early years of the last century—Teresa was sure to be one of its first heroines. Liberty leading the people!

Teresa saw herself as well as her husband in heroic terms, then. And so did I. That explained the nobility of her singing. The only other explanation was magic, and Wolfgang and I were having none of that no matter what the neighbors thought. Her voice, her graceful manner, her goodness—all of it seemed to spring from a nobility that she was too modest to acknowledge. And let it be said, Wolfgang resembled a god when I first knew him. Never before or since had I seen so much dedication to a cause. Nothing else existed for the man. What was more important to someone as young as I: there was *nothing in it for him*. He fully expected to lose his life as payment for his years of struggle to liberate his beloved United States...

Nothing I was ever shown by him could be refuted. Yes, he *looked* like a crank, but that was his disguise; Teresa had told me what to expect. True, he was fanatical about some things—symbolic things, for example—that didn't seem all that important to me, even at the beginning. For hours sometimes he would bemoan the fact that Franklin's nomination of the turkey for national bird hadn't found favor... and the United States had been stuck with the fearsome eagle, with the fasces in its claw. But he had grown up in Germany, after all, and under the *führer*—symbols meant more to Germans of his generation. Whenever I was crossways with his traits of character I simply enlarged my definition of hero to accommodate him.

I'd never been stirred to mad-bomber states of consciousness by someone stating the obvious (except, briefly, Marx). Wolfgang inspired fanatical devotion because he wanted the masses who had been trodden on to fling the words of the Founding Fathers back in the faces of those in power, much as the "enemy" in Vietnam had appropriated our Declaration of Independence to proclaim the lineage of their struggle for nationhood.

I strode behind Brian's desk, took him under the shoulders right out of his chair and into my arms. As I was pressing his bony little body to me I realized that he didn't smell. Nor had Emma given him a bath... She'd disappeared in the manner of many an enabler when the hospital had stepped in. Brian had washed himself, dressed himself, combed his hair, shaved. He was showing us navvies that worked here the same respect he'd have shown a perfect stranger—an amazing about-face.

"If you want to call off the wrestling, I'm with you, Brian," I told him, after letting him drop back into his chair. "I guess all the money turned my head. It would be great to run a replica of the Raleigh Tavern after I've seen how easy it is to make a new idea catch on. If we did it right we could have a chain. Raleigh Taverns coast to coast, with facsimiles of Mason's Bill of Rights. The chamber music would fit right in. We could do a string quartet in costume. The second violin would take the part of Jefferson, the first violin, Wythe. I think Wythe was the first violin..."

"Hold on, my friend—don't tell me too much all at once. Between you and your friend Wolfgang I feel as though I'm walking around with someone else's head on my shoulders. There's been a lot of damage." He tapped his forehead sadly. "I know I've been pointed in the right direction, but straight down is still there, too. You used to drink a bit too much, Bancroft? Do you remember the feeling? It's not quite like walking on eggs, though I've heard it described that way by a fellow in my group. Nor do I feel as if I'm walking a tightrope. I'm really quite steady on my feet. Perhaps it's a bit daunting to realize how quickly things can be accomplished without great effort. I'm not saying I feel like one of those thick sorts who goes to the light switch and has to ask himself what he came for. But it is annoying to realize that I'm accomplishing my purpose from moment to moment and have to keep thinking of some new goal. I feel as if my life has lost its *flow.* Everything that happens in the course of a day is surrounded by quotation marks of dead space..."

"Cheer up, Brian, that's merely your self-awareness kicking in. Think of it, for years your life had meaning—a simple meaning, but a meaning all the same: to get enough to drink. And for years, well-situated as you were here, you could have anything you wanted on a whim. A pig in shit, then. Now look at yourself! Sure, there's a little visible damage. People don't become avatars for giving up their bad habits. But you're neat and clean. You still eat sparingly, but you eat well, and before long you're going to have dinner invitations again..."

"Ah, you're teasing me, Bancroft."

"I promise you I'm not. You're nothing less than a miracle as you stand before me. And the fact that you've become a convert to Wolfgang, which is to say, to Jefferson and continuing revolution, is something more than a mere miracle. When you were shitfaced all the time you sounded like the right-wing simpletons downstairs who never shut up about 'welfare scroungers' and could be supporting a small town somewhere with what they spend on beer. I'll be frank: there were times when I thought of extinguishing the little bit of life you had left in you, especially when I had to move you a lot to make room for our clientele. But this change in you requires a change in me. Doing a Raleigh Tavern should have been my idea all along; I should have consulted Wolfgang before I ever thought of getting into this new end of the business. If I let you down with *Lucia*, I won't keep trying—just drag the dead horse out of the arena and bring on the syllabub and hot spiced cider. A Raleigh Tavern atmosphere with chamber music... Throw in some jigs and reels to remind the locals of their origins, and those from the old country that we Americans are their cousins... There's no end to what we could do! The Ben Jonson down at the Cannery has waitresses going around with their tits half out—now that would be good for business. All the atmosphere you need right in front of you: trencher with a roast on it, the woman bent to serve you putting her tits in your face..."

"Slow down, Bancroft. This might be more than I can stand all at once. I'm for a nap. We'll come back to this later. Please go ahead with all your plans. I trust you completely. Wake me at the dinner hour, when the shouting stops. Surely important things remain to be discussed..."

The alliance between Wolfgang and Brian worked wonders for Teresa's morale, and when Teresa was in good spirits, she was a publicity machine for me, she rolled over obstacles like an all-terrain vehicle.

She went with me to Volodya's place less than an hour after I found where it was. From the moment the huge, blinking Russian answered the door with nicotine-stained fingers and food in his beard she turned on the charm, swung her hip ever so faintly as she entered, throwing her head back to look down her nose at his host's apartment... calling attention to the luscious pallor of her neck and shoulders... and the structures at the base of her neck which would have exalted an emerald but were best unadorned, crying out for Vermeer.

What Teresa called her *prancing* behavior was misleading; it was appropriated stage business which made it easier for her to meet strangers such as Volodya with a dramatic presence. He responded appropriately with big smiles and winks. When she was satisfied that he was capable of throwing himself in front of a truck for her she touched his cheek lightly once, and gave his ankle a little kick moments later, a gesture full of significance, though beyond understanding.

Volodya was ours. We had him commit all his afternoons. We left him with elaborate directions to the Fife from the house where he had been given hospitality, out in the small White Russian colony in the part of the Richmond District called Close In. Teresa couldn't resist a look over her shoulder as we walked away.

I gave Jørgen his schedule over the phone when he was home after work, telling him to cancel everything else he had planned for the next week or two—which he promptly agreed to do. God, it felt good to be blindly obeyed for a change, even by a fellow madman.

Anneliese wouldn't be able to stay for a full rehearsal each afternoon—she made eighty dollars an hour to coach internationally prominent singers who were passing through town, and maybe fifty or more coaching local wannabes. She would have an assistant take over when she had to go—Robert, the very gentleman who would be playing piano number two (to be rented) in our performance. He was wafer-thin and had a penetrating nasal voice. Robert had the self-assurance to look frankly between men's legs the way other people looked in their eyes, expecting to read important things there from moment to moment.

Robert had rehearsed us for the last *Lucia* (though it was ultimately a one-piano performance with Anneliese). I loved Robert's pianism as much as Anneliese's: his touch was perfection and he only made honest mistakes.

At the COC Robert had never let a rehearsal go by without announcing that he was in love with my voice, so I was a little worried when he started saying that about Volodya's at our first cast meeting.

Perhaps I wasn't pitiful enough for a bucking up now that I was an impresario of sorts. I was not only singing as well as I ever had, but I had somehow brought into being what everyone liked to call a *venue*: not just a new place of employment for my colleagues, but one where I could reward artistry and inculcate high standards of vocalism and performance. From now on, if I was as tough on others as I had always been on myself, Nothing But The Best need not have been an idle, mercantile boast where the Pit were concerned, or rather, the Raleigh Tavern. I sensed that I was starting to look good to Teresa again, which was a sure sign of pending good fortune whether or not Wolfgang had fallen from favor for a reason. Actually, all was well on the home front except that he'd rededicated himself to serious garlic-eating, and since the Raleigh Tavern got off the ground, spur-of-the-moment clog dancing, sounds of gunfire arising from his square-toed shoes at inappropriate times.

I responded to Teresa's encouragement by pointedly ignoring the comings and goings of our wrestlers and the reasons the crowds roared. I was hardly there putting my orders around. I was swinging like an ape through the bars of *Lucia di Lammermoor*.

How I feared cycles. Women were cycles unto themselves, true enough, but they involved you in cycles with them. You fought, you made love, you fought again... You needed her more, you needed her less, you needed her more. You never could believe your good fortune... then you had her, and then you lost her forever... wait, there she was again!

There were no cycles in opera production. Maybe the divas had their ups and downs but down in the trenches where I now found myself it was *marche ou crève*, a strictly linear proposition (no one ever went back for the fallen). Whenever I felt Teresa's allure having an effect, I forced myself to see the ruin of everything I had built in the past year, the death of my plans to get my career back on track and escape to France. The danger of backsliding was reduced somewhat because I could put on a good show of being too busy with all I was trying to accomplish *for art, for the people* to bother with even the most rudimentary self-gratification. The right response to such an attitude (a wayward maternal pride) had been carefully inculcated by Wolfgang since the time he was filling his first basement with flyers. Anyway, "son of Wolfgang" was one of her favorite ways of thinking about me.

Realistically I knew I wouldn't be able to hold out much longer, of course, but living with Brian's condition had forced me to take one day at a time, and I was probably as good at it by now as some of the masters of brinkmanship I'd encountered in alcohol programs.

I decided not to do anything about the hall being too lively—Wolfgang's huge revolutionary flags were pitifully inadequate to damp the sound we were making. Opera at the Raleigh Tavern was going to hurt a little, which was the way fanatics liked it.

There was ample precedent for the behavior I was counting on. Presumably the Brooklyn Paramount Theater had been around before Alan Freed's rock and roll shows, and so had the Fillmore Auditorium before Bill Graham came along, but the volume of sound had been different, and that was the main difference between everything that went before and everything that came after. Fanaticism no longer festered in the upstairs rooms of private homes—it had taken over the largest halls in town, proclaiming itself at such a decibel level that communicants could obliterate their sense of the other, both creating and celebrating their new world by swamping their senses.

My hunch had been given credence by what had happened to the wrestlers after they'd grown accustomed to hearing

Melchior at the upper limits of the comfort range. Quite simply, they'd become addicts. I couldn't have nudged the volume down by the merest fraction of a decibel without howls of protest. Yet I could have advanced the volume well past the pain threshold and they wouldn't have deigned to notice me. I could have slain them with it and they'd never have taken their eyes off the ceiling. Melchior was theirs now.

They'd all seen the writing on the wall—had seen the flags, that is, and read Don't Tread On Me... They had asked their questions, and sufficiently understood Wolfgang's longwinded answers, shaking their massive heads.

The times had changed a little too much for any of us to share Wolfgang's excitement. Perhaps the wrestlers felt as I did at times that a secret society had been driven out into the open, and that something like Freemasonry, after all, could be blamed for the Vietnam War.

Wolfgang's hand was everywhere. The wrestlers now left their dressing room and ascended to the ring on an exact replica of Thomas Paine's iron bridge. As Wolfgang explained it Paine had been "shafted" out of U.S. citizenship after all he'd done for this country, wouldn't even have been welcomed back had it not been for Jefferson. Though his scholarship may have been faulty, the miniature bridge, with carpet and pad to damp the considerable sound of traffic perfectly exemplified the passage from oblivion to essential service and back.

Wolfgang wasn't the only one with tears in his eyes when he told this story. Paine had become Brian's patron saint. When he was asked by his tory friends what he thought he was doing going around in a *bonnet rouge*, and in a homespun jersey encrusted with slogans, he was likely to summarize the Rights of Man and give a ringing endorsement of its author, whose contribution to the freedom and liberty and justice for all Americans had never been properly acknowledged.

The bunting which festooned the wainscoting was a big mistake, I thought. It made me think of a political speech by Hayes, Garfield, Arthur and their ilk, though I'm sure Wolfgang had carefully researched its use. (In his book all the late 19th-Century politicians were buffoons.)

In addition the wrestlers seemed to resent being made to feel like intermission entertainment at a rally of some kind—indeed, many of them had thought the new name of the club was Rally and were bewildered when the new sign went up (at street level, with black script and white scrollwork, swinging above our oaken door). Our fight crowd in general sensed that wrestling as they had known it at the Pit was about to become a fond memory. Gone were the glory days when the women locked in combat on the mat were alive with mysterious impulses. Game after game was won or lost for no perceptible reason; no longer did I try to separate the sweat and tears.

After rehearsing all afternoon I was worn out putting plates around. Our customers sensed my urgency and stared at their food and at me with the same suspicion. I could have been asking for back rent instead of my fifteen percent. They were starting to stiff me.

All the firsts in our *Lucia* deserved to be advertised but there wasn't time. Anyway, some of them were only important to a certain San Francisco art underground whose members didn't think of opera as art, and probably thought Hilliard was doing his career a disservice by taking a role in our production. More to the point, advertising that Hilliard was to be taking the part of Lord Arturo Bucklaw in our production would have made it impossible to keep the rest in the cast, except for Volodya, who didn't know Hilliard and would have been impressed by his beard. I hinted at a surprise Arturo after the principals had put in some rehearsal time.

Anneliese and Robert had taken my word that the part was covered. They knew the part was musical piffle even though, as the leading tenor's rival for Lucia, there was no story without him. (We needed to know who Arturo was in order to be satisfied when Lucia knifed him to death on her wedding night.)

Arturo had little music of his own to sing, frequently doubling the chorus, or yipping his outrage in unison with Enrico (me). Sure, he mouthed off a little prior to signing the wedding contract (as who wouldn't, when rumor had it the woman he was about to marry was madly in love with someone else). In the concertante that followed I couldn't help remarking that *my* character was the one who really confronted Edgardo when he showed up too late to rescue Lucia and felt betrayed to find her contracted to another. Arthur started by asking guidance from heaven and complaining that he had a tiger in his bosom; then in unison with Enrico he told Edgardo to beat it; finally, with the entire chorus behind him as well as both low-voiced leads, he told Edgardo to get lost in even stronger language as the music raced to a climax.

Great as singers were in those days the Signor Giacchini who took the part of Arturo at the first performance in 1835 (Naples) was surely someone who had never posed a threat to the lead tenor, Duprez, the first Edgardo di Ravenswood. Even in those days there must have been white-voiced, nasal singers, who stood with their hands at their sides, or when they'd had to pull a sword for some reason, held it over their heads until their entire bodies were trembling. Anyway, regardless of the importance of Arturo to the story, I didn't have anyone on hand to take the part. The wretch who had done it at our last production had left town for some reason. A relative with a cold?

Eureka! In thinking of how to do a *Lucia* without an Arturo I had the brainstorm that would save the entire production from being just another underfinanced attempt to do something grand without enough voices, without even enough room for the voices if they could be found and paid.

Do *Lucia* entirely in the dark! My thinking: much of the action takes place at night, anyway, or might just as well. Our brave cast is only indoors when they're at Enrico's "apartments." Otherwise it's the dark gardens of Ravenswood castle in the beginning, then after the brouhaha at my place, a place outside Wolf's Crag Castle (where illuminated rooms are seen in the distance—just so!) and then among the tombs of the Ravenswoods nearby, with no break in time. All that would be necessary to keep the whole production in darkness would be a suggestion of activity within, while we did our sword-wielding out on the verandah in the dark, surely a more seemly place for quarrels over women, then as now.

Before telling him about his promotion to second lead in the forthcoming *Lucia di Lammermoor* I brought Hilliard into the rest of my plan. We could knock down the wall between the dressing room door and the double doors to the serving area by the dumbwaiter, replace it with a scrim the size of a Cinemascope screen...

"I get it. You put the chorus back there."

"Wrong. We import a crowd from the Fife, give them Ivanhoe headgear, make them promise to keep the noise down, give them free drinks, backlight the hell out of them...!"

"So it looks like a bigger production?"

"That's part of it. You'll see."

"Give me one day," said Hilliard. It was clearer than ever why I'd always loved him.

"I don't want a small crowd that looks like a big crowd..."

"Right. If I use enough light we can pack 'em in. Once I get all the sheet rock out of there I can dress the studs and posts to look like pillars supporting a medieval hall. The studs will look like they're marching back inside and the whole interior space will look offset. Then you can put the big guys on the left, the little ones on the right. How about that? Way I see it, your big problem is finding people who can drink all they want during a long scene without hollering 'Far out, motherfucker!' or something like that. You don't want them to sing?"

"I think I've got that covered. If I'm right, we tear down that wall tomorrow morning. Fuck what the wrestlers think is going on. I'll clean out the scenery and junk that's behind that wall, and you'll have the scrim in place before they can start making noises about their modesty."

"Right, but that still sounds like a lot of trouble just to suggest a crowd. Sure it wouldn't be easier to project the whole thing?"

"You'll see what I'm up to soon enough..."

The crucial call I had to make was to a bosomy Finno-Guatemalan mezzo-soprano who was still very much a member of the chorus at the San Francisco Opera, as I had once been—my first professional job. It was getting difficult to find female singers who hadn't quarreled with Teresa at some point—because of slights involving Wolfgang, yes, but often because they were secure enough in their talent to invite comparisons. Teresa was peerless, of course, but she was handicapped when a part was contested or prize money sung for at an audition. She was sworn to Wolfgang, or me, or both of us, really, and wouldn't reward someone interested in her with anything but thanks. Lucky for me June was not one of those mezzos who was waiting to "go up"— that is, to fill in for a soprano and surprise the world with her beautiful high notes. June was born to play Alisa.

Nor would there be any bad feeling between my Lucia and her "companion," when Alisa's breasts were pushed out of her dress. Except for Teresa's alabaster skin, they could have been the same breasts. And both women were five and a half feet tall, had the same dark hair (when they wore it the same way) and if one took the other's hand on stage would have looked like a Rorschach test. Yet they'd sung together a number of times without having their similarities noted, so different were their voices and stage deportment. Teresa was definitively the prima donna, the star, and June the lady in waiting. Even when she was alone on stage attention passed quickly from June to the wings—where was the star?—or to the crowds behind her for signs of making way.

What set June apart from her colleagues—how she would have dreaded hearing this!—was her earnestness in wanting to improve her fortunes as a singer, her doggedness in ignoring years of evidence that she was a mediocrity, ignoring even the quiet testimony of the tape recorder she carried everywhere.

It was her tape recorder, not her breasts, that got her the part of Alisa. For the fifteen or so years that June had been waiting in the wings for her big break she had tape-recorded every bit of singing she had ever done, including, with the smiling consent of her beloved chorus directors, all her rehearsals. Most of these rehearsals were a waste of tape, surely, since it was common practice to rehearse by section, even when everybody was present, but there were plenty of examples to be heard of the full chorus in a state of readiness. In its rehearsal room the full chorus of any opera company is thrilling to hear, especially in the *forte* passages with everyone trying to out-blast his neighbor. Such pure singing never happens on stage when so much is going on that choristers often refer to themselves as "living scenery." They aren't much more, in fact, because they must be careful *not* to draw attention to themselves, histrionically or vocally. Even with a chorus that's very sure of itself it would be hard to imagine *fortes* such as can be heard in the practice room when no one present can get enough distance to pay attention to them in the first place—least of all the chorus director, who's just waving his arms around to keep from drowning. I remember those evenings as a pleasant three-hour wallow in the shower, but with eighty voices in there with me.

"Sure you can use my tapes," June told me right away, delighted to be approached at one in the morning for any reason, "but is that why you thought of me for the part this time? You didn't use me in your last *Lucia*... I bet I could have done better than Hilda. Why aren't you using her again?"

"June, I didn't cast that show, but it's not such an important part, you know? And I'm paying... Look, I'll pay for the use of your tapes, if that's what's bothering you."

"Don't be ridiculous. Won't you get in trouble with the opera, though, if they find out?"

"How are they going to find out? Who's to say who's making the sound? There won't be any speaking voices, no director telling everyone to shut up and take it from the bottom score of page whatever. We'll edit the tape and tune our pianos to it."

"I don't have a problem. It's a good idea! I wonder why no one ever approached me before. Look, if it works for you, maybe this would be the start of something. If it weren't for the cost of choruses and the time it takes to rehearse them there could be a lot more opera going on. God knows there are always enough singers to cover the leads."

"So you know the part already? Alisa? Alice?"

"Sure. I did it in a workshop years ago, just to help out..."

"Sounds good. Well, you'll have ten days to brush up. And you haven't put on a ton of weight since I last saw you? I can put you in a costume like Teresa's?"

"God, I hope so. Has she taken a bunch off, or something?"

"Nope. Same as ever. Count on lots of cleavage showing."

"Oh, I could figure that," she said with some pride.

Perfect. The wall went down the next day, creating momentum for subsequent bright ideas, and I was ready with them.

Anneliese and Robert were the first people to find out that our Lucia was to be an exclusively nocturnal creature. They didn't take me seriously.

"We can do everything with lighting. Six people singing? We use six spots. Fixed spots to make up for the fact that no one will be able to see their marks. Maybe not even their feet, but the riser all around the back of the platform stage will be a slope they can handle. Nothing to trip over but each other's feet. Fixed lighting for the sets. Intense blue and green dappling for boscage, dark blue for the stone, if we've got any. We might be able to throw some pink on the principals during the singing and clinging."

What about the wedding contract scene at Henry's? they both wanted to know. I was ready for them, primed with the confidence Hilliard had given me.

Since they didn't know yet that we'd be going without an Arturo, they still thought the idea of doing opera under cover of darkness was farfetched.

"Robert, you've never seen our Normanno in action. Go ahead, tell him, Anneliese."

The point was, there wasn't much to tell. If there had been some way to eliminate him I would have, but Norman was all over the place, he was the whisperer, the plot driver, the one who had the gift of launching tirades and outpourings of love with the ordinary details of his day. Our Norman the last time out had been a fellow named Throckmorton, a tall and slender pawn who stood at attention while awaiting the conductor's hand. He had a fierce little beard, a rictus tight against tiny teeth, and he showed his little incisors when he sang, as if inviting his tones high into his cheeks (which is where most of them ended up). He was reputed to be a Ph.D., and might have run a school of some kind over in Marin County. He was full of secret health information, and frequently ate raw liver, which was why I never got in a conversation with him and gave him a wide berth when we were onstage together. But he was polite, always available, and cheap.

"Actually, it's a little frightening to think of Throckmorton loose in the dark with me," I told Anneliese, "but I'll take my chances. The main thing is, we've got some weak sisters in some of these parts, nose-pickers and ass-scratchers, you know the type. If we're giving the audience nothing but music and atmosphere, it might be enough. I've got a genius for the lightboard..."

I did, too: the last wino I'd hired to cue the music for our wrestlers. Most of the winos who worked for me were just trying to make the price of a drink. They'd get roaring drunk on payday and forget all about me. Max was different, though. He looked like the other winos and drank enough to be one but he was uncharacteristically steady in his job. Drunk or sober he got everything just right, and I knew he'd be no different following lighting cues, which are a lot easier than cueing a record.

Anneliese and Robert didn't want to dump on my ideas yet, but I could tell they thought they could talk me out of them before we opened. Let me proceed in my folly! We'd still need the spotlights later, and the lights that bathed the wrestlers every night were more than enough to light the stage and environs when I came to my senses.

Jørgen was the crucial hurdle. First I had to swear him to secrecy about everything we were about to discuss. Then I told him his rival, Arturo, didn't exist. I didn't have the guts to tell him he never had. The guy I'd tapped for the job had left town for some reason, no one knew where he was. I even had to invent a name for the missing tenor since Jørgen thought he knew all the tenors in the state and he probably did.

"What are we gonna do?"

"You've heard about doing the whole production in darkness, haven't you?"

"I thought you were kidding."

"Nope, I was getting the cast ready for just such a contingency as Franz running out on us. You can't take loyalty for granted with a budget like ours."

"Right, but how does doing the production in the dark make up for the voice that's missing? People that will come to a place like this to hear people like you and me are going to know this opera. They'll walk out on you if you try to marry Lucia to someone who's not there."

"They probably would if I didn't have a body of some kind where Arturo is supposed to be. And we'll have one. Hilliard, if I can get him."

"Your buddy with the beard? Can he sing?"

"Of course not, but we can fix his beard so no one will know the difference. You're going to sing for him!"

He looked up from his shoes in terror. "Oh, no you don't! Jesus, we've got a great cast with you and that Russian guy and Teresa and me. This is a chance to do something right for a change. The papers will be all over a new company in a space like this. Call an agent in New York and pay to fly out someone who can do the part cold."

"I can't spend that kind of money, man! What, for someone to stand around and double me and the chorus? There are only five times he sings alone in the whole opera, I counted. We get Hilliard in the right spot and you sing through your nose. Stand right behind him if you have to."

"What about the times he's brandishing his sword and telling me to fuck off!"

"Hilliard can brandish a sword with the best of them. The point is, Arturo is singing with the chorus at that point, and I'll make sure the volume is so loud he won't be missed. You've heard how much Melchior my system can take."

"I hate the whole thing, starting with your recorded chorus. I want *people* back there, goddammit! If something goes wrong with your system we're going to have a terrible mess on our hands."

"Is it any different at the big houses? If something goes wrong with the way they're flying their scenery or the way they've constructed their second floor balconies you'd be looking at a bunch of dead singers. But it doesn't happen. And we're going to bring this off. I've heard you imitating bad singers before when you were having fun. You can do the same thing when you're serious. Hilliard will be easy to block, I'll get him on it tonight. I promise you, Jørgen, this will be a first if you can bring it off. A stunt like this could get you national publicity!"

"You think so?"

I'd always known that getting Hilliard onstage wouldn't be easy. He absolutely wouldn't have to sing. He wouldn't even have to mouth the words if he couldn't remember the cues. Could he just be a supernumerary and brandish a sword now and then? That was all I was asking.

After a bitter argument wherein it was explained to him that the success of the production rested on his shoulders, he consented to "try."

That afternoon we worked under the lights that Max and I had installed and blocked our reluctant Arturo into the action. There was open mutiny when Jørgen started singing for him, but the chance to be in a spot every time they soloed turned out to be more agreeable than any of them had thought.

Everyone felt we had a long way to go, but had done well, under the circumstances. Friends in the audience thought the way the singing characters popped out of the dark was a refreshing way to do a concert reading. Pressed, they felt our highly dramatized *Lucia* might have been what the opera would look like in their heads had they sufficient imagination to reconstruct it while they were dreaming.

I wouldn't brook comparisons with concert readings, even the splendid ones that Pippin had been doing. The crowd behind the scrim would be the decisive step in achieving my goal: a *Lucia* that would make people's hair stand on end.

Hilliard fleshed out Arturo magnificently, which made it all the more essential that Jørgen give him a voice that wasn't ridiculously reedy. Since Hilliard was more robust than his vivifier, the latter's generosity was taxed trying to find the right voice for him. Jørgen had been a merchant seaman before he settled into high-rise windowwashing. He was the furthest thing from a mama's boy, and acted as if he felt compromised by the melting pianissimos he could manage at the top of his range, tones that female operagoers of a certain age frequently heard as a plea for adoption. He invested his roles with all the hairychested brio he could muster. He had none to spare Hilliard.

"Let's take a look at Arthur's character," I told him, trying to round up support from Anneliese with sidelong flashes of desperation. "Sure, he's a blockhead, but how do we see him personally? Tense, *nicht wahr?* Scared of what he's getting into, but trying not to disappoint Lucia's reckless brother. Doesn't that suggest anything to you?"

Apparently it didn't.

"Imitate *me*, Jørgen. Do a white-voiced, vibratoless imitation of *me*.There are no flaws in my technique to exaggerate, but you can make it clear that Arturo is riding piggyback... I'll have Hilliard imitate my pose of body. You can do it, Jørgen! The dark color of your voice will be false, much shallower emotionally than the inherent virility of your resounding tenor!"

Volodya whinnied once again. Impatient to get on with rehearsal? Scornful of my grandiose characterization of Jørgen's voice? No telling with Volodya. His whinny; his belly laugh, which began with the hum-roar of a tidal wave; his vocal eases, which resembled gulping or gargling: he'd picked all of it up somewhere at an early age and it was too late to change. He knew his music and could find his spot in the dark. What more could I want?

Trying to imitate me Jørgen found the perfect voice for Arturo. Even Hilliard was happy about it. Some heard the whiny exasperation of Jack Benny hollering "Rochester!" It was the voice of someone whose will had been tampered with to the point that exasperation and admiration sounded the same. Arturo had been perfectly characterized as the obstinate, misshapen echo of Lucia's implacable brother, Henry. To those of us on the inside Jørgen's malicious parody of my singing style deepened the meaning of Lucia's wedding-night tantrum by giving it the psychological coloration of attempted incest and fratricide.

What more could we ask? I say "we" because I refused the title of Director. As much as possible we followed the COC version of the opera with which all of us but Volodya and June were familiar. Its director had moved on to better things and wouldn't have minded our borrowings. Nevertheless, because I was responsible for our minimalist set design and for cloning the voice of Arturo everyone felt more comfortable with me telling them what to do from moment to moment. I was made to feel that the members of our cast were house guests. (Except for Hilliard, who had clambered up and down the risers in this room for longer than he would have liked to remember.) Of course the others were lost in surroundings unlike any they'd known and needed to be yanked this way and that until they began to "get the production in their feet."

Technically we were having closed rehearsals but we didn't turn away the curious who stood by the door with drinks in their hands, even if they'd wandered up from the Fife. Brian and Wolfgang attended every rehearsal sitting at the table nearest the prompter, where the apron would have been. Sitting there with matching red caps, keeping their opinions to themselves—it was quite a sight. True, there were titters at first—their comical aspect was undeniable since Wolfgang was so much taller, so much nobler, a returned mariner par excellence, with a Whitmanesque twinkle and melancholy sumptuousness of demeanor—Brian scrawny, handsome in a sharp-faced way, dapper, ill. When the Weasel showed up it was clear that Brian was much more deserving of the cognomen. They had the same sleekness, but the Weasel was so much more padded out these days I thought of a sea lion peering out of its blubber. As they quietly observed the fraying of our nerves the two or three of them seemed to belong to another time, as did all the ghostly red, white and blue decor. They relaxed us and gave us a crazy continuity with the excesses of our ancestors. Drunk with oxygen (all singers are after a time) I no longer saw our red-capped friends as guests at our rehearsal. Rather, our personnel—with their warlike posturing, elegant Italian wooing and heavily ornamented insanity—seemed the somewhat outlandish guests of the Raleigh Tavern.

Eleven days after *Lucia* went into rehearsal and three days before opening night the entire league of women wrestlers decamped for a bar over in the Castro Valley.

The wrestlers had seen the end coming. I had. Brian had wanted it.

All I'd had the courage to ask for when I went to the wrestlers was a second dark night, so we could do two performances a week. A respectable number, the most heavy singing we could expect of our leads.

When I got no immediate answer from the steering committee I knew the wrestlers were going to leave. A number of little things had added up: the newsletter had never been circulated because it "embarrassed" the wrestlers. I was never told why, but was made to feel it had something to do with me. The way the opera people invaded their dressing room and stored props there had been a deeply resented violation, even though opera people and wrestlers were never there at the same time. Brian's head injury months ago now had cast a pall over the company: Brian had been despised, but despising the owner of their arena had lent panache to the whole camp exercise. The wrestlers might have deplored Brian's obsession, but they'd been more comfortable with how it made them feel than they'd let on.

The fact that I ignored the wrestlers while I put plates around might have done more than I would have thought to promote an exodus. I'd been their champion early on, but it was all I could do these days to keep their names straight.

The dressing room was bare of their presence except for a bottle of body soap in the shower and mammoth torn panties dangling from a faucet handle.

I felt a wary relief as I dragged off the mat and stored the ropes for future use as stage properties.

The night of our dress rehearsal all the places were taken out in the house, but no one was being served, we'd stopped dinner service for a few days after the wrestlers had cleared out to help air the place of their disgruntled fans. I made a short announcement to the effect that we'd be serving five-course sit-down dinners again in the near future. In the meantime all the tables were laden with cheese, fruit and wine courtesy of the Raleigh Tavern, as they would be on opening night; people should take a certain way out if they felt obliged to leave; they should not applaud; they should expect the production to be stopped again and again since we had been short of rehearsal time and were attempting an experimental staging...

I glanced at the prompter's desk (below the lip of the stage) and saw my talismans, all three caps tonight. *Liberty or death! Rebellion to tyrants! Join or die!* Nothing so comforting. I felt as if I were about to open a chest of vocal gold. One principal with such a feeling could yank the others into alignment. It wasn't common but I'd heard it done.

The guffaws and scraping of chairs gave way entirely when Robert struck the wooden floor three times with his wooden staff, and then for good measure his water glass three times with a knife.

Anneliese began the introductory music alone, playing with authority, then Robert joined her on his black Steinway during the *allegro giusto* and there were two midnight riders and much excitement. The pianos were turned to hide the light fixed to their music stands, which barely reached the keyboard. Even those who knew the show were no doubt wondering what about this production was giving them the creeps.

Now the chorus burst into moonlight, dressed for the hunt, facing more or less the same way there behind the screen (because sober enough to follow instructions at the top of the show).The men on tape were singing prettily about some execrable truth that needed to be revealed. Throckmorton was trying to sing *forte* over the tape, urging them on, but it was clear that the chorus was unaware of him, while Throckmorton was carefully trying to be one of the boys.

The music still had force because of light shifts behind the "chorus" which made our supernumeraries seem like they were getting somewhere. For verisimilitude I'd selected these men from the stalwarts among Brian's Scottish regulars, pint-bibbers who'd stayed loyal to Brian's Fife as it had once been, hoping to see it that way again. Still, they were mine to do with as I pleased as long as the free drinks were coming... My instructions about silence were being ignored, but to good effect, since the strong singing of the professional chorus needed to be scuffed a little by spoken English. And the way my guests rubbed shoulders seemed very natural: little drunken boats on different wavelets, nudging each other.

After the chorus I left for my spot on cue taking care not to make the riser boom. Norman was right behind me, breathing Manchurian mushrooms, which was the reason, though he was first to sing, I was first out of the chute. It was also the reason we were making small-talk from opposite ends of the stage. I wasn't going to risk letting Throckmorton gag me so close to my big aria. *Cruda, funesta, smania* set the standard for male behavior right to the end of the show: haughty, bellicose, bullying. Lucia's doomed amour is no different unless she's turning on the charm. Only Raimundo Bide-the-Bent, played by Volodya, now close on my heels, could be touched by Lucia's lovesick laments. Until she knifed Arturo, that is, and went mad. Then it was "the poor dear!" all around.

Norman was managing his spotlight, I saw at a glance. He had learned to approach it without occupying it, so that it picked up the projecting parts of him but left him mostly in doubt. His voice was still a terrier's, but even a terrier can frighten coming out of the dark at you with nothing but its snout and bared teeth.

His entrance took a split second, his first words to me—in essence, "you seem upset"—scarcely more, but he really settled me down. The confidence I had felt about my voice was begining to extend to the whole production. My god, if we could make Throckmorton ominous we could project anything! I began to revel in all the inner torment that was about to spew from me, measure by measure, as from a berserk machine unreeling tickets.

Volodya Bide-the-Bent made his spot like a train coming out of a tunnel. As he gave us the first of his patented "take pity on the poor girl" speeches I could sense the disappointment of the audience that the mountain of black sound that had shocked them had issued from the slow-moving, cape-clad, fatherly advisor. There always had to be an old priestly type, but why him? What a waste!

Launched on my big aria I felt the immense relief of knowing that for some minutes my throat was all I had to worry about. Oh, Volodya and Throckmorton came in briefly along the way and Volodya bolstered the finale (we cut the chorus there), but nothing they did wrong would matter as long as my singing was solid. I'd never sounded better. People were knighted for less.

We exited to wild applause, but before going off we dragged Paine's iron bridge out of the shadows to suggest garden whimsy and pulled up a downed chandelier of Brian's which, recently garlanded with living ivy and lit, suggested the all-important fountain where Lucy is awaiting Edgar. She dreads the sight of this landmark, she tells Alice in her famous aria, because one of her ancestors slew a woman there in a jealous fury and there, too, Lucy had communed with the woman's ghost.

In mere seconds the lighting was changed and the darkness was speaking to our audience in a slightly different way. All of us going off had a good look at the ladies about to enter. My relief at having got so far into the show without a glitch was doubled or quadrupled by the sight of the breasts about to precede Lucy and Alice into the moonlight: bare to the nipple, bulging with impudence. In spite of themselves auditors both male and female would find their attention buried in these inviting bosoms until they were hurled back in their seats by the sudden sound arising there.

Ah, but they could sing. At least Theresa could, with the best of them. When her caprices began one could almost forget she had a bosom. The whirring. The chirring. I thought of a bird of paradise being stuffed into a box. A mating call to Woody Woodpecker. The nineteenth century equivalent of the strobe light. She was everywhere at once. Notes like gnats were storming our ears.

Edgar was out watching now, too, waiting to go on, or waiting for the ladies to turn around so he could see if they'd really dared to go with as much tit as the rest of us were saying. The drunks were carrying on in darkness beyond a screen. They'd have been out of hand by now if the enchantresses had had to enter under their noses.

"The show must go on" was no longer a mere slogan to inspire us to care more. The show itself seemed to care this time; it wouldn't be denied. It was all Anneliese could do to keep up with the notes that swirled into each successive tableau, or call it a cameo, when successive characters came spinning out of the dark.

Another good omen: Alice remembered to exit stage left and cheat along the wall in the dark to the dressing room door, foregoing the opportunity to vamp Edgardo as he was going on. Anything was possible after this Edgardo's manhood had been called upon. On stage with him I often felt as if I were looking over the shoulders of a bull as in a film I must have seen, watching the object of his attention become centered between the tips of his horns.

Logical though they may have been none of my worst-case scenarios came close to happening. Everything was so smooth that my uneasiness felt completely out of place. The moments that had made me shudder looking ahead were passed with no more than a tic.

Though Jørgen's horsy face often looked as if it had straw coming out of it I was sure the audience saw him as a perfect romantic lead. They had fallen into idolatry as a consequence of so many things that had gone right, one after the other. Lucia and Edgar were godlike in their coyness, revealing with every small gift of themselves how much more they had to give. Though such behavior is maddening in mere mortals, say out on the street, where people in love should never have appointments to keep, where being together should remove the possibility of being elsewhere alone, in opera the illusion that the singer always had more to give never comes across as a cheap trick (though it is, having to do with the husbanding of breath). Far from feeling disgust that the singer is holding out on them they want more, more, encore, bis. They never get enough until the singers who've been nourishing their habit step out of character at the end of the show. It's like the kind of sex that only ends because of exhaustion: I know you love me, I love you too, but let's forget the god I was, and I'll forget how much I needed to become that god. Let's put clothes on and drink coffee and go our separate ways before any of this gets old...

Yet while there was still plenty of show left, and we had two full acts to go when Edgar was through with Lucia, the well-known success effect was operative and one of us could have let go. When an audience drives a singer's doubts away with their applause even a mediocre talent can give an outstanding account of itself. And just as an audience can become quasi-addicted to what a singer has to give, singers can become quasi-addicted to applause from the audience, or the utter stillness of awe, which is sometimes more intoxicating.

The success effect is especially lavish in bestowing confidence in the singer's upper register. To return to the bedroom for comparison, something like the same thing happens when a woman is told she can have multiple orgasms, and the person telling her sounds convincing because he has convinced himself. When the belief is mutual she starts letting them rip... It might be a disaster for the hypothetical couple, creating unrealistic expectations about what they ought to mean to each other, but opera is a matter of moments, and singers have an easier time of it than other lovers because every new performance, no matter how many times they've appeared in that particular opera, is like having a new partner in a new bed. All the experience with audiences will stand you in good stead. They can be won the same way, but they're always composed of strangers.

When Edgar gave Lucia her ring he was required to move into a new spot between them. If the different ones they were occupying were armchair-sized, the new one was a love seat, oval from most vantages in the house and flattened further because the beginning of the ramp leading backstage cut across it like a secant. Perhaps because he was afraid of a misstep that would start him sideways Jørgen stepped into the daddy spot too much downstage and became a talking head instead of someone with a ring. Teresa saved the scene by entering upstage and pulling Jørgen's proferring hand high above her to admire the ring as she placed it. When she brought forth her own ring, breast-hot, and slipped it on, Jørgen could take no more. In the grand pause that followed, for which an embrace had been planned, he put a tango move on her and when she was bent back so far as to be completely dependent on his strength of arm, buried his face in her bosom.

Applause made the grand pause even grander and Anneliese buried her face in her hands to disguise her smile. When the lovers continued to sing, their exultation was orgiastic. They wrapped each other in music, trapped each other in their vocal lines, pecked and pulled at each other, pizzicato'd and spiccato'd, spinnareted each other with flung silk. It was a Kama Sutra of vocalism. So much excitement on his scaffold would have been the end of Jørgen. As for Teresa... Wolfgang might have been having second thoughts about his Revolution, or if that was going too far, at least his memory was being jogged a little. I know mine was.

One act down, two to go, and we hadn't stopped once. Too good to be true, but now was no time for such thoughts. All of us prepared alone, wishing the minutes by. There were only going to be ten of them—time for the audience to freshen their drinks. Carrie and Lulu would have been working overtime. Brian himself might have been helping in spite of recent vows.

The first half of the next act was a cinch to get right if Teresa could calm herself. All of us had told her how well she'd done, but it was dangerous to meddle with a soprano aroused by her audience. Born performer that she was I'd seen Teresa seize up from excess of emotion, forget where she was in the music momentarily and spend the time between acts thinking she was about to die. All of us knew we were having a great show and left each other alone. Best if we went out for the second act and started from scratch.

The next big section of music, *Il pallor funesto, orrendo,* a duet with me and Teresa, ought to have been a sure thing. This was one of the first scenes we'd ever done together, and we were as sure-footed by now as a couple of old goats. Barring acts of god I couldn't see what would prevent me from bullying Lucia into a frenzy to protect the feelings that had been so important to her the last time out.

And Teresa responded. This wasn't the first time I'd belittled her in matters of the heart. Probably half the words I'd spoken to her were designed to make her feel foolish for clinging to Wolfgang or for not consecrating her career to me à la Jeanette MacDonald. As well as we knew this scene, something entirely new came into it tonight. She may have sensed that I was trying to deprive her of the ecstasy that had just been hers with Jørgen. Never mind that months had supposedly passed, and I'd been suppressing the letters Edgardo had been writing her and was about to present her with a phony letter that would make her long-lost love appear to have been unfaithful. To the audience and to our Lucia her Edgardo was still a lingering presence. During the break it must have occurred to Teresa that a partnership with Jørgen might lead to her goal of becoming the nation's *prima donna assoluta*, or it would if the heights they had just ascended could be regularly attained. It might also have occurred to her that Jørgen had never caused or suffered much trouble up there where he was scraping the windows of buildings that scraped the sky. In the three COC *Lucia*s, and in a stage rehearsal and a dress rehearsal to boot, when Jørgen had presumably gone all out, the earth had failed to move. Jørgen had made a breakthrough, and after one such there was no going back.

Enough evidence was in for me to try to annihilate her with the fire in my eyes, to leap across the abyss between us and force the forged letter against her bosom with the maniacal smile of a cuckold, crowding into her precious light to watch her respond to the lies. I forced her to bow her head and cover her face with her hands. I forced her to lash out in her pain and drive me from her spot. When I returned to gloat at her from my original position on stage, Max had the spot ready. We'd staged passing the letter to her this way, but forcing it against her breasts had been improvised, and so had staying in a spot that was just big enough for one of us. The scene was improved, I thought, but I had to be careful not to be too inspired around Norman and the rest. I knew perfectly well that Throckmorton would be struck dumb if I forced him to change his stage business. I never had to deal with Jørgen, but Volodya was dangerous because his English was insufficient to ask directions.

Everything we'd tried had worked so far. The system of fixed spots hadn't been an embarrassment. With banks of lights such as any well-equipped small theater could supply, the technique could have been more supple still, offering performers almost unlimited possibilities for surprise and disguise. As a practical matter, it was of great importance during a scene that was falling apart, when two or more singers were at different places in the score, for example, that it should be possible for singers to detour into darkness and wait for the prompter or the conductor, however rattled, to put them back in the show.

Thanks to a scene that was traditionally cut we could take a break before the scene in the "festive hall," which was identical, when visible, to "the apartments of Sir Henry Ashton" where I'd just finished with my sister. Now, however, all was in preparation for the nuptials of Sir Arturo Bucklaw—Hilliard. We put up the lights instantly on the crowd that was yukking it up behind the scrim, roaring drunk at this point, and so what? We took turns telling them to keep it down, but a milling crowd was just what we were after, so that the fine line not to be crossed was perceptible to no one.

Hilliard gave us all a fright by not being found for a minute or two. He'd slipped in among the revellers, thence into the serving area and out into the lounge bar. He'd stayed at the bar long enough to hear how great everything had sounded to Carrie. He'd had one drink to settle his nerves, but was certain that he wouldn't forget anything he was supposed to do, anyplace he was supposed to be. I put away the smelling salts.

If we were going to be ridiculed, the most likely time for it was right ahead. Arturo had a short solo before the ensembles took over. At last I would learn whether there was something innately comic about Hilliard's stage presence or whether I thought it comic because I knew him. When he started to fake his part I was sure there would be some tittering of the Japanese sort: hands over mouths and sidelong glances only—no pointing, no loud comments.

Hilliard came upon the scene, opened his mouth and left it open. He was swaying a little and I wondered if he'd lied about having one drink. What the hell, this was a wedding party, there was no time like it for carousal. Jørgen's voice rang out too much, maybe. I doubt there was a musician in the house who would have expressed disbelief if told that Jørgen was singing Hilliard's music. But that was a far cry from being able to identify exactly what was going on, just as it was easier to answer multiple choice questions than to come up with one right answer.

Hilliard's Arturo was no worse than the job the rest of us were doing. Inspired, perhaps, by what they'd seen me do in the last scene with my sister, all were trying to get too much drama out of sudden appearances and disappearances. Pretty soon no one knew where to look for the person who had the same music, or was at least on the same side of the issue. That shouldn't have been too hard because the situation was basically everybody against Edgardo, but Raimundo was making the usual noble noise for appeasement. Like a ringmaster I spent the entire act glued to my spot, trying to look people back to their marks as they flashed in and out of the light. Confusion about who and what and where was rampant, but the recorded choruses accounted for some musical steadiness. There wasn't any point in stopping, either. If everyone kept singing the right notes we'd end up brandishing our swords at the same time. As long as we recognized Edgardo and didn't turn on each other, there'd be enough sense to satisfy most operagoers.

In hindsight, Hilliard had been the most confused. Prior to Jørgen's official entrance, Hilliard's job had been to stay in front of him, so that Jørgen could aim his notes where Hilliard was looking. After Jørgen became the embattled Edgardo it was Hilliard's job to stay as far from him as possible. Hilliard's response when he heard Jørgen open up behind him was to run behind me. It may well have been that all of us thought Arturo was that kind of guy, and there was no doubt that my character was the one who was most eager to moisten his sword with Edgardo's blood, but when moments later we were confronting Edgardo single file with drawn swords, we were so tattered by the light we must have resembled a dappled Chinese dragon.

Max had done well, bless him. None of the problems were his fault. He stuck to the cues no matter what, just as I'd told him. The big little moments went all right. The wedding contract on its little table had a spot on it throughout the scene, so there was light when Lucy signed it and when Edgardo read it later and questioned Lucy about the signature. In the same spot Edgardo ripped off the ring and bounced it off the table, so there was a flash of gold before it entered the void.

Volodya had corpsed a number of times when people ran into him. He was having a great time, and unlike other unkempt Russians of my acquaintance he didn't have a problem with vodka. Everyone loved him by now, and before long he'd be making friends at the Met, we all thought. He knew that it was the lot of the basso to play fuddy-duddies, and he never complained. His natural flamboyance took over the moment he stepped out of his part, but in spite of his language problems he could be counted on.

The huge ovation we got at the end of the second act was the low point of the evening. Gone was the high opinion we'd had of the show to that point, which might have been a lot more ridiculous than we had thought. Since I had virtually no important singing in the last act it was my job to buck up the rest. Volodya was ready for his big aria right after the opening chorus. One look at him told me he was going to nail it. Teresa was furious about the lapses in the concertante, insisting that we should start running that part of the act with the lights on and a real Arturo in the part... It was a disservice to Edgardo... Made him appear to be a clown... With someone so young it was my duty to think of his career...

I'd had a premonition that Teresa would be sticking up for Edgardo so that I wouldn't take her for granted as a singing partner. Politics at this level was child's play for someone who'd been able to stay a step ahead of Brian for so long. I agreed with everything she had to say about Jørgen and his voice. He was the biggest talent I'd come across in years! We should do everything we could for him, exploit all our contacts. If we couldn't make a go of it with *Lucia* I'd dedicate the Raleigh to concert music just to give him a program...

"You'd do all that for him? How come you never thought of helping me that way?"

"I know better than to try to pressure you to sing. How many times have you complained about not having time to pursue your career. Whenever there's a chance to do music you know, I tell you about it, don't I?"

That was the last I heard of Jørgen and his stalled career. But I meant what I had said, whether she knew it or not. I would gladly have have given Jørgen a chance to do a solo concert, and Volodya, too. I couldn't see a full house for them at the Raleigh Tavern, but what did I know? I'd always counted on Brian's wrestling to be a bust. I was only too happy to take credit for my brilliant business strategy, but the truth was, I'd just tagged along with him and Nina. I'd wanted to understand Brian's eternal optimism, which came close to something that could be called love of life, and never made any sense, considering his prospects; I'd wanted to understand the way Nina cared for people she didn't know and gave herself fully to everything she did and, past providing for her kids, seemed not to care about the payoff.

With Volodya's aria, Teresa's mad scene and Jørgen's soliloquy and suicide, I stopped being a character in the drama. I was another member of the audience with tears in his eyes. It was a wonder I didn't applaud spontaneously from where I stood on or off the stage.

I was lost, finally lost the way I needed to be, not in booze or work or sex, but in beauty. Not a kind of beauty, either, not a kind of singing. This was It.

Oh, there were moments of self-consciousness when Teresa couldn't believe how a row of notes had fallen or risen so exactly without effort. There was internal shuffling and scuttling because of her important guest; she hid for a moment, tried a fixed smile, took refuge in her training the way a woman will run "to put something on." This was the human seasoning that keyed our responses, that made perfection a cause for tears.

Volodya and Jørgen were smoother in surpassing their expectations of themselves, but no less moving.

Volodya let go of the sadness he'd been carrying by allowing it to annihilate him. Instead of pushing with a tense belly and making his dark sound in his throat he let sadness reach bottom, and lo and behold, the bottom wasn't the "diaphragm" beloved of pedagogues, it was deeper than that. It was impossible not to think that his tone had come from a far place and his lips and our ears were both part of its destination. He wasn't singing *to* us at all, then, but *with* us. Yet his tone wasn't "swallowed" in the least—as basses' tones are said to be when they are entertaining themselves. We were getting lightning glimpses of his depths while braced against his black sound as against a hurricane.

There was no question of Volodya making way for what was in him—he was subsumed by it, soggy with it. Our hearts were touched in his case because of a painful, inflamed place that could be heard along with all the black sadness, a place he couldn't reach where there was a tiny goad. An autopsy of Robeson's voice would have turned up the same filament of gold.

So the sadness was just a mood, after all. However certain its relation to annihilation, it was a black cloud that could be moved. But the source of his pain remained and hooked us all.

Was there a wound deep in us where identity originated, from which we measured all our states? Was sadness our inherent inner air? Were all the feelings, which seemed to come from nowhere, in reality a reflection of inner accumulations or of our agility to escape? Wasn't all freedom and relief merely an escape without end, a movement of energy away from pain that didn't slip back, that stayed ahead of inertia?

To hear Volodya was to feel the truth of the above assertions. One could hear the inertia sucking him down, feel the pull of it, but he never seemed to be doubling back to push against it like so many of his low-voiced colleagues—like a drowning man in quicksand, that is, in deeper trouble the more he struggled, at last just blowing bubbles. Bubbles in the treacle. The usual thing these days, no dark surface was complete without them. The sign of something alive in there, but it was a stretch to call it human.

It uplifted us to hear Volodya because we sensed the power he was escaping. Hell couldn't have yawned up any less invitingly. One misstep would have been fatal. One look back and he'd have been swamped. From moment to moment he risked everything. Again and again he survived.

But *Dalle stanze* wasn't such a long aria, after all. Before the strain was too great his courage had given way to Teresa's humility. And when Teresa had received as bravely as the basso had given, descended a staircase of sound or run back up a dozen times, flounced and floated, skipped and swooned, she yielded to Jørgen.

Our little crowd already loved him. All the ladies had had their G spots tuned to A. Lucia had expired, and when Edgardo realized it, he had to die, too. He had to make his grief so unbearable that the audience wanted him to die, but so beautiful that they didn't want him to stop singing.

In 1968 at the San Francisco Opera, Pavarotti had done the Edgardo of all time, primed by Rinaldi's mad scene. Full of heartbreaking *pianissimi* the mad scene had revealed a Lucia so crushed that there was nothing left but her sweetness. Never mind if it was possible to sing with real grief—supposedly Gigli broke down on stage when he allowed too much real emotion to take over—Pavarotti did honor to the great mad scene we had all witnessed, and over three thousand people stayed long after the show doing honor to Pavarotti with tears pouring down their faces. For a while that night the war in Vietnam was no longer possible. The will existed to acknowledge tragedies besides our own, the heart existed to feel them. Yes, roly-poly Italians in tartan skirts.

Jørgen had just the right naiveté to bring back the memory of that great night. I mean no disrespect to Pavarotti: it may not be true in the bull ring, but in opera there's nothing like the suffering of a brute to arouse compassion in a mob. (The only worthwhile emotion that can be felt *en masse?*) Too much nobility would have spoiled the last scene—whereas a gentle, stricken Everyman howling in pain could create a holy communion.

How would I readjust to the lie I would have to go on living? My struggles down in the kitchen of this dive, and even up here as a plate distributor and small time impresario, seemed pointless. Pathetic. Why had I designed such an elaborate purgatory for myself when it was as clear as anything that this was where I belonged, in a theater of some kind—this was what I should have been doing? If it was all I was good for, so much the better.

Teresa had been right all along: go for broke. She'd have stayed to pick up the pieces, too. And I had done just that prior to my father's passing, enjoying support from a host of people besides Teresa. More support than I deserved to judge by my résumé.

Damn the money! I thought; that was what condemned me. I had no experience of the damned stuff, and there was just too much. It called up some crazy conservative instinct I didn't even know I had.

Sarah came up while I was in this foul mood and covered with cold cream.

"I loved it, Gordon," she said simply.

"I didn't see you out there. How much did you watch?"

"I saw it all. I was in the back."

"I wish I'd known."

"What do you mean? I had a good seat."

"Maybe I could have cared enough to get more things right."

"You sang well."

"Thanks. What about the others?"

"I'm going to trade shifts again so I can see the opening. I'll come to every show."

"What did you think of Alex up there?"

"Well... He looked good on stage. I know he tried."

"He did fine, don't worry. Hey, it's good we've got some problems to work on. When a dress goes too well you worry about a letdown."

"Let Alex worry, then. You singers don't have anything to worry about."

She bent to me and kissed me on the cheek. Again, and kissed the other side right by my ear. I smelled whiskey, but it hadn't showed. There was perfume, too. She and Hilliard could celebrate, but none of the rest would want to. It was deadly to do a dress the day before an opening. You had to have one day off at least... But we had to open on a Saturday night. We'd already sold out the seats.

There was no reason to keep her. I had nothing more to say. I had to turn in early after a hot bath. Hangover or no hangover Hilliard would have to be there tomorrow afternoon to run through the blocking in act two. Tell him...

There was still time. Sarah could never keep him sober, but if she wanted to, she could keep him from getting drunk. I tried to catch her.

Wellwishers. Wolfgang: "Good job!"

Brian: "Brilliant!"

Another opening, another show—ah, the breeziness of *Kiss Me, Kate*, of musical comedy in general. It was all the smiling, maybe. The brotherhood and sisterhood known to whores and waiters, to all who live by peddling their manufactured smiles and moving fast to show they care. I'd tried my hand at musical comedy until I was told by a distinguished director of it that I could be a "character lead" but never a "romantic lead." All because I didn't look delighted when I had to sing or dance. I didn't have an artificially ferocious expression, either. I'd never seen a movie of myself as an amateur doing the lead in *Kiss Me, Kate* or *South Pacific*, but the word "neutral" probably described everything but my singing. Could more have been expected of a very young man playing an old man? The memory still warmed my cheeks.

All the memories hadn't been poisoned by failure, however. The camaraderie in that little "community showcase" had convinced me that the pervasive ennui, cynicism, and sour backbiting of opera singers, particularly choristers, as they waited to go on was not an inescapable fact of theatrical life. Though opera singers couldn't pronounce the names of musical comedy performers without a snort to indicate their contempt it wasn't lost on me that this supposedly more unevolved species was better paid than we were, had a stronger union, played many more houses and had more opportunities to tour... and had more fun doing it than any of our crew. What our opera singers had to get through their heads was that whores can have fun, too.

"It can feel good to shamelessly court favor," I told our little cast where we were assembled in the communal dressing room, standing first on one foot then the other next to the viciously carved private areas behind our little screens. "Granted we've all seen too much of each other, but put that aside and try to charm and attract. Excite each other, feel real hatred. Remember, with such a small house, an audience can see inside your pores—no games. No holding the girl to one side so you can sing straight to the audience. Trust the room to put your voice out, Jørgen, and put your high notes right between her eyes."

"Are you out of your mind?" shouted Teresa. "Everybody accepts those conventions. You think I'll be able to remember all my words if he's putting his garlic breath right in my face like the last time? Jørgen, press my cheek against your chest if you must, but sing to the back of the house the way you're supposed to..."

"Second-guess me, please!" I concluded, "but brilliantly. And make it clear where you're coming from if you improvise."

As soon as I heard Anneliese's first notes my stage fright left completely. I looked around at my fellow performers for a sign that they were looser now, too. They were, surely! There was something so reassuring about hearing the piano played exactly as we had heard it so many times. In fact, one new flourish would have frozen us.

The moment it started everyone thought "Earthquake!" and

my stage fright vanished in a microsecond, affording me a long moment's relief.

I poked my head out to see how many people had run away. Some had begun to, but had stopped to look hurriedly about and decide where they were going and what was happening.

The bass guitar was the giveaway. I'd been to rock concerts in the days before there was talk of damage to the tympanic membranes. I remembered how strange I'd felt about my folkdancing internal organs. Now I could identify the other notes as those of a synthesizer and more guitars. There was a drummer too. A sound we could have survived, strangely traditional in the midst of so much cacophony like a red-lit exit sign amid strobe lights.

Anneliese was bravely playing on, though no one could hear. I was screaming and waving my hands—out of character, of course—calling for our customers to remain seated until the disturbance could be stopped. I had the annoying feeling that I was amusing certain members of the audience as I stood center stage waving my arms around, my kilt hiked up, my horn having slid around in front where it was vying with my sporran, my wide mouth producing what must have been a tremendous unheard sound.

I whispered to Anneliese that we'd have to take the show from the top when I found out what was happening.

My appearance below was completely unremarked, kilt and all. None of the participants in this madness were capable of knowing who they were dancing with, much less noting a new arrival. By comparison one of Dante's circles of hell was a Victorian parlor. This was the real thing, the real end of something. Here time was being spilled the way I remember it during explosions on the infiltration course or the time all the hay in a barn caught fire at once and blew me outdoors.

Fiona was smiling behind the bar. Makeup accented her ghoulishness.

Since she could hear nothing I mimed "badge," "gun," "telephone call."

She seemed amused. Was there no recourse under law so long as the Fife had no residential neighbors? Sure, opera was loud, I'd been hearing it all my life. Surely some of Fiona's customers down here had been complaining about how loud we were while *Lucia* had been in rehearsal. Didn't the law distinguish between acoustical and amplified music? If ever there were a need for equal protection under the law...

There was a hand on my arm, then Brian's familiar red cap pushing past me.

Fiona was backpedaling. She got to the gun first. A forty-five, it was huge in her hand. She fired at the floor next to her father's foot. I saw the bullet tear up the floor, never heard the report. Brian was backing off. He may had been considering another weapon, a surprise move of some kind—if he had been frightened he'd have run for it, I thought—or perhaps he was remembering all the trouble he'd caused the last time he went behind the bar to challenge a woman who was fed up with him...

When he got behind me he was pulling me along, indicating the kitchen, then with a high swoop of his hand, a further retreat into the alley. With the heavy barred doors thrown shut behind we could hear ourselves think...

"I won't have it," he said, wild-eyed. "I'll put them out for this! They've been warned!"

"Your daughters? The band? You've seen them before?"

"Of course. Their minds are completely gone. That noise has been going on since the sixties. Fiona knows they've been barred. She and Deirdre invited them to play once when I was out on a spree and our regulars had to look all over town to find me. I had to force them out at gunpoint, though. Oh, there are other guns upstairs, don't worry. I wouldn't have to kill one of them, just fire at their noise machines. But things are different now. Fiona would shoot me if I came downstairs with a gun. Things hadn't gone quite as sour between us by then as they are now. No, she'd love an excuse to plug me with that forty-five. As you can imagine, I've lost what little pull I had with the local gendarmes."

"I see. Well, we're in a spot, aren't we? I guess this might be one of those times that the show must simply not go on. What about one-armed Tony?"

"Who?"

"With the artificial arm? That was sticking out of our old television set? You bit his ear off once."

"Oh, sure. The gambler. You want to call *him*? What good would that do?"

"I thought he was your bookie. With connections."

"Oh, he runs bets for me. Or he used to. No, he was just an old friend. If I bit his ear off I'd better look him up one of these days to say I'm sorry."

I was in no mood for kidding.

"I thought... maybe... if you knew any mob guys... I used to have a fan from that milieu who would put me on stage with his strippers to sing Verdi. Teresa had a bunch of admirers, obviously, but her parents wouldn't let her have anything to do with them. If some of the oldtime mobsters are still around we might turn up an operalover who'd be willing to run off these guys with the noise machines and no eardrums."

"Sorry if I gave you the impression... Look, I've met a lot of people in this town, and there are a number who make their living dishonestly, I'm sure, but I've never known anybody who would stick up for an opera company like yours, or for that matter, a tavern like ours. I hate to tell you this, but having that Russian in the production, and that Norwegian, or whatever he is, isn't helping you a bit with the local gentry. Now Teresa is another story... Besides, she's female. People are used to paying big money to hear an Italian girl go on in her native tongue... Oh, I don't know. I keep telling myself that a nucleus of people will get used to you. But you can't expect an opera crowd to come back again and again, can you? Not the way they might for a nightclub pianist, for example, or a group playing chamber music, such as we discussed. I'm not trying to back out, don't get me wrong..."

"You really wish I'd forget it, don't you?"

"Not at all. Come on, we'll muddle through somehow!" He pushed me ahead of him back into the madhouse, then pulled me after him around the corner and up the slow-spiralling stairs to what was left of our opening-night audience.

Thanks to his nasality I could make out some of Wolfgang's words, but they didn't fit the gestures he was making to the dressing room, where the cast of *Lucia* was listening, where I soon stood speechless with some others.

I pushed past my friends in the cast and retrieved the wallet from my pants where they hung on a recent nail behind my dressing screen. On stage with Wolfgang I mimed refunding their money and pointed them back to the ticket desk (which was also our coatcheck room) at the top of the street stairs.

Before the room had emptied the music stopped and Wolfgang's voice was the only irritant. He wasn't raving or talking in German but too much had been missed of what he'd already said to make sense of where he was going. "The sense of the people..." was in it. Perhaps it was the set speech calling for Jefferson's precincts and wards.

"It was all my fault," I told the cast later when they agreed to hear me out at the quietest public place we could find at that hour—Foster's, an all-night cafeteria. "I'd been listening to that jukebox for so long at top volume I was sure that was all we would have to contend with. You remember what dress rehearsal was like. You could tell that there was a jukebox playing down there, but you couldn't make out the notes or words... How did they get through to us with the live music? Are there hidden speakers? Any ideas?"

"We've got to call the whole thing off," said Anneliese. "That could have been a nice little room, but without the goodwill of the tenants below... too many things could go wrong. But cheer up, singers. It never hurts to brush up a role. And there are plenty of halls we could get on short notice. What about the Russian Center, Volodya?"

Volodya had never heard of it, though he might have been there long enough to see all the grey hair.

"They might have us," I said, forestalling Anneliese with a raised hand, "but what about my restaurant? We'd never be able to pay ourselves anything on ticket sales. I was hoping to make enough on our dinners to pay you guys some decent money. Start rehearsing another opera..."

"But we're not in the restaurant business," said Jørgen. "And if you want to do something with that voice of yours, you should get out of it."

"That's not fair," said Teresa, staunchly. "That place would have been perfect to showcase our voices. He had no way of knowing what those people downstairs were up to. It's bad luck, is all. A tragedy."

"I agree," said Anneliese, in the deadly, conciliatory tone I recognized from times I'd heard her telling people of little or no talent that they should stop thinking of a career in music. "Gordon has been hurt the worst, but all of us have just watched all our hard work go for naught..."

"Wait! I'll pay everyone as if we had two performances before the public. Please don't fight me on this. I should have had the foresight to realize those people would sabotage me."

"That's very generous of you, Gordon," said Anneliese. She wrinkled her nose and looked sideways at the mop pail that had just glided up beside her. There was always someone mopping the floor in these places, someone who looked as if he'd worked twelve hours today already. I stood and said a few words to him in restaurantese. The little castors immediately swung 180 degrees and the pail began to leave Anneliese's periphery.

"We all know what a generous person you are. But Gordon... This is painful. Most of us remember when... drinking was a problem for you. Will you forgive me? I hate to bring all of this into the open, but I can speak for everyone who knows you, I'm sure: we're really happy that you aren't that kind of person any more. There's no limit to what you can do. You have the discipline to make a career now, but you've got to make new friends. I hate to be so blunt, but you've got to stop associating with people whose lives revolve around alcohol. Bars. Even restaurants. There are plenty of other jobs you could get."

Everyone but Volodya seemed to agree with this pious pronouncement. He seemed to understand the gist of Anneliese's remarks as she was making them, since they caused him to screw up his face in sufferance, and when the rest concurred he seemed ready to say something violently pro-Bancroft.

He did say something—in Russian. He looked quickly from face to face for signs of comprehension. Then he began babbling English words, among which I could make out "shits," "program," "glory," and something that sounded like "pantywaist."

After a phone call to Hilliard to secure his consent to my new plans I went to Brian's office and, finding him alive, arranged for the transfer of all my interest in the restaurant/club variously known as the Fife and Drum, the Open Pit and the Raleigh Tavern to himself and Hilliard, who was going to stay on and run the coffeehouse with him (with plenty of help from Carrie, I was sure). Brian cashed me out with one check to cover all my improvements, chattels, and what I thought was a reasonable amount for the energy (so much of which was Nina's!) which accounted for the fact that a surprisingly large number of neighborhood folk and *bons vivants* now thought of his establishment, by whatever name, as a place to eat their lunch or dinner—instead of a place to imperil the lunch or dinner they'd eaten elsewhere.

I told Brian about the separate deal I had with Hilliard to let me have a third of his profits for six months—as before, from food and entertainment, not liquor—if there were any profits. Hilliard had agreed with me that I deserved at least that much for working all my long hours and for my ideas.

Carrie wanted to stay on and so did Lulu after Carrie called her and told her what she thought the Raleigh Tavern would be like. It was hard giving the news to Melanie, who said she hadn't been looking for another job during the few days we'd suspended service upstairs. But we'd told her of the changes, and weren't much better than she was at staying abreast of them. She offered to help us get started and thought she could cook whatever Hilliard and "Mr. Steele" would want. *Mr. Steele, already...*

Sooner or later I had to stop torturing Peckham and let him tell me his version of what happened last night and why he hadn't warned me... Since I'd never had words with him last night at the "noise happening" he must have known I'd reached decisions about the business that didn't include a nasty firing.

"They had a hired crew taking out the tables in my busiest section, over by the pool table. When I asked them, 'By whose authority?' they said, 'Ask Fiona,' and she just said, 'We're gonna have a band tonight. That's the dance floor.' 'But that's my restaurant,' I told her. 'Not any more.' Hey, I asked what kind of band and she just said, 'What we've always had.' She said they always had their best crowds when they had bands. They thought I'd sell a lot more hamburgers, and believe it or not, I did."

"How? Where do they sit?"

"They were eating standing up or at the bar. They had a big piece of plywood over the pool table so that was a surface. Look, man, how could I figure you didn't know about it?"

"And you didn't see them bring in the monster speakers?"

"Not till it was too late. You won't believe me, but I couldn't figure them for doing something like that. They knew it was your opening. But right along you've worked with the jukebox on down here, and that gets pretty loud. I've been up in the theater while it's on, though, and you can't tell me that's more than a minor nuisance. A distant roar."

I remembered his visit during our staging rehearsal. He'd had a few nice things to say about the production. Of course the jukebox hadn't been a problem during the dress rehearsal. The daughters had been cagey: kept it down to make my disappointment all the keener when they brought in their doomsday machine.

"I went to them as soon as it started to make them stop. She said straight off—Fiona—'We'll be so loud they won't be able to hear their fucking opera. That's our plan, to blow out Bancroft and his dykes.' I know, the wrestling was already over, but they think everything you do is for gays. I should have quit on the spot. Dammit, how could I? I've been making a small fortune down here. I could buy you out if it keeps up. I don't know, that noise is like nothing I've ever experienced. I crammed soft wax into my ears... But it's the vibration in my chest I'm worried about. My heart is skipping too many beats. I don't think I can handle it. Do you think they'll stop if you take your opera somewhere else?"

I shrugged.

"Look, I'll keep the lunches going and serve the guys who come in from work and need something quick. A few early dinners, then I close the place. It's a shame because I was really doing well between eight and midnight."

"A lesser hamburger man might be throwing in his greasy towel."

"It was a lot easier when Carrie was here, even if the money wasn't as good. I miss you and Hilliard, too. I don't think I've had a single intelligent conversation since the two of you went upstairs. I think it would be a shame if we still can't be friends. Childish. I saw an opportunity down here where you guys didn't."

"Come on, Peckham, the daughters have had you in their pocket ever since Brian was at death's door."

"I'm not sticking up for them. I think it's great that Brian is doing so well. If a guy that far gone can turn his life around... Look, if I stop serving late at night you'll have to expect less revenue after I take my guarantee."

"You'll probably have to take that up with Hilliard. Or Brian. But Hilliard will be running things for me. Brian cashed me out for my improvements. The rest of my stuff is on loan to Hilliard. So you see, Brian will have Carrie."

"He hates Carrie!" Face bright red.

"Still dreaming of the day, Peckham? When you gonna get over her?"

"I don't know. I was man enough to put up with all the attention she got—she's a spontaneous person—but I don't think I could put up with it if she's going to let Hilliard grab her ass whenever he wants and won't let me take her arm."

"It's the way you overlook her weaknesses that makes me think you two will work something out. It's not often that smart people like you are so compassionate. I admire your courage in allowing yourself to appear stupid enough to blame drink for everything that's wrong with Carrie."

"I'm going to feel like a complete imbecile if I let you go on praising me."

"I'd say be patient if you care as much as you say. Stay aloof and you'll get your chance. Scintillate a little and she might think intimacy with you would be more interesting."

"You sure know how to play on a person's good opinion of himself. But I guess I've blown it. I can't even get to her now."

"Sure you can. They're going to have a glorified coffeehouse up there before long, chamber music. Come up and hang around. I'd like to see your dream come true. You'll capture Carrie's heart, wean her from the bottle and live happily ever after."

"Nobody's that altruistic. And if somebody could be, it wouldn't be you."

"I'm not your fairy godmother, but there's no reason I shouldn't think well of you. You didn't know me that well when I was a falling-down drunk, but it was a serious problem for me that nobody thought I was good for anything. Nothing I said was real, nothing I wanted or didn't want was taken seriously. Others always knew what was best for me, knew better than I did. What I did was distrusted no matter how well it stood up. Well, that's where Carrie is, only it's worse. Because of her beauty, perhaps, early in life she might have begun to feel that she was nothing but a shell to people, to men in particular. When she drank and neutralized what was on the inside she found that people didn't miss her, they carried on exactly as if she were still there. Why should she bother letting her real feelings lie close to her skin if she was only going to feel the hooks go in and see herself pulled every which way by desires and needs that didn't have much to do with her? She took a leave of absence and donated her body to mankind. Hence it's not really important to her who gets the feel."

"I think you're really onto something. You're saying things I must have known or sensed in some way."

"Don't forget, I've known Carrie for years. I knew her back when we were both on automatic pilot. You can imagine the stunner she was eight years ago. Too young to know what to do with all her talent. She can still sing, though, and I warn you, Peckham, if she ever gets off the sauce for any length of time, you're going to hear a lot of singing. I hope you like her voice."

"I'm crazy about her voice. The fact that Hilliard wasn't was the reason I lost respect for him."

"Hilliard's hypersensitive, that's why he likes easy listening."

"You're welcome to your opinion."

I saw that he hated Hilliard in addition to disrespecting him. It must have put him into a fury to hear Hilliard say, "Her voice is OK, I guess."

I was back at the rooming house I'd left when I went to stay at Nina's—this time in a suite on the top floor where there were longtime lodgers and less puking and fistfights. Peckham was checking in most every day and I was seeing more of him than of Hilliard, who was spending all his time at his studio.

Peckham had already taken on the cooking chores. If this was a fulfillment of one of his lifelong dreams, he was quiet about it. Hilliard had cut him in on a third of the profits as well, since he didn't want to bother with the kitchen. He was taking a small salary as manager and collecting tips when he felt like putting plates down.

"We've got to get rid of Hilliard unless he's willing to do more. He's not on time. There's no way he's worth a third."

"If you're really doing all the cooking I can understand how you feel that way."

"You're damned right! Or we could do something about that salary he's getting. He comes to work with dirt under his nails! And that art work of his just doesn't belong up there side by side with Americana."

"If you take over the place, believe me, you'll need Hilliard. He's loyal. He's someone you can always count on, and he has a way of giving you confidence and inspiring you to think boldly. Nothing is ever too farfetched for Hilliard to consider, and he's not one to poke fun at you, whatever he really thinks. Also, Hilliard is lucky. He's the luckiest guy I've ever known, and you can be sure of success if you've got him on your side."

"Enough about his virtues. The rate you're going he should get a third of the take to be our mascot."

"Carrie's sweet on him, isn't she, Sid? That's why you've got it in for him."

"I suppose," he said glumly.

"Hasn't it occurred to you that if you lose Hilliard you might lose Carrie, too?"

"We'll lose them both anyway when Brian succeeds in making

it dry."

"He still on about that?"

"He won't go against you, but what about us when you're out of it? Anyway, he's making offers again. Wants you back to help him run it. Arrange for the entertainment, at least. He thinks he needs you to help make the place a success since so many ideas about it were yours to begin with."

I was noncommittal, though I felt I'd walked away for good. Maybe someday it would become the place I'd dreamed of having. Hard to believe if Peckham had anything to do with it.

What had made me so lazy? Why was I turning my back? The way I saw it the place that Hilliard and Brian wanted to run was too improbable, tainted top to bottom with ideology they were picking up from Wolfgang. As in *Peter Pan*, you had to believe. If you could believe that Peckham would put one minute into the place after he passed his bar exam or pulled off a big drug deal... If you could believe that Brian would spend the rest of his life dispensing good music and good cheer... I'd been on solid ground when I'd been in business with Brian while I was rooting for him to stay alive, but to go into business with him and root for him to stay sober?

I didn't see Peckham for a couple of days and found out why when Hilliard caught me in the afternoon.

"I guess you know by now that Carrie quit."

"No."

"Yeah. She's had enough. Brian's been treating her great, but Peckham has flipped out. It's getting hard to work with him. *For* him. Cooking seems to bring out the worst in him."

"Is he getting the job done?"

"We could live with him if he would just stay downstairs."

"He was pestering Carrie."

"Yeah. Maybe I shouldn't tell you this... Carrie's been modeling for me."

"Peckham knows about it?"

"No way he could unless he's been following us around."

"Aha! You've been messing around with Carrie all this time! While Sarah's at work!"

"Look, I was going to tell you. I've been meaning to break

with Sarah but I don't know how to tell her. I keep putting it off. Carrie doesn't pressure me."

"They like each other?"

"Carrie wouldn't mind being friends. Nah, Sarah doesn't suspect anything."

"I'll tell her for you, Hilliard. This is my big chance."

"You're going to France, though, right? You don't want some dame tagging along."

"I think there's still time. I was planning to leave the end of this week. You could have ruined my life."

"I don't get it. Anyway, all I've been trying to do is help you by staying on and making sure you get your money. As long as I'm there Peckham won't try to screw you."

"I know you've done your best. Man, I'm glad I found out while I've still got time to change some of my plans. The big favor I want to ask is: trust me to tell Sarah how it is with you and Carrie."

"She won't believe you, shit. She'll think you're trying to pin something on me to get in her pants. If she believes you, she's going to be steaming mad."

"I'll know how to tell her. I'm the one. If it were up to you, you'd be screwing up your courage for weeks. Anyway, she must sense something's going on, if I know Sarah."

"Oh, she doesn't like me having so much time to myself down at the studio. She hates the place but she knows how important it is to me."

"I'll wait for her at the hospital. What time does she get off?"

Hilliard gave me the details. I was so excited I wanted to leave now and wait for her on the ward, but I knew I had to control myself. I'd have my hands full when she saw me on the lot instead of Hilliard...

He had to meet Carrie somewhere...

"Are you sure you know what you're doing?" I asked before he was gone and I was stuck with my plan.

"You're the one who's doing the doing."

"Giving up a woman like Sarah."

"Yeah. I wanna be friends, but she just isn't someone a guy

like me could ever live with. If my life is going to revolve around Artaud, it's better if things are a little looser with women. Know what I mean?"

When she came out and scanned the lot I felt oppressed by the ideas I had to get across. Sarah was a cool head in a crisis. Trouble was I'd never seen her in a crisis of her own.

After all the times she'd seen me in that Mercedes... but no.

If I pursued her she might want to go off by herself and cry.

There was too much at stake to be "supportive."

I needed to get her in my car and start running her life. On the surface it looked very much as if I wanted to kidnap her, but I thought of it as a deprogramming.

I honked the horn impatiently. If I were thinking of myself enough to be impatient she wouldn't think I had bad news for her.

"This is a surprise." She got right in. She didn't like what she saw on my face.

"Is he all right?"

"He told me to come. He's dumping you for Carrie, our ex-barmaid."

I started driving in case she changed her mind.

"Couldn't he tell me himself? I could have come to work in my car, you know. Did he set this up?"

"No!"

"Why am I such a sucker for WEAKLINGS?"

"To stay out of rush-hour traffic I'll crawl down some side streets, OK?"

"Fuck you will. What?" She didn't know who I was.

"You all right, Sarah? Want to tell me about your day?"

"No. I want to hit you over the head with it. All day I'm hitting my fucking head against a wall with these patients of mine while he's fucking around with the fucking groupies at that fucking place. I know the score. It's a great life."

"The patients do this to you?"

"Goddammit, I lost another one today. Yes! It's driving me crazy! The poor broken bastards. I have to be there for them, browbeat them into giving a damn, fight them for their own fucking lives. Then they talk someone into doing it when I'm not there."

"What?"

"Pulling the plug on their respirators! Where have you been, Bancroft? I thought you knew about this line of work. Hah!"

"You might need a drink. I'll pick something up on the way to your place."

"My place my ass! Half my shit's at Hilliard's. You know where I mean. Not the studio where he does all his living as you very well know. Anyway, I've got a roommate now, another fucking woman, and she doesn't know me very well. Except she thinks I'm a stable good influence. What a joke. If the fucker comes by his place with that slut and finds me, so much the better!"

"Don't forget, I'll be there. He won't even come in if he sees my car."

I gave her a long look for someone driving but she wouldn't look back.

She rambled all over the place till we got to the house. Nothing incoherent, but I saw a lot of moods and needed a drink as much as she did when we pulled in.

Ever since Hilliard had taken his studio the drawing room had been barren of his art, some of his furniture, the drawing table. The end of his life here was so obvious that even Sarah should have seen it, bad as she wanted not to.

"I know where he is. Yeah, the barmaid. I've already seen some pictures. He just leaves them lying around."

"Sorry I didn't know how rough it was for you at work, Sarah, but if you want to talk about Hilliard I might have something to say."

"Forget him. Not worth talking about. What do you care, anyway, Bancroft? You're off to France in a few days."

"Not right away. I'm going to drive to New York and sell my car first..."

"So you want to keep me company for a few days, have a

little loveless sex, then it's off to France to be with your girlfriend?"

"I was going to ask you to go. I know it's selfish of me when your patients need you so much."

"What?" A shriek. She was coming apart at the seams. "I took it for granted you were following your girlfriend there." She took a smaller swallow of her scotch, then changed her mind and took another big one. "Why not. I'm game. Fuck this scene. I'll take a leave of absence, a burnout leave. I'm overdue. Fuck everything."

"All of you get like this from time to time?"

"What do you expect? Hey, it's a great time for me to split. I lost another one last week, but the rest of the ones I have now are ready to come out soon." She could have been talking about teeth. "So what's the plan when we get to France? New York, is it? What do we do there? How much money do I have to bring?"

"Sure you're not on something?"

"Take drugs and drink? I'd never try to end it that way after what I've seen. I want to live. That's why I'll go with you."

"We've only got three days to find out if we're compatible."

"You want to fuck me?" She was on her feet. "Want to see if you'll like me?"

"Sure I do, but calm down first. Jesus, Sarah, I've never known you like this. Mind if you're a little more like the person I know before we do it?"

No answer. I took her empty glass. "You want the same?" I was expecting tears but she nodded quickly and seemed to be coming out of it.

"I'm sorry. I'll be all right." This was the voice I recognized. "Scotch."

Late that night Hilliard tapped on the front window and came in after I pointed at the double doors to the middle room and mimed unconsciousness.

I followed him into his bedroom.

"What have you done to her, Hilliard?"

"That's what I should be asking you! She never snored when she was with me. Shit, that's why I left Carrie's. Thought I could get some sleep here..."

"And I suppose she never got drunk on her ass when she was with you either."

"Sure, once in a while. When she gets fed up with that job of hers. You're not going to tell me she got drunk because of me?"

"I'm sure that's part of it. She lost a patient today."

"Wow. There was another one last week. I just tell her not to bring that shit home. She's the one who wanted to work around all those people who can't breathe."

"So you just tell her to shut up when she has a problem about it?"

"I haven't told her anything in a long time. She knows better. She could find something to do that doesn't burn her out so much. I mean, she could still be a nurse. Not everyone in a hospital is about to die or so fucked up they aren't good for anything."

"What a soothing effect you must have had."

"No, she still gets carried away. She's real emotional, you know. I've told you that before."

"I thought you meant 'passionate' or something."

"You didn't find out yet? You'll see."

"All I want to know is what she was like when you picked her up from work. Was she a fruitcake sometimes?"

"I don't know. I don't think so. Depends what you mean."

"G'night."

"There's an old saying, ya know. Be careful what you wish for—you might get it."

Hilliard was up first, yawning loudly as he clattered about, then suddenly on tiptoe. I didn't even hear him leave, but recognized the sound of his truck out on the street.

What a beautiful shape under the sheet. The ass on her. Sarah herself where I'd dreamed she'd be...

In my bed, that is. But on the old mattress where I crashed when I was wrecking my life?

There was still time to back out. If her head was pounding as bad as mine she might feel like taking back a lot of things she'd said last night and give her true feelings another chance.

She couldn't be as impulsive as she had seemed. How would she and Hilliard have lasted a year? Hilliard planned all his moves and the only deviation was when he got stuck somewhere or tried not to.

I got a sneaky hard-on watching her. Wouldn't I, with a hangover and no woman for a while? She was on her side facing away. I tried to roll her gently from the shoulder. She gave me no help and came onto her back with a soft thud, the sheet slipping down.

Had to make sure she wasn't playing possum. Breathing was the best way to tell. I eased my head into the crook of her shoulder feeling like a saboteur, a landing party. Above me her nipple slumbered sensitively, a dolmen covered with scribbles. Beyond was a drowsy continent waiting to be taken, shrouded in mystery.

Actually the shroud was one of Hilliard's mottled bedsheets, and I called off my expedition to remove it from the morning light. There were no better sheets in the closet. Hilliard had always washed them, but he sat on the bed.

As I covered her with a blanket she woke, groaned, stirred, let me kiss her neck. I worked my way down to her dolmens before she fell asleep again.

I removed the blanket and meditated on her body while perched on a crate in the corner. In the days of wine, women and song around here I'd have gone to meditate in a coffeeshop, cutting a breakfast into bits, drinking coffee. She'd have been gone when I returned and wondering what I thought of her. The next time I saw her she'd believe me when I told her how much I wanted to see her again.

It didn't take me long to do the right thing: cover her up and walk around the block a dozen times. It was a typical San Francisco morning: sun bright in the trees, bits of trash frisking in the streets.

I finally made up my mind. Someone with a body like hers had to be the right woman for me. There wasn't anything wrong with her mind, either. The display of raw emotion I'd seen last night was just what the situation called for. It was a wonder she hadn't started smashing things.

I was the loony. In the Fife and later in the Pit I'd been the reason for the routines, the manager of them—the only one with an interest in seeing everything run smoothly. The restaurant had been hanging by a thread. Not one. Dozens. I'd known where they were. On a given day every one of them went taut at least once.

I'd become exactly like the zombies, insisting that my imitation reality was the norm. Genuine emotions, actual pain, cries of rage, the heart laid bare... not here, thank you. Not in my place.

She was in her underwear calling work when I came back.

"Sorry I didn't think to call in for you."

"Glad you didn't. I tell the truth."

"Do you tell the truth when you've had too much to drink?"

"I'll stand by anything I can remember."

"Good. We're off on a cross-country trip. I'm going to sell the Mercedes in New York where I'll get top dollar. This baby's never been through a winter. Where we'll be staying I'll wait for the rest of the money from my restaurant, and maybe from my father's estate."

"I told you I'd go?"

"Do you still want to?"

"Yes, but I think we should know each other better. Is there any reason we have to leave right away?"

"I've never had this much money and I'm afraid I'll spend it here. Especially if Teresa gets hold of me. There are others who think they know what I should be getting out of life and might convince me."

"I don't know. Something not right about going three thousand miles away to wait for money that's owed you... Haven't considered that?"

"I can trust Hilliard. I'm giving him everything. You probably think that's like turning both cheeks and bending over, but he's the main reason I could make a go of it at the Fife. How do you feel?"

"Awful."

"Why don't we take the day off together and treat this place as ours? He won't be back. Yeah, he came in last night while you were out of it."

She frowned, but drunks tend to worry less about humiliation if they've been passed out.

"You could use one of his bathrobes. Ever notice that about our old buddy? The shit he doesn't have to wear out on the street is always top quality."

She went to his wardrobe and came back in a maroon terrycloth robe. I brought her the breakfast special: black coffee, dry toast and 3 TUMS.

"I've thought of a way to speed everything up. I say we answer questions about ourselves the way they do at one of those computer dating services."

"I have to fill out a questionnaire before you'll kidnap me?"

"Think of it as elopement brought up to date. You know, we don't have to get married because we aren't coming back."

"I've often wondered what you'd find out about someone from those computer places... Wouldn't it just be a projection of what people want you to buy about them? If they have any use, I guess it's to take away some of the risk that you'll be going out with someone crazy."

"After last night that might be a risk that both of us are taking."

"The technology is useless if it puts me with another workaholic. Crazy? For the last year you've been killing yourself to make a success of that restaurant of yours, and when the payoff comes, you want to turn your back..."

"Did Hilliard tell you? The basic idea of the Raleigh Tavern was mine all along. Even if I didn't have the Americana, it was only a matter of time. If you're a friend of Wolfgang's..."

"Right. But don't tell me that little old drunk doesn't know it's yours and want you to run it."

"It's their headache now, Sarah. I'll be in the land of milk and honey. Anyway, that's one of the questions we need to ask each other. How do we define success?"

"If I'm happy with my life I feel successful. I wake up in the morning and it's all right there for me."

"Right there—bravo. Your patients aren't going anywhere. All your love objects are right in a row."

"Give give give until I drop? No thanks. That's where your pal Hilliard was so cagey. When he saw that his hopelessness was getting me down, he started looking elsewhere. A gentleman in a weird way. Very careful not to dish out more than you can take."

"I know what you mean, but his gloom has always been bracing to me, like salt air. When he goes on a tear and tries not to say anything for a couple of days, scowling and slashing at his work, his tongue and his lips all stuck together, I feel like I haven't got a care in the world. There are so many things I want to do I have to run to keep up. Ideas overwhelm my notebooks, I've got to sprinkle them through the cafes."

"Yeah, I've often felt that I have more energy to give to life because I'm living it for so many others..."

"Oh, I've never done any living for Hilliard. He's slow, but he covers a lot of ground. He's my idea of a success. He gets an idea, makes the most of it, moves on. He doesn't get boxed in by his discoveries."

"Let's talk about us. Is any of this really going to happen?"

"I sure hope so. Look, we know each other. We've been flirting for a year from the decks of our different cruise ships. We just don't know *about* each other."

"Speaking of which... last night... did anything...?"

"Almost certainly not. I haven't had a drinking problem in

quite a while. If I don't remember it, it didn't happen."

"Then you might have blacked out too."

"Maybe that's what it sounds like, but what I'm really telling you is that I'd remember something like a hard-on after all that drinking. It might be a sign that I'm recovering the potency I had before drinking became such a problem for me. If so, I can see some sense in the last couple of years I've spent facing the world without a drink in my hand."

"Jesus. This stuff that you want to know *about* me, then—I didn't just put Hilliard's robe over it?"

"Well, sure you did, but tell me about yourself first, the way you might talk to somebody holding a microphone next to your mouth and pointing a camera. I can be patient about the other part. We've got three whole days."

"I was always tall and strong. I was a tomboy..."

She was off. I heard the things that Hilliard had never mentioned... or had already forgotten. How she didn't play with dolls... Got out of track and field when her boobs and her ass were too big. Jewish parents and she didn't want to go to med school because "once I got my hands on the patients I couldn't let go." Lots of brothers and sisters. She'd had uncontrollable maternal feelings toward the end of high school. A lot of the sex she had was "using."

Her whole life story couldn't have taken more than twenty minutes. "That's it? You sure? Everything else was a waste of time?"

"Completely."

"Then it's my turn. My father put in a regulation pitcher's mound and plate on our front lawn. Anything else you want to know?"

"Did you want to be a pitcher or a catcher?"

"Neither, but he wanted me to be a pitcher and so did the guys on my team and the other baseball nuts in town. Anything else?"

"I'm sure I should ask about your drinking. Hilliard told me the funny stuff..."

"I think I drank my twenties away to diminish expectations of me. I could come up with bursts that put me at the top momentarily, but I could never stay there. I was only interested in proving it was within reach. How about your boozing?"

"It scares me. A Jewish background makes for more guilt about drunken behavior... But you know that. I drink too much sometimes to put the day behind me. And because I want more to happen."

"Please never think you have a problem, OK? Normal is no place to be. It's a tightrope. You're just lunging at life as it passes you by and don't know what you're missing. Extremes are OK for us as long as we go to them together."

"How can you be so dogmatic about stuff like that? That scares me."

"Maybe I'm just fighting dogma with dogma. If it's true that problems thrive on attention, what about cutting them off?"

"Then they fester."

"Not necessarily. I had some pretty strange assumptions about the world in my early twenties. I'll go into the gory details when I haven't got a hangover, which better be damned soon. Or when you really think you need to hear all that shit. Anyway, I'm not the same person. I don't think the way I did then, I don't see, I don't feel things the same way. Booze even tastes different. It's a little insulting when people want *me* to be the helpless person I used to be."

"Quite a cop-out. Still, I've got to admit, the whole time I've known you I never saw the kind of person Alex was telling stories about. The bastard."

"Him?"

"Yeah. He never portrayed you that way."

"What else did he say about me, though? Maybe it would save time."

"He was impressed by your voice. Singing professionally. He thought the women in your life were a disaster."

"The ones who went with him first, sure."

"Please. He told me once that you were too soft, you felt sorry for too many women, and those were the ones always hanging around, while the ones that really attracted you got away."

"That might have been true while I was living here, but if

you'd seen some of the places I've lived... The Hotel Vacancy... You know the one? Wouldn't it be a sorryass woman who'd want to hang around? Anyway, the pretty ones... Those were the ones who got away, OK? A mattress on the floor wasn't what they wanted. They may have stopped here briefly but they were looking for someone in Pacific Heights, a man with a view."

"That was never me."

"Don't I know it. You stayed with Hilliard longer than any woman since I've known him. Don't get me wrong! That was never the same thing as hanging around. Not when looks is all he goes by."

"It's not. But don't paint yourself as some kind of loser. Not after what you did with that restaurant. That's another thing Alex admired."

"I can't believe he told you that."

"Managing a big restaurant and club didn't mean anything to you?"

"I couldn't manage a lemonade stand."

"Why did you try so hard?"

"I had all this money from my father I wasn't supposed to have. I took it in trust as a last chance to prove to him I could get something right."

"And you did."

"Well, I fucked up my dream of producing operas that would showcase great overlooked singers, but I guess the restaurant was a winner, thanks to Nina. And Brian. If it weren't for his wrestling idea I'd have gone back to a life of selective hallucination when Nina left. My imagination took a hell of a beating, all those months in my little galley... We'd never have got off the ground without Brian to do my hallucinating for me. The wonder of alcohol. After a while you can't dream any more, but your brain needs to, so you have to start bending reality a little. That's all Brian was doing. He caught me in the mood."

"You sound like someone who's been through hell."

"Where did you think I'd been?"

"Well, some people might think running a restaurant is a glamorous occupation."

"Don't bring 'em around here!"

We were out of the house by lunchtime. With Sarah in my life I could think of food again without a "no" down below.

At one point she said she'd have been more optimistic about us if she thought she were having a relationship with a businessman.

"Is there some way you can travel with me indefinitely without having a relationship?"

"Then we wouldn't be going anywhere. I'd be the next Nina."

"Not fair. Think how much we're alike. I've got the same tendency to take on jobs that depress the hell out of most people. We've both made a career out of the abnormal, writing poetry while all our friends were watching the Big Board. We both put sex ahead of security as the ultimate in life. We both drank too much at times. We were both too big and aggressive... at least, part of our lives..."

By that evening we'd found still more common ground. For one thing, Hilliard was still gone and we both felt like interlopers in someone's getaway place.

Sarah's hangover subsided that night and she felt exhausted, as if she hadn't slept in days. She was a fiend for sleep, I was finding out. A bad sign if she weren't so right for me in other ways.

I was someone who could fall asleep all wrapped up in a woman, even one as big as Sarah, and four good hours were enough...

She wanted to go home to sleep, and I complained that I'd been wanting to have sex with her all day. Today I'd become convinced that our compatibility wasn't the kind that led to friendship. With an optimism I remembered now more than felt I told her that our compatibility did away with the need for privacy. Since she could never be an intruder, I had no more refuges. I would always be there for her...

"I remember you telling me we'll always be strangers..."

"From the time we met we were friends of the same friend. We've known each other in a superficial way. Maybe that's why I feel so comradely about you. But I keep waking up to your presence: my god, look at you. Another world, so fresh. Words just don't get it. Try it this way: knowing you doesn't make you more familiar."

"It's flattering to hear all this when you want to fuck me, but you really don't know me at all if you think you're going to tell me I can't go home to my own bed and get some sleep when I want to."

"Do you think we should break the continuity?"

"Who the fuck do you think you are, Werner Erhard? You really think you're going to brainwash somebody who's been through as much shit as I have?"

"Come on squiggums, I know you don't mean that." That cracked her up. "I'll put on a pot of Ovaltine. You know you want it as much as I do."

She held my hands and looked hard at me. I didn't feel a bit like one of her quads.

"Let's face it," I went on, "if we get sick of each other in two days, what are the chances we'll stay together when we're on the road, and it's you and me for six weeks straight?"

She decided to stay, saying only that she wanted a change of clothes. She knew where everything was so I didn't have to tell her which pyjamas and risk another escape attempt.

She fell asleep right away, breathing easily. No snores to-night.

Instead of being grateful for the quiet sleeper she had turned out to be, I was eaten up with dread. Everything seemed to be going against us. All day long she had been collecting insights that would benefit her quads. She only seemed to approve thoughts that would play to that passive audience she tried so hard to please.

Drink wouldn't help but I had another small tumbler of Black Jack anyway. The facts were all too plain. I was taking her away from her patients, or trying to. She'd have to be crazy to think I was more deserving of her goodness than anyone on the ward. She had turned out not to be crazy, ergo she had her own reasons for going with me, selfish reasons. She was setting herself up for a loss of self-esteem and I'd be her scapegoat.

I may have had selfish reasons for wanting her to go with me, but they weren't the only reasons. She needed a break from misery, she needed to be with someone who would dedicate himself to making her happy. I had twenty-three grand worth of dedication, even if my love turned out to be less precious to her than the love of her quads with their shining eyes.

I was fairly crocked when I joined her on the floor. I remember wanting to wake her to ask, "Who do you think you are?" but had the good sense to let her sleep—the only encouraging sign that evening.

The following morning we were wandering on a stretch of beach we both knew about, out between the Coast Highway and the Pacific, among the dunes and iceplant, getting hungry. I loved the big holes she trod in the sand. I loved the height of her that never obliged me to stoop when we walked with our arms around each other, but let me rest my hand on her hip.

Between the dunes we were like two boys in a hut, or two tomboys, discovering her body. Two boys with her breasts in our hands. Then she was a tomboy wanting my *thing* to do tricks, but the woman was already husky in her throat.

The fog came in and we finally got hungry enough to go to a hole in the wall in Japantown. She knew about it from Hilliard who had known about it from me. We took turns watching each other be ravenous while the waitresses went about on tiptoe and whispered about us. I may as well have brought her wrapped in a sheet.

Right after lunch, headed for the park, there was a breakthrough.

"How did you feel about the hippies?" I asked.

"In the sixties? Maybe I still feel a little bit the same. Envious. Sometimes skeptical. Nothing I'd have liked better at the time than to drop out and let everything slide. All that's changed. I could never understand why so many people with the luxury to do it wanted to destroy themselves. Great to find out about yourself and the nature of reality, but what good is self-knowledge if there's no more self? I mean, you don't become a seeker to get lost."

But that was precisely why! I held my tongue. "Could you think about being hippies, kind of, when we leave?"

"I don't want to rough it. Don't want to be that dependent on you."

"You're damned right. I never roughed it while I was in my right mind. Oh, maybe once, in the army. I was reading Kerouac. Got a three-day pass from Knox and thought I'd like to stomp around Kentucky with a backpack. Nuts and raisins and T-bird wine. I was the only creature in the woods who had heartburn. I was shot at by moonshiners. It rained the whole time. My first night I found a rock overhang high on a hill. Couldn't keep a fire going. A huge animal was circling me all night while I made menacing cries. I thought it must have been a bear that wanted my spot."

"This was the beginning of your thing for motels?"

"Maybe so..."

"So what does it mean to you, being hippies—just smoking a lot of pot?"

"No, I guess I just meant, bum around together, no plans."

"The trip to New York? To France?"

"I'd like to end up in New York if we can. I'd like to go on from there to France."

"It's too soon for me to think about France. That part worries me. Bum around, though—sure. You were never a hippie, either?"

"I looked like one, I thought like one and all the straights thought I was one and treated me like an outcast. But the leaders of the movement in the Haight didn't always accept me. I smoked pot, but I still drank a lot. I'm sure some of them thought I was a derelict trying to pass."

"How'd you manage to leave that life?"

"Friends. Hilliard and other artists. I realized I could rise above my circumstances. I wrote about them."

"That poetry about the vermin..."

"Yeah. Some of them were written then."

"Now I'm really excited. We'll make a scrapbook. We'll memorialize the trip. No postcards to anybody. We'll take pictures, write poetry, do drawings and watercolors. We won't have to worry about making the trip a series of delights. That would be hard on a low budget."

"I've got more'n twenty grand."

"I know, but we're going to last out our trip as long as we can, right? I'm really tight, Gordon. You'll find out. If we avoid the tourist spots we'll miss the spectacular scenery... But we'll make the scrapbook as juicy as possible. Every day we'll find a few things that we'll always want to remember..."

I loved to spin slowly through art museums with a woman, but she would have done a lot of that with Hilliard, and she'd already done it with Hilliard and me at the Palace, my favorite museum.

"Would it be too much like pissing on Hilliard's grave to go to museums with me?"

She felt like the DeYoung, the stars and the fish.

We found ourselves wanting to stay with the crowds. Outside, among the rhododendrons, we dawdled with families who had time for the plaques with variety names. We were swept along by the tourist hordes that the busses were disgorging wide-eyed like the newborn of an ancient species with one primary instinct.

We watched the fish drift in their contiguous eternities, amazed at the safety of so many species. Increasingly we watched each other, stopping to search each other's faces, parting a torrent of the curious. It was like being at the beach with the sound of the sea, the screams, the jostle of bodies, while we conversed through the sand, her slightest movement a message to my bones. Her sudden breath on my neck was no surprise—her ideas like a fragrance in it.

We were starting to respond as one and needed to escape the places we knew. We were already wandering... forgetting... lost.

We were alone as you can only be alone in a place that is half-abandoned.

"I guess you know what has to happen now," I said. "You're going to have to see stars. For at least twenty-four hours you should have difficulty focussing your eyes."

She slid into the next room taking off her clothes and came back in a blue canvas smock looking like a mental case.

"It doesn't have to be anything, Gordon. I want to leave with you no matter what it's like. Anyway, why won't it be wonderful?"

"Because of the need for it to be wonderful, that's why. How can we turn our backs on all the places we know and our work and our friends and take a one-way trip into the unknown unless we're stoned on each other? Tonight I expect a miracle. After tonight, motels can do the trick."

"Tell me more about these motels of yours, what they do for you."

"We should take one tonight. It's no good being around all these places where Hilliard has lifted his leg."

"You want to go to a motel?"

"Right. Go home and get your own bathrobe."

She uncrossed her legs was all, briefly showing me the whites of her thighs. Waiting for an explanation.

More motel madness. "As soon as the door shuts behind

you everything is ordinary and the room is making you a present of it. Gift-wrapped glasses. A gift-wrapped toilet. Here the ordinary is virginal. Motel room sheets are so neutral that a body you know as well as your own will come alive like a drop of pond water on a slide. Give me your body in a motel room and I'll find things to love that Hilliard doesn't even know you have."

She sealed off the view between her legs.

"Couldn't we simply take those sheets of his to the laundry?"

"You want us to spend our last evening together in San Francisco at a laundromat?"

"I don't want to be at a disadvantage when you make your slides. We'll have our fill of motel rooms soon enough."

A bit later Hilliard's sheets, pyjamas and towels were giving up their secrets to a room full of gumchewing inquisitors. It was an inspired delay. By the time she was getting out of her clothes again I was sure this would be a night that her body would never let her forget.

"C'mon, let's take a shower."

"I had my shower this morning," I protested.

"C'mon, we'll soap each other."

I followed along.

"It'll break the ice, you'll see."

"Spoken like a true nurse trying to get someone to pee."

"You'd better not."

"Promise me you and Hilliard weren't in here playing in the shower. That'll ruin everything."

She was in charge of the faucets and getting the right temperature.

"Never. With Hilliard sex was always the same. Maybe he was superstitious. C'mon in."

She went for my prick after mere seconds of soaping. The sheet metal sides of our stall faithfully recorded our changes in position. She managed to coax a dark-red, soapy hard-on out of me, but what for? Surely she didn't think I was going to let a woman her size put her arms around my neck and jump me! No, she was going on her tippy-toes and I was supposed to scooch down. I was in, but this was some kind of hoochy-coochy dance.

What with the water slashing down and the stall going "bong" things were too confused for us to feel completely ridiculous, but it was excruciating.

Digging my fingers into her ass I said the hell with my lower back, and up she went. She immediately locked her wrists behind my neck. Even so, on the way out of the stall it occurred to me that if I lost her she'd break my prick off on the way down. On an evening like any other a thought like that would have wilted me in a flash, but my cock had a will of its own at the moment. It was immune to panic, ridicule, pain, and I was so proud of it for once I started to think the not-prick part of me was going to come through, too.

Hilliard's bed was handy. I got us over there with a flurry of short, safe steps and heaved us onto his bedspread, a relic of his college days that deserved to have gone to the laundromat as much as anything we'd taken.

"Oh, no. We'll get it wet."

"True." She was either losing lubrication at an alarming rate or she was one of those women who peed when she got too excited. But in the latter event, wouldn't there have been a strong smell of urine at Hilliard's place? "Throw your legs back and save some for later."

She did as I asked, but she was edgy about it, the tomboy peering out again. That's right, I'd given her another order.

"I hate this bed!" She was screaming to be heard over the shower senselessly blasting away next door.

I rolled onto my back and took her on top of me, saw the thrill on her face.

"You'll be on top, but not yet."

I walked on my elbows until my feet were well over the edge of the bed, then walked us off. Doing the coolie step as before I carried her down the big hall to the telephone, where there was a wooden chair, no arms.

When I had her wildeyed in my lap I knew she hadn't done it this way before. Hilliard had thought my advice to him was a trap! Still thought she was too big, too heavy, it wouldn't work. Prolonging her misery I left her balanced on my lap and reached to unplug the phone, bouncing her slightly by closing my legs.

The movement inside her was minute, but the thought of what I had in store for her was swelling me; she must have felt it.

She saw it was easy for me to bring her back each time she slid away. She saw that she was meant to watch. She saw herself laid open, huge, wild with life. She watched me enter as I drew her toward me, she watched herself cling as she eased down and away.

She was biting her lip. Her nostrils were wide and straining. The breath hung in her mouth, her cheeks were flapping, a panting horse. She groaned when she was gone and her strength left her, but I kept on, relentlessly gentle, nourishing her ripples until they were waves with teeth.

Some time after, I followed her into the abyss. We left the hall on four feet, not a word between us. Made straight for my old bedroom and stretched out on the clean sheets. The moment I realized she wanted to sleep I heard the shower, our background music, our thousand-and-one strings.

Should I let the dust settle? I was asking myself as I went to turn off the water. Should I assume I'd won the battle? What if I awoke in the morning to find myself the only casualty on the field?

Romance was what women were pleading for these days, but it was too late for that. Her fault, starting with Hilliard's shower. Then his bedspread, a faded but cumulatively powerful document of pigfucking since he was an art student, full of wine stains and menses. The little chair in the hall? I was still proud of that inspiration. Bold, minimalist style, with so much of Hilliard's art missing. The experience, even in mid-July, conjured the ghost of Christmas parties past, and even if she'd never worked in an office a woman so beautiful must have been assaulted at a Christmas party before by a man who'd been dancing in and out of her periphery all year wanting to hold her in his arms...

"Please, I just want you to hold me. I'm already sore. It was wonderful though... Don't think.."

"I do think, though. I could have bought roses. Imagine a motel room, one of the expensive ones where everything has been steamed or boiled, full of roses and your naked body. I feel as if we had our wedding feast at Joe's Diner when we could have gone to *La Tour d'Argent*."

"It's sweet of you to think... But think of all the times that lie ahead of us, all the motel rooms, if you like."

"I don't think, especially when you never stop talking about your quads and new ways to keep their interest."

"You don't believe I want to go with you?"

"I believe you want to but I'm afraid you'll want to come back right away because you're so unselfish and have such a saintly idea of what you've got coming to you that you aren't good for more than a couple of days of vacation every other year."

"I've already had that, though, haven't I? No, this is something I want to do."

"Sure. Do you mind if I pass along a little of the folk wisdom that's been handed down by generations of guys like Hilliard? All that conquest business is for lightweights. A woman who goes to bed with you is no more of a conquest than something you've run over on the road. Anyone can fuck a girl. The important thing is... how long does she stay fucked?"

Not a sound. The light was out.

"Love is like a disease I'm supposed to catch?"

"Don't mess with folk wisdom just because you've had a little experience. It sounds callow but I've never known it to fail. To be sure of a woman she has to have a peak experience that she'll be drawing on for the rest of her life..."

"I'll take the one I just had. Seriously. From the ridiculous to the sublime. It was total. And through it all I could tell how much you wanted me."

"About wanting you, fine. But the ridiculous aspect was nothing I'd counted on."

"Of course not, but you didn't let it get in your way. You must have wanted me a lot."

"Wanted you?" The temptation to tell her about my homage came on strong, but I had to wait. So much musing about her would have been flattering but it would take her a month to tell me all the ways I had her wrong. No, the way things were going, I might not need my homage until she started making her first divorce threats. "If you only knew how many nights my pillow has been your stand-in."

"Oh, I knew you liked me, but on the physical side you were too respectful. If you'd wanted to start something, you could have."

"I didn't want you to think I was the kind of person who'd try to steal his best friend's woman away. Don't worry, Hilliard's had it much too good for too long. I'd have stolen his woman in a minute if she were just another woman, but I really did want to have your good opinion."

We caressed each other for a while: the last trickles of love, nothing happening inside.

I thought we were having the same thought when at some point we both seemed to be watching our big, long bodies stretched out together.

"The first time I lived with a woman," I told her, "it was with another couple—lesbians. One of them had been a friend of my girlfriend's in college. I was impressed by the way they made love. A slow fire. Or call it a long slow heating up, then suddenly the world's on fire."

"They come on to me a lot. I guess I'm not as nervous about it as I used to be. But I like the way you are, Gordon. Don't hint around. I like you to be gentle... knowing how rough you can be."

"Rough?"

"Haven't I praised you enough?"

No!

Sometime later I told her I didn't think she was sore anymore. "I don't think you ever were."

"Have it your way. No, I want to. I want to get lost in this."

She swung herself up and rode me. I could see in the dark now. Dark shapes. Dark lips, parted teeth. Breasts very large when she leaned to me, hair a dark curtain. The sounds were a young girl's. That was the beauty of it, that was what had me in awe. Gentle goodness contained her. Just as she felt a roughness somewhere beyond me when my hands were gentle, and trusted my hands, and trusted what she meant to me, I felt the rages of her life out there beyond her, all the pain and suffering she'd dealt with squarely, and trusted her wildness to be more joyful than a mere escape.

The child was never lost. We had been the same child once, caring for nestlings. Worried about all the animals and bewildered by the senseless human pain. We'd become adults the same way, uncomfortable in our skin, that dead skin, aghast at all the stupid games and the deadly serious results. We'd put on adulthood like armor, always ready for the worst. We'd staggered on, we'd made it this far. All the wreckage was somewhere else now. The world was gushing smoke right outside our door, and we were children together making sounds of caring for a wet fledgling, whether mine or hers.

Now that the adults were out of the way truly anything was possible, and nothing was wrong. From years of peering out of our masks we knew that this time there had been no mistake.

We said goodbye to Hilliard down at his studio. He saw the glow on our faces and his surprise was captured by a sneaky guiltlessness. He'd been preparing that guiltlessness for months with lowered eyes.

"Well, I guess I send the money to Sheridan's then. You'd better give me his new address."

"There's a note on your pillow. You'll get the new details in the mail, if there are any."

"Whatever happens to you guys, there are bound to be some details."

"Yeah, well, I'll try to write, is what I'm saying."

"I will, too, even if I haven't got the money yet. How long do you want me to wait before I sell off the stuff he hasn't paid you for?"

"The minute Brian becomes his old self. Or see if Peckham has enough law in him to keep things going. Hey, you don't have to listen to me any more. It's your place now."

He pulled his beard for a minute till it became apparent there was nothing more to say. He kissed Sarah once on her cheek, holding her hard against him. His face was very tense, yet he looked paternal, of all things.

"You're still a son of a bitch, Alex," she said through her tears, "but I'll always love you."

Since I had no plans to come back I had to have a hug, too. This might have been a first. Ever since I'd known him Hilliard and I had always been in close touch, only separated from time to time by futile escapades.

We really let the tears come when we got back to the car.

"You'll see each other again," she said.

"I don't know why I love that bastard so much."

"I do," she said with a smile. And we were veterans in other ways. It was good to know that, starting out.

TAHOE. We had come to Tahoe, I told Parker ("just Parker"), my pick-up golf partner on the course at Incline, because my girlfriend didn't want to leave California without seeing it. She was from Seattle originally. We were headed east, her first time in Nevada, she had never gambled before. A nurse. Me? Had a restaurant in the City by the Bay. Just sold it. The Fife and Drum.

Parker had been in insurance. Commercial lines. Made more money than he knew what to do with. Well-paid people ran it for him now. He was hanging around resorts and spas a lot these days looking for a woman to replace the young one who had been his wife until a few months ago when she ran off with a younger version of himself. I shouldn't feel sorry for him, she had been a high-maintenance sports model. He wasn't looking for a type this time, just a person. The right person could be almost any age or size. He didn't want any picture in mind in case the right person came along and he didn't recognize her.

He'd been at it a few months, then. Well? Nice shot by the way.

No luck. He had to watch it, a man in his position. They only wanted his money, especially the young ones. High-priced hookers was all. All you find up here.

But I wasn't looking, I told him after one of my patented three-hundred-yard down-the-middle drives that scared sports gamblers on first tees everywhere until they found out my short game was for shit. The woman I was with was it. Since we were in the land of Harrah, the antique auto czar, I'd call my model a Facel-Vega, Aston-Martin, Hispano-Suiza... In the shop at the moment. I hadn't wanted to wake her. Drank too much last night when we got here. I left her a note.

Parker thought it unwise to have left her alone in a place like this, crawling with available guys who had dough. The place was like a supermarket for babes where all the rich guys in the country did their shopping. I shouldn't expect her in the room when I got back.

I wouldn't. I'd go straight for the bar.

He'd join me.

In the bar Sarah was sitting at a table with a college professor named Bud Weinstock who claimed not to be a millionaire out shopping the babes, and introduced himself to the man at my side, who turned out to be Colonel Parker out shopping for the next Elvis. No, really just Thomas. Ol' Tom. But it was true about the shopping. He still had a wife but she wasn't at home any more. No telling where she was. She might blow right by us in this bar.

Sarah's eyes were still red but the scotch was waking her brain. She remembered last night. Sorry she lost so much, but now she felt lucky, ready to try again. We had all the time in the world was what I had said, so we had time to stay around Tahoe till we got even. Go on from there. There was still Reno and Vegas—hah, hah. But the Grand Canyon—definitely. The desert. Yes.

Afternoon, she'd had no lunch or breakfast. I took her for prime rib and asked the men to join us because I knew she would ask if I didn't, and I didn't want her to think I was worried about them. I wasn't worried about them. Sooner or later Sarah would be off the bottle long enough to remember who she was. When she woke to herself these men would look pathetic, especially Parker. Weinstock wasn't rich, wasn't even a gambler. English professor, probably a writer, but elliptical like all the practitioners these days. Wouldn't say what he wrote. Never came right out with anything. I was watching his hands and keeping an eye on Sarah's away leg when Weinstock was walking or sitting on that side. He was tall, too. Another fit.

Last night at the blackjack table a woman sat next to me and nudged my leg and then stroked inside it and nudged my penis with the heel of her hand when my pile of chips got high. Looked like a college girl. Beginner's luck, everyone said. That was the only time the girl looked right at me and smiled. I wasn't the beginner, I said. That was my wife, Sarah, here. Sitting to my left at the moment, immersing her upper lip in an ice-filled glass of scotch, watching the girl across my lap. The girl's hand didn't move, and she was still smiling when she looked back at the dealer. Sarah whispered she wanted to have sex with me right away. The whore was making her hot.

The prime rib was good but Weinstock and Sarah were both more Jewish than I had thought, liking the butt end, well-done.

Parker said he didn't eat any meat unless it had blood in it: you two can look away. Then looked at me trying to show special regard, as if we were long-suffering the same way. Both men aware of my surprise at Sarah's choice. I couldn't have known her long, must have thought. Didn't know her as well as I thought was true. But told them: I didn't know Sarah ate meat at all. We were fish-eaters, and all fish was well done except that Japanese stuff she wouldn't touch.

Sushi. Sashimi.

Right. I knew all the different kinds of sushi, had been gorging for years, but kept my mouth shut. If I were reticent around these men, let them be the experts, Sarah would see a new side of me. I had always been an expert in running my restaurant the way a man can become expert in caring for his lawn. By default I'd been the expert when we put on *Lucia*, or tried to. I'd been the expert in sex because Hilliard and so many others, if it was true about all her lovers, had never taken her beyond the speed limit or left the road. I'd convinced her that a body was just machinery, and we'd done the experiments together to explore its possibilities, talking lewdly to each other about what we were doing and later, when she began to fade, about what we had done. Proclaimed herself addicted to sex as well as alcohol before we hit Tahoe. Last night, late, thought she could be addicted to gambling. Too drunk to remember saying that. Good. Wouldn't have remembered all the sex, either. Just the drinking and gambling. But sex would be a broken connection now as well. So there were three live wires, hissing and thrashing. Parker and Weinstock had seen and heard them too.

They became dispirited when I didn't drink with them at lunch, though I'd had a beer with Parker after the golf round. Parker and Weinstock stopped circling Sarah hypnotically and started waiting in ambush. They sensed the weakness in her will to live, in other words, but were too lazy to wait for it to die. They needed to do away with me first, though, and I was a match for them, even if they were confederates.

I hated gambling, always had. I'd played beside my brother Tom a few times. Knew about craps and blackjack from watching him. We'd been winners at times and losers, and through some mathematical trick, though we'd won as many times as we lost—and had been big winners quite a few times, and never lost an amount that could be called large—we had been losers overall, I felt sure. Maybe not by much.

I'd always known that gambling was nothing but a complicated self-deception. My brother thought not, but I had the evidence from watching him. It would have been unbearably boring to watch myself the same way, hour after hour, night after night.

The men took heart when they found out how badly Sarah wagered, while I did nothing to correct her. My first big flaw! I wasn't a protector. I wasn't experienced enough. Now they were staying with her drink by drink, giving advice every time she played. She started to win. She even got hot. At the end of a good run at the craps table they talked her into quitting while she was ahead (or while she could still stand without bumping into different men so much) and she agreed! Then while the next player was trying to make his point, she put her winnings on DON'T COME and lost everything.

The men had seen the bet coming in time and tried to talk her out of it. They'd even appealed to me before it was too late. They cared that much for her. I thanked them and told them that it showed a lot of concern for Sarah to let me be the one to stop her from making an ass of herself. As I thought they would, they missed the sense of my remark, except that I was calling Sarah an ass. Not really an ass, I corrected. A loser. No harm in that. There were winners and losers all over the place. What did it matter whose side you were on, since all the losers were trying to be winners and all the winners were trying to be losers?

This made sense to everyone, even Sarah, who put her arm around me for the first time that afternoon. Then she took it away when I said that nobody but Sarah had an interest in being Sarah. She didn't want to recognize herself, she said then, scaring the men, who started looking around the bar.

We were in another casino, another bar, Sarah hadn't liked the low ceilings at Harrah's. Win or lose was nothing compared to the height of the ceilings, and whether you felt elegant about what you were doing. This wisdom was applauded by all except me, including some drunken Texans at an adjoining table. I stuck with my Campari and soda the whole time, watched by both men and Sarah with suspicion, but given admiring glances from time to time by the cocktail waitress and the wife of one of the Texans. I was the quiet type. I liked watching my friends have fun. I was having a great time, too. With someone like me a smile was as good as a laugh.

When our new friends saw how much money I was giving Sarah to gamble with we almost lost them to people they had to see. But those people could wait, they decided, they were having too much fun. Weinstock gambled small amounts and stayed even. Parker went ahead at blackjack and got behind at craps. Then he went back to the blackjack table and won some more, insisting that Sarah watch him play.

Weinstock and I played roulette where we could see Parker and Sarah. Weinstock doubled his bets on black and came out ahead. I stayed on number fifteen with one chip and finally hit it before I was a loser no matter what. Weinstock and I, black brothers, were utterly bored. Obviously passing the time, waiting for the real players to finish their game, I was surprised to have been offered free drinks. Weinstock took his, a scotch and soda, and drank it all. I declined mine, still full of golf and the outdoors, glad to have chased the slight hangover I'd given myself by staying with Sarah last night. Or trying to. She had been drinking two to my one toward the end of the evening. She'd have been blotto if we hadn't had to run to the room every two hours for more sex.

Unusual, I thought, that the alcohol showed in her gait before it affected her speech. Noted the same thing today. She was a wild, blundering drunk. I wouldn't have been surprised to see her pull a man's cock out in a public place. She was only alive in all the little moments that came and went. Things were happening fast, but nothing seemed to be happening to her, the scope of everything was so intimate. Her behavior was childlike, but slowed by her adult's body and her adult needs. Her attention seem to stick to something everywhere she looked, and her fingers kept fumbling. She threw away the money, held the flesh and teased, touched her clothes a lot to correct her appearance. She was wearing her best clothes and was radiant now that her eyes were no longer red. Her color was up and gave her a peachiness that had been missing entirely that morning when she lay like a wreck on the bed, bloodless and reeking. She had a dissolute beauty that none of the cool whores about could match. She had the attention of all the men in the small rooms where we went, all of whom knew she was not a whore, and she created unusual traffic patterns in the large rooms. I could imagine her in a simpler time being followed down a cobbled street by townspeople and cheering boys, flinging her generous body about, facing down strangers with a smile.

Her smile was slightly crooked when she was drunk. A little curl in the lower lip. Never noticed that before. Last night and tonight.

Is she Italian? someone wanted to know. She's a star, said someone else. How long have you known her? still another. I told everyone the truth for some reason. She was a nurse. She was new to everything that was being done. She was disoriented. Didn't know quite where she was. She would get her fill before long. We were driving to New York.

Later she and Parker were playing blackjack side by side. Weinstock and I were both watching. I went to the john and spoke French to some Canadians, which seemed to provide something they had come for. Back at the blackjack table Weinstock was alone and playing. The two high-rollers had gone to play craps again. I went after them. They were making side bets and didn't see me come up behind them (the reason I'd circled the room going over). They were encouraging each other. Touching. Fondling? It was only discreet because Sarah didn't seem aware of her body at the moment, all her attention was on the table.

Well back from their table in a dark recess there was a bar. I had another Campari there, and watched. I couldn't see exactly how she was touching him in the press of people, but I knew it was happening because she was starting to look for me in the direction she expected me to come. I could see everything on her face when she lifted her head above the crowd. Probably just stroking her ass, she liked that. By now she would be fondling him, though. She did it all the time when she was drunk. How's my pal? Playing with my money. Playing with Parker. No stakes. Playing with all our plans, our future. Trying to convince herself that none of it mattered.

The future had been covered. It only belonged to me now, she'd said. It flattered her that she had been invited along. She'd come as far as she could, but couldn't promise more than that. So bad? She had been dead sober when she said that. Not so bad. Along for the ride but she could tell me where to stop and where to go. It was up to me to see that we made our destination, but if I hurried her too much she might pull out. After all, she hardly knew me. And I didn't know her at all. She didn't trust me to still want her if I did, that was the main thing.

I finished my drink, crept up behind them and stroked her fanny. She thought it was him, backed her hand up between his legs. Found out, she blushed red. With all the blood already on her skin, a very dark color. Parker knew what had happened, too, and wanted out. But my face was friendly turned to him. I saw him file the information, all the busy computation behind his eyes. I could have peeled that happy face away like dead skin.

She whispered something in my ear that I couldn't understand and said goodbye to Parker. Weinstock was nowhere. Pulling me outside, asked where was the car and pulled me that way when I told her. There were too many people in the lot, she said. We could do it in the room if I would only hurry.

She sucked me in the car, manipulating herself under her dress. She was already coming before we made the hotel. I kept driving fast so no one could look in. Found an empty place to turn around. Came back. I had the feeling she was trying to make the orgasm happen in the back of her throat as well, or trying to create pain there. Come in my mouth, she begged, her eyes shivering but unseeing, huge when she raised her head. Lipstick smeared around her mouth. Greed on her face and anger about her interrupted feeding.

I would try, upstairs. All the spunk she wanted, give her. Easy. I wasn't drunk. It wouldn't be enough, though. Nothing would satisfy her. OK?

She got out of the car pulling her light coat, dragging it for a bit while she stumbled toward the hotel entrance, then bunching it under her arm. She turned to see was I coming before we came to the valets who should have parked our car. The others who might remember us from last night. (Oh, yes.) She wanted to leave this crazy place. She thought the desert would be better, where no one was around. She was drunk, she said. Sorry. We could stay if that was what I wanted. We hadn't won back our money yet.

She was too drunk, that was all; nothing was unspeakable. Shit would have tasted good. I ignored the request, refused to beat her up or tie her up with her pantyhose. Still a pretty good job of going around the world, as a pro from the old days might have put it. (How many lived long enough to retire? Maybe then, not now: drugs.) She wanted every obscene, vile thing to happen. If I crapped out on her she would leave me to look for more. Insisted she was no good. Always suspected it, now she knew for sure. Worse than a whore. At least a whore needed the money for something, if only a drug. Kept some dignity. Told you your time was up. She only wanted more. Everything was too clean, too soon over. She didn't care about orgasms any more. Wanted the sense of sin to stay.

There was no sin, I told her. She was just learning how to be a hippie and do her own thing. She could have all the sex in the world, but it would just get worse if she kept opening new doors. She could abandon every value dear, abandon her identity, I would still be there. Couldn't shock me by what she was capable of doing because I knew that anything was possible when a woman wasn't herself because of drink or drugs. Sex was much stronger in her, in all women.

Once in a while. They called it satyriasis. That was it. She'd heard of that. Yes, it had happened to me. But the only pleasure was making the woman crazy, becoming her god. Little sensation for me except soreness. Drunk? The same thing, sometimes, but it wouldn't stay up. No orgasm either way. Still best, I thought, were lots of heavy scenes with light scenes in between. I'd already sucked and licked all the obvious places (the toes and armpits maybe only obvious to us) but not every square inch of skin. I would look for new sensations. She would be right there with me.

Like a hippie, she gurgled on the way downstairs, alone with me in the elevator. I love this. I can do anything. No line drawn.

She would have to find her own way back if she got lost. If she wanted to leave I would give her money. No limits. No. But if she was gone all night... If she was gone in the morning... By checkout time I would be leaving.

We would stay together no matter what, she said. She would never leave me again, even in spirit. She wanted to see the desert. Stay in the desert a day. Did I promise? She was drunk tonight, but the desert sun would bake her right. We would replace all the bad things with spring water. We would take gallons and gallons of water with us when we crossed the desert. Sweat in the desert and drink in the car. Swim in the water that night. Not just a motel, houseboat on the Colorado the way I had told her on the way here before she got drunk. It had meant too much. She would never let me forget.

How it happened, according to the old man at the desk who gave her the blanket: she went stark naked down the fire stairs, all the way. Got into the kitchen where the early crew, all spics, were getting ready for the breakfast. They were all over her. No telling how many got her before the beverage director saw them.

Early riser. German. He don't put up with that shit. Said it wasn't their fault, though, our guys. They's away from their women, a lot of the spics that work here. Sending money home. She's the best thing that ever happened to them—no offense. You find her up here?

You brought her? Man, that's too bad. Seen the booze do that to some women. What it was, the fast lane, see—they don't know nothing about it. Don't even know when they're in it.

Rivulets of semen all down the inside of her thighs. For the scrapbook she'd begun? Not funny, good thing she hadn't understood. There were already some wildflowers. Pictures of Donner Pass (maybe) and Bowie. The silver mine with her alone, smiling in the sun. A roll of film to be developed as soon as we were one place long enough. Three, four scrapbook pages to be filled. All memories she would want to have someday. Soon, even. Sundazed.

Nothing memorable here. Pierce Arrow. Bugatti. A Doozy. No sense. Babbling about the desert tomorrow, the sun.

If we showered now I would never have to tell her about this one. The desk would be a different man—men—but everyone would know. Check out while she slept, get her out quick. Onto the highway, into the desert. I loved it too.

Passed out in the shower she weighed a ton. I was still happy to know how much I would do for her, how far I would go, how far I would drag her. The burden of her helplessness brought all my muscles up hard, muscles I'd forgotten I had. The things that were too much about her were nothing. So much love for her, helpless in my arms.

III

The last day on the road I'd had the car detailed at a place near the motel so it didn't look that different from a lot of other cars on the streets of Manhattan. As we emerged from the Lincoln Tunnel the car was making all the usual noises, what I was going to call a purr when I met its next owner. I pulled over as soon as I could.

"We made it. We're hippies no more."

She snorted to mark the sarcasm. She was doing it a lot these days.

"Damn the expense, we'll take a hotel. You'll have all afternoon to rest up."

She snorted to mark the euphemism.

"I'll go look for Sheridan," I went on. "If I don't head him off after work he might not come home till the middle of the night and we'd have to hit every bar in town to find him."

"You're trying to give me more time to get my act together. I know what's going on. You need to be with your friend alone and tell him what to expect."

"For the last time, you're going to look perfectly normal to him. I've been crashing at Sheridan's for years, and he's been crashing with me. He's not entitled to an opinion."

"Go on then. Waste a few hundred more on your 'baby.'" A smaller snort, but fiercer, with a toss of the head thrown in.

Then she hung her head and covered it with her hands. Missed everything, and she'd never been to New York.

I had plenty to tell her about parts of town I remembered, about things that had changed. I was too excited to shut up so I told New York what I remembered, and then the valet...

It was a good thing I was standing right next to the exit when Sheridan came out or I might have missed him. He must have put on eighty pounds in the last year, all from empty calories to judge from his blotchy skin, the boiled look of him. Now that he weighed close to three hundred pounds he walked differently and his face wore the expression you'd expect of someone in a runaway vehicle.

"Bancroft? Thought you might have fallen into the Grand Canyon. Where's the lady? I've got mail for you guys. Christ, it's almost November. Good thing you didn't get here on Thanksgiving. I'm going away for a few days. This is my bar, here. First drink's on me. The lady all right? Why she hiding?"

Assured that "the lady" was resting up from the long trip, Sheridan started lining up the shots and beers while he tried to grapple with whatever it was about me that wasn't quite right.

"I expected you a month ago."

"We got carried away."

"She was Hilliard's lady. He wrote me a letter, too. Do I know her? Any chance I saw her with him?"

"He was keeping her away from the Fife while you were coming in."

"How'd he let you steal her from him?"

I told him about the studio, Carrie, the last feverish days in San Francisco, our trip. Sheridan's eyes were too puffy for me to tell what he was feeling, but I could tell by his mouth that he was listening.

"She gave up the scrapbook in New Mexico? That wasn't very far along."

"Yes it was. We were crisscrossing. We'd hit six states by

then."

"But you said that was the purpose of your trip. You were going to make a scrapbook... What would be a travel book, someday, or a shelf full... Which might even be a movie... A whole new life for both of you. Sounds like you were on the right track, if you were attacked by Indians."

"Cowboys, too, in Wyoming."

"Then after New Mexico you came the rest of the way without notes?"

"We left out some states. The Dakotas, the Deep South. We were afraid of being attacked by Southern Christians. She had the wrong kind of slurred speech..."

"I think I see what you mean."

"She'd never been a lush before."

Sheridan raised a hand to indicate he was thinking. Then he ordered another round, went to the john, came back and told me he'd forgotten what he wanted to say.

"You probably wanted to tell me that it might not be a good idea for us to move in with you if I'm looking for a place for Sarah to sober up in."

"No, that wasn't it. I don't mind having you, especially if you'll keep the refrigerator full of beer in case I wake up in the middle of the night. It's dangerous to shop in my neighborhood. Oh, I know what it was. Do you still care about this woman as much as you did when you started the trip? If she's been partying as hard as you say, her looks couldn't be what they were..."

"I doubt she's put on more than five pounds. People with young strong bodies like hers aren't going to degenerate in ninety days. In fact, she's got a bloom on her. The first blush of something."

"What if it's shame? Someone who's never been out of line before... Those times she took off on her own? She could have been with men. She might have a disease!"

"I told you there's nothing definite about other men."

"I don't know, if she's got a disease I might not look so bad to her."

"I never caught her, OK? I couldn't be bothered. Exhausted doing all the driving, always being the responsible one. I'd better warn you, she walks in her sleep."

"Just my luck to be such a heavy sleeper."

A swallow of whiskey went down the wrong way and he rerouted it with a deft movement of his upper body, a convulsion that was over the moment it had begun.

"Sorry, Bancroft," he said hoarsely. "Fourteen thousand... whew. I think I'd have seen the writing on the wall after the first thousand. Even in New York a thousand will get you a whole room full of whores. Anyway, it speaks well of you that you brought her all the way across. A lot of guys would have dropped her off in the middle of the desert somewhere."

"Figure it this way: she'd never put herself first before. No one had ever let her. Hilliard—you know how he is. She was nothing but someone to help him load his truck."

"I know what you mean. Hilliard is a great guy, but when I think of all the times I helped him, I can't remember a single time he did anything for me."

"Time to go get her?"

"No! Tell me more. We might not have another chance to talk with her around."

"What more do you want to know?"

"Why you're so crazy about her. You really going to take her to France? I was there in my destroyer. Went ashore in Cannes. French people might not drink as much as you think."

"Hilliard and I went..."

"I couldn't believe the women. If she doesn't wear makeup she's going to feel out of place. She might be ostracized, even if she speaks French."

"She had Latin and German."

"So did I! What's the matter with you, Bancroft, don't you know how the French feel about people who don't speak their language?"

"She'll want to learn. She talks about broadening her horizons."

"Then why would she go with you? You want to sing opera. What kind of horizon is that for her? She could teach English, maybe, but that doesn't sound like a job for someone who's been fighting to keep people alive."

"I know. She should stay here under your protection and fight to keep you alive."

"I think you should both stay in New York. You wouldn't have to be my guests for long. Till you get started. There's a check in the letter you got from Hilliard."

"We'll see. I had a couple of good years here with my first wife."

He gave me a pained look and seemed to be protecting his glass from me.

"In France a cafe owner asked me what I did and I said, sing a little opera. He asked to hear me. I never bought a drink after that. I sang a lot that night and those French people had tears in their eyes."

"Hilliard stuck by you all that time?"

"We had French girls at our table. He doesn't speak French."

"That one night is the reason you want to change your life?"

"Things like that were happening all the time. Wherever I sang—out in the street!—no one thought I was crazy."

"Hilliard must have been sorry he went with you if you were singing all the time."

"We might not admit it but Hilliard loved the good treatment we were getting, he was proud of me. You don't know what it's like to make an anti-American cry. I've got to go back. I was singing way over my head. When I came to the high note I got the feeling they were rooting *for* me."

Sheridan waited at his bar while I went after Sarah. She was in acute withdrawal but it was too early for DTs. A few belts would have her right. We took a cab.

I could see him at the bar through the front window, sagging. I didn't point him out but it was strange to think I was about to introduce someone to him.

They seemed not to pay much attention to each other, but when she went to the toilet Sheridan couldn't contain himself.

"She's beautiful! Ah, Bancroft... What good fortune!"

"Now you understand."

"Everything. With a woman that beautiful, what's a little disease?"

"Stop acting like you're trying to get the truth out of me."

"Everyone has one now," he said with satisfaction. "You've been away too long. Had dinner? No? Good, don't bother. The finger food is great at this place. Stock up. What say? Have a bite here, another round, then I know just the place."

He had a piano bar in mind for us. Not exactly an inspired compromise of our different interests. I didn't have to sing. We sat as far from the piano as we could and told stories about our trip, leaving out the robberies, the bail I'd gone for her, the breakdowns... The car was the only thing that had come through without one.

Before the night was up Sheridan was telling stories about the old days, remembering fellow tenants of cheap hotels.

We were too devastated to come by before noon the next day. I didn't trust him to remember, but he claimed that he didn't start driving till 1:00 p.m. on Thursdays. He swore he had his hours of work straight. To stay in touch he had written them on a slip of paper with a work number for messages.

Sarah was having bad withdrawals but was still happier than I'd seen her in quite a while. Perhaps excessively relieved that she liked the fellow who was giving us a place to stay. Sheridan often made a good first impression no matter how drunk he was because of his friendliness and the good background that hadn't completely succumbed to his alcoholic blitzkriegs. He was mannerly, and even if he were at the stage where he couldn't keep straight anything you were saying to him, you still got the feeling that he wanted to and would keep trying.

Sheridan was living in a gentrified neighborhood on the fringe of Spanish Harlem. Beyond his street the next three were rubble—a no-man's land that was patrolled by what signs proclaimed were VICIOUS ATTACK DOGS. There were places to park, which seemed ominous to me, so I left the Mercedes in a metered spot five blocks downtown.

He finally buzzed us in and looked more dead than alive when he came to the door, but we'd expected that. His apartment was a complete shithouse, but we'd expected that, too.

Sarah had to use the bathroom right away and I was worried what for.

"I've said good things about you, Sheridan. She thinks you're respectable."

"Why wouldn't she? I work for a living."

"Maybe so, but this place smells like dirty socks. You used to keep your room at the Vacancy in better shape."

"I know. Dammit, I'm not this much of a slob at heart. I haven't missed any work, though. After work I go to the bar. After the bar closes I come here to crash, and then the whole process repeats itself. On weekends I borrow my sister's car and get out of town. When have I got time to clean house?"

"Let us clean it for you," said Sarah, coming back.

"We'd like that, man. We don't want to feel like we're sponging. Let us buy some groceries and keep the place clean for you... If you're worried about Sarah seeing the mess—don't forget, she's seen mine."

"Hey, that's really great of you."

In his murky world it may have appeared to Sheridan that we'd dropped by on our way to Europe to give him a hand with the chores.

He was reading my mind. "I'm not going to start staying home, though. I hate regular meals." He tore away and thundered down the stairs.

I'd underestimated Sheridan. The way he saw the arrangement we were just guests in an apartment that he didn't really need. If it made us feel better to fix it up, fine, but he wasn't going to change his habits because of us. Perhaps his world wasn't as murky as I thought. A better word might be *bleak*.

The check was for four grand. The letter was for laughs.

Hello Bancroft—

Hope you guys had a good trip. Wish I could say the same.

Pekm wants everyone to kiss his ass now he's the chef and business is falling off which is all his fault, if only he'd stay down in the kitchen. He's an idiot.

I won't let him cheat you. May not be as much money as you thought, but I swear I'll get a third. Daughters never come up but wait till we're a coffeehouse. Shit.

Best wishes from Your Pal Hilliard

PS— I've got a new girlfriend who doesn't sing. I still like my studio at Artaud. These guys really want a place without alcohol and that's when I quit and don't expect much money. My idea is, maybe a comedy club. H.

I wrote Hilliard a long letter to his studio address giving him the highlights of our trip. I told him that Sarah always spoke well of him and of their days together.

With what I had left from the trip and the money from Hilliard and the twelve grand minimum I expected for the car we'd have as much trip money as when we started. If dad's estate ever cleared probate (always a matter of days when I talked to my brother) I'd have an even bigger windfall. Tom wanted to invest the money for me, of course, and I would give him some for that purpose, never expecting to see it again. However, I'd just about made up my mind to open an account in the American Express Bank in Nice, where my trip through Europe was going to end up, and I would settle—with or without Sarah. Of course I trusted my brother and Hilliard to keep the money coming when I was abroad, and didn't need to stay in New York even to sell the car—Sheridan would have done that for me. I was holding back because of Sarah. If we'd crossed the country expeditiously and made straight for France I'd have arrived at an important audition time. Now I had to make new plans, write more letters, make more overseas calls. I had all winter to evaluate Sarah and me and create interest in a future full of Chinese boxes, with France the big box, and me the last little one—until the baby.

While he was at work Sarah and I gave Sheridan's apartment its first real cleaning in years. It was Armageddon for all the mice and roaches.

When Sheridan staggered in that night in time for the dinner he didn't want, his apartment was only fit for human beings, but barely. All the wood surfaces were soaked with disinfectant, and the nooks and crannies were brimming with poison. His clothes had gone to the laundry and he'd have to stay in his dirty ones till morning. His books had been crammed into a makeshift bookcase, his newspapers had been thrown away, his sex magazines were neatly stacked, his cooking utensils had all been rounded up, washed and stored, the porcelain and painted surfaces gleamed and no army barracks ever smelled so bad.

Sheridan wanted to take us out to dinner, but Sarah had already prepared a sumptuous meal. Unfortunately, the smell of it had been overpowered and not even the tastes had a chance. We might as well have been eating soap chips.

After dinner Sheridan had a bar in mind for us where "you don't have to scream to be heard over the fucking piano." Sarah was marginally sober from working so hard but she was ready to start throwing them down and I knew enough about booze to let her decide how much for how long. My job was merely to reinforce any feeling she might have that enough was enough.

We left with the windows open to air the place. In spite of the iron grates on the window Sheridan was worried that he'd find his TV set missing when we got back.

"I know it's not so," he said as we were going out, "but I can't help feeling you guys are trying to get me out of this place."

"What do you mean, 'get you out?'"

"That you want me to move, or something. How can I live in a place like this? I mean, it's beautiful, but it's not mine."

"What are you saying, man? Don't worry, Sarah, he doesn't mean it. He's glad as can be, he just doesn't know how to show it."

"Of course I am. Don't think I'm ungrateful. I can't believe how much you did. It's the best thing that ever happened to me in New York, no kidding."

Oddly, Sarah and Sheridan seemed to hit it off again that night. Whenever we were alone I would ask her, was she having a good time?, would she like to stay longer?, and each time she said "yes" as if she meant it.

When we rolled in no one was feeling any pain and it was just as well because of the slobbering sound Sheridan made in his sleep.

His broken-down sofa was supposed to turn into a bed, but you could have found a softer place in a wrecking yard. Sarah pulled off the thin foam mattress, doubled it and slept next to me on the floor.

I slept on the cushions from the sofa, and woke up on the floor with the cushions everywhere but under me. Sarah and I had hot showers and coffee without waking Sheridan, who was snoring. The apartment looked bleaker than ever by morning light, and the dog that woke us was still howling. The next-door neighbor was throwing his or her body on the floor for some reason and the vibration was enough to bounce our coffee. Various kinds of music moved through the building like a tingle up your spine.

I tried to console Sarah for the grim end of our trip by telling her all the things we were going to see and do in New York. She reached for my hand, and hers wasn't trembling. Still drunk, of course.

Suddenly a nearly naked Sheridan streaked from his alcove with a belaying pin and started pounding on a pipe that penetrated the neighbor's apartment.

"All right, Friedlander, cut it out!" There was another thud next door. "You motherfucking bitch! I'll fucking kill you! I'll hit you over the fucking head!"

A woman's voice came through the wall, as deep as Sheridan's. "Try it, you stupid drunk motherfucker. You'll be wearing your balls for earrings."

"So it's a woman," I was saying to Sheridan as he started back to bed. He didn't seem to hear me or even to know I was there.

Sarah and I wanted to go out for a walk, but we didn't want to have to wake Sheridan to get back in. I decided to take his keys and leave him a note to say that we went out to pick up some danish along with his laundry.

We were gone a while, but careful to come back an hour before he had to be at work. He was fuming.

"What's the fucking idea? Why'd you take my keys? There's not a drop in the house! You should know better than to leave me like that, Bancroft. Do you have any idea how far it is to a bar where I won't get killed? What did you want me to do, buy a six-pack and sit on the stoop waiting for you to get back? I'm sure the super would love that. Fuck him, he only takes the neighbor's side because I'm never around. What's this, danish? Later, maybe. I've got to make a run."

When he came back he had two big bags with four six-packs of tall cans inside, but two cans had vanished on the way back from the store. Jesus, a quart of beer and he hadn't even brushed his teeth. Bad as she'd been lately, Sarah didn't know about morning drinking on this scale and must have felt Sheridan needed to drink because he couldn't bear to face us in his apartment at the start of the day.

"Before you're well on your way, why don't you tell Sarah that you didn't mean anything by bawling us out first thing in the morning when all we were doing was running errands for you."

"I wasn't addressing her! Doesn't she know that? Come, you must have told her. I'm sorry, Sarah, he should have explained. Gordon knows better than to leave me here like that with nothing in the house. I know it's depraved, but after a quick one or two I'm myself again for the rest of the day."

As long as they keep coming, I was thinking. "What about this Friedlander woman...?"

"I'll kill her!"

"What's going on? What does she do in there?"

"You won't believe it. She practices falling."

"I should have known," said Sarah. "My little brother used to take judo."

"Who'd have thought you could practice judo alone. She throws herself down on the bare floor?"

"She's got a mat, but you should see her. She's as big as I am."

"If she's that big, why does she have to learn judo?"

He pointed to the belaying pin.

"Seriously, she must be taking it to lose weight."

"Like hell. She never does anything but put it on, and she's all muscle."

"Why does she want to disturb you?"

"She doesn't like me coming home late. Says I wake her up. She gets even by doing her falls at the crack of dawn."

"I don't see where her falls are half as bad as that howling dog."

"Guess I'm sensitive to vibration. I know about the dog, though. Thank God for him. He keeps her awake, too."

To live in a neighborhood that was an armed camp, to put up with the distant wail of humanity, the howls of an unseen brute at the window, the plummeting of an unseen brute next door—one had to be drunk. It was perfectly reasonable of Sheridan to start drinking as soon as he came awake each day. I'd have done the same if I were him. He needed more money to afford a better place, and he couldn't change jobs. It was a miracle he could keep the one he had.

I'd have thought twice about getting into a cab with a three-hundred-pounder whose eyes were swollen shut, but I doubt New Yorkers ever gave it a thought. They only asked him to speed up—or so he claimed. No one ever asked him to take it easy. I believed him. Everyone knew what a tough town New York was. A fare never had time to worry about getting where he was going, he was too busy thanking God that he was alive from one moment to the next.

The squalor at Sheridan's was congenial to Sarah. She was constantly on the lookout for things that needed doing. It was clear that she was still doing penance for the trip.

"I don't know what came over me," she told me more than once. She felt awful about all the money we'd spent because of her. "Why did you let me pull you down, too?"

"Being there with you wasn't such a bad place to be. You'd have done fine if we had a style."

"A style? A style was lacking?"

"Everything was against us as hippies. Money, a decent Mercedes..."

"You were serious about being a hippie?"

"I don't know. Maybe there's no such thing anymore. You're either a bum or you're slumming."

She was in the mood all of a sudden. We were on a studio couch we'd bought and planned to leave behind. Sheridan was having one of his late nights.

After, out of the blue, she said, "I don't want to go to France with you."

"I was afraid of that."

"I don't want to lose you, but now that I'm more together I should go back to work. I know I can make it here. I don't trust myself to travel with you again."

I gave her my blessing but we agreed that we wouldn't decide about France tonight. We'd only decided to stay together.

Before Sarah started work we did the usual sightseeing. We were both tourists because I hadn't been much of a sightseer when I'd been a young married New Yorker.

Climbing the Statue of Liberty had been a sublime experience of my childhood, but when Sarah and I went up the spiral staircase in the dark with perspiring humanity pressed tight up ahead and pushing up from behind, the experience was as sublime as work in a coal mine. Other side trips were more successful. She loved the art museums. She dragged me into the big stores. New York was where she wanted to live, she told me—a visit wouldn't satisfy her no matter how prolonged.

I wasn't sure how I felt now. In my teens and early twenties New York had been my religion. At that age I'd been in awe when I went on errands. When I handed over a nickel for a fat New York Times I thought I had the rest of the world under my arm.

Now the traffic was slower. The cabdrivers didn't seem to have any grievances, and they weren't as reckless. One of them actually told me, "Have a nice day." This in the mouth of a New York cabdriver? As a joke, maybe, out of the side of his mouth, tempered by a wet cigar. Where were the cigars?

Next thing the salesclerks would be asking if they could "help" me.

As ever, New York was full of success stories: sharp-featured, clear-eyed men whose cheeks were pink and gray, impeccable in cashmere overcoats. Every night I regaled Sarah with the splendors of France. I had travel books now, color pictures that vastly improved what I remembered.

To be safe I'd bought photoessays on London. We would spend two weeks there steeping in English culture. We'd take the night ferry to France as Hilliard and I had done. She'd get a feel for how close England was, how cheap it would be to go back when France was getting too much.

"Wake up, Sarah, someone as beautiful as you will be welcome anywhere."

She wasn't buying. She'd heard too much about the difficulty of work permits abroad. Sheridan had told her some of what she heard. He was pumping his passengers now for any bad word they might have about Europe. Going on the wagon for two days at a stretch in response to Sarah's temperance.

"I never could have done it for myself," he told her, negating decades of doctrine.

Sheridan's pitch for Sarah was so clumsy that it would have

been hard to check without being cruel to him. It was practically out in the open anyway since I laughed out loud at so many of the things he told her.

Nevertheless, he was making headway. Sheridan was well-placed to engage Sarah's interest; people on the brink of disaster had as much going for them as those who'd just passed it. It didn't hurt that she was ninety percent of what he had to live for. He didn't clump around the apartment when Sarah was in or bang on the walls. He tried to make himself useful like a mother at her kid's first birthday party.

Staying at Sheridan's put me at a disadvantage. He knew it and was forever telling us to stay as long as we liked. "I'll probably remember these days as some of the happiest of my life." (This to two people who'd seen his withdrawals and heard him thrash around at night.) He was eloquent telling me not to waste my money trying to find our own place.

"You know how outrageous the hotels are now. And rent control's a thing of the past. An apartment this size would cost you twice what I pay, and twice that again with first and last."

Sarah was a frugal sort at heart, and prevailed on me to stay with Sheridan, stay home some nights. I shouldn't forget that her experience in helping Sheridan to stay sober had given her a host of insights about herself.

I could have done without all the insights. They were coming at a time when we'd been unable to talk about ourselves and have sex. Now that Sheridan was off the grape he wasn't coming home at two in the morning. He was coming home for dinner with journals of opinion that he'd had with him all day in the cab, a host of topics to explore.

Having to screw in the daytime with all the hammering outside wasn't that different from being economically disadvantaged. Heretofore I'd made up for being economically disadvantaged by trying to work miracles in the sack, but I'd found it was hard to work miracles again and again with the same woman. Miracles had nothing in common with habits. Nevertheless, I had to stick with miracles, habits had always been much too difficult to acquire.

She noticed a trend.

"You're not taking so much time with me."

"I guess not. That was a far cry from a quickie, though, don't you think?"

"But I remember when you were never tired of me."

"I'm not tired of you now. I'd be all over you if we could do things at night, but the way it's been lately we don't even touch each other, we're so afraid something will squeak and we'll hurt his feelings."

"I know. But will it ever be the way it was before? I want that to look forward to. I want it as a goal to be the person I was that you wanted so much. If I had to swear off drinking for good I'd do it to be wanted that way again."

I'd created a monster.

"I resent being the one to make sure a woman of thirty has had this experience of life, but Sarah, dearest darling, sex doesn't always start at the extreme upward limit of human possibility and get better from then on. In fact, it tends to become increasingly casual and you might even let a day go by without having it, all the more to appreciate your next go."

"Don't talk to me like that, Bancroft. It makes me want to slap your face."

"Still another way to make sex interesting. In your case, a knock-down, drag-out fight could make things *very* interesting, even without Friedlander to spur us on."

"I could never strike you, don't be silly." The fight went out of her without affording the least relief. All that was left was sweat.

"Sarah, by now you should be taking me for granted. I'm not going anywhere without you. All this talk about France and London is just to see if I can't get you fired up about doing the things I want to do... Pure selfishness. If you hadn't wanted to take the trip, or had wanted to turn back, I'd have canceled everything. I might even have gone back to the restaurant and moved in with you and who knows? started a family. I know I didn't want to lose you."

"All that? You son of a bitch! I don't believe this! You mean I gave up everything for a whim?"

"Not exactly. Something I felt I had to do, but I was sure

you needed a vacation..."

We had other conversations that matched this in vehemence, though neither of us came close to renouncing the relationship.

In the meantime I was picking up $25 parking tickets every day. To stay ahead of the red flag I'd have spent all day looking for a place to park. Of course I tore up the tickets, but when breaking the law becomes part of your daily routine it's easy to think of doom.

I decided I had to be less halfassed about selling the car, dropped the price slightly and put more facts in the ad. The day after the new ad appeared I sold it.

Sarah had decided to be less halfassed about going to work as a nurse in New York. That is, she stopped waiting for some quadriplegic to come to her and went to two hospitals to ask for a job. They both offered her work on the spot at the same pay and she chose the hospital nearest Sheridan's.

I had plenty of money for France in my hands and Sarah wanted to wait for her first paycheck... Preferably, for two paychecks. Couldn't I let her see how she liked the job before we had to chuck everything? Wrestling. "France can wait. It's winter."

"I've told you before, that's the best time to tour. Nobody else goes then so everybody will be glad to see us."

"Isn't there enough to do here? Spend more time with that accompanist." I'd been renting practice space in the rooms behind Carnegie Hall and had made some friends who were musicians. "I'd be a fool to leave when everything is going right for me."

"I'm the fool to stay. I'll leave and wait for you. You can come when I've got a place. You say it's the constant travel that's hard to take."

"I don't trust you. I don't think you could live without a woman for that long. More than a month? In France? I'd never see you again."

These discussions were excruciating now that she was at work all day and there was no way to patch them up in bed. Finally we went to a hotel. The note to Sheridan said to expect us late, not to wait up.

Sarah was off the next day and Sheridan wasn't. He was still in the apartment when we got back and we knew right away that he'd been drinking, the big baby. Neither of us said anything, of course, but we both expected him to come home plastered in the middle of the night and that was what happened. The telepathic self-fulfilling prophecy, his specialty.

It was quite a performance. I think he drank in his sleep for the next few days.

For the sake of getting him to snap out of it Sarah was letting herself be used as bait. She let Sheridan throw his arms around her and sob on two occasions. On another he grabbed her in what he must have thought was a hearty way and started rooting around under her collar with his swollen lips. Big as he was he was easy to fend off thanks to the amazing courtliness I may have mentioned already.

Gradually Sarah sobered him up, though I must admit that the sight of him that way was no more uplifting than the sight of Brian had been.

No, I didn't fear for Sheridan's health anymore, I feared for my sanity. What kind of person would adjust to a bughouse like this? Why should I be conditioning myself to get along with Friedlander and company? And the ever-shifting population of bottles... Bottles which came as friends and quickly made a nuisance of themselves after their caps were off and their story had been told: vodka, bourbon, wine, beer. The same old story. A hundred thousand times the same. Between times the shattering refrain.

It was a strange life that produced so many illusions and so much broken glass. It was a life I knew. The American dance fever needed an antidote and for years I thought I had found one in booze. No more. My personal nightmare hadn't eclipsed the collective nightmare—ever. There was no refuge from insanity within or without. The only alternative was exile.

Unawares Sarah was making it easier for me. It was a change

in the way she looked at Sheridan, the way she considered his opinions or sought them. Drunk as he was at times he must have been aware of the change in her, and he must have been pleased with it in spite of what he told me about the wisdom of staying, and Sarah and I belonging together. She was sizing him up.

He wasn't out of the question. Sheridan was warmhearted and he'd been the manager of a department store in Manhattan once; booze hadn't been a problem then. In other words he wasn't someone who'd been a loser since the age of thirteen. He'd been badly hurt by a wife. It was just another story of infidelity, but Sheridan's reaction to it was unusual. He'd decided he hadn't had enough punishment. He hadn't been the greatest husband perhaps, but he'd been faithful, a good provider. Why he blamed himself for losing his wife was what the rest of us wanted to know, and none of us ever found out because Sheridan didn't tell the story anymore.

Sheridan was someone to feel sorry for *par excellence*. His good qualities were near enough the surface for anyone to see them, so there was no need to explain giving him a helping hand. It was a wonder Friedlander hadn't offered hers by now.

I had a key to Sheridan's by this time, and I was used to letting myself in when no one was home and waiting for Sarah and Sheridan to arrive within thirty minutes of each other.

When Sarah and Sheridan both failed to come home at the usual time, and when neither could be found in any of the locals, I didn't know what to think.

I felt like getting drunk, but that was the way I expected them to come in and they wouldn't be quite ashamed enough if they found me in the same condition.

Struck with the fact that I wasn't going to do anything but wait it dawned on me that I was jealous. And angry. How could I become one of those possessive types who were anathema to beautiful women?

Finally I decided that she was a disgusting bitch and unworthy of me for finding Sheridan attractive just because he had one foot in the grave from drinking.

It seemed I'd been waiting forever but it was only 10:30 when they came in.

Sober, and not looking guilty. I held my fire. An emergency? Sheridan looked better than he had this morning.

"I've just been to my first AA meeting," Sarah said. A quiet, resentment-seeking eye.

"I should have known..."

"Maybe you should have, after all. I was afraid to tell you. Afraid you'd tell me not to go. I'm an alcoholic, Gordon. I've been trying to deny it all my adult life. In the back of my mind I knew something was wrong. Especially at parties. I knew I was different."

"What low cunning, Sheridan! To use the guilt she felt about our trip after all I'd done to expunge it!"

There was something sanctimonious about the way he was making the decaf. "I told you, Sarah," he shouted over his shoulder. "I know this guy. If you ever get any help, he has to be the one who gave it to you."

"So you went to a meeting and sat around with Sheridan afterward and discussed my drinking problem."

"Very briefly," said Sarah, lying through her teeth. "We did discuss some of the ideas you have about drinking now, and how they might not be the right ones."

"You two both make me sick. The right ideas. Sarah, were you ever drunk on duty when you were caring for your quads?"

She knew the answer was no, but she was brainwashed already into thinking of herself as a problem, she had to search her mind anyway. "No."

"As I thought. Why?"

"Because I'd have been a danger to my patients, I might have caused their death. But I wished I could have been drunk many times and I didn't waste any time getting that way when I went off duty. I didn't just look forward to a drink, I had to have one, whether I got drunk or not."

"So you didn't always get drunk. According to Hilliard you got plastered very seldom in the whole time he knew you and he never heard you snore."

"That was because he slept like a log. And he always drank a lot himself and didn't pay much attention to how much I was drinking. Gordon, we've been over the criteria for alcoholism and they all fit me."

"You won't get anywhere with him, Sarah. If he doesn't want you to admit a problem after you were stiff for ninety days..."

"Shut up, Sheridan. Or if you're going to put in your two bits, get your tremulous ass in here and look me in the eye when you tell me I haven't got Sarah's best interests at heart."

"I'll be in as soon as the coffee's ready." Instant, by now it should have been, but the measuring took him a lot of time. "Don't worry, I'm going to give Sarah all the help she needs with you."

"I suppose I'm meant to admit my alcoholism now, too, or you won't play with me any more." I said this to her in a softer tone.

"I'm not asking you to admit anything," she replied. "But I'd be curious to hear your views about drinking. And if you're sincere about them I hope you'll go to meetings with me."

"The hardest thing is to admit you've got a problem," said Sheridan, coming in with the coffee.

"I admit I used to have a problem. I admitted it all over the place. I've been through detox units, longterm hospitalization, and I used to get a great kick out of AA meetings. I know they're the best way to sober up and stay sober. I've been in rehab programs and I've done volunteer work, outreach to help my fellow drunks."

"Then reach out to me!" said Sarah, sounding like a holy roller and slopping her coffee.

"I know what you think," said Sheridan. "You think I'm making a play for Sarah, but really we're just trying to keep each other sober. I wish you would try to help her, too. She loves you and needs your support."

"All right, Sarah. I'm reaching out to you, and I want you to take my arm and accompany me to a nice hotel where we can have it out. You've let Sheridan fill your head with his propaganda..."

"He had nothing to do with it! It was my idea!"

Sheridan's turn to gloat again.

"Your first AA meeting? Out of the blue you decided to go on over and see what kind of wild times the folks at AA were having this evening?"

"I didn't think I could help Sheridan unless I was willing to face my own problem. I've felt wonderful since I finally had the guts to do just that. I've cried my eyes out. I've had insights tonight that no one can ever take away from me. If you loved me, Gordon, you'd want to share these feelings. You'd be proud of me."

"Do we get to discuss this in private or do I have to be treated to that holier-than-thou look of Sheridan's for the rest of the night?"

"I'm too tired..." she said. "I have the day after tomorrow off, so we can take a hotel after tomorrow night's meeting."

She was trying to shock me but I knew she'd be going to a meeting every night for a while and maybe some days.

We didn't have much to say right away when we took up residence in our hotel room the next night. In a quick series of interrelated actions we set up the bathroom and hung out the Do Not Disturb sign, turned down the covers and got out of our clothes.

She was dying to show me that our sex would be better than ever now that she'd taken the pledge. I felt I was putting more into it than I had in a long time, but sex was always more intense when I was sober.

At first. Before I got bored. Long periods of enforced sobriety diminished the importance of sex in my case. True, I'd never waited three or four or eight years or whatever, as suggested by various medical doctors or Ph.D.s, to conquer the depression that was a problem for recovering alcoholics. For one thing I'd never been depressed when I was on the wagon, there were still plenty of things to like about life, new things to like, it was just that some things I used to like a lot, like sex, became a tad boring, especially with the same person.

We were awake before dawn ready for serious talk.

She'd been to three meetings by now. She had all the answers. I hadn't been bored at all, most likely. Just not "in touch with my true potential."

"I have a feeling you've been hearing about 'a higher power.'"

"Does that bother you?"

"It did when I was going to meetings. But really, I was looking for any excuse at all to be someone they couldn't help."

"There, you admit it. Maybe you've grown since then."

"I'm afraid I've only grown more sure of my reasons for staying away."

She didn't say anything for a while, and as eager as she was to proselytize, that meant she was crushed. I got good value from our luxurious mattress and surrounded her without bouncing. To let me know that she didn't mind being in the grip of her ideology she didn't yield right away, but after all that had transpired already that night a rejection of me on ideological grounds would have been unbecomingly narrowminded.

"It may have been very stupid of me, very romantic and naive, but I believed in you when we left San Francisco." Stupid, romantic, naive—full of sympathy for herself she stressed these words. "I believed in what had happened to us. I'd known you for a long time, yes. I'd been attracted to you. Still, I wouldn't have believed that it would be possible to feel so sure about living with someone after three days unless it had happened to me. It was so easy to walk away from the life I had there that I was convinced."

"I know where this is going. You went along to drink your fill. Bancroft the Enabler was going to pick up all your bar tabs..."

"I never thought that. I'll bring that up at the next meeting. I wanted to say that I was sure you cared about me as something besides a body."

"I did. Enough to see beyond your escapades."

"Then if you still care about me, get behind me now while I'm trying to change my life. See your dreams of an endless vacation in France and who knows where next for what they are:

a refusal to yield to your caring feelings. You know you have these feelings. I know you do, too, because of the way you stuck by me."

"Now, wait a minute. There's more than one way to look at this. If caring for your quads was the only thing keeping you sober you must have been terrified of going to France where there wouldn't be any quads to care for."

"I was. I have been all along."

"Afraid of where you were going with me..."

"Afraid of losing control."

"You've got so much self-control, though, Sarah. Not once in eight years as a nurse were you tipsy around one of your patients."

"It was one of the first things they told me. Alcoholics have a tremendous amount of self-control, much more than the average person. They know just how much they need to get through the day. Or in my case, get through the night."

"It's sad to think you had to drink to get through the night. Maybe it even became a habit, booze. But using it as a medicine that way is still a far cry from being addicted. Look, I was addicted for years, I ought to know something. Haven't they told you about hitting bottom, finding your bottom?"

Her bottom was such a big part of our encampment at the moment that we both snickered at the double entendre. This wasn't the time to make such a point, but in all the years I'd been listening to alcohol totalitarians using this jargon in mixed company, no one had given any thought to finding each other's bottoms instead of merely their own—not even in jest. A measure of how seriously folks with alcohol problems took their soul-searching.

"Of course. And I found mine. I'm a binge drinker and I went on a ninety-day bender. All of them were shaking their heads when I told them how much I was drinking each day. They thought it was a miracle I was still alive."

"Did you tell them how you were eating everything in sight? How you were making me stop to read about all the points of historic interest or even climb them? Then dancing your ass off every night?"

"I told them everything. I vomited on thirty states."

"The way you were being sick by the side of the road was health personified next to the kinds of things most drunks get up to. It was all the rich food coming up. It was your body trying to protect you."

"It was alcohol dependency at its worst. A need for something that's killing you."

"All right, have it your way. Booze, the bane of a decent life. The home-wrecker. The killer on the highway. It's all those things, I'm not a stooge for some distillery. But I still think you're getting the wrong picture of yourself from the people at your meeting. It would be just like Sheridan to steer you to a bunch of hardnoses."

"I told you, I picked the group. I knew there were all kinds. These are mostly professional people, very bright."

"Then they ought to know what a lush is. That's all you were. A pig in shit. Someone so repressed that she had to give herself every thrill in sight, all of life... And sure, you got out of control, sometimes, but maybe you wouldn't have if you hadn't known I was looking after you."

"I don't want to go through life needing someone to look after me."

"Of course you don't. Especially *you* don't because you know how easy it is to feel possessive about the people you care for."

"I resent that."

"Good, then see how this grabs you. Those people at your meeting may not want to possess you, but they want their system to possess you, as it possesses them. You know how it works. With corporations, sometimes. Fundamentalist religions work this way in spades. These people belong to the group and everything it stands for, they know they belong to it, body and soul, and while they sit around solemnly and watch you relinquish your former identity they're enjoying your secrets as if they'd seduced you themselves."

"What a lot of lurid nonsense. Nothing like that was going on. I've never been with friendlier people, more open about themselves. My God, Gordon, you're paranoid. I can tell you've made yourself sick worrying you'll have to face yourself someday."

"I've faced myself and I've faced these new friends of yours. Since I rebelled from the church at an early age and was never crazy about team sports it was probably the first time in my life I knew what brotherhood felt like. It overwhelmed me to realize I had so much in common with all those people."

"So what happened? My God, what happened?"

"I failed."

"Oh, you poor one. My darling..." Sarah when she was excited could put a hold on you that was worthy of college wrestling.

"Don't push me away!"

"I'm not. You're crushing my balls."

"Gordon, all of us fail. All of them have failed. I don't plan to, but after what I've heard, I won't be surprised."

"You're jumping the gun. I was going to say I failed a few times and it changed my perspective. I began to realize that a vast body of knowledge had been accumulated about alcoholic behavior. I realized that nothing I ever did would come as a surprise... to anyone... Especially to the professional listeners who wanted me to ratify their theories about life without dirtying their hands."

"You deny them good will."

"I don't trust their good will any more than I trust the good will of God's anointed."

"I don't think you trust anyone."

"I might have trusted the Founding Fathers to care about me. They were drinking men."

"I don't believe it. You're exalting people who drink."

"It was harder to be a menace to society in those days of no superhighways. The Founding Fathers really put the stuff away. Even the leading lights like Jefferson were big boozers. Paine was a drunk. Ethan Allen was a giant to begin with, but when he got started on his Stonewalls it would have taken a whole room full of dainty types like Sheridan to keep up with him."

"Tell me this is all a joke."

"People didn't judge you by your personal habits, but by your natural endowments, your energy and heart and mind, and the uses to which you put them. People were allowed some complexity in those times. Today you get a label like 'alcoholic' slapped on you and your behavior is a given. I remember telling you, it takes a lifetime to prove you're not a problem drinker. But you don't have to be a drinker: if you're capable of having problems, there's no such thing as all right. It doesn't matter who's studying your behavior—your boss, your pastor, some social worker or other professional meddler, or your pal at AA. Once you admit to a problem it's like telling them you want to talk about it for the rest of your life. I need you—or someone—to help me resist this massive attempt to explain us to ourselves and in effect to tell us how we should behave...

"I see myself as you did leaving San Francisco. Romantic and naive. Because of a few things I saw in France and the way I felt I want to try living there. That's what it means to be romantic and naive. You take a chance on something before you know very much about it, the way you took a chance on me. You said you 'believed in me,' but that's wrong. You were just giving me a chance to be right for you. No one ever believes in someone who doesn't believe in himself."

"No way I'll swallow that. Someone as cocksure as you doesn't come along very often."

Dawn was at the window like the face of a giant.

"For some reason a lot of men get off thinking about the big picture," she went on quietly. "Always the doom and gloom, then silence about how to put a little light in the picture."

"If you'd caught me a couple of years ago I was full of schemes."

"What happened?"

"I stopped believing in solutions when I took a closer look at the problems. They start in the lower grades of school: telling children what to think. When I started reading Maria Montessori I was swept away. She could make a real difference. Much more potent than Marx, a much greater revolutionary. She wasn't making hay out of people's problems, she was interested in starting children off right with the tools to get the most out of themselves and out of life. Every year there are more Montessori schools and I rejoice."

The gloom was all hers for a long few moments. "You really

are a bastard. You know there's something right about us. It's just not fair to come so close."

"What about Sheridan?"

"There's nothing going on with him. How can you say that after the way it's been with us tonight? I was up in the night, sometimes, drinking with him. We never made it. I resent you for thinking I could."

"I was jealous of the way he has all the right ideas."

"Don't bother, we're getting all our ideas from the program. I'm not going to stop trying to involve you right up to the moment you run out on me. I haven't been a part of it long, but I'm damned proud of the job they're doing. I know I can lead a fuller life if I stay dry, and I'm going to. Think you'd have the guts to repeat what you said to me tonight to a room full of AA members?"

"Not on your life. They'd know I was one of them. They'd think I was another smartass who thought he knew better than The Book, was smarter than the system, or more charitably, they'd dismiss me as someone who didn't want to stop. I always did fall on my face at Step One. 'Powerless over alcohol,' powerless to stop drinking. I couldn't get over the idea of giving all that power to some crap in a bottle."

Her anger passed into sadness. We slept two hours, I think, hatred separating our bodies in the bed.

We went back to Sheridan's at midday and found him home with a sandwich in his mouth and a letter for me.

Hello Bancroft—

Maybe you better give me a call at the place so I know you got the check I sent. Sorry, no phone at Artaud. By the way we haven't sold any of the stuff you bought. Pekm says he needs it, you never know. It would be nice if someone besides me could check to see if he peddles it on you after I quit. (I hate this place now.) I'll keep anything you could use to furnish an apartment case you come back. There's room at the studio. Sorry the check is only for two grand but Pekm says you're lucky to get that, there really aren't any profits. He might be right. Anyway, he lets me watch him do the books. Say hello to Sarah. Drop a line sometime.

Best wishes from Your Pal Hilliard

I decided to call Hilliard late that night, his evening. Meanwhile Sheridan was hanging around to see if we'd decided anything.

"Looks like you'll have Sarah to yourself, man," I said breezily. They were sitting close together on a studio couch I'd bought which he'd inherit. "She wants to get established here. And I want to get disestablished. Fast. My brother will open the lines of communication as soon as I get to Nice. And I have enough to do all the sightseeing I want and take a place for a year in the south of France."

"You bastard." A vicious tone of voice Sheridan had seldom heard.

"Do you feel deprived? Come with me while I tour, then, Sarah. I owe you at least that after all the publicity I've been giving Europe. You'll have your return ticket right in your purse. Being with me is too rough for you, turn back anytime you want. Sheridan has room for you. You'll get your old job back for sure. I don't care if you've only been there a month, they know how good you are by now. Why so quiet? Because I'm right."

"Maybe you are. Narrowly. But you're also wrong about a lot of things and it's time someone told you. I'm tired of you telling me who I am and what I should do with my life. You've been wrong from word one. The very first advice concerning me! 'Carry her a lot, Hilliard. Tall girls love to be carried. They love to feel small and pretty,' or some such rot."

She looked to Sheridan, back to me.

"Go ahead and say it in front of him," I volunteered.

"I don't like being carried and made to feel passive. The kick for me is being on top, being in control. That's why I always had a thing for men a lot smaller than I was. Right. A control freak,

I'm sure I qualify. So it's no accident that I gravitated to a nursing job like mine. I had the power of life or death over my patients. I was their god. A special bond with every one, special relationships. More give and take there than what I had with Alex. Almost more sexual, sometimes. So now you know what really turned me on. Having their lives in my hands."

A quick look at Sheridan convinced me that he might have trouble accepting the way Sarah had passed herself around.

"So now you have at least one accurate picture of the person I am." A *vicious* self-satisfied grin! "But let's go on. The trip. Of course I knew I had a drinking problem before we left, but I'd had it under pretty good control. Why did everything go haywire? Hey, one thing: I'm glad it did. I'm glad I went off the deep end. It needed to stop. I could never have been happy the way I was going. Why, though? Because I was scared to death of you! Sure I was attracted. But you were no one I could ever control. Alex was another story. It's true that he was very independent in his way of seeing and working on his paintings, but he couldn't have balanced his checkbook without me. Then you stepped in... spinning me about the town with you or across all those state boundaries. I couldn't see myself crossing Europe that way, or being dependent upon you in a place like France, where I wouldn't have been able to make myself understood. And there were scarier things. You wanted a career as an opera singer... Why? You had no music degree. By your own admission you never even had any courses in music. You told me yourself that you were old to be seeking leading roles in the big houses. And if that weren't enough to discourage the sappiest true believer, you had a record of being fired and making enemies. And why all the ruined chances? A drinking problem you refused to do anything about. If this isn't the profile of a loser, what is? You told me yourself, lots of singers never make it who have better voices than the top stars. What kind of picture do you suppose I was getting...?"

My merry smile was disconcerting her. You bet she hadn't taken the fight out of me! I was already laying for her. "You just said. A loser."

"Oh, I don't know. Maybe not. You had a voice. You were

god-awful determined. I'm sure people like you do move a mountain from time to time. I was damned if I'd be the one to say you couldn't. But there were a few other details that made the picture even less promising. For one thing, even though you were a dry drunk, or a non-practicing alcoholic, you'd become one of the world's worst workaholics there in that grungy kitchen. All you did was work, eat and sleep—until Nina came, anyway. And when Nina showed up you took on all the duties of a family man, a father to her children, without any of the rewards. A glutton for punishment. Care to correct the picture I had of you at that point?"

"You said it. The glutton. Low self-esteem. I guess I didn't try hard enough to get what I deserved."

"What are you talking about? Who would have dreamed you'd be able to make so much money on a place like that in one year? A lot of people might think you got more than you deserved, considering Nina's contribution. Carrie's. Even Alex's. No, the picture I had of you was of someone expiating the guilt he'd amassed over a lifetime of failed relationships. Most important among them, probably, the one with his father. But Christ, what was it? Two marriages? Never did talk about them, not even to Alex. He had nothing to confide. The way I saw it, you worked all the time because you were afraid to have fun or felt you didn't deserve any. That's right, fun. Of the shallowest kind. In fact, I might need good times more than the average person. Just to piss away an evening like the people you hated in that Fife place. So I was impressed that you did so much with your restaurant. No one could ever doubt your capacity for hard work. And you're a hell of a pragmatist. But what for, Gordon? Why is getting there all you care about? Why are there no interim goals and interim satisfactions? You're always a step closer to your eventual goal—I guess, the top. I'll go on record right now: I think you'll be a wreck by the time you make it. You'll have a commanding view, no doubt. The rest of us will look like ants to you. But you will have forgotten how to enjoy life. I rest my case."

"You need to give it a rest, all right. If what happened last night doesn't qualify as interim satisfaction..."

"Did you enjoy me, Gordon? Or were you just trying to prove something?"

"You were the one with that agenda. Trying to show me you could be uninhibited without drinking."

"What a convenient way to remember it. I get it—I'll never get credit for being myself as long as there are limits. Well, if I have to keep surprising you to keep your interest, it's best I get out now. I've got news for you: being in endless flux isn't the same as *being yourself*. Not to me. I want to be happy with the person I am. Even content a little, heaven forbid. I want to be happy with my work and content that it does some good. And I want the person I love to need me and be content with me *as I am.*"

Sheridan was flipping about on the couch to keep from hatching a powerful *aye*. He was canny about self-revelation, though, and knew she'd bite his head off if he added one word against me.

"Do you want to leave it there? That's an impressive argument. I don't mind you having the last word."

"Leave it, Sarah," said Sheridan, hoarse from not speaking, but I heard his fear—he knew I wasn't one to butt out of an argument right after I'd been shit upon.

"Of course I want to hear what you have to say. And you don't have to be defensive, either. You're an incredibly interesting person..."

"I think so, too, Sarah. Anyway, I saw that you were a control freak, and understood why you couldn't trust somebody to think of you as a cuddly sweet thing. But I also saw the cuddly sweet thing. I'm surprised you don't think I'm looking for a mother. Oral-fixated alcoholic seeks six-foot mama who likes to make noise in the kitchen. Eureka!"

She was nodding eager agreement!

"Would explain the liking for boobs I've had lately. Never felt that way until I became obsessed with you. No kidding, all I ever fantasized was eating it. The way yours were practically in my face? But it's all too simplistic this way. I liked being the mama more than you did. Your head lolling against my chest. You'd tongue my rudimentary dugs and make me feel like I was falling off the earth. Anyway, I always understood why it scared you to hear how high I thought my talent would take me. Still, in the Golden Age there was a correlation between great singing and lack of school time. Ruffo, my hero, never spent any time there at all. As for being a mope and keeping my nose to the grindstone for a year or so—that was me, all right. Another experiment."

"Well?"

"Well what?"

"Is that all you've got to say? 'I see where you're coming from?' Now that I've figured you out you'll try your Svengali routine on someone else—is that it?"

"What routine? Someone so transparent can't afford any routines, Sarah. That's how come I've always got the element of surprise on my side. You know, walking back and forth in my kitchen all that time, who would have figured I was cooking up an assault on European opera houses? Anyway, what opera singer in his right mind would allow musical garbage to be dumped over his head all day and half the night? The fact that I was in hell may have accounted for the fact that I didn't always appear to be having a great time back there."

"Lay off, Sarah," said Sheridan. "I know where Bancroft is coming from. There are jobs that can ruin your sense of fun..."

She gave him a significant look.

"There have to be some laughs," she said. "I don't need anyone to tell me how tough my job is, but I refuse to be grim about it. The way Bancroft was charging around with his head down..." She faced me again. "You did! Like a hunted animal. I always felt like telling you to start a restaurant somewhere else. Why that place? Alex was just as crazy. You don't put up paintings about despair where there's so much despair."

Sarah kept after me a while longer, but the fight was out of me, and not only because I was tired from last night.

On our trip Sarah's behavior had made her certifiable a number of times, or considering where we were at the time, jailworthy. So what? I'd never known a woman with so much anger and appetite for life. She was a pain in the ass in predictable ways when she was drinking, but there were other times, drinking or no, when she had been superb. Such a beautiful, big soul nodding out of her eyes.

She felt she'd run out of chances? Well, maybe she had, with me, if she needed to redefine our circumstances to include a burdensome *mea culpa*. I'd gone through orgies of problem-solving when I "came to grips" with my drinking years ago. Blessed by my attention, and that of equally miserable committed company, my problems had achieved the complexity of an overgrown English garden. The more attention I gave them, the bigger they became. My healthy impulses had been strangled. How could someone in such a degraded and decrepit state even think of going ahead with his life? It took me a while to find my way, but the right method was quite simple when it came to me (like all good ideas): I should transfer my obsession with alcohol to something else, and when that started to go badly, to something else again. Sarah had been quite right to identify me as a workaholic during the time I was trying to make a go of the Fife. She had been wrong to think that my workaholism was in some advanced, irremediable state. If she had said the words, "I'm through with Hilliard," presto!—I would have swapped my obsession with restaurant work for one involving her. I came very close to doing just that when Nina and I became involved. Yet Nina hadn't wanted to be my one and only. She'd have looked for another job if she thought I was slacking off on her account. Why a rap like workaholic is hard to beat: practically everyone is an "enabler."

I let Sarah and Sheridan go off to their meeting feeling very superior about all the new strength they had found to face up to the unpleasant truth about themselves, etc. There was no irony for them in possessing a superior understanding of the ways of the world at a time when the ways of the world were endangering the very survival of our species. Oh, I was bitter, make no mistake. Talk about my lack of a degree in music could do that every time. Of course I'd have been better off going before the mandarins of the music world with a résumé that oozed the names of famous universities and teachers and masterclasses in this country, private study in that, as well as a long list of roles I'd taken for companies besides our scrofulous COC ensemble, widely perceived by academicians as a place where people who thought they could sing were enlightened by fiasco.

So she was right—was that it? There was simply too much to overcome? I was aiming too high? But wait, maybe she had it all wrong. Maybe I wasn't aiming anywhere in particular. "Great" was all I ever heard about my voice, but I wasn't someone who needed to hear kind things to be encouraged. No, that was going too far. A famous old Italian tenor had told me, when I was something like twenty years old, that with a particular high note I would "have many blowing-nose kids," by which he meant, support a large family. I'd been gratified to have someone so eminent see so much in me. Nor did I outgrow the need to hear good things about myself, because it had felt good later on to hear about all the wonders I would accomplish when I "settled down." Later still it was "stop drinking and I'll make you a star." Pure desperation. Anyway, I may not have had the best voice in the world, but I was close. The point was simply to keep singing and growing where the right people would be paying attention and the wrong people wouldn't be whispering in their ears. As a practical matter, then, I needed to start conducting all my affairs in a language besides English.

The real reason Sarah and I would have to separate now was because she didn't want to learn French. I was already rehearsing the exchange: "I never dreamed learning French would be such a problem for you." "I always told you it was." "I never believed you. You hadn't seen France. My own preparation was inadequate. They were speaking some kind of argot that wasn't in my argot books."

Sarah would want us to separate because I refused to get involved with AA—though I needed to for my own sake and hers, too, if I loved her. I would back her against the wall with a promise to set up house in France where she'd be able to attend AA meetings in English. She couldn't accept such a compromise, nor could she think of any but smallminded rebuttals to keep the argument going. My best parting shot, after some thought: "If this is what love is about, I want to find out what happened to my stamp collection."

Sick at heart about having to give up Sarah, not at all sure I could, I called the Raleigh Tavern, listed now. With Hilliard on the line I could keep it short.

"Raleigh Tavern."

"Peckham? What are you doing up there? Don't tell me you've got a phone down in the kitchen?"

"That's not it. Jesus, how are you going to take this? Brace yourself. There's been an accident. I've been meaning to call. We weren't sure if he'd live. We didn't want you to come all the way back for nothing. With Sarah..."

"Hilliard? What happened?"

"Rearended by a drunk driver. Middle of the night. Was waiting at a stop sign in a fucking Volkswagen. His own, can you beat that? Just got rid of his truck. That's all there is to it. Snapped his spine. Right at C2-C3, I think. They think he's going to live, but I don't know for how long. He'll be paralyzed. Totally. A quad. Now can you see why we were thinking it might be better if he died? For you and Sarah, I mean. Say something."

"All right, Sid." I was so calm. It wasn't right. "Don't call here. Don't write. And make sure that no one tries to get hold of me here at Sheridan's. Far as I can tell, Sheridan has been completely out of touch with the old crowd he was running with, and they weren't friends of Hilliard's. Look, Sarah's been trippy lately, and she's been going to AA. Something like this could kill her. Where have they got him, Ralph K. Davies?"

"Right."

"Great. Right in there with all her old co-workers. I know she didn't tell anyone how to find her, but they're going to try."

"No they're not. I've been over there and met with them. They all knew Sarah, the kind of person she was. They loved her, man. And they knew that Hilliard meant a lot. When I told them how things were for her now..."

"You told them she was here? Shit!"

"I didn't. I thought of that. She might get in the same line of work and they'd have a registry or something."

"Thank god you've got a head on you, sometimes."

"I was wondering, though, do you think Sarah sent them some postcards while she was traveling? She could have told them her plans..."

"Don't worry about that. She kept a scrapbook, or tried to, but she didn't write any postcards. Look, maybe she never felt sure about being here? It's been quite a winter. What do you think, Peckham, should we be deciding all this for her? Supposing things don't go well for Hilliard and she finds out later and starts thinking she could have made a difference?"

"I've thought about things like that, but I don't know any better than you. If it's any comfort, all the girls who worked with her said, keep her out of it. They said: no, definitely, if she's got another life now, keep her out of it."

"Good. Let's see if we can."

"What are *you* going to do? You don't want to see him?"

"Of course I do. I'll call each day and see what I can find out. As soon as he wants to see me I'll find a pretext to get away. It's getting close to audition time over in Europe and she doesn't want to go. Look, this campaign to keep her in ignorance might be a flop, but at least we'll have tried."

Before I got off I asked about Brian, who was "doing just fine," and the Raleigh Tavern, with Hilliard gone, which was "catching on," or at least the red caps were. Wolfgang and some of his friends were helping out. After I got off the phone it made me sick to think of business as usual at that place so soon after Hilliard's life was ruined, but at the time it had been important to talk about things that hadn't changed, or—praise the lord, could such a thing be?—had actually taken a turn for the better.

Since Sheridan's place was alcohol-free now I went out to find a bar where I could drink whiskey in the near dark and sort through my options. Or maybe someone would come up behind me and hit me on the back of the head. Hilliard and I would have the same options and spend our declining years drooling chess moves into the telephone.

The first order of business was to rationalize taking a drink. It didn't feel the least bit wrong because of the recent vows of the sorely wounded Sarah or Sheridan, but I did have to wonder about the drunk driver who had rearended my great old friend, and about the outsized importance of drink in my life and all the people who gave it to me, drank it with me, stopped drinking it with me or stopped drinking altogether. I did wonder, if only for a moment: would this be the right moment to swear off the stuff? Was there something sacrilegious about taking this drink instead of calling Hilliard to see if he was well enough to have anything to say?

Premonitions could be fed attention the same as problems. And I'd been down in the dumps too long, guilt didn't have a chance. Anyway, doom never snapped at my heels, it was well out of view up ahead somewhere. I had no interest in how soon, where. The so-called demons that lived with me from day to day were exhausted too. Tired of trying to woo me, steer me, get me to run off with them to the end of the night. I'm sure it would have alarmed my former would-be therapists, and I had no desire to rub their noses in it, but the practice of denying myself nothing had taught me that there was nothing in life I needed. As I looked at my glass now there was no danger in it. A pleasant warmth going down, a pleasant taste. Just the sort of low-level distraction I needed to contemplate Hilliard's extremity. Scenarios began to unreel and unravel. Possibilities were hanging in the air.

Sarah had said that the worst time for quads was the first four to six months. They wanted an end then. Nothing to live for. Get them past that point and they'd make the best of it. Give Hilliard something to shoot for. Offer to take him to France with me.

I had cared for a quad, once. Sarah had never asked for the story, but I'd done a good job of it except for the five suppositories I was supposed to shove up his ass every other day. Dave had forgotten to tell me about the second seat which fit over the low one on the toilet and left room for his nurses to reach beneath and do the deed. Longstanding routines had blurred a lot of details for him. Anyway, a bit later, in the course of more intimate housekeeping, five suppositories were found to be studding the folds of flesh between leg and scrotum. Good for laughs.

French people dove into empty swimming pools, too. They had the hospitals, the nurses. Money would be the hard part. All I knew from experience was that car maintenance was incredibly cheap over there. They didn't hold you up for things like windshields. Still, I suspected that caring for a quad was likely to be too expensive for any provider but the government, and that the government would frown on the importation of people in need of such care. Smuggling him in wasn't completely out of the question. People routinely came to visit and stayed: the main thing was to prove you had plenty of money to throw away while you were touring.

Touring and auditioning would have a lot in common in my case. I would have to make one round of the country to come face to face with the *administrateurs* and *régisseurs* who would arrange to audition me and another to keep my appointments. It might well be a year before I was settled somewhere, plenty of time for Hilliard to decide if he had anything to live for. And there really was something to live for in France besides a remote control device to operate your television and food out of a microwave. Italy, Spain, even the northern countries. There was art all around you. Looking would be enough for him. Hard to overestimate the importance of his eyes in keeping him interested in life so far.

One possibility.

I ruled out going back to San Francisco to nursemaid him. It would have been too easy for him to talk me into a mercy killing. What if he wanted me to come back and unplug his respirator when no one was looking? Happened all the time, according to Sarah, and was never punished, even when the nurses did it. Could I do something like that, though? My initial response was too macho. I was his best friend, wasn't I? Hadn't I always put friendship above god and country like any true brigand? Hadn't I faithfully despised the opinion of my fellow man when I knew I was right? Who was better qualified than Hilliard to decide if life as he knew it was worth living? Why the sales pitch unless Sarah and her fellow psychobabblers were pretty sure themselves that their primrose path had nothing to offer?

I wasn't the one to judge. I couldn't make any of his decisions for him. Sarah had been dead right about my being depressed over the past year insofar as the term suggested anger about one's circumstances and conditions in general; extreme annoyance with the sound of drunkards smacking their lips while eating (though I liked to think of myself as a provider of cheap, nourishing food to the downtrodden); a sense of pointlessness that extended even to screwing, so that I enjoyed it most when I felt "not there" (Sarah had been right about that, too); feelings of panic and suffocation when singing for small audiences (surely one of the reasons I had been so eager to perform *Lucia* in the dark: ever since my tour of duty as a chef I'd let myself go, and much as I liked to blame space limitations for my pacing and other caged-animal characteristics, there had been a certain conscious desire on my part to be someone nobody would mess with [singers in huge houses, particularly the low voices, cultivate just such a presence, so it was more an annoyance than a cause for hand-wringing]). All? Oh no. What about jealousy, whose ugly head had never reared itself at all before sometime last year? Not just jealousy of Hilliard, either, which would have been understandable in view of the way the very sight of Sarah could make me weak in the knees. No, I was jealous of all the revelers yukking it up at the Fife every night without a care in the world, their arms around comely women or even not-so-comely women. Envious of all the different destinations they could have and things they could do with their time if they wanted. With all the time they had to piddle around with those women they could have worked up to things that would have been deliciously lewd, while Nina and I were so constrained by convenience and fatigue most nights that what we could manage had more in common with a piss call.

The pros and the cons could go on endlessly when I was alone in a bar. Could anyone consider it depressive mentation to have wanted to punch Peckham in the nose as much as I did most days, or wring the necks of Brian's daughters? Could there be anything sick about the last fantasy as long as I had no plans for their dead bodies? Get 'em the hell out! Better yet, let them live! Send them by container ship to Valparaiso.

Undoubtedly I would have enjoyed watching the life go out

of them, but that was precisely why I could never have throttled them. I knew very well from certain combat veterans and weirdos around the neighborhood who had probably done a little killing that there could be a high, a feeling of well-being, associated with it. From the moment I first heard of the high I was thanking god that none of the blows I had struck thus far in my life had been fatal. Then I was vowing I would never strike another, even against Peckham. I was so turned off by the idea of pleasure in death that if Brian's daughters got what they deserved, which would have meant a lot of little pieces, I wouldn't have betrayed the slightest satisfaction. Who knows, by the time Nina took over I'd mellowed so much I might not have felt any. Was that the mind of a psychopath?

And if I was such a depressive that I had no right to help Hilliard decide what was right for him, why was I still so intoxicated by beauty? Not just the women with their languorous eyes and mouths and their exquisite sex compartments, but nature, every square foot of wilderness, and the city too, which after the wilderness seemed such an ingenious arrangement for the wellbeing of man that it compelled Dionysian dance steps?

I had to wonder how tough I'd be when I was faced with that respirator woofing away, the sight of white-clad beings rushing every which way to do what was needed. I couldn't be the reason for his endless, unbearable suffering.

What would I do, set him up with a sort of hit man who would have the guts to do his bidding? The thought had more appeal than I wanted to admit. The problem for me was in feeling responsible for Hilliard. I'd shared too much with him. I'd be killing all the old stories, the meaning of all that we'd gone through together. How could I ever do that to someone I loved? How could I bring myself to think that all we'd been through had no meaning for him?

The possibility hardest for me to face was sure to be the one all the nurses and social workers would be pushing. Hilliard would settle for a life as close to what he had before as modern technology could make it. He'd learn to feed himself, drive a car or at least one of those battery-powered buggies such as Dave had, nearly as fast as one. He'd round up a crew of slaves from

Social Services to help with the shopping and spend the rest of his life down at Project Artaud with a paintbrush between his teeth.

If he chose that course, how could I abandon him? I'd had to psych myself up now for months to so much as contemplate walking out on Sarah—or flying out, really—to pursue the career that had always seemed so important to me when I had lacked the means to pursue it. Now I had the time, the money, the talent—and I still loved to sing. How could leaving Sarah assume such importance? Especially now that she was intoxicated by all the drinking she *wasn't* doing, the bitch... Ah, my frustration with her gave me my answer. She was bedeviled by problems now just as I had been. How could I turn my back on her when I felt so much power to help her find a path she would want to stay on? And I knew I had that power, even though I'd let her win the argument today. I knew I could make her feel loved, create the trust in a loved one which would enable her to cede control consciously for once, not because she was disoriented from drink.

If she trusted me to love her and protect her always, nothing could prevent me from doing so. If she persisted in distrusting me, I could drag out the "novel" she thought I was writing and start deciphering my scribble. I had no doubt that her ability to inspire more than three hundred pages of devotion would help to make her feel loved. However, it was the great defect of the manuscript in its present state that there were no entries at all after we made New York. Someone with her latent esteem problem would be certain to conclude that I had adored her before I really knew her well, and was having a much harder time these days thinking of sweet things to say.

If she kept going to meetings right and left outside of work I'd have plenty of time to doctor my "homage" with entries purporting to have been written when she went AWOL during our trip, or during my long stints in rehearsal rooms, while she was at work or shopping. Much as I hated resuming my oblique prattle about her now that I could bare my soul any time I felt like it, I was tempted. Even with Hilliard lying in a hospital bed, trying to get used to his skull prison, I could well imagine myself putting the finishing touches on this falsehood.

If she entrusted her life to me as I felt she should, all her problems would be over. She would be loved. We could go back together to help Hilliard die. If he weren't in constant pain he'd probably like to see our joy.

Thus spoke Jack Daniels after two deep consultations.

When I got back to Sheridan's later that night I was given the silent treatment. A stranger to the scene would have been sure to conclude that Sheridan and Sarah were the lovebirds.

And what was wrong with that scenario, which I seemed to have left out of the argument I'd been having with myself all night? Sheridan could lose eighty pounds. I'd seen him take off twenty before in what seemed like days. He had a great Celtic face with curly black hair (large curls, not small). He knew lots about literature, quite a bit about art, and like Sarah, was good at sports and service-oriented. (They used to say "approval-seeking.") What's more, Sheridan was a smart prick. At the moment he may have been clumsy, irritable (especially when he wasn't drinking) and pathetic, as well as physically repulsive, but after four months or so of clean living he might very well present to the world as a man of dashing appearance, subtle wit and roguish charm. Sarah would have been taller in heels, but Sheridan had big ears, a big nose, big hands, a big prick. When he got over feeling stunned that pails of booze were no longer passing down his throat as a regular thing he had a mouth on him every bit as persuasive as the one he shouted for drink with. He might have taken some getting used to, but I predicted bliss for him and Sarah, especially if they let themselves be pickled in the same doctrine, say, for another month.

I may have been mildly drunk but I was pretty sure this hunch would hold up: it wouldn't hurt so much to lose Sarah if Sheridan picked her up. It wouldn't hurt at all if I got the feeling she was sweet on him. One sign of affection from her, one peck on the cheek that wasn't quick enough, and I'd sweep her off her feet for Sheridan and dump her in his lap.

The three of us were edgy from that night on, but for quite different reasons. Sarah interpreted the sadness that had come over me as the result of my decision to leave for France without her. I didn't care what Sheridan thought was going on as long as he stayed in the dark about Hilliard's accident.

Each day I called the hospital from a hotel while my roommates were out working or attending meetings. I had a rapport with a nurse called Nancy, and was on fairly good terms with another named Megan. On the third day they let me speak to Mr. Hilliard.

It wasn't his voice, but after I got used to the sound of the respirator I recognized little snatches of resonance from his nose. Between whooshes these were his first words:

"There's absolutely no... hope for me so don't start... thinking it might get better... All I want you to do... is help me get out of this... fucking place. I know they... try. They're giving me... a lot of care. I'm... not complaining... They're all right. I'm... just tired of having people... bend over backwards..." There was more. Nancy had been a one-night stand just before or during Sarah's reign. Not a friend of Sarah's, maybe. She'd transferred to Davies to care for him. And she cared too much to take his life. So I was supposed to care less than one of his one-night stands?

It was a mere ten days after first talking to him that I made the break. A short note for Sarah; money. A short thank you to Sheridan; more money. Every scrap of mine gone. Quite a bit thrown away.

I had seen no sign of love blossoming between the two of them, but they were spending all their time together. When they were likely to be home I made it a point to walk the streets for long hours, or in bad weather, to sit in theaters alone. I might take a drink before coming home to make sure they wouldn't think me worthy of their deepest thoughts, but I was never intoxicated. They'd have been too compassionate to write me off, and that would have spoiled everything.

Loading up the cab in the morning went smoothly. As soon as I was rolling to the airport, though, I couldn't get her out of my mind.

Thoughts of her continued to occupy me while I was in the air over our country, the states which had recently sponged up so many acts and thoughts gliding by like years to someone thinking back to a path not taken. I spent no more than moments wondering what Hilliard would look like, what I would find. I was certain he would be alive.

I thought of what I was doing to Sarah in terms of things I had never done, couldn't have done. Taking a pet from its home, our home, where it was loved and cared for. Leaving it in a long-forgotten vacant lot in the burned-out heart of a great city. Driving off while it poked around.

I couldn't bring myself to think I was the kind of person to do something like this, but something like this was exactly what I was doing. The worst reproachful words that came were: *this is a coward's way to kill someone.*

From the old Palace Hotel on Market I could jump a streetcar up to Divisadero. After checking in I realized that I wanted to visit the Fife before I went directly to the hospital. I didn't really want to see any old faces, even if they were friendly. I didn't care whether the Raleigh Tavern had chamber music these days, or if Teresa was packing them in with her new singing partner, or Wolfgang had singlehandedly raised the consciousness of an important number of citizens. I needed to see Peckham for a bit before I went to the quad ward, and anyone else who had known my friend, to make an event of what I was about to do, and help me prepare, the way I would have for a performance. Because that's what this would be, an acting job. To Hilliard, to me, the meaning of my visit would be settled between us in the twinkling of an eye. *At the last trumpet...*

I loved the place right away, the way it looked these days. The bunting was gone—alas, it was Wolfgang's idea of festive decor and would have been put back in mothballs right afterward if our opening night had opened something. The risers were gone, too, and the place looked more like other cafes. The differences now had to do with the museum feel of some of the displays, and the *liberté, égalité, fraternité* of so many of the patrons. The *bonnet rouge* was on a great many heads now, and a house full of this new, high-spirited rabble resembled inn scenes I remembered in certain operas.

I sat with Peckham and Brian drinking cider. After a while Wolfgang arrived with a fresh issue of the newspaper he was producing now which really set the record straight about certain Tories, Whigs and Federalists who had been tormenting him all his life. After carefully sliding his papers into a homemade wooden dump he came to my table and said how sorry he was about Hilliard before he said hello.

It was apparent after fifteen minutes in his company that Wolfgang was no longer a voice crying in the wilderness, would no longer be rousted, investigated and exhibited on television as a radical freak. Now that his operation was out in the open it was evident that no friend of justice had anything to fear. Like some poor Japanese soldiers who were still fighting World War Two when they were discovered on remote islands long after the end of the war, Wolfgang saw the American Revolution as neverending, the way Jefferson had *hoped* it would be. His loud calls for the imprisonment of pretty nearly everyone currently involved with our "de facto" government was based on the way they had subverted the intent of the Founding Fathers as to the kind of country we should be. He cared not a fig for all the reams of legislation being quarreled over in our courts and legislatures.

"Everyt'ing is politics dese days," he said with a shrug, still sounding a bit like Popeye. "At least you got a choice when you come in here. You want to hear what the swindlers are up to, want your product from the bullshit machine? Buy your paper out on the street. If ya want someone to tell ya straight what's goin' on, you got it, there, and it's free."

Brian was so changed I didn't recognize him. Or else I'd been unable to eradicate the memory of his beard colored with different liqueurs, of the red-eyed, wild-haired, ranting madman who teetered into the kitchen asking for soup from time to time. When he'd sobered up he had had a big bandage on his head, then a *vélo* helmet, then a liberty cap, and it had been harder to see facial changes. Most amazing to me now: he was a handsome man, a sort of pint-sized Cary Grant. The boyish, gentle side predominated, complementing Wolfgang's very German good manners—not quite cold enough to be called "correct." They were a team.

And Peckham? After all the time I'd spent hating him for trying to promote a deal of his own when he should have been looking out for my interests, I thought of him as a friend again. He was still about half bullshit, but the same could have been said about my words to Sheridan and Sarah lately. It was hard to be straight with each other concerning the business, or future plans that didn't concern the business, for that matter, but we had a lot of the same feelings about Hilliard when our feelings came. He promised me he'd visit with me soon. He'd only gone the one time he'd told me about, when Hilliard had been unconscious, and he was ashamed. It would be easier if we went together. He admired me for going alone today, and that was the main thing I had wanted from him. A sense that someone besides Hilliard and some nurses I didn't know were counting on me.

The horrible truth was, or might have been: I could have run out on Hilliard the way I had on Sarah. Sure I could have. Let him live out the few miserable months or years he had left with a new set of friends. Would I have cared what anyone said of me? I wasn't really tempted, even though running off and assuming a French identity had appealed to me for years. Maybe there was something in the Buddhist thought I'd tried to imbibe along with pots of ale. Maybe there was such a thing as right action. Maybe all the weird spirals that had been gusting me here and there constituted a path of some kind and not a mere trail of devastation.

I wasn't expecting a pretty sight when I got to his bedside, but the changes were still shocking. Any change in his Smith Bros. trademark beard would have been a mutilation, but there was a world of difference between a conscious mutilation and the result of carelessness. The central part of his beard had been cut away so that there was only stubble under his chin and two barbs to either side. There was a lot of chin sticking out, he hadn't worn his beard all those years to hide anything, but my first thought was, why wear a beard at all if it looks chopped up like that? If they shaved him clean at least they'd have something to do to make him look better and even feel better, since he still had sensation in his cheeks. *Venison*, I was thinking. The word just popped into my mind.

He was about half asleep and I was waiting to come into focus for him. I wanted to ask what had happened to his beard, which would have been a reasonably gentle way to lead up to what had happened to him. Then one possible explanation occurred to me. He might have tried to commit suicide by swallowing his beard. After all, only his mouth moved, or so I'd been told.

The nurse who'd taken me to him touched his face and said his name again. This time his great black eyes stayed open and his mouth was saying my name. All I heard in his voice was recognition. He might have been coming out of a coma instead of a nap.

I took his hand and had another shock. It was already much smaller, pink and clean like a baby's, and it felt as if I'd just taken a handful of wieners out of the fridge. I held on tight to these souvenirs of the old Hilliard because I didn't want to deal with the question of what to do with my hands.

The respirator kept whooshing. He was on oxygen for a minute but didn't seem to be getting a rush. After, he spoke as much as he could, then waited patiently for enough air to continue. These uniform chunks of utterance reminded me of a heavy smoker speaking, though it was easier to bear with Hilliard.

The machine seemed to be aiding him merely to empty his lungs, which were quick to fill again, like the sponges I imagined them to be, but before I'd ever got much of a conversation going with him a nurse came along and pumped him full of air. The way the machine intervened was less and less adequate, until finally another violent intervention was required to keep him from suffocating. As far as I could tell, the violent interventions, which were scary, weren't required at closer and closer intervals. This wasn't exactly a cause for celebration, but it kept me from thinking about his plug for the time being.

"This is a hell of a way for two old friends to meet." So much for my prepared speech.

"Do it today please.... get to know Nancy. You... won't have a problem..."

The nurse bending over him at the moment just kept going about her business.

"Can I ask her something in private, man?"

The nurse turned to me, startled. Robin.

Hilliard assented somehow. Robin followed me into the corridor.

"Sarah Schwartzman was my friend. You knew her?"

"Sure. You're her new boyfriend. I know all about you."

"Please forgive me for cutting to the chase, but Nancy..."

She seemed blank.

"Who works here?"

"Sure. His girlfriend."

"Well, that's what I wanted to ask you. She knew him before..."

"She was a one-night stand!" Not laughter...

"Maybe something more."

"Oh, I'm sure it was. Nancy's a special girl. But if you're worried, is it real, I mean, you want to know how much she cares? A lot. It would have to be."

"Sarah told me some things, but she wasn't specific. I'm not asking you to be, but what the hell does she get out of it?"

"More than she got out of it before when she went out with him. That's what she told me. Look, don't worry so much. Be yourself. He'll be living through you."

"Thanks, Robin. It's been great meeting you."

"Good meeting you, and thanks for coming. All the way from New York, I hear. Hey, don't spend too much time today, OK? Come every day and he'll be able to handle more and more of you."

When I came back to bedside he'd stopped taking oxygen and his lips were a very bright red the way they used to be when he'd had a lot of beer. The whooshes were really getting on my nerves in spite of all the good they were doing him.

Nancy came and just touched the top of my hand when she introduced herself. She took his oxygen away, and when she came back, introduced herself as his girlfriend. She was a dark-haired, blue-eyed looker and I could sense that he was damned proud of her interest in him.

Hilliard told me in his labored way that Nancy had been trained to take care of quads, it was her "major." She'd never known Sarah. Was sorry she hadn't from what was said of her here.

"There's no one around," said Hilliard when Nancy bounced away. "You could do it right now."

"I'm not ready to, man. I don't know if I can. You may not feel much like one, but you're a human life."

He pleaded then. Complained that none of his other friends would have the guts to finish him. Too many of the nurses were pro-life. Nancy wasn't, but she was in love with him.

"Some girl. The best I've ever seen you with."

It was amazing how he could communicate disgust with no change of expression.

"Anyway, what's with all this pro-choice, pro-life shit? They think of you as a fetus?"

"What's the difference? Got... to stay hooked up... to survive. Maybe... a fetus would be... better off, wouldn't you... say? It doesn't have to... listen to the arguments..."

"What about the mouth drawings I heard about? Once when I called, I think it was Megan who told me you were still doing your art."

Hilliard claimed that he only drew that way to get people off his back. "They try so hard... to make me give a... fuck..." Not Nancy, though. She wasn't afraid to hear what he really thought. I was, though.

He went on to tell me that Nancy was top dog here. A nurse and a social worker, too. This time he suggested I know her better by taking her to lunch. "The best lady I ever knew." He'd have been serious about her if he had his body back.

For the rest of my first visit I answered his questions about my plans for Europe, and he answered mine about the Raleigh Tavern. The answers were brief on both sides, he was wearing down. Robin came again to pump his lungs and told me she thought he'd had enough for today. She followed me out again and told me I had done really well with him. Then she gave me a big hug.

My surprise was showing.

"We're real affectionate around here. You'll get used to it. Touchie-feelie. It's kind of a morale trip. Come again tomorrow." A saucy look over the shoulder going away. At one time I'd thought of Sarah as the most beautiful woman I'd ever known, but both Robin and Nancy were just as striking. Was it pure torture to be around beauties like this all day?

Was I going to be a good enough buffoon to keep Hilliard interested in living? Would I have to keep falling all over myself every time I came? Would I get better at being pleasant? Would I want to kill him to keep from bombing? Questions no less hard for being ridiculous.

I went back to the Tavern to give Peckham a detailed description of Hilliard's life-support equipment, meaning not only his respirator but the beautiful women who cared for him.

Peckham countered with a caring trip of his own. Brian had had a small *slip* before I came—AA lingo for a relapse into drinking. Peckham had found him drunk, taken him home with him and locked him into a spare room until he dried out. For twenty-four hours Brian had sworn he'd kill Peckham, then when he was sober again, swore that Peckham's intervention was the kindest thing anyone had ever done for him.

Alone with Brian I asked him why Emma wasn't looking after him any more.

"My daughters. They've turned her against me. Think I'm exaggerating how little I'm earning here. Think I've ruined business for the Fife because big drinkers mistakenly assume alcohol is no longer served down there. They have a point, but the hell with them. After what they did to sabotage your opera I've disowned them both. Changed my will. They'll never get a dime."

"What about Emma, though. She'll see they do, the way my mother is seeing that I get mine."

"But Emma won't be getting it all. I know what I'm about, you see. Of sound mind, as they say."

He really was, that was the big surprise. And as likable now as he was formerly obnoxious.

Hilliard didn't appear as glad to see me the next day when I brought Peckham. He marked Peckham's presence with the word "Peckham." Nancy was favored with some grousing about his care. His night nurses, the lazy bitches, had been neglecting him again. That was their game. First they gave you reason to believe they were going to be there for him at specified times, then they made him wonder if he were forgotten.

"If they made their appearances like the cuckoo in the clock," I offered, "you guys would be saying 'It must be three o'clock' when they come instead of 'Oh, boy, am I glad to see you.'"

"Any time Mr. Hilliard is glad to see someone, be sure to let me know," said a hardnosed older nurse working nearby. The place was such a beehive everything you said was overheard.

"What I want to know is how come it's OK for the nurses to let you live but your friends have to risk going to prison to do away with you?"

"Because I want it... to be someone who... cares about me. Not... just lazy..."

Peckham was getting uncomfortable. Probably there was no precedent for this kind of approach.

"Wouldn't you suffer less with a pillow over your face?" Did I really think I could do such a thing, or was this some kind of macho routine to impress Peckham?

"It would be quicker... I suffocate either... way."

"What's all this?" said Nancy stoutly, coming up.

"The best way would... be to shoot me up. If... one of them had a heart... I'd be gone that way... already."

"They monitor the dosages very carefully," said the same

nurse who had piped up before, the older one—Sally. She joined us. Getting rid of Hilliard had turned into a symposium.

"So what?" said Hilliard, glad of his chance to do battle. "Who's going to know?... Who's going to ask for... an autopsy? You think... my mother or my sister... would want you cutting me... to pieces to make sure... I didn't die of a ruptured... appendix?"

"You don't know who you can trust," said Sally, becoming pensive.

"Alex is going to find something useful to do with his life," said Nancy. "Just you wait."

"Provide employment for... all these idiots in... white," Hilliard droned.

"I know what I'd do," said Peckham so firmly that he had the rest of us waiting to hear the last word. "Volunteer for experiments to advance the frontiers of science."

Hilliard could move his head and Peckham would have been better off not seeing what was in his eyes.

"In six months, or nine months, or a year at the outside, Hilliard could be painting masterpieces," Nancy drooled.

"That's right," said Peckham, as if angry with himself for having forgot. "I've seen Christmas cards designed by a guy who held a brush in his teeth."

"How exciting," said Hilliard, his teeth clenched as well. "Maybe I could... go the guy one better... and learn to chew up... the pigment and spit out... reindeer and sleighs."

Nancy was chuckling. I appreciated her sense of humor, but I didn't have the stomach for much more of this.

"Perhaps you could put down a wash that way," I said, trying to be helpful. "I knew a Japanese painter once, Masando Kito, who threw glue onto the canvas before laying on the paint."

"Show him. Go on... Nancy. Let them... both see..."

She gave me a guarded look while opening a compartment near his bed. It was the look of someone who would have no problem at all not being a friend.

She was holding them up too long.

"Just whiz through the... stack, Nancy. One's... the same as the next."

"I don't think so."

"They all stink. I... told him what to ex-... pect."

"I agree, Nancy. I don't think he was trying when he did these. I think the mistake is trying to use pencil or charcoal, though. What about a calligrapher's brush? What do you think?"

"You're right. I haven't... been able to get... into it."

"You might come up with something like the doodles of a Klee, Kandinsky, Miró. There's plenty of room for wit. They'd be more interesting if you could be playful. Maybe when you aren't so frustrated..."

"Klee's pretty cute. He knew... what he was doing... Nobody else could get... away with it... Nobody ever tried... Maybe if I worked in that... way long enough I... could get something of my... own going."

"Of course you could," said Nancy. "And you will. You've got to try."

"Don't let on that you're handicapped, man. I think that's the way to put these over. It has to appear that this is the way you want your finished work to look. Make all your limitations appear self-imposed."

"Maybe so. I don't... see myself in any of... the ones I've done... though. I see the... record of a struggle... I remember the struggle... and I remember thinking... what's the point?"

"The point is to keep struggling and see what you find." Nancy.

Hilliard didn't feel up to starting anything today. He'd had enough of us (I thought). We were subdued when we went our separate ways.

Nancy had given me her number and I called her that night to talk about Hilliard. She told me that he'd smiled that afternoon. She'd cried hard at the time and she was crying as she told me. Then I was. Hilliard had a great smile. It was incredible that she could have cared so much for him for weeks now without seeing one.

When she recovered, I did, and we talked about Hilliard's

"mouth art." She appreciated what I was doing in trying to be tough enough to make him trust my encouragement.

With the sense of someone making a life-threatening mistake I told her that honesty was everything. Suicide insurance for artists of all kinds. Without it there was just money to pay for time to feel shitty about yourself.

We fought very quietly. I sensed her resources of compassion and wondered why Sarah hadn't had an easier time disposing of my arguments.

When I was off the phone and trying to sleep, it started. Nightmares of the sort that had kept me awake once after smoking hashish. Strange prehistoric scribbles... Arcana of all kinds peeling, crisping, breaking off. Magical etched signs crumbling, great architecture, old stones collapsing. Words and formulae in a writhing black heap, hopelessly interlocked. Horror at myself so extreme that I wanted to die, I wanted to blow my brains out, perhaps I would have, had I possessed a gun. The sense of sin scorching my soul was raising a suffocating smoke.

I called Nancy back and woke her, feeling like the coward I was.

"I'm sorry, but it's all come to me just now... My mistake."

She was calm and sentient, asking me to go on.

"How could I have been such an asshole? Such a posturing creep? I just had a kind of nightmare that ended with the art being done right now. The limelight that's everywhere for artists in every discipline. All the egos trying to get into it... All the critics barring the way or putting people out... The mighty struggle for judgment, egotists everywhere who know what's best..."

"Gordon, you'll depress Alex if you go on like that."

"But I've only said what I intend to repudiate. I want to tell him my mistake! He can go someplace with what he's doing. He and I fell right into the trap as if we were nothing but a couple of brainwashed college graduates. Why should anything he does be compared to the great artists of the past? That's the trip all the jostling egotists are on, and I've been even worse, wasting a dozen years trying to sound like Titta Ruffo because my ego wouldn't let me be any less esteemed. Fuck what anybody says about what Hilliard does, or what they think. The record of a struggle, remember? Some artists today are pretty slick, you'd never get the idea that they had to work at what they do. They want to be cool. But the struggle is there when something great is going on. You can feel it. Dostoevsky. Van Gogh. Nijinsky. Ruffo. Anything cool about *them*?"

"I'd love for you to tell Alex all this, because I've been telling him every day." I heard a sigh, as if she were exhaling smoke, but she didn't smoke. "I didn't know him long when he was a working artist." She actually chuckled. I waited. "But I knew him enough to sense the importance of his work to him. We need more artists who *have* to work the way they do, *see* the way they do. Not more million-dollar works of art to sell magazines. More people doing it. I put it to him this way: now you've got uninterrupted time to work on your art. To want to die is to destroy the meaning of your life. It sounds cruel, and maybe it is, but my work is trying to get them to care more about what they're doing and less about what they've done."

"Or wish they could do."

"Exactly. See you tomorrow. I'm glad to have an ally. Two p.m. will be a good time."

I put down the phone bathed in sweat. A sense of wellbeing was teasing me. I'd felt that way before, but not since I was twelve. The feeling was quickly submerged by panic about how I would handle everything that lay immediately ahead. I'd let Nancy be my guide. Watch, listen. I didn't trust myself to give Hilliard the right help, but I was beginning to feel I might be of some help to *her*.

The Raleigh Tavern was serving lunch again, so I went, desperate for the company of weak fellow mortals.

Brian seemed to expect me. He came to sit with me and smiled a long time before saying anything.

"You have a wild look about you, Mr. Bancroft."

"I didn't get much sleep."

"Mr. Peckham said you were tough on our good friend's drawings yesterday."

"He forced me to be."

"All you artists are so hard on yourselves." He appeared tired himself. An insomniac, too? "You were about to leave for Europe I think. France, was it?"

"Yes."

"You should go. According to Sidney your friend has asked you to kill him."

"Yes, but I couldn't now. His nurse has shown me a way I can help."

"It may seem cowardly to you, but you should leave him with his nurse friend. If she's all that Sidney says she'll offer him something to live for. Perhaps when he's more accustomed to his condition he'll care more about her happiness."

"Thank you for saying this."

"Send him picture postcards when you're in Europe. Something tangible. Share your travels with him. Have you ever kept a diary?"

"Of sorts. The entries were erratic."

"Well, a few words on a card is easier than a diary. If you avert the young woman, she can keep them for you. Someday they'll be an excellent way to remember the uses of your time. If only I'd had the sense in my day!"

This was no one I knew, but he'd made me wish for time to know him.

"I'll visit your friend as well. Should have gone before this, but Wolfgang keeps me busy. Don't worry, he won't lack for visitors that care for him. I'll poke around down at the studio where he was living. There's no phone, I understand, so some of the boys down there may not even know what happened to him."

"Very good of you, Brian. I'm glad you're his friend."

"I'm yours as well. Please drop me a line now and then if you've the time, or a little card. I'd like to know what comes of all your singing—you really do have an impressive voice. It may sound a bit strange coming from me after all the trouble I caused you, but I think of you as a son. And if you think of me, remember—I believe in you."

On the way to the hospital I saw the future. There was never anything frightening about such premonitions. I'd had them before, twice. Images flitted through my head like pictures to go with a joke someone was telling. No different from the images in daydreams except that I knew, though it didn't seem particularly important, that I was seeing *right.* (In the main, I was.)

I saw Hilliard start to get excited about what he was still able to accomplish as an artist. I saw Nancy fall ever more deeply in love with him. When I was leaving for France—directly for France, with less money than I had now—Hilliard and Nancy would be talking about the van he was going to get, and how his studio would be equipped.

I didn't have much luggage. The money and papers I needed were stowed conveniently upon my person. I was calm and sober as never before in my life. All my small acts and words had an exquisite quality, as if I were an extremely able intelligence operative, secretly exulting in his ability to get everything right. I was killing Hilliard with my footsteps. Walking on his "art." When I turned on my heel I scraped his eyes.

His smiles would be less frequent in time. The postcards that were such a delight at first would have less to say. Triumphs, always mine, would be announced long distance, but all the emotion would seem very noisy at the time, and in retrospect, false. My life would be spread out in front of my friend like a banquet in front of a man who had lost his appetite.

One day in a drizzle of ordinary French life I'd be called to the phone, and it would be an overseas operator, then my brother Tom. He would have been in touch with Alex Hilliard all this time, and Nancy would have called him in the middle of the night. Tom would tell me, sounding bewildered and regretful: of unknown causes, my friend had died.